Apocalypse

Grand System Vending

Book One

By

Ryan maxwell

APOCALYPSE

Contents

APOCALYPSE

APOCALYPSE

Nai elen silatha melme a'na vian e' imladris.

Chapter 1

Current Earth: System Integration

Attention, people of planet 35956390246, also known as Earth. We are pleased to take this opportunity to congratulate you! Your planet has been selected as the newest member of the Intergalactic Federation of Planets, or IFP. This prestigious honor is bestowed upon you by the IFP High Council to ensure the continuation and prosperity of your species.

At this moment, your planet is undergoing conversion to be integrated into the Grand System. A mana generator is being placed at the core of your planet to provide you with the resources you will need in the coming months.

Please remain calm as we integrate each of you into the wondrous life that comes with being part of the Grand System. A brief tutorial will be provided to every human on Earth to assist with the integration process and ensure you have the best possible chance of survival.

Do not be alarmed by the changes you will experience during this new phase of life. These adjustments are perfectly natural and will ultimately strengthen your species in the long run. Once again, congratulations on your integration, and welcome to the Grand System!

A large, androgynous, but kind-sounding voice boomed out of a projection in the sky, reverberating off the buildings around it. The projection had appeared from the completely black stone obelisk that had erupted from the ground suddenly in downtown Dallas.

The day had started like any other. Tom had woken up, gotten ready for work in his apartment, and made his coffee, which he drank every day on his way to work.

Sipping it carefully so as not to burn his mouth, he called to his roommate and coworker, turning to look down the hall to his closed bedroom door.

"You ready, James? We're gonna be late if we don't get going. You know the traffic on 75 is fucking brutal."

James stepped out of his bedroom, adjusting his superhero t-shirt under the backpack he had thrown over one shoulder.

"I hear ya. I just had to send in my PR for the graphics on the Dungeon. Boss was not gonna be happy if we didn't have that ready for review today," James replied, hurriedly searching for his keycard to access their building.

"Great! You fixed the walls that kept turning invisible when you got too close?" Tom asked.

"Yeah, that wasn't the big issue. The worst part was the recurring issue with using Mage Hand to open doors. But I finally got that solved, too. Now, let's get out before we lose any more time."

Finally stepping out the door, Tom and his friend descended the stairs of their apartment building and climbed into Tom's car, which was parked in its usual spot out front. The two lived on the outskirts of Dallas, where rent was more affordable, making their daily commute into the city a necessary inconvenience. They both worked for a company called Underdark and had been with the firm for the past six years. Over time, their shared interests and long hours fostered a close friendship. Perhaps inevitably, they decided to move in together, both to carpool and to save on living expenses.

Underdark was a game development company known for its popular titles, primarily Massively Multiplayer Online Role-Playing Games, or MMORPGs. They had released several big-name games in recent years, and their latest project—highly anticipated by fans—was slated for release at the end of the year.

As they navigated the usual morning traffic on I-75, frustration mounted with each stop-and-go stretch. They cursed their luck, glancing at the clock and hoping they wouldn't be late. Suddenly, a deep, resonating rumble shook the ground. The reverberations were so intense that Tom, along with nearly every other driver on the road, was forced to slam on the brakes. Cars skidded and swerved, narrowly avoiding collisions as the entire freeway came to a jarring halt.

Tom gripped the steering wheel, eyes wide, as the vibrations subsided. Whatever had caused that tremor was unlike anything they had experienced before.

"What the hell was that?! SHIT!" Tom asked, trying to keep control of the car as he slowed down and swerved to avoid a car that had come to a stop in front of them.

"No fucking idea," James replied, turning his head back and forth while he gripped the door handle and center console, trying to see if any other vehicles were going to hit them. "Earthquake?"

"In Dallas?" Tom asked.

"They have been doing more fracking recently," James offered.

"That's all west Texas shit," Tom replied. "The only fracking happening in Dallas is on Friday nights when your mom goes out."

"Oh, real classy. Going after my poor..." James trailed off as he caught sight of something in the distance. "...mother?"

"What is it?" Tom said as he tried to follow James' line of sight. When he finally saw it, he wished he hadn't.

Out of the ground, a giant obelisk was rising higher and higher into the sky. It was jet black, and polished so smooth that the light from the still-rising sun glistened across its ebony surface. It appeared to have come right out of West End, towering over the aquarium.

"What the *actual* fuck is that?" Tom gasped in shock.

James shook his head, staring slack-jawed and unable to find the words to describe what he was witnessing. The obelisk, having finally stopped its ascent, towered over the Dallas skyline, dwarfing even the tallest buildings by hundreds of feet. Its dark, gleaming surface cast a shadow over the city—an imposing presence that felt both alien and ominous.

The crunch of metal from behind snapped the pair out of their stupor. They turned to see two SUVs that had collided, their drivers distracted by the rising obelisk and unable to swerve in time. In their panic to avoid hitting a mid-sized sedan that had stopped abruptly, the vehicles had smashed into each other. All traffic had ground to a complete halt, and people were beginning to get out of their cars, craning their necks to gaze up at the colossal structure.

Suddenly, a massive projection shot out from the top of the obelisk, beaming into the sky. A giant screen formed, its bright rectangle displaying the image of a robotic-looking creature's profile in stark relief against the blue sky. Its metallic features glinted in the light, and its presence was not only felt immediately but was viscerally unsettling.

The projection's announcement boomed out, its voice resonating through the city with an overpowering force that drowned out the blaring car alarms and the shouts of bewildered onlookers. The sound was deep, mechanical, and unmistakably commanding, cutting through the chaos with an intensity that left no room for misinterpretation: something extraordinary and terrifying had just begun.

The creature spoke about joining a Federation of planets, but the words that stuck out the most to him were tucked neatly in the middle of its speech.

"Strengthened in the long run…" Tom whispered. That phrase had left an ominous pit in his stomach about how things would look in the *short* run.

"*…There will be many changes to come in the near future. The introduction of mana to your otherwise woefully depleted world will spawn monsters, Dungeons, and many other unexplained phenomena.*

"*This is to be expected, and it is all part of the normal process. Pay close attention to and follow along with the instructions during your tutorial on how to handle these situations and how to go about your new lives,*" the creature continued. "*Again, please remain calm while you await the Grand System integration.*"

The screen folded in on itself, shrinking and disappearing as mysteriously as it had appeared.

Another rumble shook the ground, causing Tom and James—who had now stepped out of their vehicle and were gripping the car doors—to stumble as they struggled to keep their balance.

They exchanged wide-eyed glances, standing in stunned confusion, trying to process what they had just witnessed. Suddenly, Tom felt an intense, stabbing pain shoot through his head, like a knife being driven into his brain.

With a gasp, he grabbed the sides of his head and collapsed to his knees, the pain overwhelming him. He fell to his side, writhing on the pavement. Just before squeezing his eyes shut, he caught a glimpse of a woman in the car next to him experiencing the same agony, her body slumped over the steering wheel, accidentally blaring the horn as she fought against the searing pain.

APOCALYPSE

A scream tore from Tom's throat as he tried desperately to release the agony consuming him. His vision was filled with swirling stars, and he could do nothing but curl up on the ground, clutching his head as his world dissolved into a cacophony of excruciating pain.

The pain intensified, reaching a level beyond anything Tom had ever endured. It felt as though his skull was on the verge of shattering. His body finally rebelled, causing him to retch violently, emptying the contents of his stomach onto the highway. Just when he thought his head would explode, the pain abruptly subsided, leaving him gasping and disoriented.

Tom slowly opened his eyes, half-expecting to find himself soaked in the blood that he was sure must have wept from every orifice in his head. Instead, he found himself squinting against the harsh sunlight that pierced his vision. Tears blurred his sight as he wiped them away with one hand and cleared vomit from his mouth with the other. The light felt sharp, stabbing into his eyes like needles, forcing him to shield his face as though searching for shade in a blinding desert.

As he blinked and his vision cleared, Tom noticed that nearly everyone around him seemed to have endured the same excruciating experience. People were hunched over, clutching their heads, some still on the ground, others slowly trying to recover from the brutal assault on their senses.

Grunting, Tom attempted to stand and called out in a voice that broke as only a whisper, "James?"

"What the actual fuck was that?" James half whispered back, as though the sounds were going to make the pain return. "I thought my head was going to split open and spill my brains out on the ground."

"Not a clue," Tom replied, also unable to bring himself to raise his voice as the sounds of the car alarms and sirens around were already threatening to bring on another migraine. "But it looks like everyone else also…"

Tom trailed off as a screen appeared in his vision.

Welcome to The Grand System!
You have been initiated into the most advanced AI system in the known universe, which means that your planet has recently been integrated into the Intergalactic Federation of Planets (IFP). I am here to guide you through the initial tutorial process of this System.
Refined over the past seventeen centuries by dedicated Administrators, this System serves as the primary model for tracking your personal growth.
Throughout this tutorial, you will be introduced to the key facets of the System, ensuring you understand how to utilize it to enhance your experience in the new world you are about to enter.
Most functions of the System are controlled through a neural network that has been recently integrated into your brain. To access different features, simply think about the screen you would like to view, and it will appear in your interface. Let us begin by thinking "Character Sheet."

Standing stock still, eyes wide, with the pain of a moment ago forgotten, Tom stared at the notification in his view. It was a golden-bordered prompt with white text on a nearly see-through background. Reading the notification several times over, his confusion was no less prominent even though he understood the words.

"What does it mean, 'Think Character Sheet?'" No sooner had he thought this than a new window opened as the prompt closed, and on it was a set of stats.

Tom Harris	
Race: Human	**Class:** None
Level: 1	**Total XP:** 0
XP To Next Level: 1,000	**HP:** 100/100
MP: 100/100	**SP:** 100/100
Attributes:	**Unused Attribute Points:** 0
Strength: 10	**Constitution:** 10
Dexterity: 10	**Endurance:** 10
Intelligence: 10	**Wisdom:** 10
Charisma: 10	**Luck:** 10
Non-Combat Skills:	
Inspect	**Level:** 1 **Rank:** Beginner
Combat Skills:	
N/A	

"This looks just like a video game screen. James, are you seeing this?" Tom called over to James in awe, not looking away from the screen.

"I'm seeing a notice of some kind. What are you seeing?" James replied distractedly.

"Think Character Sheet."

"What do you mean think… Holy shit!" James exclaimed.

"I know, right!? But level one kinda sucks. Figured at our age we'd be further along than that," Tom said excitedly.

"Yeah, but we're brand new to the 'System,' so it kinda makes sense. I think most of these stats are simple enough to understand, but I'd love to know what they actually *do*," James said. A prompt appeared in his vision when he thought this. "Dude! Think about what the Stats mean!"

Tom thought about the Stats, and a prompt appeared in his vision as well.

Attribute Definitions:
Strength - Determines the amount of weight you can carry and how hard your attacks hit.
Constitution - Represents your toughness. Each attribute point placed here increases your Health Points by 10 and slightly boosts your resistance to poisons as well as environmental conditions.

Dexterity - Governs your mobility, ability to use ranged weapons, and raises the regeneration rate of your Stamina Points.

Endurance - Measures your ability to keep moving. Each attribute point placed here increases your Stamina Points by 10.

Intelligence - Affects your ability to use magic. Each attribute point placed here increases your Mana Points by 10 and determines the number of spells you can learn.

Wisdom - Impacts your ability to continue to use magic by increasing your mana regeneration rate.

Charisma - Influences your ability to interact favorably with others. Each point increases the likelihood of favorable outcomes in personal interactions.

Luck - A mysterious attribute that affects your fortune. Each point can impact your luck positively or negatively, though the true outcome is known only to the universe.

You can also enhance these attributes through physical and mental exercise, similar to how you would train your body to become more fit and healthy.

"This is interesting and all, but we really need to figure out what's going on, don't we?" Tom asked.

"Yeah, you're right. But what do we do? We're kind of pinned in here," James replied.

"Maybe we can see what we can do to help people get back into their cars to get traffic flowing?" Tom offered.

"I'm actually a bit more concerned about something else that *thing* said." James shook his head. "What did they say about spawning—"

A scream answered his question from the road ahead of them. Turning quickly to see what caused the commotion, both of them froze in fear at what they saw. More screams rose to join the first as something headed their way. Soon a group of people were running toward them, masks of complete panic on their faces.

"—monsters!" James finished.

"No fucking way," Tom said. "Get in the fucking car NOW!"

Chapter 2

Goblins

Ducking quickly into the seats and slamming the doors behind them, Tom and James locked their doors as fast as they could. Out of habit, both of them also put their seatbelts on.

"Are those... goblins?" Tom asked, horror gripping him as he stared through the windshield.

James struggled to get the seat belt buckled, his voice filled with both panic and frustration. "It's either that or I hear really ugly banjos off in the distance. I mean, let's tick the boxes." He held up the fingers on one hand, ticking them down as he spoke. "Short. Carrying primitive weapons. Looks like someone took the Wicked Witch of the West, tossed her into a blender, then put her back together using only half the parts. I'd say they're goblins."

"What do we do?" Tom asked, unable to peel his eyes away from the horrors in front of him.

"I don't know... Try to get to work and see if anyone is there? Safety in numbers?" James offered, his frustration mounting until he was finally able to get the satisfying click sound he had been looking for.

"Alternate idea," Tom held up the index finger of his hand. "We can Mad Max this bitch and see what kind of loot the trash mobs drop..." Tom revved the engine, gesturing to the people running past them.

A new scream pierced the air, louder and more frantic than the rest. Tom and James looked up just in time to see a woman pulled to the ground, her desperate cries filling the air as three goblins descended on her with spears. Blood spewed from her back as the goblins twisted their weapons, repeatedly stabbing her in a frenzy. Her shrieks echoed in agony, eyes wide with panic as she reached out toward the fleeing crowd, only to be swallowed by a writhing mass of green bodies.

The goblins, seemingly lost in a bloodlust-driven fervor, continued their relentless assault, chasing down anyone within reach. They threw spears with deadly precision, leapt onto fleeing people to drag them down, and sliced at legs with their short swords, leaving chaos in their wake.

A man stumbled, crying out as he hit the pavement. Goblins pounced on him immediately, knives and short swords tearing into his flesh. His scream cut off abruptly as a blade slashed across his throat, silencing him in a brutal instant.

People rushed past Tom and James' car on both sides, sheer pandemonium erupting around them. The crowd surged, shoving and trampling each other in their desperate attempts to escape. The goblins were nearly on top of them when Tom threw the car into drive, slamming his foot on the gas and veering left toward the shoulder.

Tom's eyebrows drew down as a mixture of burning rage and sheer panic lit his gaze. "Mad Max it is, mother fuckers."

"What the hell are you doing?" James shouted, gripping the door as the car lurched forward.

"There's two ways off this road." Tom gestured at the wrecked cars behind him, as if to demonstrate their inability to retrace their path. "We get out and walk…"

James took another look at the green-skinned goblins attacking every pedestrian in their path. "You know, I'm good on that, thanks."

Tom nodded, pointing out the windshield at the writhing horde in front of him. "Then quit your bitching and grab your oh-shit handle."

A primitive-looking arrow suddenly bounced off the windshield, causing both men to yelp in terror, instinctively raising their hands to shield their faces. Tom swerved, the front of the car bumping into another vehicle that was blocking the way. Metal crunched as Tom shoved it aside, pressing the gas pedal even harder.

They made it to the shoulder, Tom scanning for a clear path. Just as he found an opening, a group of goblins jumped in front of the car. Tom growled, gritted his teeth, and floored the accelerator. The car barreled into the pack of goblins; the impact sending bodies sprawling across the pavement. The sickening sound of bones crunching reverberated through the vehicle as it jolted and bounced, rolling over each goblin like speed bumps. Black blood sprayed out from under the wheels, splattering the sides of the car, but Tom didn't dare slow down.

"Holy fucking shit dude! That was like running over a group of situationally unaware preschoolers!" James shouted, banging his hands on the dashboard.

"I've always wanted to do that…" Tom muttered, though not quite silent enough.

"What?" James blinked.

"What?" Tom jumped, staring back at James innocently.

"Whatever. I'm just saying… You know what? You're right. Fuck it," James swore. "Mow those green bastards down like we're back in fourth grade trying to get enough money for a new game system."

"I hated that job," Tom scowled, stomping on the pedal.

"Yesss…" James hissed, his voice taking on a deep, scratching cadence that wasn't quite deflecting the fear he felt. "Let the hate flow through you…"

Tom kept the pedal down, barreling forward as goblins continued to throw themselves in front of the vehicle in desperate attempts to stop them. Others hurled weapons at the sides of the car, arrows and daggers bouncing off the metal and windows, their aim frantic and wild. After mowing down a good number of goblins, the creatures seemed to wise up, realizing that charging head-on wasn't working. They began to scatter, avoiding the path of the speeding car.

Suddenly, one particularly bold goblin leapt onto the windshield from the hood of a nearby vehicle as they passed. It snarled ferociously, brandishing a dagger that it slammed repeatedly against the windshield. When the glass didn't break, the goblin paused, glancing at the tip of its weapon in confusion before trying again, its frustration growing.

Tom and James screamed in shock at the sudden appearance. They quickly regained their composure as Tom flicked on the windshield wipers. The wipers smacked the goblin in the face repeatedly, stunning it and disrupting its grip. The goblin slid off the side of the vehicle, tumbling onto the pavement and disappearing from view.

The wipers continued their now vastly more squeaky, rhythmic journey as they smeared the blood and other questionable fluids from the creature's stained hands and clothing across the windshield.

Tom quietly and deliberately pressed the button for the washer fluid, pointedly refusing to look into the rearview mirror at the chaos they were leaving behind them.

The shoulder of the freeway seemed relatively clear for most of the way, though there were occasional obstacles where vehicles had pulled over to avoid collisions. Tom navigated around these as best he could, carefully maneuvering past when space allowed. A few times, he had no choice but to use his car to push other vehicles out of the way. Slowing down, he gently nudged the back end of the obstructing cars, hoping for minimal damage to his own vehicle.

As they continued down the road, Tom and James caught glimpses of other drivers who had adopted a similar strategy, using their vehicles to run down goblins in a panic. However, most people still hesitated, unwilling to hit anything humanoid, likely out of a deeply ingrained fear of legal consequences and police intervention.

At one point, they passed a group of three men taking cover behind a car, engaged in a shootout with goblins on the other side. Gunfire cracked through the air as the men fired desperately, using the vehicle as a makeshift barricade. It was clear that chaos had taken over, with everyone trying to survive in whatever way they could.

"Sure makes you wish we'd gotten a fucking conceal carry license right about now. We could have guns to kill these little fuckers too," James commented.

"If I've said it once, I've said it a thousand times," Tom frowned. "Just because you *can* own a gun, doesn't mean *you* should. You'd shoot someone with it."

Tom glanced over at James, clearly seeing the man's unbelieving expression as he gestured animatedly at the invading goblins.

"Oh, come on," Tom shouted, exasperated. "I meant you might hurt *people*."

James folded his arms, clearly intent to stand his ground. "Goblins are people, too."

"Whatever," Tom scowled. "For now, let's just get to the office to see if anyone else made it there."

APOCALYPSE

There were only a few other times they saw goblins on their journey, and each time they tried to either throw themselves in front of the vehicle or throw their weapons or rocks at it. The glass and sides of Tom's car had dings and holes in it now from the barrage of objects, but it continued to run despite its new paint job of black goblin blood and green skin fragments.

Finally making it to their office, Tom and James practically leapt out of the car, running full speed for the office building. They scrambled into the door after scanning their security badges, Tom dropping his once in his haste to remove it from his pocket, and pulled the door shut behind them. Rushing up to their cubicles, the pair sat down in relief, panting heavily.

"Holy cow man. That was the shittiest drive to work ever," Tom said, his head leaning back over his chair.

"Right? What the hell? We work our ass off to make a living, and then this has to happen?" James replied. "Guess this means I don't have to turn in the fix for that ticket now."

Tom noticed a blinking icon on the right side of his vision as he sat there staring at the ceiling. Focusing on it, a prompt appeared, telling him he hadn't finished the tutorial yet.

"Really? You want me to do that now?" Tom said aloud.

"What?" James asked.

"It's telling me I need to finish the tutorial," Tom replied.

"It sure is insistent. That blinking is going to get annoying after a while," James said, his eyes unfocusing to look at something Tom couldn't see.

"Maybe we can get some answers about what the hell is going on and what we need to do about it," Tom pointed out, James grunting in agreement.

"I mean, I guess this is our new normal. We may as well get it out of the way so we can find out what's going on," James said, opening his notification as well. "Looks like a lot of basic information, but if it's the only way to make these damn pop-ups go away, I guess we don't have much of a choice. This had better not end up like those games where you can't do anything until you read the prompts, because unlike there, we can't pause real life. I can't just hold up a finger and ask the bad guys to 'hold on a sec while I read this System message.'"

HUD Display:

Your HUD (Heads-Up Display) provides vital information about your current status. It is designed to keep you aware of your health, resources, and immediate surroundings. Below is a guide to understanding the key elements of your HUD:

HUD Elements:

1.   **Red Bar (HP - Health Points):**
   - Represents your current Health Points.
   - As you take damage, the bar will decrease. If it reaches zero, you will die.

o   Regain HP through healing items, spells, or natural regeneration, which only occurs outside of combat.
o   Keep a close eye on this bar during combat to avoid critical health situations.

2.   **Blue Bar (MP - Mana Points):**
o   Represents your current Mana Points, used for casting spells and activating abilities.
o   Each spell or ability costs a specific amount of MP. The bar will decrease accordingly.
o   MP regenerates over time, or it can be restored instantly with potions or certain skills.
o   Manage your MP wisely to ensure you have enough resources for crucial moments in battle.

3.   **Green Bar (SP - Stamina Points):**
o   Represents your current Stamina Points, used for physical actions such as sprinting, dodging, and using heavy attacks.
o   Physical exertion reduces SP. If the bar depletes, your movements will become sluggish, and you may be unable to perform certain actions until it regenerates.
o   Stamina regenerates over time when you are not actively using it.
o   Balance your actions to maintain a healthy level of stamina during engagements.

Additional Features:

●   **Critical Alerts:** When any of your bars drop below 20%, they will flash to indicate critical status. Take immediate action to recover and avoid dangerous situations.
●   **Positioning:** Your HP, MP, and SP bars are positioned in your peripheral vision to minimize distraction while providing constant awareness of your status.
●   **Customization:** Adjust the size and placement of your HUD elements by concentrating on an item in your view to best suit your preferences and needs.

Tips for Managing Your Resources:

●   **Plan Ahead:** Monitor your resource bars frequently and plan your actions accordingly.
●   **Use Potions and Skills:** Keep a stock of potions and utilize skills that enhance regeneration or reduce resource consumption.

> - **Avoid Overuse:** Avoid unnecessary actions that deplete your resources. Conserve your HP, MP, and SP for critical moments.
>
> Mastering the use of your HUD will enhance your awareness and increase your effectiveness in any scenario. Keep these displays in your sight and use them to your advantage.
>
> ### Continue?
>
> | *Yes* | *No* |
> |---|---|

As Tom glanced upward, he noticed three colored bars now visible at the top of his vision. Their appearance reminded him of the health, mana, and stamina bars from most video games, so it made sense to him. Intrigued, he concentrated on the bars, experimenting with their placement in his mind. After a bit of focus, he managed to rearrange them: one bar shifted to the far right, another to the far left, and the third remained directly in the center of his vision, instead of being stacked on top of each other.

Satisfied with the new layout, Tom selected "Yes" to continue, and a new window materialized before him, adding to the growing sense that his world had suddenly become much more like the games he was familiar with.

> ### Skills:
>
> Skills are abilities that enhance your combat, survival, and interaction capabilities. They are essential tools for navigating challenges, defeating enemies, and optimizing your performance. Understanding and managing your skills effectively will significantly impact your success.
>
> **Skill Overview:**
>
> 1. **Skill Types:**
>   - **Active Skills:** These skills require manual activation and consume resources like Mana Points (MP) or Stamina Points (SP). Examples include offensive spells, healing abilities, and special attacks.
>   - **Passive Skills:** These skills are always active and provide constant benefits without requiring activation. They enhance attributes such as critical hit rate, damage resistance, or regeneration rates.
>   - **Ultimate Skills:** High-impact abilities with powerful effects. They often have longer cooldowns and can turn the tide of battle when used strategically.
> 2. **Skill Acquisition:**

o   Skills can be learned through leveling up, finding skill books, completing quests, or training.

o   Some skills have prerequisites, such as certain attribute thresholds or prior mastery of related skills.

3.   **Skill Levels:**

o   Skills can be leveled up to improve their effectiveness, reduce resource costs, or enhance their effects.

o   Skill rankings are determined based on skill levels and are categorized as follows:

- Beginner (Levels 1-9)
- Novice (Levels 10-19)
- Initiate (Levels 20-39)
- Apprentice (Levels 40-69)
- Journeyman (Levels 70-99)
- Master (Level 100)

o   Skill experience is gained through repeated use or training.

4.   **Resource Management:**

o   Most active skills consume MP or SP. Monitor your resource bars to ensure you have enough to activate skills when needed.

o   Some skills have cooldown periods after use. Plan your actions to avoid being left vulnerable during these downtimes.

Tips for Effective Skill Use:

- **Know Your Skills:** Familiarize yourself with each skill's effects, resource costs, and cooldowns. Understanding when and how to use your skills is key to maximizing their impact.
- **Synergy and Combos:** Some skills work best in combination with others. Experiment with different skill pairings to discover powerful synergies and combos.

Mastering your skills will give you a significant edge in any scenario. Experiment, adapt, and evolve your skill set to become the ultimate adventurer.

Continue?

Yes	No

It was at this moment that Derek came running over to their cubicles.

APOCALYPSE

"Have you guys seen what's going on out there? Why are you just sitting at your desk like it's a normal workday?" Derek questioned, true concern in his voice as he looked to the door.

Derek was another work friend. They had played video games online together and even formed a D&D group with him and a few other people who met monthly to run different campaigns.

"We're trying to finish the tutorial. If we're going to live in this world, we figure we should know what's going on, and it's the only thing offering any information," Tom replied, not looking up from reading his prompts.

"Oh. That actually makes sense," Derek said, completely dumbfounded

"Pull up a chair, shut the fuck up, and let's figure this shit out," James said, pointing at an unoccupied office chair.

Derek pulled over another chair and sat down to go through the tutorial as well. Tom selected "Yes" to continue.

Vending Machines:

The humans of Earth have shown a fascination with vending machines, so the Administrators have decided that this will be the most efficient way to distribute items. All vending machines have been upgraded to function as automated storefronts, providing adventurers with a convenient way to purchase items tailored to their Class, level, and the specific Dungeon they are preparing to enter. This System is designed to streamline your preparations, ensuring you have the right equipment and resources for the challenges ahead.

Key Features of Automated Vending Machines:

1. **Class-Specific Items:**
   - The vending machine automatically identifies your Class and offers items that are best suited to your role, such as weapons, armor, consumables, and Class-specific accessories.
   - Each item comes with a brief description, including its stats, effects, and any requirements or restrictions.
2. **Level-Appropriate Gear:**
   - Items available for purchase are adjusted to match your current level, providing equipment that scales with your progression.
   - Higher-level items become available as you level up, offering improved stats and abilities.
3. **Dungeon Preparation:**
   - The vending machine has the option for Dungeon selection and suggests items that will enhance your chances of success, such as resistances to specific damage types, consumables that counter Dungeon-specific hazards, and gear that exploits the weaknesses of anticipated enemies.
4. **Resource-Based Transactions:**

> ○   Items are purchased using Monster Cores. Each item displays its cost, and the machine will notify you if you lack the necessary cores.
>
> **Usage Tips:**
>
> ● **Review Recommendations:** Take advantage of the tailored recommendations to optimize your loadout for each Dungeon.
> ● **Plan Your Purchases:** Consider your current resources and prioritize items that will provide the greatest benefit based on your Class and the upcoming challenges.
>
> With these automated vending machines, you can efficiently gear up and customize your equipment to suit your needs, ensuring you are always prepared for whatever challenges lie ahead.
>
> **Continue?**

Yes	*No*

"Seriously? Vending machines are how we get items?" Tom laughed.

"Appears so," James replied bemusedly, now nearly fully reclined with his feet up on his desk.

"What? What are you guys talking about?" Derek asked, frowning.

"Just keep reading, you'll get there eventually, cupcake," James replied sarcastically, waving a hand at him to continue through the prompts.

Tom noticed that even though he had the tutorial up, he still had an icon flashing for his attention on the right side of his vision. He mentally focused on this, and a different pop-up appeared in his vision.

> **Level Up:**
>
> You have earned enough XP to advance to the next level. You are now level 2! Continue to work hard and push yourself to gain more XP to continue to level up. You receive 10 Attribute Points to distribute as you see fit.

Level Up:
You have earned enough XP to advance to the next level. You are now level 3! Continue to work hard and push yourself to gain more XP to continue to level up. You receive 10 Attribute Points to distribute as you see fit.

Level Up:
You have earned enough XP to advance to the next level. You are now level 4! Continue to work hard and push yourself to gain more XP to continue to level up. You receive 10 Attribute Points to distribute as you see fit.

Level Up:
You have earned enough XP to advance to the next level. You are now level 5! Continue to work hard and push yourself to gain more XP to continue to level up. You receive 10 Attribute Points to distribute as you see fit.

"Holy shit," Tom said quietly.

"Yeah," James sighed. "The whole *Dungeon* part's a real kick in the balls."

"No, I'm level five now," Tom said, amazed at the quick progress.

"What? No way. How the hell did you manage that?" James asked in disbelief, moving over to be closer to Tom.

"I'm not sure," Tom said.

"Did you check your experience?" Derek asked.

"What? How do I do that?" Tom asked, turning to look at Derek with a quizzical look on his face.

"It's in the combat log. You can configure that in the settings. Are you still on the vending machines page of the tutorial? Come on bro, the world is ending, and we need to get this info," Derek chided.

Going back to the tutorial, Tom selected "Yes" to continue.

Combat Log:

The Combat Log is a powerful tool that provides a detailed record of all actions taken during a battle, helping you analyze your performance, track your progress, and make strategic adjustments for future encounters.

Key Features of the Combat Log:

1. **Experience Tracking:**
   - Every time you defeat a living creature, you earn experience points (XP) that contribute to your character level. Leveling up grants Attribute Points that you can allocate to enhance your stats.
   - The Combat Log records XP gained from each kill, allowing you to track your progression in real-time.
2. **Detailed Battle Records:**
   - Access the Combat Log by simply thinking "Combat Log." This will display a screen with a comprehensive record of the battle, including each strike, the damage dealt, and any spells or abilities used.
   - Healing actions and their effects are also logged, providing a complete view of all restorative actions taken during the fight.
3. **Customizable Filters:**
   - The Combat Log can be overwhelming due to the sheer volume of information it captures. To manage this, you can customize the log by mentally configuring filters to display only the events you wish to see, such as:
     - **Damage Dealt:** View only the damage your attacks have caused.
     - **Healing:** Focus on healing actions performed by you or your allies.
     - **Buffs and Debuffs:** Track status effects that impact your performance.
     - **Critical Hits:** Highlight critical strikes for a focused view of your most impactful attacks.
   - Adjust filters at any time to refine the information displayed, keeping the log relevant to your needs.
4. **Full Log Access:**
   - If you wish to review the complete details of a battle, think "Full Combat Log" to remove all filters and display the entire record of actions, including all strikes, spells, healing, and more.

o   This is useful for in-depth analysis or when reviewing the performance of your party as a whole.

Tips for Using the Combat Log:

•   **Analyze Performance:** Use the log to identify strengths and weaknesses in your strategy. Review critical hits, misses, and overall damage output to refine your approach.
•   **Track Enemy Behavior:** The log also records enemy actions, allowing you to study their attack patterns and adapt your tactics accordingly.
•   **Adjust on the Fly:** Filters can be adjusted during combat to help you stay focused on key events, such as incoming damage or healing needs.

By mastering the Combat Log, you can gain valuable insights into every battle, optimize your combat performance, and make informed decisions to enhance your character's growth.

Continue?

Yes	*No*

Thinking "Combat Log," a log showed in the bottom right of Tom's vision. Reading through the information there, he realized what had happened.

Congratulations!

You have killed a level 3 goblin archer. You gain 500 XP. Continue to fight to reach greater heights in your abilities!

Congratulations!

You have killed a level 3 goblin warrior. You gain 500 XP. Continue to fight to reach greater heights in your abilities!

Congratulations!
You have killed a level 3 goblin scout. You gain 500 XP. Continue to fight to reach greater heights in your abilities!

Congratulations!
You have killed a level 2 goblin archer. You gain 400 XP. Continue to fight to reach greater heights in your abilities!

Congratulations!
You have killed a level 4 goblin scout. You gain 600 XP. Continue to fight to reach greater heights in your abilities!

On and on the log went, with kill notice after kill notice. Tom began to feel a bit sick to his stomach, thinking about how he had killed the creatures. It looked like there were a little over twenty of the goblins that had died from his death plow. Tom had never killed anybody. He'd just reacted in the moment to try to save his life.

"You feeling okay, Tom?" Derek asked, concerned at Tom's expression.

"Looks like I got credit for all the goblins we ran over on the way here," Tom said softly, feeling even more queasy as he remembered the sounds their bodies had made as they were run over by the car's tires.

"What?! But I was there to help, too," James exclaimed, outraged at being cheated out of the experience. "I'm a contributing member of the team as well, you know."

"Apparently, because it's my car and I was driving, only I get XP," Tom replied, still not totally believing what had happened.

"So, what?" James asked. "This whole System interpreted your car as essentially a weapon used to kill the goblins?"

Tom shrugged. "That's my guess, yeah."

"I think if you were to have formed a party, then you would have shared the XP," Derek added.

"How do I do that?" James asked, looking through the prompts to see if he had missed something.

"Just keep reading. You'll get there eventually, cupcake," Derek replied sardonically, putting his feet up on a desk and smiling.

Chapter 3

Tutorial

Dungeons:

Dungeons are special, high-risk areas filled with powerful enemies, traps, and hidden treasures. They are designed to challenge adventurers of all levels and reward those who can successfully navigate their dangers.

Key Features of Dungeons:

1.   **Difficulty Levels:** Dungeons are categorized by difficulty—Common, Rare, Epic, and Legendary. Higher-difficulty Dungeons yield better rewards but pose greater threats. Choose wisely based on your party's strength.

2.   **Party Size and Roles:** Each Dungeon has a recommended party size. Balance your team with roles like Tank, DPS, Healer, and Support to maximize your chances of success.

3.   **Objective Completion:** Each Dungeon has specific objectives such as defeating a boss, collecting items, or clearing waves of enemies. Completing objectives unlocks rewards and progress within the Dungeon.

4.   **Loot and Rewards:** Defeating enemies, completing objectives, and exploring hidden areas can yield valuable loot, including weapons, armor, potions, and rare items. Don't forget to check every nook and cranny!

5.   **Exit Points:** Dungeons have designated exit points. Exiting a Dungeon before completion will not save your progress. Use exits strategically if the challenge becomes too great.

6.   **Traps and Hazards:** Dungeons are filled with traps and environmental hazards. Keep an eye out for suspicious tiles, hidden triggers, and environmental cues. Using skills like Perception or Disarm Trap can mitigate these risks.

7.   **Boss Encounters:** Each Dungeon culminates in a boss fight. Bosses have unique mechanics and abilities—study their patterns, work as a team, and adapt your strategy to take them down.

Tips for Success:

- **Preparation is Key:** Stock up on potions, repair your gear, and ensure your spells are ready before entering.
- **Communication:** Coordinate with your team to handle tough encounters and avoid traps.
- **Adaptability:** Be ready to adjust your tactics based on the challenges you face inside.

Good luck, adventurer! Your bravery and skill will determine your fate within the Dungeons.

Continue?

Yes	*No*

Mana:

Mana is a newly introduced concept for the people of Earth, serving as the primary energy source for casting magic. Due to your planet's previously low mana levels, a Mana Generator has been installed at the Earth's core, which will gradually increase the ambient mana available. This influx of mana will result in significant changes to the environment, including altered flora and fauna and the potential for random monster spawns.

Understanding Mana:

1. **Accessing Mana:**
   - As a user of the Grand System, you now have access to this mana, allowing you to manipulate it to cast spells and perform magical feats.
   - Your body has been equipped with a **Mana Network**—a complex system of channels that direct mana from your core throughout your entire body.
2. **Mana Network:**
   - The Mana Network channels mana efficiently, enabling you to direct it to specific areas of your body for casting different types of magic.
   - Familiarizing yourself with your Mana Network and learning to control the flow of mana is essential for mastering magic.
3. **Casting Spells:**

o   To cast a spell, focus on channeling mana from your core, through your Mana Network, to the desired part of your body.

o   Spells require varying amounts of mana depending on their complexity and power. Monitor your Mana Points (MP) bar in your HUD to ensure you have enough mana to cast your intended spells.

4.   **Mana Proficiency:**

o   Regular practice circulating mana through your channels will increase your proficiency, improving your mana efficiency and enhancing your magical abilities.

o   As you level up and invest in Intelligence or other mana-related attributes, your total MP and mana regeneration rate will increase, allowing you to cast more powerful spells more frequently.

Tips for Effective Mana Use:

•   **Practice Control:** Regularly practice mana control exercises to improve your ability to channel and manipulate mana precisely.

•   **Manage Your Resources:** Keep an eye on your MP bar during combat to avoid running out of mana at crucial moments. Use mana potions or rest when necessary to replenish your reserves.

•   **Learn and Adapt:** As the ambient mana levels continue to rise, new spells and abilities may become available. Stay adaptable and continuously explore new magical techniques.

By mastering your Mana Network and effectively managing your mana resources, you can unlock your full magical potential and thrive in the ever-changing world around you.

Continue?

Yes	*No*

"Is this really all necessary?" James asked, throwing his head back in frustration.

"I know," Tom sighed, not looking away from his screens as he continued reading. "But hey, we do the same to the people that play our games. Besides, you never know what info will be helpful later."

Forming Parties:

Forming a party is a crucial aspect of combat and survival in the new world you now inhabit. Working together with others allows you to combine strengths, cover weaknesses, and tackle a wider variety of challenges. Some monsters possess unique defenses, such as resistance to magic or enhanced physical protection, making a balanced party essential for overcoming these obstacles.

Key Features of Parties:

1. **Party Composition:**
   - A well-rounded party with a mix of Classes—such as Tanks, Damage Dealers, Healers, and Support—can handle a broader range of enemies and situations.
   - Specialize roles within your party to counteract specific enemy defenses, such as using magic users to exploit vulnerabilities in physically tough opponents, or melee fighters to break through magical resistances.
2. **Forming a Party:**
   - To form a party, simply think about extending an invitation to someone nearby. This mental action will send a party request to the selected individual.
   - They will receive a prompt to accept or reject your invitation. Once accepted, they will become part of your party.
   - Parties can consist of up to 8 members at a time, allowing for a diverse range of skills and strategies.
3. **Experience Sharing:**
   - Experience (XP) gained from defeating enemies while in a party is divided equally among all party members, typically based on their individual contributions.
   - This system encourages teamwork and ensures that all members benefit from collective efforts, promoting growth and progress for the entire party.
4. **Party Interface:**
   - Once in a party, you can view your party members' status, including their HP, MP, and other relevant stats, through your HUD.
   - Use this information to coordinate tactics, provide support, or call for assistance when needed.

Tips for Effective Party Formation:

- **Balance Your Team:** Aim for a balanced mix of roles to cover all bases. Too many of one Class can leave your party vulnerable to certain types of enemies.

- **Communicate:** Keep in touch with your party members and plan your strategies. Clear communication is key to overcoming tough encounters.
- **Adapt to the Situation:** Be ready to adjust your party composition based on the challenges you expect to face. Don't be afraid to swap out members or change roles as needed.

By forming a party, you can enhance your combat effectiveness, tackle more challenging Dungeons, and increase your overall survival rate in the new world. Embrace the power of teamwork and lead your party to victory!

Continue?

Yes	*No*

Monster Cores:

Monster Cores are valuable items dropped by monsters when defeated. These cores are a key currency in the new world, used primarily for exchanging items at vending machines found throughout the world. Understanding the value and use of Monster Cores will significantly aid you in your journey.

Key Features of Monster Cores:

1. **Acquisition:**
   - Each time you defeat a monster, it will drop a Monster Core. The type and rarity of the core depend on the monster's strength and classification.
   - Collect these cores as you progress; they are essential for acquiring gear, potions, and other useful items from vending machines.
2. **Core Rarities:**
   - Monster Cores come in various rarities, each representing the value and power of the monster defeated. The ranks are as follows:
     - **Common**
     - **Uncommon**
     - **Rare**
     - **Epic**
     - **Legendary**
     - **Celestial**
     - **Demonic**
     - **Artifact**

o   The rarer the core, the more valuable it is. Higher-rarity cores can be exchanged for more powerful and rare items.

3.   **Core Conversion Rates:**

o   The value of each core rarity can be converted into lower rarities using the following rates:

- **1 Uncommon Core** = 10 Common Cores
- **1 Rare Core** = 25 Uncommon Cores
- **1 Epic Core** = 50 Rare Cores
- **1 Legendary Core** = 100 Epic Cores
- **1 Artifact Core** = 5 Legendary Cores

o   **Celestial and Demonic Cores** are special categories and cannot be easily converted or exchanged like other cores. They hold unique properties and values.

4.   **Usage:**

o   Use Monster Cores at vending machines to purchase items tailored to your Class, level, and the Dungeons you are preparing to enter.

o   Keep track of your cores and plan your purchases wisely, using conversions to maximize the value of your exchanges.

Tips for Using Monster Cores:

- **Collect and Save:** Be sure you keep track of your Monster Cores, as they all hold value and can be exchanged or upgraded for higher-rank cores.
- **Strategize Your Purchases:** Use your cores to obtain items that best suit your immediate needs or long-term goals. Higher-rarity cores can secure powerful gear and abilities.
- **Watch for Special Cores:** Keep an eye out for Celestial, Demonic, and Artifact Cores, as they can have unique uses beyond standard exchanges.

By mastering the collection and use of Monster Cores, you will gain access to powerful resources and equipment that will aid you on your journey through the evolving challenges of the new world.

Continue?

Yes	*No*

Guilds:

APOCALYPSE

Guilds are powerful alliances that can greatly enhance your capabilities in the new world. Forming a Guild provides strategic advantages, collective strength, and access to special features that can aid in your journey. Here's how to get started and make the most of your Guild:

Key Features of Guilds:

1. **Formation Requirements:**
   - A Guild can be formed by a group of 10 or more members. To create a Guild, the following conditions must be met:
     - **Member Agreement:** All founding members must agree to join the Guild.
     - **Base of Operations:** A designated base of operations must be claimed, which will serve as the Guild's headquarters.
     - **Guild Name:** A unique name must be chosen for the Guild to establish its identity.
2. **Guild Structure:**
   - Once a Guild is formed, additional features and ranks become available, defining the roles and responsibilities of each member.
   - Higher-ranking members have access to special privileges, such as managing resources, distributing bonuses, and organizing Guild activities.
3. **Bonuses and Perks:**
   - Guilds provide significant bonuses that can be distributed by higher-ranking members during battles. These bonuses may include increased damage, enhanced defense, improved healing, or other strategic advantages.
   - The strength and type of bonuses available will grow as the Guild levels up and expands its influence.
4. **Raid Parties:**
   - Guilds have the ability to form raid parties, which consist of multiple standard parties working together to tackle larger, more challenging creatures and Dungeons.
   - Raid parties allow for coordinated attacks, strategic planning, and the pooling of resources to overcome formidable foes that would be too difficult for a single party to handle.

Tips for Maximizing Guild Potential:

- **Strategic Formation:** Choose Guild members who complement each other's skills and roles to create a balanced and effective team.

- **Utilize Guild Bonuses:** Make use of the bonuses available to your Guild during critical moments in battle to turn the tide in your favor.
- **Coordinate Raid Parties:** Communicate and plan with your Guild to form raid parties that are well-equipped and prepared for the challenges ahead.

By forming and participating in a Guild, you gain access to powerful allies, strategic advantages, and enhanced resources that will aid you in your journey. Embrace the strength of unity and lead your Guild to greatness!

Continue?

Yes	*No*

Crafting:

Crafting and Alchemy are essential skills that allow you to create powerful items and potions to aid you on your journey. By combining various materials and using your mana, you can enhance the quality and capabilities of your creations. Understanding the crafting and alchemy systems will help you produce items of higher value and effectiveness.

Crafting Overview:

1. **Combining Materials:**
   - Crafting involves combining different materials to create new items, similar to traditional methods. However, with the addition of mana, you can now imbue items with enhanced strength and magical properties.
   - The quality of crafted items is determined by the materials used, your crafting skills, and the amount of mana infused during the process.
2. **Item Ratings:**
   - All crafted items are assigned a rating based on their quality. The basic ratings are as follows:
     - **Poor**
     - **Average**
     - **Good**
     - **Well-Crafted**
     - **Excellent**

- **Master Craft**
  - o The rating, combined with the rarity of the materials, determines the overall value and effectiveness of the item. Higher crafting skill levels in the specific type of item you are creating increase the chances of achieving a higher rating.

3. **Blueprints:**
   - o Crafting requires a blueprint, which serves as the instructions for creating your desired item. Blueprints can be acquired through quests, vending machines, or designed by yourself with sufficient crafting knowledge.
   - o Ensure you have the correct blueprint and materials before starting the crafting process to achieve the best results.

Alchemy Overview:

1. **Potion and Poison Crafting:**
   - o Alchemy involves mixing various ingredients with mana to create potions or poisons. These concoctions can serve a range of purposes, such as healing, enhancing attributes, or inflicting harm.
   - o Similar to crafting, the quality of potions and poisons is influenced by the ingredients used, your alchemy skill level, and mana infusion.

2. **Potion Ratings:**
   - o Potions and poisons have their own ranking system based on their effectiveness:
     - **Diluted**
     - **Weak**
     - **Basic**
     - **Enhanced**
     - **Fortified**
     - **Perfected**
   - o Higher skill in alchemy increases the likelihood of producing potions with superior ratings, resulting in stronger effects.

3. **Recipes:**
   - o To craft potions or poisons, you will need a recipe that outlines the necessary ingredients and steps. Recipes can be found in various locations, purchased, or learned through experimentation.
   - o Follow the recipe closely to ensure the desired outcome and avoid unintended effects.

Tips for Successful Crafting and Alchemy:

- **Practice Your Skills:** Regularly practice crafting and alchemy to improve your skills, allowing you to create higher-quality items and potions.

- **Experiment with Mana:** Experiment with different amounts of mana during the crafting process to discover new enhancements and enchantments.
- **Collect Rare Materials:** Gather rare and valuable materials to increase the overall quality and rarity of your creations.

Mastering crafting and alchemy will provide you with powerful tools and resources, giving you a significant advantage as you face the challenges of the new world. Use your skills wisely and continue to refine your craft!

Continue?

Yes	*No*

Inventory System:

As a user of the Grand System, you are equipped with a personal storage space known as the Inventory. This feature allows you to securely store items in a small dimensional space that can be accessed at any time, providing you with a convenient way to manage your gear, resources, and valuables.

Key Features of the Inventory System:

1. **Accessing Your Inventory:**
   - To access your Inventory, simply think "Inventory," and a visual representation of your storage space will appear in your field of view.
   - From this interface, you can view, add, or remove items with ease. Simply focus on an item to retrieve or store it, and it will be moved in or out of your Inventory.
2. **Secure Storage:**
   - Your Inventory is a private, dimensional space accessible only to you. Items stored within are secure and will not be lost or expelled, even upon death.
   - This ensures that your most valuable items remain safe, regardless of what happens in the outside world.
3. **Storage Capacity:**
   - The initial storage capacity of your Inventory is limited, but sufficient for basic needs. To expand your Inventory, you can purchase upgrades from vending machines located throughout the world.

4. **Item Management:**

- Upgrades will increase the number of slots available, allowing you to store more items and better manage your resources.

  - Organize your Inventory by sorting items into categories such as weapons, armor, consumables, crafting materials, and more. This helps you quickly locate items when needed.
  - Use filters or search functions within the Inventory interface to find specific items without scrolling through your entire collection.

Tips for Effective Inventory Use:

- **Prioritize Important Items:** Keep essential gear, healing items, and valuable resources in your Inventory for quick access during emergencies.
- **Regular Maintenance:** Periodically review and clean out your Inventory to remove unnecessary or outdated items, making space for more useful gear.
- **Plan for Expansion:** Invest in Inventory upgrades as your needs grow. More storage space means more options for gear and resources during your adventures.

By mastering the Inventory System, you can effectively manage your items, keep your gear secure, and stay prepared for any challenge that comes your way. Remember to check your Inventory regularly and make use of upgrades to maximize your storage potential.

Continue?

Yes	*No*

Intro Tutorial Complete

Congratulations! You have successfully completed Phase 1 of the tutorial. You are now equipped with the foundational knowledge needed to navigate the Grand System.

As you continue to grow and explore, more information and features will become available to you. Remember, you can reference any of the information you've learned so far through the Help Menu at any time. The Help Menu will provide details on topics you have already covered and will expand as you gain more knowledge and experience.

Good luck on your journey, and continue to strive for greatness!

"Finally finished?" James asked.

"Yeah. Sorry," Tom replied. "Just trying to take it all in. I was really expecting something more like a traditional game tutorial."

"You mean, you expected it to ask you to pick up a sword, walk forward, swing the sword, then crouch under some convenient obstacle before learning how to jump gaps? Come on, man. Be realistic," Derek added.

"You know what I mean. But you're also right. Now what do we do with this info?" Tom asked.

"Why don't we form a party first?" James asked. "You in, Derek?"

"Sure," Derek replied.

Thinking about extending an invitation, Tom reached out to Derek and James and was rewarded with a prompt.

Party Formed:

James Sanders and Derek Calloway have joined your party. You can see their health information on the left side of your view.

Sure enough, on the left side of his vision were two smaller red bars showing James' and Derek's health. While staring at his view, he noticed another blinking notification on the right side of his vision.

Mentally selecting it, a new pop-up appeared.

Class Selection:

Congratulations on reaching level 5! You now have the opportunity to choose a Class from the list below. As a bonus for reaching level 5 so quickly after the Grand System was implemented, you will also be granted an additional bonus. After selecting your Class, you will be given the option to choose one of three randomly selected bonuses. Choose wisely, as your Class cannot be changed once selected.

Classes:

Warrior – Neutral Alignment - The Warrior is the most basic combat Class, excelling in close combat and physical attacks. While Warriors have a strong physical presence, they possess a weaker affinity for spellcasting.

Ranger – Neutral Alignment - Rangers are skilled with ranged weapons and typically fight from the backline. They have bonus affinities for using projectile weapons, making them excellent marksmen.

Cleric – Light Alignment - Clerics have the strongest affinity for healing magic. Valuable on any team, Clerics also possess offensive magic granted by their chosen deity.

Paladin – Light Alignment - A holy warrior imbued with magic from their God, Paladins are frontline fighters with an increased affinity for heavy armor.

Spellblade – Neutral Alignment - A balanced fighter with affinities for both close combat and magic, Spellblades offer versatility in battle. While not as strong as Warriors or as magically adept as Wizards, they combine the best of both worlds.

Wizard – Neutral Alignment - Wizards are the most powerful magic casters, capable of learning more spells than any other Class. Their focus is almost entirely on offensive magic, but this often comes at the cost of physical capabilities.

Barbarian – Neutral Alignment - Barbarians are the most brutal physical Class. They have little to no affinity for magic, instead relying on raw berserker rage to overwhelm enemies. Barbarians can withstand significant damage with minimal armor.

Rogue – Dark Alignment - Masters of stealth, Rogues excel at ambush tactics and have magical affinities for secretive magics. Their ability to cloak themselves and deal damage with small weapons makes them ideal assassins.

Druid – Light Alignment - Druids are magically inclined fighters who specialize in earth and nature magic. They can bond with animals and transform into a beast form during battle.

Bard – Neutral Alignment - Bards are a Support Class gifted with musical abilities that allow them to cast spells that buff allies and debuff enemies. They can learn more spells than most physical Classes and are generally more agile.

Warlock – Dark Alignment - Warlocks, like Wizards, are primarily magic based, but their power comes from a pact with their patron. They can summon creatures to fight for them but must follow the will and whims of their patron.

"Sweet! I get to choose a Class now! They offer a fairly good selection. Not as many as I have seen in some games, but it's not just a basic list either," Tom commented. "Not sure about these alignments though."

"Really? What do we have to choose from?" James asked.

Reading through the list of options and their descriptions out loud, Tom shared the information he had with his friends.

"What are you going to choose?" James asked Tom.

"I'm not really sure. It looks like it's a permanent choice, so I have to think about it. Do any of them stick out to either of you? If we're going to be a party, then maybe we can pick things that work well together," Tom offered, looking at each of them, hoping they would help make the decision easier.

"Cleric," Derek suggested right away. "I want to be able to help when people need it. I was a medic when I was in the military. So, I think that will suit me well."

"Right on! It's great that we have our Healer already taken care of. I'm probably going to be a Ranger. I don't mind being in the back and using some kind of ranged weapon. I wonder if guns count?" James puffed out his chest with pride as he bragged.

Derek and Tom had a chuckle at this thought. Then Tom stopped and thought about it. How cool would it be to get guns and use them against monsters? It would be much more effective than a bow and arrow would be.

"Actually, that's not a bad idea," Tom replied, now eager to find the answer.

He brought up his storage and noticed he had twenty-four items stacked in one slot of his Inventory. They looked like a grey-colored coin in the image of the icon. They had the face of a goblin embossed on the side of the coin.

So they automatically go into my Inventory. This was great news.

"Don't we have a vending machine here in the building?" Tom asked as he connected the dots.

"Sure, it's on the third floor in the break room," Derek replied casually, then sat up in his chair. "Wait! Are you thinking of going to try it? It's just a snack machine."

"I think we need to go look at it," Tom replied and stood up to head toward the stairs, Derek and James following behind after staring at each other for a moment.

Climbing the stairs two at a time in his excitement, Tom raced from the first floor, past their work desks to the third, where the large break room was located.

Chapter 4

Vending Machines

Coming to a stop, slightly out of breath from their rush, Derek and James found Tom standing in front of the vending machine in the third-floor break room. But it wasn't the same machine they remembered. The old vending machine had been a standard, unremarkable device, adorned with a massive decal of a bag of chips bursting open alongside a bottle of soda fizzing as its cap was twisted off. What stood before them now was something entirely different—almost like a work of art.

The new machine appeared to be crafted from antique metal, with intricately inlaid designs and delicate silver filigree adorning its surface. The front of the machine was a deep, rich red, while the sides were painted a soft sky blue. Near the bottom was a retrieval bay, elegantly designed, and beside it was an oversized coin slot, paired with a sleek digital touchpad that was clearly intended for making selections.

A soft, ethereal glow emanated from within the vending machine, casting an otherworldly light that illuminated the items inside. However, there were no visible bulbs or LED strips; the source of the light seemed magical in both nature and truth. The interior was arranged with seven rows of items, each neatly displayed in individual slots, ready to be dispensed.

Each slot held a sixteen-ounce can, reminiscent of those used for popular energy drinks. The front of each can featured a detailed image that hinted at its contents: a battle axe, a sword, a bow, a quiver of arrows, and many other items that seemed to belong to a world of fantasy and adventure. The cans gleamed under the machine's mysterious light, each one promising something extraordinary within.

"Hello, how may I help you today?" The machine said in a female voice that sounded like all the other automated assistant voices.

"It talks?" Derek asked, stepping back from the machine in surprise.

"If you would like to make a purchase, place your hand on the touch screen to begin," the machine continued.

Tom reached forward to place his hand on the screen.

"Wait, dude! You don't know what that will do!" James exclaimed, reaching forward and trying to stop Tom. But it was too late. Tom's hand touched the screen.

"It appears you have not yet selected a Class," the vending machine explained. *"At this time, I can only offer you basic selections of starter gear instead of being able to tailor your selections to your Class. Please make a selection and enter the appropriate number of Monster Cores to complete your*

purchase. Or you may select a Class, retouch the screen, and I can give you an updated selection of items."

"Incredible! It's way more advanced than I'd assumed. I wonder how it gets stocked?" Tom said in awe of the machine, his hand still touching the screen. "I don't see guns as an option, though."

As he said this, the machine glowed brighter. It reconfigured itself so that one of the items in the machine drew back into itself and was then replaced by another row of cans. This time, the picture on the front of the can was a handgun. After this change, James pressed his face up against the glass, pushing Tom to the side slightly.

"Are you shitting me?!" James exclaimed, practically drooling on the glass as he smooshed his face against it in an attempt to get closer. "You know, we could just break the machine and take all of these things."

"I would advise against that course of action," The machine suddenly said in its deadpan voice. *"Any act of aggression taken against a machine will be seen as a violation of the Grand System rules and will be met with swift and harsh punishment."*

"Orrr we could *not* try to conduct a smash and grab on something that was created by a powerful entity completely unknown to us," Derek said, a hint of nervousness in his voice at the warning. "Seriously, dude, you need to see about getting some help for your kleptomania."

"I'm not a klepto! I just don't like paying for things. Big difference," James explained emphatically, trying to defend himself. "Besides, I'd never liberate things from someone who needed it. Only from those who have more than their fair share. Think of me as more of the Robin Hood of this tale."

"How magnanimous of you," Derek replied sarcastically, with not a small amount of derision in his voice.

"It looks like the gun costs three Monster Cores," Tom said, looking at the numbers next to the can's letter and number selection combinations. Pulling up his Inventory, he selected the Monster Cores and imagined three of them. They suddenly materialized in his hand out of thin air. "That's pretty cool. They are bigger than I expected as well."

Each of the coins was a dull silver color and was about three times the size of a silver dollar, making them quite cumbersome to carry.

"I guess that explains why the coin slot here is so much bigger than normal," Derek pointed out, looking down at the opening beneath the touchscreen.

Tom reached down, put one coin in the slot, and released it. There was a metallic sliding sound and then the telltale thud at the bottom that showed it went into the coin repository.

"One common core entered," the machine said and a number one appeared on the screen next to the word "Common," while zeros still remained next to the other rankings to indicate how many cores were put in.

Tom placed the remaining two cores into the coin slot and entered "D-6" on the keypad, selecting the can labeled with a handgun. With a metallic clatter, the can dropped from its slot and landed in the bottom receptacle of the machine. A moment later, a new can slid into place, replacing the one that had just been dispensed.

Reaching into the receptacle, Tom grabbed the can. It was cool to the touch, but not uncomfortably cold. He turned it over in his hands, inspecting it briefly before holding it out to James.

"Are you sure? Those are your Monster Cores, man," James asked, a little hesitant to take it from him. "I don't want to steal your thunder."

"Of course you do, you kleptomaniac," Derek jabbed.

James gave him a dark glare as Tom and Derek chuckled at the joke.

"It's for your Class. Use it. We're a team here," Tom said, pushing the can into his chest. "I just want us to have the best chance of surviving this, so I'll buy our first round of gear. You can always pay me back later if you feel you need to."

James accepted the can, almost reverently. He looked up at Tom and smiled.

"Thanks, man. I never really had friends like you growing up," James said solemnly. Then, with a smirk, "Now give me a kiss."

Tom rolled his eyes, but as he let the moment settle, he couldn't help but reflect. James hadn't had much growing up. Even now, he still sent money back to his parents when they struggled. Tom felt lucky to have him around.

He clapped a hand on James' shoulder. "Dude, you're like my best friend," he said, voice steady. "We're in this together."

Then, with a grin, he added, "Also, I'd be failing as your best friend if I didn't say—stop whining, you little bitch. The machine already warned us, and I'm not interested in getting smacked down by the System. I'm kind of attached to living."

The jab landed perfectly.

All three of them burst out laughing.

"You just had to add that last bit, didn't you?" James joked, shaking his head. "I really thought we were having a moment there. Finally got past all that 'you're a man, I'm a man bullshit' and found something special. Guess not."

"Oh, stop with the sap and just open it already," Derek chided, looking at James with his hands on his hips. "I'm curious how the can-o-gun works now. Doesn't look like it just fits inside the can."

James took the can and popped the top open. There was the familiar and satisfying "Chhhhttsssssss" sound that comes from opening a can of cola, and then a "POOF" as a cloud of smoke erupted around James' hands. When the smoke cleared, he was holding a Glock G17 9mm handgun.

"Holy shit, it worked!" James exclaimed, waving the gun around in his hand.

"Hey, hey, hey! Point that thing down, you son of a bitch!" Derek yelled, covering his face with his hands and ducking to not be in the line of fire. "Didn't anyone teach you gun safety?"

"Nope," James said, smiling evilly.

"Well, then I'll be the first. Rule number one: never point it at someone unless you're willing to pull the trigger. Number two: James doesn't get any more guns," Derek recited, reaching to take the gun from him.

"Nuh-uh! This is mine! Tom gave it to me," James said, dancing away and pulling the gun to his chest. "Besides, there's plenty of things I'm willing to shoot right now. Like all those goblins we ran into on our way to work."

Rolling his eyes, Derek reluctantly acquiesced, "Fine, but you have to learn how to use it properly. Plus, you only have like fifteen shots with that thing. You're going to need more magazines and bullets."

"Don't you mean a clip?" James asked, turning the gun over in his hands to look at the magazine slot.

"No, I don't. That's why I don't think you're ready for this," Derek stated emphatically. "A magazine holds the bullets in your gun. A clip is used to load the bullets into a magazine that then goes into your gun. Just let me see it for a moment. I promise I won't keep it from you. I just want to check it out."

Reluctantly, James handed the gun over to Derek. Looking over the outside of the gun carefully, Derek turned his body so he wasn't facing the others. Taking out the magazine, he pulled the slide back. He spent about two minutes looking it over and then placed the magazine back in the gun, loaded one bullet in the chamber, and handed it back to James.

"I thought it was a Glock 19. Apparently, it's a Glock 17," Derek told James. "So, it has a seventeen plus one capacity, which means it can hold seventeen rounds in the magazine and then one in the chamber. We still need to get you some more rounds. Are there any in the machine?"

All three turned back to the machine to look through the available options. It did in fact appear that there were some bullets down at the bottom. Though it didn't say how many came in a can. The picture on the front of the can just seemed to be a generic picture of one bullet standing up and a pile of them lying down behind it.

"I guess we'll just have to buy them to find out. It's only one Monster Core, so here goes nothing." Tom said. He summoned another core from his Inventory and put it into the slot in the machine. Selecting "G-1" on the keypad, the can for the bullets dropped into the bottom of the machine.

James reached in and took the can. Turning his head side to side, he looked at the weapon in one hand and the can in the other for a confused second. Shrugging, he put the gun in the waistband of his pants and reached to open the can.

Derek facepalmed.

"You're doing this to piss me off, aren't you?" Derek asked, annoyance evident in his voice.

"Oh, definitely," James said, opening the can.

This time, when the cloud of smoke appeared, the sound of metal tinkling as it hit the ground sounded over and over. The smoke cleared and James was holding two handfuls of bullets, with quite a few more on the ground. James began to stuff them into his pockets.

"Use your Inventory, you moron," Derek scolded him.

"Oh, right," James said, looking sheepish.

He then touched a single bullet, thinking about his Inventory, and all the bullets disappeared into his Inventory.

"So, how many did you get?" Tom asked.

"Looks like I got two hundred," James replied, his eyes unfocused and clearly staring at a screen the others couldn't see.

"That's a pretty good number. But it's hard to tell if that's a good price. I assume it is based on the fact that it only costs one common core, which is the lowest rank of the cores," Derek mused.

"Let me see the gun for a moment, James," Tom said, having an idea.

James handed him the gun, and Tom used Inspect on the weapon.

Item: Glock 17 9mm Handgun	
The Glock 17 is a highly reliable and widely used semi-automatic handgun. Known for its durability and simplicity, this firearm is a favorite among law enforcement and military personnel worldwide. The Glock 17's reliability, light weight, and 17-round magazine capacity provide a balance of power and precision. Its Safe Action system ensures safe, easy, and quick usability. The Glock 17 is renowned for its accuracy, minimal recoil, and ease of maintenance, making it an ideal choice for both self-defense and tactical scenarios.	
Item Type:	Weapon, Ranged
Durability:	50/50
Attack:	8-10 Damage
Item Quality:	Average
Item Rarity:	Common

"I don't really know if this is great or crap. It's likely a starter weapon, seeing as we started at level one. But I assume once you get a Class, they'll become better and do more damage," Tom commented after looking at the stats. "Here, use your own Inspect skill on it to see the stats."

James took the weapon back and used Inspect. He frowned slightly, looking at the stats.

"Well, it's still a weapon I didn't have before. Besides, I'm sure a headshot will be lethal to most smaller monsters," James added, holding the gun up in a Charlie's Angels pose.

"True, and speaking of that—Derek, what kind of weapon do you think would do well for you?" Tom asked, looking over to Derek this time.

Stepping up to the machine, Derek looked at all of the available options. After a moment, he stepped back and pointed at one of the cans.

"A mace. That's the standard starting weapon for most Clerics, and I think I would love to go with a warhammer at some point, so let's start with that. It looks like the best option in the starter gear for that line," Derek said thoughtfully, imagining being on the battlefield smashing goblins with a weapon like the legendary Mjolnir.

Tom pulled out three more Monster Cores and inserted them into the machine, then punched in "D-1" on the keypad. The can clattered down into the retrieval bay, and Derek quickly reached in to grab it. Without hesitating, he popped the top of the can, and a familiar "poof" sounded as a cloud of smoke erupted and quickly dissipated. When the smoke cleared, Derek was left holding a basic flanged mace.

The mace featured a sturdy wooden handle with a leather-wrapped grip, offering a secure hold. Its metal head was flanged with eight sharp protrusions, and a pointed spike topped the weapon, adding to its menacing appearance. It was clear that this was a weapon designed for inflicting serious damage—it looked like a strike from it would be incredibly painful.

"What weapon are you going to choose?" James asked, suddenly realizing Tom needed to get something and looking to his friend.

"I'm still not entirely sure what I want to be. I'm leaning toward Spellblade so I can use both weapons and spells," Tom said, contemplating all the choices the System had given him. "It just feels like a big choice to make, considering I can't change it."

"What about a Paladin?" Derek asked.

"I think if I was going to go the route of tying myself to someone, I'd rather go Warlock. The ability to summon creatures sounds pretty cool, too. Though Paladin is on my shortlist," Tom replied, not completely convinced it was the right choice for him.

"It sounds like you might be able to get either a sword or battle axe for any of those choices," Derek explained, putting a hand on his chin in contemplation.

"Wouldn't a Warlock use a staff?" Tom asked, picturing a dark wizard in his mind when thinking of a Warlock.

"No. They could if they went purely magic-based. But most Warlocks can also do some up-close combat. It all depends on the pact that's made," Derek replied, gesturing with one hand, his elbow resting atop the other arm across his stomach.

"You sure know a lot about this stuff, Derek," James interrupted, surprised by how in-depth Derek was going into the explanations of so many Classes.

"I was on the team that did most of the research into Classes and races for character development in the last several games we released," Derek replied, smiling at the compliment.

"Well, then I think I'm ready to decide my Class!" Tom exclaimed.

Chapter 5

Path of the Warlock

"Warlock?" James asked, almost sounding incredulous. "That's what you're going with? Don't they normally have, like, a limited number of things they can do?"

"I'm thinking about the long game, James. Warlocks start out a bit weaker than the rest, but usually can summon super powerful creatures to wreak serious havoc," Tom replied slightly defensively. "Besides. You guys can help with the beginning and having the extra firepower seems like it would be a good deal for us."

"He has a point, James," Derek interjected. "The Warlock Class only seems slightly lacking at first because the relationship has to be built up with the one they make the pact with. If he can show them his abilities, then he'll gain power really quickly."

"Well, what about the whole slave-master prospect? You don't want to be a fucking slave to some demonic sicko, do you?" James asked, beginning to sound genuinely concerned.

"James, not all pacts are ones between a master and a slave. In fact, few are. Most people are wary of anything 'slave' related, and those that form pacts with Warlocks know that. Many are just to benefit the other being. Some need souls for power in their dimension, so simply killing monsters here grants them great favor with the pact holder," Derek explained. "There are almost as many kinds of pacts as there are creatures and beings to make pacts with."

"Fine, but if you end up tied up to a bed by your wrists and ankles, yelling for your master with an ass-blaster belted to your waist, don't come crying to me without sending a video first," James said smugly. "And always remember your safe word."

"Aaaaaaand he's back," Tom said, laughing at James' antics.

"Sounds like you've made up your mind," Derek said. "Why not pick your Class so we can see what Class-specific items look like?"

"Sure thing," Tom replied and pulled up the notification in his vision.

Class Selection
Would you like to make your Class selection now? You can choose to wait, but please note that items specific to your Class build will not become available until you make your selection, and you won't gain as many benefits until you do. **Choose now?**

Yes	*No*

After selecting "Yes," Tom was presented with a new prompt displaying the same previous list of available Classes to choose from. He scanned the options and chose "Warlock." Immediately, another prompt appeared before him. This one had a completely black frame, with wisps of shadow billowing off the edges like fog drifting from a bowl of dry ice submerged in water. The effect was eerie and otherworldly, adding to the mystique of the choice he was about to make.

Path of the Warlock	
Choosing the path of the Warlock requires you to forge a pact with a powerful being from another dimension. Before selecting an entity to bond with, you must first decide on the type of pact you will be making. Each pact type will grant you different abilities and access to a unique list of entities to choose from.	
Slave/Master Pact	This pact requires you to follow the will of your master at all times. They will dictate your path and set your goals. While this type of pact offers immense power, it also grants the least amount of freedom.
Soul Provision Contract	This pact requires that the souls of all creatures you kill be sent to the entity with whom you've made the agreement. While this pact offers you the most freedom in your actions, your power will only grow based on the number of souls you deliver to your patron.
Pact of the Tattoo	This pact allows you to form a contract with a being that will mark you with sigils of power. These sigils can be activated in times of need to grant you additional strength. This pact is a balance between freedom and obligation: while the being will make requests of the Warlock, you have the

	choice to accept or refuse them. The more requests you fulfill, the more power you will receive.
Pact of Sacrifice	This pact requires you to make live sacrifices to your bonded being in exchange for power. The purer the sacrifice, the greater the power bestowed upon you.
Pact of the Assassin	This pact requires you to carry out contracted assassinations of powerful entities to gain favor and power. Although this path is difficult and dangerous, it offers significant rewards and the potential for immense power.
Pact of Knowledge	This pact requires you to provide new sources of knowledge from your world to the being of power. The more valuable and unique the knowledge you offer, the greater the power you will receive in return.
Pact of Religion	This pact requires you to bring followers to worship the being with whom you form a contract. The more followers you can recruit to serve the patron, the more power will be bestowed upon you in return.

The options laid out before Tom seemed straightforward enough, but several were immediately out of the question. The Slave/Master Pact was a hard no, as were Soul Provision, Sacrifice, and Religion. Tom wasn't willing to compromise his morals for power, and he'd rather choose a completely different Class than be forced into one of those paths. One option, however, stood out to him: the Pact of the Tattoo. It promised the potential to gain power quickly, but on his own terms, without the sinister and obvious strings attached to the other choices.

After making his selection, a dark void materialized in a perfect circle in front of him. Black and purple lights swirled within, creating a mesmerizing, nebulous effect right before his eyes. From the twisting vortex, a black, leather-bound book with intricate red inlays floated out, landing softly in his hands. The cover was inscribed in elegant gold lettering that read, "The Path to Power, Embedded in Your Flesh."

As soon as the book firmly settled in Tom's grasp, the portal collapsed on itself with a soft pop, disappearing as quickly as it had appeared. The three men stared in awe and wonder at the book, still processing the sight of it materializing out of thin air.

"Well, go on... open it," James encouraged him excitedly.

"I will, just give me a minute. I'm soaking it all in," Tom said, slightly annoyed.

"Not sure you have that kind of time." Derek's voice was oddly resonant as it lightly echoed from the open space he was looking toward.

Tom and James turned around and looked through the window across from the break room door. They could see that the building across the street was now engulfed in flames.

Rushing over to the window for a better view, the trio peered down at the chaotic scene below. From their vantage point, they saw goblins dancing wildly with spears raised above their heads, chanting and shouting in what appeared to be some kind of celebration of the fire they had obviously set.

A group of goblins had gathered around the entrance to their own building, but fortunately, the door was a reinforced steel security door—installed to protect the sensitive data housed inside. Additionally, there were no windows on the first floor, a design choice meant to prevent easy access during a potential break-in. However, the second floor did have windows, and it was clear that if the goblins were determined enough, it would only be a matter of time before they managed to break through and gain entry.

"Well, no use standing here with our thumbs up our ass, regardless of whether some might enjoy it... Open that motherfucker!" James exclaimed, never taking his eyes off the goblins out the window and gesturing at Tom.

They had the bodies of several people that they were proceeding to cut the intestines out of and wrap around their necks like macabre scarves.

One of the little ankle biters had a man's head that he had rammed onto the end of his spear, and he was waving it around and chasing other goblins with it, laughing at the game he was playing. Another goblin grabbed the head off the spear and threw it at the spear wielder's face. He screamed something at him and then stomped off.

"You think I could kill one of those bastards from here?" James asked evilly, stroking the pistol in his hand.

"Sure, but then they'd know we were here, and the glass would be broken," Derek said. "Best *not* to give away our position until we're fully equipped and have a plan of where to go next."

"Good point. We can shoot their dicks off when we exit the building," James replied, suddenly pausing his gun-stroking while shaking his head from side to side.

"Might want to aim for their other heads, so they don't get back up," Tom offered.

"You guys are no fun," James said, pretending to mope slightly. "Fine, we'll go with your plan. But I want it on the record that I'm only complying under duress. You forced me to do this. You're a monster."

"Says the guy wanting to shoot dicks off," Derek added, a concerned look on his face.

"Touché," James replied.

APOCALYPSE

Tom walked away from the window and back into the break room, leaving James and Derek still talking by the window.

Standing alone, he held the book in his palm, spine down, and carefully opened it to the first page. As soon as his eyes fell on the text, the words glowed with a bright pinkish-purple hue, and the letters seemed to jump off the page. The words and images flowed directly into his eyes, and Tom found himself unable to move, captivated by the strange process unfolding before him.

A sudden gust of wind, seemingly from nowhere, whipped through the room, causing his hair and clothes to flutter as if caught in a storm. The knowledge contained within the book began to flood his mind, seeping into every corner of his consciousness. The pages turned rapidly, faster and faster, as the glowing text continued to leap off the paper and into his thoughts.

Tom felt a sudden pressure building behind his eyes, as if his mind were stretching past its limits to contain the flood of information pouring in. The sheer volume of knowledge threatened to tear through him like his brain couldn't keep up.

The book reached its final page, snapped shut with a sharp crack, and crumbled to ash in his hand. He staggered backward, dropping the remnants as he fought to stay upright.

His hands gripped the sides of his head as the storm inside his mind raged on, fragments of foreign knowledge flashing too fast to process.

Moments later, he found himself on his knees, breathing heavily as the mental assault finally began to ease. The crushing pressure ebbed, and the chaotic fragments slowly began to thread themselves into something comprehensible.

Breathing heavily, Tom tried to steady himself as James and Derek rushed over, alarmed by what they had witnessed. They knelt beside him, concern etched on their faces as they checked to see if he was okay.

"You good? You look like you just took a shot of Jäger and forgot the chaser," James said, one hand on his back, and his concern evident in his voice.

"Yeah. Just… took in a lot of info all at once," Tom replied, gasping slightly from the exertion of sorting all the information in his mind and the toll it had taken on him. "That book was no joke. But it taught me a lot about my Class. I need to perform a ritual to finish up and make the pact."

"That's pretty standard. Do you need some kind of chicken to sacrifice or special ingredients?" Derek asked.

"Dude… that's dark," James said, a pretend note of disgust in his voice. "I like it."

"Nah, just need to draw a symbol on the floor and imbue it with some of my mana," Tom said, dismissing the question.

"Well, that's anticlimactic. Next time, choose something that wants more death and destruction," James said, clearly disappointed.

"You've never killed anyone. You don't know what you're talking about," Derek said accusingly, looking at James with a bit of anger.

"True, but I've always been good with blood. I bet I'll be great at it. Just like most other things I put my mind to," James added, a smile coming to his face as he thought about all the video games he had played.

Tom and Derek just rolled their eyes. Derek moved to a drawer and opened it to pull out a marker for Tom to draw the sigil with. He took the marker and looked for a place on the floor to draw the circle.

"All the tables are bolted down. Can you just do it on the wall?" Derek asked.

"That's what she sai—" James began before Derek slapped him in the breadbasket with the back of his hand, briefly knocking the wind from him.

"No clue," Tom said, rolling his eyes and moving over to a large white wall and drawing a circle. "It just said to do it on the floor. I don't see why it would matter."

Halfway through drawing, he noticed a blinking icon in the right of his vision. Selecting it, a prompt appeared.

Bonus
Now that you have selected a Class, you will be given the opportunity to choose a random bonus for reaching level 5 so quickly after the System initiation. Please select one of the following: • **Attack Boost** – Receive a 10% bonus to attack damage • **Defense Boost** – Receive a 10% bonus to your defense • **Speed Boost** – Receive a 10% bonus to your speed

The choices weren't overwhelmingly great, but any boost would help. Tom opted for the bonus to his attack, reasoning that Warlocks typically functioned as DPS—damage-focused characters specialized in dealing consistent damage. Once he finished with the prompt and noticed no new icons appearing, he turned his attention back to drawing the summoning symbol.

After about ten minutes of careful work, Tom had completed several concentric circles, each filled with intricate runes and complex patterns. At the center of the design, he drew a large star, and along the outermost circle were words inscribed in an ancient language that none of them recognized, wrapping around the entire perimeter. He finished the design with symbols resembling flames at four points, corresponding to the north, south, east, and west positions on a compass.

Stepping back to survey his work, Tom raised his hand and focused intently. Closing his eyes, he concentrated on the mana flowing through his body, visualizing it coursing through invisible channels within him. Slowly, he guided the flow of energy, directing it to manifest in his palm as a tangible force. With a focused push, he sent the mana into the summoning circle. The lines and symbols began to softly glow with a blue light, gradually intensifying as the mana infused every part of the design.

Tom lowered his arm and took a deep breath, then spoke a string of words in a language none of them had heard before. The air around them seemed to hum with energy, and the glow from the summoning circle grew brighter, pulsing with a faint, otherworldly power. The symbol radiated with the promise of something extraordinary about to unfold.

"Admoneo te, magne spiritus, ad nutum meum accede et da mihi potestatem quam cupio. Habeo crustulum," Tom chanted, a guttural sound echoing behind his voice as he spoke the words making him sound slightly possessed.

The light from the summoning circle suddenly flared, intensifying in brightness. Derek and James instinctively took a few steps back, shielding their eyes from the glare. As the light grew stronger, the rest of the room began to dim. The glow from the circle cast long, eerie shadows along the walls. Smoke started to pour out of the circle, creeping across the floor and curling up the walls. The effect added to the increasingly ominous atmosphere.

In the center of the circle, the air seemed to ripple and distort. Another portal began to form, swirling with dark energy that twisted and pulled at the edges of reality. It expanded outward from the drawing on the wall, crackling with power, until a being began to materialize within the portal.

Slowly, it floated forward, emerging straight out of the wall. Its form was still shrouded in shadows and smoke. The room was filled with an unsettling hum, as if the very air was charged with anticipation as something otherworldly crossed the threshold into their world.

Chapter 6

The Pact and Choices

The being emerging from the portal looked like a hybrid of a professional bodybuilder and a lizard. Its entire body was covered in dark red scales. They radiated out across the creature's skin with intricate patterns and were adorned with glowing tattoos that pulsed with an ominous energy. Its eyes were a solid, unbroken red, without pupils—giving it an unsettling, alien appearance. A white bandana was tied around its forehead, contrasting sharply with its crimson scales. Muscular arms and legs bulged with raw strength, while its hands and feet ended in sharp, black talons that gleamed menacingly.

The creature continued to float horizontally from the portal, arms crossed over its chest in a pose that radiated both arrogance and confidence. Its disposition spoke a clear message, proclaiming that it was a force to be reckoned with. It was a powerful, intimidating entity, clearly expecting the world to bow before it.

However, as it fully emerged and its feet touched down on the wall, gravity took over in a comically abrupt fashion. The creature fell to the ground, landing flat on its face with a heavy thud.

"OW! What the fuck?! Who put the summoning circle on a wall? The instructions specifically say to put it on the floor for *just this issue!* You complete and utter morons have no idea what I'm capable of, and I'm really not in the mood to deal with this shit. You absolute cunt-stained, whore-bred, pencil-dicked, ass-hatted sons of bitches!" the creature yelled at the three men standing in the room.

"I like him," James leaned in and whispered to Tom, who was leaning back from the verbal onslaught.

The being smiled at this.

"It's too bad you aren't the one who summoned me. I like your spunk, kid," it said, looking at James. "I am Azroc. Great being of the plains of Porthos, far beyond the realms of the demigods. I have come to form a pact with you."

Azroc pointed directly at Tom, his red eyes narrowing as he fixed his gaze on him. His scales were a deep reddish hue, except for his chest and stomach, which were a contrasting dark cream color. Black tattoos, swirling in intricate patterns, wrapped around his scaled body, accentuating his muscular form. As Azroc moved, his muscles rippled with each flex, showcasing the raw power beneath his skin. Every movement seemed deliberate, radiating a sense of menace and strength as he continued to lock eyes with Tom.

"Let us set the terms of the pact. You will serve in the capacity that I need in exchange for some of my power. I will tattoo you with the abilities you choose from a set to be determined, based on the jobs done for me, or milestones met," Azroc said.

"What exactly does that mean?" Tom asked. "What are the requirements and milestones? I'm not signing anything without clear understanding between us."

"The requirements are quests that you will complete, and I will give you them over time. The milestones I can set as either accomplishments that you complete or based on the number and quality of souls you send to me," Azroc explained.

"Souls I send. You mean from kills or sacrifices?"

"Ew." Azroc wrinkled his nose in disgust. "Kills of course. Only those dark freaks like sacrifices. The souls are usually too pure and don't have that much energy anyway. I'm not some kind of monster. Regular old souls will do fine. The more you send, the more power I'll give you."

"Speaking of souls," Tom began, "how is what you're offering any different from the Pact of Sacrifice or Soul Provision Contract?"

"The Pact of Sacrifice requires *live* sacrifices. It's messy, and quite frankly, fucking disgusting. Not kink-shaming, mind you. If that's your thing, that's on you, but I don't like it. It also requires a lot of ritual work on your part. Very time consuming," Azroc explained. "As for the Soul Provision Contract, mine's not all that different, except that the abilities given are activated in different ways. Soul Provision will give you spells that have verbal and somatic activation requirements, meaning you're more of a spellcaster, and tattoos can be activated with a thought. You don't have a problem with tattoos, do you?"

"No, or I wouldn't have chosen the Pact of Tattoos," Tom replied, a bit confused.

"Cool, cool. You wouldn't believe how many people don't read that part of the fine print," Azroc said, chuckling slightly.

"It's… literally the name of the Pact," Tom said, frowning.

"*Exactly.*" Azroc snapped the fingers of one hand and pointed a finger at Tom. "Fucking idiots. So, you get to pick one tattoo to start with. What's it gonna be?"

With that, a prompt appeared in Tom's view.

Pact of the Tattoo

You have chosen to form a Pact with Azroc. As a gesture of good faith, Azroc offers you one tattoo to begin with. Choose one of the following:

- **Tattoo of Brute Strength:** This tattoo allows you to boost your Strength by 50% for 1 hour at the cost of 20 mana. With this enhancement, you'll hit harder, lift more, and deal greater damage to your enemies. Cooldown: 1 hour.

- **Tattoo of the Flaming Fist:** This tattoo enables you to encase your hands in fireballs for 1 hour at the cost of 20 mana. The flames can be

> activated and deactivated at will, but the 1-hour timer will continue to count down even when the fire is not active. Cooldown: 1 hour.
>
> ● **Tattoo of Bark Skin:** This tattoo thickens your skin, increasing your defense by 50% for 1 hour at the cost of 20 mana. Cooldown: 1 hour.

"These are all great options. I have no idea which one to choose," Tom said, seriously considering his choice and scratching his chin. "But there are no ranged options. These are all close combat only."

"That's because, at this level, you likely don't have a lot of mana, so hitting things ends up being the way of it. I want you to be able to defend yourself. And no, I'm not getting sweet on you, so calm down. You're an investment and it's in both of our best interests if I can help keep you alive and supplying me with those sweet, sweet *souls*. Don't worry, every Warlock gets a spell or two right at the beginning as well. But *these* will keep you out of tight spots," Azroc explained. "You don't want to be some guy with a bunch of ranged spells and then get your ass handed to you in a fist fight. That would really make you a pussy against a close-combatant."

"That makes perfect sense, actually. Thanks!" Tom said, brightening at the idea. "I think Tattoo of Brute Strength is the way to go for now. That will come in handy in a lot of places. Nothing like having someone get in close only to realize the spellcaster didn't skip arm day."

"Never skip arm day." Azroc nodded with an overly serious expression, seeming to mentally back into his mind for a distant memory. As if to make his point, he flexed his arms and legs like a bodybuilder to show off his physique. "And for that matter, never skip leg day either."

Tom made his selection, and almost immediately, a burning, stinging sensation spread across his shoulders. It felt as though a swarm of needle-like pricks was crawling over his skin—as if he were being bitten by a million mosquitoes all at once. The pain intensified, blossoming into a fiery heat that seared through his flesh. Gritting his teeth, Tom pulled up his sleeves, revealing large, swirling tribal patterns forming on his shoulders and upper arms. The black ink etched itself into his skin, the intricate designs seeming to come alive as they spread.

When the pain finally subsided, Tom noticed a faint hum of power flowing through the new tattoo. It was subtle, but unmistakable—a small surge of energy that coursed through the markings, connecting them to the magic he had just unlocked. Tom flexed his arms, still feeling the lingering warmth of the ink, and marveled at the sense of newfound strength that pulsed beneath the surface.

"Badass!" James gasped, moving in close to see the tattoos for himself.

"Our Pact is sealed. Stand by me, and I will stand by you. If you are not comfortable with a certain quest, you may reject it. But be warned that you can only reject three quests in a row before you must take the fourth, else our Pact will be broken. I will not ask terrible things of you. I do need certain resources to continue to provide you with the strength you have, though. Do me proud, young Warlock," Azroc said, beaming and again standing with his arms across his chest, looking proud.

With that completed, the portal in the wall opened again, and Azroc moved toward it.

"And if you ever summon me on a wall again, I'll teach you a terrible lesson about the pain those tattoos can cause you," Azroc threatened menacingly.

He clumsily climbed up into the portal, awkwardly hoisting one knee over the edge before losing his balance and tumbling sideways. Inside, he landed on what seemed to be flat ground, but the orientation was perpendicular to the wall, giving the whole scene a disorienting tilt. With a soft shimmer, the portal winked out, leaving no trace of its existence.

As the portal closed, a new prompt appeared in Tom's vision, hovering expectantly as if awaiting his next move.

Class Acquired - Warlock
You are now a full-fledged Warlock. You have been granted the spell: Eldritch Blast. You have been granted the spell: Dark Ball. You have been granted the spell: Dark Healing.

Tom felt a surge of power flow through him, seeping into his mind as the spells became ingrained in his memory. The sensation was reminiscent of when he had read the book, although this time it was less overwhelming, with a more focused stream of information. The knowledge settled in his mind, clear and precise, as if he had always known the spells.

As soon as the sensation faded, another prompt appeared in his vision, waiting for his next action.

Requests
Your dark patron, Azroc, has sent his requests to you. Complete the following tasks to receive further powers and gifts:
Request #1 – Kill 100 monsters and send their souls to Azroc
Request #2 – Kill 1 boss monster and send its soul to Azroc

Warlock Quest – Complete Dungeon	
You have been offered a quest. Complete a Dungeon in the name of Azroc and place his symbol at the end to show your patron that you do these deeds in his name.	
Accept?	
Yes	*No*

The first quest seemed straightforward and perfectly acceptable to Tom. There were no grotesque requirements like bathing in the blood of enemies or performing sinister acts to declare loyalty to his patron. Relieved, Tom accepted the quest, noting that the tasks seemed reasonable and aligned well with his intentions. This was shaping up to be a promising relationship for his chosen Class.

Curious about his progress, Tom pulled up his character sheet and was surprised to find that he still had forty points to distribute. As he considered how best to allocate them, he reflected on everything he had absorbed from the book. He weighed his options against the newfound knowledge now at his disposal.

"What's on your mind?" Derek asked, seeing Tom take on a contemplative stance.

"I have forty points to spend, and I'm considering where to put them," Tom said, looking at his character sheet in deep thought.

"Well, Charisma used to be a big part of Warlock builds. Is that still the case here?" Derek asked.

"Not as much. Or at least not in the same way that some games are, where Charisma affects the ability to gain spells. It does play a role in how I'm perceived by those who might be aligned with the light and can power up the effects of some spells, though. For example, if someone who is light aligned were to see me with a Charisma of ten, they would likely try to attack me because I'm considered dark aligned. But I can hide it with my Charisma, which will make people react more favorably toward me. I'm just not sure how often that'll happen," Tom explained, thinking through his new knowledge base.

"That does make sense. It seems like maybe throwing a few points in there every so often would definitely help," Derek replied, also thinking about the options. "And how does it affect your spells again?"

"Some spells have a greater effect if my Charisma is higher. Not necessarily like more damage, but some of the control spells are stronger with higher Charisma," Tom almost muttered as he was thinking about the knowledge of his Class.

"What if you just became so attractive that no one ever harmed you?" James interjected.

"I don't think that's how it works," Tom said skeptically.

"I don't know, think about it. How many men used to fall all over themselves at bars for that one woman who was so beautiful? She would literally take advantage of the free drinks, tell them she hated them, treat them like dirt, but they still wanted a shot at her," James said, reminiscing about times he had been completely ignored in a bar. "People do stupid things for pretty people."

James actually had a bit of a point. Charisma really did make people do strange things. Hell, there was a list as long as his arm of world leaders who had been able to do terrible things because of their personal charisma.

"Alright. So, Charisma might actually be somewhat useful. But in the beginning stages, I also need to be able to defend myself," Tom stated.

"That's a wise plan in the beginning. Plus, as a Warlock, you should have gotten some spells, so some Intelligence and Wisdom would be helpful," Derek added.

Tom thought about it for a moment and decided that he would split his points evenly for now. He placed five points into each stat, including Luck, to give everything a boost. Looking at his stat sheet, he smiled at the progress he had made so far.

Tom Harris	
Race: Human	**Class:** Warlock
Level: 5	**Total XP:** 10,500
XP To Next Level: 4,500	**HP:** 150/150
MP: 150/150	**SP:** 150/150
Attributes:	**Unused Attributes Points:** 0
Strength: 15	**Constitution:** 15
Dexterity: 15	**Endurance:** 15
Intelligence: 15	**Wisdom:** 15
Charisma: 15	**Luck:** 15
Non-Combat Skills:	
Inspect	**Level: 1 Rank:** Beginner
Combat Skills:	
Vehicular Homicide	**Level: 2 Rank:** Beginner
Spells:	
Eldritch Blast	**Level: 1 Rank:** Beginner
Dark Ball	**Level: 1 Rank:** Beginner
Dark Healing	**Level: 1 Rank:** Beginner
Tattoos:	
Tattoo of Brute Strength	

Staring at the screen for a moment, Tom was shocked to see a combat skill he didn't remember having. Focusing on the skill, he was given more information about it.

Skill – Vehicular Homicide	
You have killed multiple enemies with your vehicle. You have become more proficient at running things over and causing their demise. Continue to plow through your enemies to receive greater bonuses to damage.	
Current Skill Level: 2	**Current Skill Rank:** Beginner
Bonus Damage Dealt: +15%	

"Seriously?! I got a fucking Skill for killing things with my car?" Tom exclaimed, slightly mortified that he had apparently done enough murder with his vehicle that the Grand System recognized it as a skill he had.

"Dude! Right on! Now we can run more things over to level it up!" James added, bobbing his head and thinking about the possibilities.

"Only you would take joy in this," Tom said, looking over at James in resignation.

"And why not? Any fight we come out on top of in this new world seems like a win we should celebrate," James replied. "I mean, seriously, the alternative is getting our asses handed to us by those monsters out there. Remember, there's no such thing as overkill."

"Speaking of which, why don't we look at the options in the machine now? Those goblins won't stay outside forever, and I'd rather be ready for them," Derek offered, gesturing to the machine.

"You're right. Let's take a look," Tom said.

Tom walked over to the vending machine and placed his hand on the digital screen once more. The inside of the machine began to shift as rows of items were withdrawn and new selections moved forward to replace them. When the transformation was complete, the display showed a similar array of weapons, but this time with various armor options included.

Scanning the new items, he hoped for something that might catch his eye. However, despite the change, he didn't feel like his choices had been significantly narrowed down. The assortment was still broad, leaving him with much to consider before making a decision.

"Well, that wasn't as helpful as I was hoping for," Tom said aloud, his shoulders slumping slightly in disappointment.

"You were expecting a bunch of staves and robes to choose from?" Derek asked.

"Yeah. Maybe a sword or two. But not almost every type of weapon," Tom replied, scanning the rows of items in the machine.

"I told you that Warlocks were more versatile than people thought. Why not choose something that will complement your tattoo?" Derek offered.

Tom scanned the selection of weapons and immediately noticed a greatsword that caught his eye. It had the exaggerated, stylish design of a weapon straight out of an anime, and it only required five common cores. Without hesitation, he pulled out the five cores, inserted them into the machine, and selected "B-6" for the greatsword. The can clattered down from its slot into the retrieval bay, and Tom reached in to grab it.

He pulled the tab on the can, and the familiar hiss of escaping air sounded, followed by a dramatic poof of smoke that filled the area. When the smoke cleared, Tom was left holding the greatsword. It was hefty, likely weighing around fifteen pounds—a substantial weight for a sword—but with his newly boosted Strength, it felt manageable, even comfortable.

The blade was nearly black along its central length, with razor-sharp, gleaming silver edges. The crossguard was fashioned into the shape of a dragon's head, with the blade extending from its open mouth and its jaws forming the quillons. A striking red jewel was set in each of the dragon's eyes on either side of the blade, adding an extra touch of flair. The handle was wrapped in soft, high-quality leather, providing a firm yet comfortable grip. The pommel was a metal sphere adorned with intricate filigree, completing the weapon's ornate and imposing design.

Tom hefted the greatsword, appreciating its balance and the way it felt in his hands—a perfect blend of artistry and deadly efficiency.

APOCALYPSE

"Yes. This will do. This will do nicely," Tom said as he held the sword up in front of him. "I'll call you Dark-Blade."

Chapter 7

Time to Move

Breaking News:
The coastlines of every nation bordering the Pacific Ocean have been devastated by rapidly rising flood waters. Tides surged inland as tectonic shifts, caused by a massive object embedding itself into the Earth's core, triggered significant elevation changes across the globe. This catastrophic event has overwhelmed and killed countless residents in affected areas. The object, believed to be the mana core mentioned in the alien warning, was seen plummeting into the ocean shortly after the broadcast from the mysterious dark obelisks that emerged in nearly every major city on Earth.

Upon striking the ocean, the core created massive tsunami-like waves that slammed into coastlines, obliterating most islands, including Hawaii, the Philippines, New Zealand, Tasmania, New Guinea, and large portions of Malaysia. Japan is almost entirely submerged, significant parts of Australia have been swallowed, and major regions of Central America, California, and South America have been devastated. Current estimates suggest that around two billion people have been killed by the rising waters, tsunamis, and earthquakes. Scientists warn that, as the core continues to burrow into the Earth, it will likely cause further destruction.

Adding to the chaos, monsters have begun appearing across towns, cities, and rural areas worldwide. These creatures are exceptionally violent, further adding to the death toll from natural disasters. The military has been deployed to address the monster threat, and a global state of emergency has been declared.

This catastrophe has officially been deemed the greatest crisis ever to hit the world. Politicians are struggling to meet the growing demands for aid as the death toll continues to climb as rescue teams worldwide are working tirelessly to provide assistance. Experts urge everyone to band together to ensure mutual safety. Please avoid venturing out alone, arm yourself for protection, and make your way to designated gathering places, which will be posted on our news social media page. Bring any supplies you can to these locations. This will likely be one of our last broadcasts until the situation stabilizes enough for us to return to the air.

APOCALYPSE

Tom, Derek, and James had ended up spending all twenty-four Monster Cores that Tom had received to get themselves stocked when Derek showed them the news broadcast from his phone. They stood there in silence for a few moments, unsure exactly what to do.

"It's bad everywhere. There's nothing but terror and destruction in the news. The whole world is experiencing this event, and help isn't going to be coming. So, we're on our own to figure out how to survive," Derek said solemnly as he stared at his phone.

"What about the army?" Tom asked, hoping that there would be some kind of rallying force to come help with the monsters.

"Busy. They're fighting right where they are and can't make it to literally everyone," Derek replied, still looking through news feeds on his phone.

"Army? We don't need no stinkin' army," James said in a thick accent. He pointed the gun around the room, pretending to kill invisible monsters.

"We're gonna die, aren't we?" Tom asked sarcastically after looking at James for a moment.

"Probably," Derek nodded, looking at James with a mixture of concern and disgust.

After some discussion, the trio decided on their final purchases. Derek picked up a sturdy shield to go along with his mace, and they purchased three minor healing potions. At two cores each, they ensured that each of them had one for emergencies. They briefly considered getting more guns for added firepower, but quickly realized that ammunition would quickly become a problem. Once they ran out of bullets, the guns would be little more than fancy paperweights, offering no real defense.

To their surprise, they discovered that the potions were simply liquids contained within the cans and didn't require the same dramatic release as the weapons. Before each potion was dispensed, the digital screen displayed a short instructional video, explaining that the cans could be opened like a regular drink without the need for any magical exchange process.

Satisfied with their choices, and a bit better prepared for whatever came next, the trio continued to strategize their next move. Each of them felt slightly more confident with their new gear and healing potions on hand.

"So, we're equipped now as best as we can. We're going to have to head to one of the meetup points to see if we can help with the info we have already," Derek said, his military training coming to the forefront.

"Should we take the car?" Tom asked, thinking about his new skill.

"We certainly should!" James said. "I have an idea for a little game that Derek should play."

"You don't mean…" Derek began.

"Oh, yes, I do. It's time for a little drive-by goblin baseball," James said, an evil grin spreading across his face.

"As much as I hate to admit it, James is right. That's going to give you a huge advantage in power as we move. And we'll be protected by the car, plus we probably can't keep it forever, so we may as well get some kills with it while we can. You guys need levels, and we can see if we can help some people along the way," Tom said, imagining Derek bashing in goblin skulls with his mace while hanging out a car window.

"I'm still not sure how I feel about this," Derek said, concern evident in his voice.

"Look, they're still playing soccer with that guy's head over there. So, buck up, cupcake, and let's go save some people," James said, a hard, serious look on his face now that wasn't his usual demeanor.

"What's with you and cupcakes? Got anything better than that?" Derek asked, putting his hands on his hips at James' constantly demeaning attitude.

"Aw, what's the matter? Not get enough yelling and name-calling in the military? You want me to be meaner? *Cupcake* is both delicious *and* derogatory," James stated, a condescending tone taking over. "Besides… I'm hungry."

"Please. You couldn't do half as much shit-talking as the drill sergeants we had in basic," Derek scoffed.

"Don't encourage him. He'll take that as a challenge," Tom sighed.

"Challenge accepted," James said, smiling even wider than he had before.

"See, now look what you've done," Tom said in mock anger.

Derek hesitated for a moment, uncertainty flickering in his eyes. But when he saw the determination in James' gaze, he took a deep breath and nodded, steeling himself for what was to come. They moved back to the window to get a better look outside.

The goblins had noticed their presence and were now staring up at the windows, beginning to hurl rocks in an attempt to shatter the glass. Below, several goblins continued to linger near the building's entrance, still milling about and probing for a way inside.

"I'll go first through the door," Derek said, setting out the strategy for their escape. "Using my shield, I can get them away from the entrance and bash a few heads if I need to. Tom, you come right behind me and swing for the fences at anything to the left that isn't me or James. James, cover us from the rear to keep any goblins off of us to the right, and for Christ's sake, *don't* shoot us. We'll make for the car, and we'll head for the closest gathering point—which looks to be the Trammel Crow Center."

"You know which car is mine?" Tom asked.

"It's the one with goblin blood on it. Pretty sure I'll know," Derek replied sardonically.

"Good point," Tom said sheepishly.

"Time to fuck some shit up," James said, grinning ear to ear while stroking his gun.

"One last thing before we go—scour the break room and let's hit up our desks for anything we might need or feel is useful that we can put in our storage. It's such a great way to carry things, and we might be able to find some things that we can make use of," Derek ordered.

The trio began scouring the office for anything useful. They raided the fridge, grabbing leftover pizza from another team's party and a few abandoned lunches. Digging through the drawers, they found some eating utensils and paper towels. James, thinking ahead, dashed into the bathroom and returned with an armful of toilet paper, which the other two acknowledged as a stroke of pure genius.

Not wanting to leave anything behind, they also raided the women's restroom and the bathrooms on the second floor—after all, one could never have too much toilet paper in an emergency.

James came out with an armful of tampons that he quickly shoved in his Inventory as well, only to find two men staring at him.

"What?" James scowled. "You guys might plan on spending the rest of the apocalypse celibate, but *I'm* planning on having at least one lady friend in my life, and I think she'd appreciate the forethought."

Derek snorted a laugh, shaking his head.

Feeling slightly more prepared, they headed back to the first floor to gather supplies from their desks. They grabbed items they thought might be useful, such as charging cables, laptops, and whatever snacks they could find stashed away in drawers.

Just as they turned to head for the exit, a loud bang echoed through the office. Covering their faces against the smoke that quickly filled the air, they strained to see what was happening. To their horror, they saw goblins pouring into the building, swarming through the breached entryway in a chaotic rush.

"Shit!" James swore as he readied his gun.

"Form up behind me! Keep near the cubicle walls," Derek ordered, putting up his shield to prepare for a fight. "Tom, stay slightly to my left and pick any off that come too close. James, fire when you have an opening, and for fuck's sake, don't shoot us!"

"You said that already!" James yelled back at him.

"Well, it's pretty goddamned important!" Derek retorted angrily.

The trio could just make out the tops of the goblins' heads bobbing between the cubicle walls as they peered above them. With the goblins averaging only about three feet tall, the scene looked almost comical, like children running through a cornfield maze. But there was nothing funny about their intent. The goblins scampered closer, darting between the aisles as they chittered in an unintelligible language, searching for any stragglers.

Derek readied his mace, letting out a low growl to challenge the approaching monsters. Tom stood with his greatsword in hand, but its size made it unwieldy in the tight office space, limiting his movements to short, stabbing motions. Suddenly, several goblins scrambled onto the tops of the cubicle walls, finally spotting the trio. One goblin shrieked, prompting the others to climb up as well.

"Bingo," Tom muttered.

"What?" Derek asked, glancing at Tom.

"Watch this," Tom replied, a grin spreading across his face. As the goblins neared, Tom shouted, "DUCK!"

Without hesitation, both Derek and James ducked low. Tom swung his greatsword in a wide horizontal arc over the cubicle walls. The blade cleaved through three goblins in one clean sweep, barely meeting any resistance. Blackish blood and entrails splattered as the goblin halves tumbled from the walls to the floor. The remaining goblins, witnessing the carnage, wisely began climbing down, still intent on reaching the trio.

"Great move, Tom. Now we need to make for the exit. Stay behind me," Derek commanded, his voice filled with resolve that bolstered the others' spirits. "Tom, stab beside me if you get an opening. I'll help make a hole. James… let's wait till we get outside to use the gun."

James nodded, and they advanced with Derek leading the way. As they rounded the end of the row of cubicles, two goblins appeared, rushing toward them. Derek let out a roar and lunged forward, bashing the goblins with his shield. The impact sent the small creatures sprawling, and Derek swiftly brought his mace down on the head of one goblin, then swung across to crush the face of the second, killing them both.

They continued forward and soon encountered another group—three goblins this time. Derek braced himself, holding his shield ready to absorb their charge. Two of the goblins wielded spears, while the third had a sword. The spear-wielders thrust at Derek, but he blocked with his shield, shattering the weak wooden shafts and breaking the brittle stone tips against the metal.

Tom seized the opportunity and stabbed at the goblin with the sword as it raised its weapon to strike Derek's exposed right side. The greatsword skewered the goblin, nearly cleaving it in half. Tom planted a foot on the goblin's body and yanked the sword free, letting the corpse slump to the floor.

Derek didn't miss a beat, assured that Tom had his flank covered. He advanced, slamming his shield into one of the remaining goblins, sending it flying backward. He then brought his mace down with crushing force on the head of the last goblin. The flanges of the mace shattered the skull, causing brain matter and bone fragments to burst from the impact. The goblin couldn't even cry out, its death reduced to a wet gurgle as it crumpled under the blow.

Suddenly, James' voice bellowed loudly into the confined space.

"Hey, shit head!" The group turned to see James standing on a table, one of the wrapped tampons in his mouth like a cigar. "You have to ask yourself one question: Do I feel lucky?"

A dagger-wielding goblin suddenly burst through the flimsy divider separating a nearby office as it swung its knife for Tom's throat. The explosive percussion of James' gun going off caused everyone's ears to ring as the goblin stumbled, falling to the floor with a bullet wound in its head.

"Well…" James' voice was distorted from the feminine hygiene product gripped between his teeth. "Do ya, punk?"

"Good looking out," Derek said to James. "Glad you went ahead and used that to watch our backs."

"Don't worry," James said snarkily, blowing on the end of the barrel. "Dirty James' got your back…" James frowned, playing back the words he just said before slowly removing the tampon from between his teeth and storing it away. He shrugged. "Whatever. I'll work on it. Anyway, I figured the no-gun rule didn't apply to the ones trying to sneak up behind us." He cupped one hand to the side of his face. "Back door's closed motherfuckers! Exit only!"

The others rolled their eyes and faced forward again, preparing to move. They walked through the aisles, heading for the exit door.

"I just thought of something," Tom said. "These are pretty small goblins. How did they get that steel door open?"

Everyone froze, trying to comprehend what might have forced open the door. Before they could piece it together, a small object rolled into the aisle in front of them, its fuse sparking as it ignited the carpet.

"HIT THE DECK! GET BEHIND SOMETHING!" Derek shouted, and the trio dove for cover behind the nearest cubicle walls.

A powerful explosion rocked the area a moment later, sending cubicle walls, desks, and monitors flying in all directions. The concussive blast shattered nearby lights, causing glass and plastic from the fluorescent bulbs and housings to rain down, accompanied by a shower of sparks from frying electrical equipment.

Tom groaned as he pushed himself up, a cubicle wall that had landed on top of him sliding off to the side as he struggled to his feet. He spotted his greatsword just to his left and grabbed it, using it to steady himself as he rose to his knees. He wiped dust from his eyes and slowly stood up, calling out to his friends.

"Derek? James? You guys okay?"

He noticed movement to his right in his periphery, and turned to see a goblin emerging from a pile of papers and shattered cubicle walls. Tom growled, swinging his greatsword in a swift horizontal arc. The goblin's eyes went wide with terror, letting out a squeak just before the sword cleaved off the top half of its head. Its tongue twitched momentarily in the lower half of its mouth as blood poured down its throat. The creature collapsed lifelessly.

"Over here! Help me with this desk—it's on my leg," Derek called out, his voice strained.

Tom rushed over and helped lift the desk off Derek's leg. Thankfully, the leg wasn't broken, but Derek winced in pain as he tested his weight on it. Just then, James emerged from behind a cubicle wall that had miraculously stayed upright, having used it as cover since he had been at the back of the group.

"We have to get outside!" Derek groaned as he gripped his injured leg. "Time to move out!"

With Tom and James in agreement, they formed up again and Derek led the way, hobbling slightly from the pain. The companions found no more goblins on their way to the door, but once outside, there were eight goblins waiting for them.

"They've got us surrounded," Tom said ominously.

"Those poor bastards," James said, looking over the other two's shoulders. "They've got us right where we want 'em. We can shoot in every direction now."

Tom leaned in toward James and whispered. "Patton?"

James tilted his head to one side, keeping his eyes on the enemies. "No, thanks," he whispered back, rubbing his stomach. "I'm full."

Derek's head almost spun around like an owl as he looked back, his eyes wide. He aggressively tilted his head toward the small army of goblins in front of them.

"...Sorry," James whispered awkwardly.

The goblins were grinning at them and brandishing weapons. Derek raised his shield and stepped in front of the others.

"So, what's the play here?" Tom asked.

"I try to help tank," Derek replied. "You and James pick off as many as you can while I'm busy. Try to keep them off me. You have good reach so you should be able to really do some damage." His voice turned serious. "And always remember: the key to a fight is committing to your actions. Don't hesitate, or you die."

"Alright, let's do this," Tom agreed, readying his own weapon in what he hoped was a proper fighting stance.

"Hehehehe… some bitches gonna die," James laughed evilly.

A moment later, chaos erupted. The goblins charged with their weapons drawn, shrieking as they rushed forward. Derek swung his shield horizontally, swiping left to deflect as many weapons as possible. Tom moved to the right, swinging his greatsword in a wide, sweeping arc, aiming to cut down as many goblins as he could. James, positioned behind them, leveled his gun and fired down the center, tracking the goblins that Derek and Tom hadn't engaged.

Derek's shield knocked the spears of two goblins off balance, sending them staggering backward. The third goblin, wielding a sword, wasn't fast enough to take advantage of the gap in his defense that the blow created. Derek's mace smashed into the goblin's blade, shattering it into pieces that flew through the air. The goblin stared in shock at the hilt of the broken weapon, and Derek quickly followed up with a brutal backswing, caving in the creature's face.

The other two goblins recovered from their stumble but quickly realized they were outmatched. Derek stepped forward, delivering a powerful front kick to one of them, sending it flying backward into the door of a nearby car.

"Hell yeah! This is Sparta!" James' manic voice howled as gunshots rang out in applause.

The goblin crumpled to the ground, clutching its chest in pain. The second goblin tried to stab Derek again, but he deflected the attack with his shield, blocking the jab with ease. With a fluid motion, Derek spun to face the goblin and swung his mace in a devastating cross blow.

Teeth and bits of viscera sprayed from the goblin's mangled face as blood gushed from its wounds. It collapsed lifelessly to the ground.

Derek didn't waste a second; he advanced on the goblin he had kicked into the car and brought his mace down hard, ending its struggle with a single blow.

Meanwhile, Tom activated his tattoo at the cost of twenty mana. He felt a familiar heat radiate from his shoulders as his mana bar dropped to one hundred and thirty. Power surged through his limbs, and the greatsword in his hands suddenly felt lighter, almost as if it were an extension of his body. Tom roared, channeling his enhanced strength into the swing.

Three goblins charged him, two wielding swords and one with a spear, all aiming to strike him down. Tom's powerful horizontal slash cleaved through their weapons—and their bodies—with ease. The force of the swing sent the goblins flying backward, their severed halves landing in a bloody heap ten feet away, staining the pavement with dark, pooling blood.

The last goblin hesitated, caught between deciding whether to attack Tom or Derek. Its indecision sealed its fate. James took aim and fired, the bullet striking the goblin squarely in the chest. It squealed in pain, clutching at the wound as it dropped to its knees. Desperately, it tried to stand, but blood poured from its punctured lung, and it began to cough violently. James fired again, the second shot piercing the top of the goblin's head. The creature slumped forward, its struggles finally at an end.

"The car! Let's move!" Derek called, pointing his mace toward Tom's blood-covered vehicle.

The trio closed in on their target quickly, with Tom leading the way. Reaching the car, Tom stowed his greatsword in his Inventory, unlocked the doors, and they all climbed inside. Derek sat heavily in the front passenger seat, and James settled in the back on the driver's side. After starting the engine, Tom rolled down the windows. Derek popped up, perching himself on the passenger door and hanging halfway out the window. James simply aimed his gun out from the back.

"Let's fucking go!" James shouted, adrenaline surging.

Tom shifted into drive and sped out of the parking lot. As he turned right onto the main street, a goblin leapt out in front of the car. Without slowing down, Tom kept his foot on the gas, and the car barreled over the goblin. The sickening crunch of bones and splatter of blood marked its end.

As they tore down the road, more goblins sprang out from behind parked cars, attempting to attack. Derek was ready, swinging his mace from the passenger side window like a baseball bat, crushing the skulls of goblins that got too close. James fired at any that approached, his shots ringing out as he picked off goblins one by one, dropping some instantly and wounding others.

When larger groups of goblins appeared, Tom swerved the car deliberately, aiming to plow through them. Sometimes the sight of the oncoming vehicle made the goblins scatter, giving Derek and James clearer shots at the stragglers. Other times, Tom's maneuver turned the goblins into nothing more than gruesome speedbumps, with the car jolting as it rolled over multiple bodies at once. They left a trail of black blood and shattered limbs in their wake.

"Keep it up! We'll reach the center in no time at this rate and have plenty of experience to show for it!" Derek called out, swinging down at another goblin and shattering its face in with his mace.

Chapter 8

Trammel Crow Center

It took the trio about twenty minutes to reach the Trammel Crow Center; a journey that should have been much shorter under normal circumstances.

The city was in chaos—abandoned vehicles littered the streets, and panicked pedestrians ran in every direction, desperately seeking safety. As they navigated the congested roads, the sounds of gunfire echoed through the city, mingling with screams and monstrous roars that reverberated off the skyscrapers.

Along their route, they saw people taking up arms, fighting back against the creatures that had invaded their city. Groups of civilians and police alike fired at goblins and other emerging monsters, creating sporadic bursts of violence on many corners. Some managed to fend off the creatures, their gunshots dropping goblins in quick succession, while others found themselves overwhelmed, struggling against the relentless onslaught.

The Trammel Crow Center, rebuilt in 2017 to attract businesses with a modern design, now stood as a temporary refuge in the midst of the crisis. The building's owners had offered it up as an emergency space, and as Tom and his friends approached, they saw teams of security guards stationed at the entrance, currently locked in a tense standoff with a group of goblins.

Gunshots cracked through the air as guards fired sporadically, trying to keep the goblins at bay. The creatures snarled and hissed, hesitating just behind a line of concrete barriers. Only a single dead goblin lay in front of the building's entrance—a grim indication that the creatures had already attempted to breach the building at least once. The remaining goblins eyed their fallen comrade warily and brandished their weapons, some pacing while ducking slightly to avoid being shot, clearly agitated but unsure whether to advance or retreat.

The scene was one of desperate defense, with what appeared to be about eight to ten guards doing everything they could to protect those inside the building. The companions exchanged glances, realizing the gravity of the situation, and prepared themselves to join the fray.

"Bet the people of Dallas are wishing they hadn't required people to put so much glass in buildings now. Looks pretty from afar, but fucking stupid at the end of the world," James commented.

"I'm sure goblin attacks weren't something they took into account when building the structures," Derek replied.

"No, but what about all those zombie movies? They didn't think to make even *one* building that was mostly concrete just in case?" James asked scornfully.

"Maybe you should've been a city engineer," Tom chuckled. "It's not too late. You still haven't picked your Class."

"Pfft," James scoffed. "Me? A government drone? Not a chance. I'd prefer being the one *testing* the structural integrity of buildings to the one designing them."

"Regardless, all of that was pure science fiction until now. No one makes plans for those kinds of eventualities," Derek argued.

"Preppers do," James stated.

"Fine… no one in their right mind prepares for those kinds of eventualities," Derek corrected.

"Not really so out of their minds *now,* are they?" James scoffed.

"Shut up," Derek shot back.

"Oh!" James held a hand up to one ear. "Did you hear that? It's the sound of losing an argument."

Derek scowled.

"Look, we need to focus. There appear to be a lot of goblins biding their time there at the entrance. I'm pretty sure if I go goblin bowling, we can take out most of them, but you guys need to be ready to pick up the spare," Tom said with finality.

"Got it," Derek responded, and James nodded.

Revving the engine drew the attention of the goblins clustered around the front of the building. Spotting a new target beyond the armed guards, the goblins turned and began advancing on Tom and his friends in their vehicle. Tom released the brake and gunned the engine, driving straight toward the goblin pack. Derek and James leaned out of the windows, ready for another round of battle.

Having already dispatched over thirty goblins on the drive over, the trio had become surprisingly adept at their deadly game. James opened fire from a distance, picking off goblins as they charged. Just before they rammed into the goblin frontline, Tom yanked the wheel hard to the left, sending the car into a sharp slide. Derek swung his mace with brutal efficiency, taking out a couple of goblins just before the broad side of the car struck.

The vehicle spun in a chaotic circle, mowing down goblins as James and Derek continued their assault, clinging to the car's OS handles to keep from being thrown out.

Time slowed.

The trio unleashed war cries of fury and defiance, their voices mingling with the chaos around them. If it had been a scene from a movie, "Happy Together" by The Turtles would have played in the background, the camera cutting to each of their faces in slow motion as they screamed in battle.

Tom gripped the wheel with white-knuckled intensity, his brow furrowed as a fierce cry erupted from his throat. James, his face lit with a manic grin, aimed and fired at the goblins that swarmed the car, picking them off with deadly accuracy. Derek, his expression set with unyielding determination, let out a bellowing battle shout as he swung at any goblins that dared come within reach of his mace.

In a single, sweeping sideswipe, the car took out ten of the fourteen goblins gathered at the entrance, including the ones Derek had already crushed. James swiftly dispatched three more with well-placed shots, leaving only one goblin to flee in a panic.

The creature scrambled away from the three relentless figures and their mechanized beast. With calm precision, James opened the car door, stepped out, aimed over the top of the vehicle, and fired. A bullet wound sprouted squarely in the back of the fleeing goblin's head.

He blew on the barrel of his gun with a casual air, then closed the door and took a few nonchalant steps away from the car.

A couple of goblins trapped beneath the vehicle groaned weakly, but Tom simply shifted into reverse, rolling over them again until the noises stopped. Satisfied that the threat had been neutralized, the trio took a moment to catch their breath, glancing at each other with a mix of exhaustion and adrenaline-fueled triumph.

"What the fuck was that?! You can't just go running people over like that… can they?" One of the security officers cried out indignantly, turning to look at his partner.

"I mean… technically, they aren't people," another security guard replied, scrunching his face up at the sight of the mangled bodies. "Were you guys some kind of serial killers before all this?"

"Not until today. But once you see a goblin playing soccer with a man's head or cutting down children on I-75, you learn to kill first and ask questions never," Tom called back as he exited his car, now completely stained in goblin blood.

The security guards looked at each other, unsure how to feel about the people now standing in front of the building.

"He's got a point there," the second guard admitted. The two stared at each other, seemingly coming to a decision to just be grateful someone had come and handled the problem.

"We need to set up a system to defend this area. If it's not in place—and soon—we'll eventually get overrun," Derek said.

"You come in here, murdering everything in sight, then just assume we're too stupid to know that we need to secure and defend the area?" The first security guard said disdainfully as he looked toward his compatriot. "What a douchebag."

"Yeah, who are you to order us around?" The other security guard asked.

"Yeah, what the fuck, guys?" James called cheerfully. "How dare we not even introduce ourselves." He turned toward the two men. "Pardon us. With all the commotion, we've quite forgotten all our manners." James stepped forward, offering a florid bow, the gun in his hand depicting a smooth arc across the bodies of two guards, who flinched uncomfortably. "They call me King James the sixty-ninth." He winked. "And this here," he continued, gesturing toward Derek, "is Derek Calloway, who—I realize I may be stating the obvious here—is the Royal French Maid—"

APOCALYPSE

The sound of James' breath exploding from his lungs interrupted his speech. Withdrawing his elbow from James' stomach, Derek kept his gaze locked on the two guards.

Deciding not to continue talking, James defaulted to a wide smile and making uncomfortable eye contact, letting the moment hang.

"We're the ones who cleared this entrance for you," Derek replied, trying his best to ignore James' diatribe. "And so far, I'm the only one with military experience and the balls to do what we must to keep people safe. So, unless you feel like you have this whole Grand System thing figured out and can do a better job, I'll handle the orders for now. Got a problem with that?"

All the security guards shook their heads.

"Good. Now, the next time those ugly fuckers come back here… you shoot to kill," Derek ordered. "You need to gain experience so you can level up. It's the only way to get stronger right now. Might makes right in this new world. I know we're all scared. We've always had rules that said murder was going to get you punished, but we have to change that mindset and get to killing these monsters that would just as soon eat your face off as have tea with you!"

"I killed one," a security guard said meekly, raising one hand.

"One of fifteen. That still gets you killed. Now get your asses in gear!" Derek commanded.

Some of the guards nodded, others saluted, but all jumped into action and found places to take up a guard and were on the lookout.

"Now, who's in charge here?" Derek asked.

"That would be Brian. He's in the conference room on the fifth floor," one of the guards replied.

"Thank you. We'll be going to have a visit with him," Derek said.

"Best if someone goes to introduce you," the second security guard said. "Rick? Come show them to the conference room."

Tom, James, and Derek all went to the front door and were about to enter behind Rick when they were stopped by another one of the guards.

"Are you just leaving your car here?" the guard asked.

"Not sure if we'll need it again. Try not to mess it up too bad," Tom joked.

The guards stared at the vehicle, now covered in blood and gore, with dents, scratches, and even bits of goblin remains clinging to the metal. They grimaced at the gruesome sight, taken aback by the trio's ruthlessness. To the guards, it seemed like these men were dispatching the creatures without a second thought, like ancient gods of retribution.

Tom, Derek, and James followed Rick into the building's entrance. Inside, they made their way to the elevator and rode up to the fifth floor. As they stepped out, Rick led them down a narrow corridor lined with signs directing visitors to the conference rooms, which were all clustered on one side of the building.

Only one conference room appeared to be in use. Through the glass walls, they could see a man in his mid-thirties pacing back and forth. He had jet-black hair slicked back and a neatly trimmed goatee. His movements were frantic as he gestured wildly, appearing deeply engrossed in a heated conversation on the conference phone. At moments, he waved his hands in frustration. Suddenly, he leaned over the table, his posture tense as if delivering urgent instructions or dire news to whoever was on the other end of the line.

Rick approached the glass door, giving it a push to open, allowing Tom, Derek, and James to step inside.

"...I don't care what you *think* needs to be done! This is the crisis to end all crises', and we need to get supplies here now to help keep people safe!" the man, presumed to be Brian, said in an Irish brogue before looking up at the three men who had entered. "And who the fuck are you?"

"I'm Batman," James said, making his voice extra gravelly, causing the others to roll their eyes in annoyance.

"Ignore him," Tom sighed. "Sorry to just barge in, but I'm Tom, this is James, and that's Derek. We came to see how we can help. We have a bit of experience with gaming mechanics, military discipline, and..." he gestured toward himself, then Derek, and finally looked toward James.

"Egregious violence," James said brightly.

Tom just shook his head. "...We figured we could lend a hand here."

"Rick, why are these people interrupting my phone call?" Brian asked the security guard.

"Sorry, Brian. These guys showed up and killed all the goblins out front. Figured you'd want to meet them," Rick replied.

"You mean they *helped* you kill them?" Brian replied, looking at Rick with a glare that said the answer had better be yes.

"Um... technically, no. Roger killed one, but they killed the rest by themselves with their car," Rick replied, looking ashamed.

Shifting his gaze to the three who had come in, Brian stared at them for a long moment before replying.

"So, you all think you can help? What kind of ideas do you think you can bring to the table that we haven't already thought of?" Brian asked, staring them down.

"Look, we aren't trying to come in here and take over. We just want to help people stay safe. So far, we've been the only ones who seem to have been decisively killing these monsters," Derek said.

"Our security guards have the situation handled... They were just taking their time," Brian replied, trying to sound confident.

"They were taking their dear, sweet time for sure. We finished them off in under a minute," Tom interjected. "We work... well, maybe 'worked' now, for a video game development company and might be able to offer some assistance."

"Look, I play video games too and think we can manage this," the man said. Then he sighed deeply, and the three could see something weighing on him heavily. "But... I could definitely use some help in getting people organized. I have so much on my plate right now. I'm completely underwater. I'm Brian, by the way." He reached out a hand to Tom, who clasped it casually. Brian winced, groaning slightly. "Strong grip you got there."

"Oh!" Tom pulled a sympathetic face. "Sorry. It's the stats, I think. Still getting used to it."

Brian nodded, thoughtfully flexing the fingers of his hand. "Well, I wish I could say it's a pleasure to make your acquaintance, but given the circumstances, that'd be a fucking lie. Rick! Get back to your post and tell the others to shoot those green bastards instead of having a picnic. It's embarrassing to have someone else come in and clean up something we should be doing ourselves."

"Yes, sir!" Rick replied quickly and scurried out of the conference room before he could be dressed down further.

"Damn, your voice is sexy," James said. "Like butterscotch for your ears."

Brian looked at James with creeped-out confusion.

"Again, ignore him," Tom said. "Have you all made it through the tutorial yet?"

"Not all of it, but I've started it. Things just keep happening around here, and someone needs my attention about every half second. I presume you all made it all the way through the tutorial. Do you think I need to do that first?" Brian asked, an air of desperation in his voice.

"Yes. It'll stop the prompts from popping up for a time and tell you more about some of the things happening," Tom said.

"Fine. I'll do that now. These little blinking icons are pretty annoying when I'm trying to handle everything needed to support the people who keep coming to the building. Mind giving me a hand with some of it?" Brian asked.

"Sure thing. What would you like us to do?" Tom asked. "We came to help. So, tell us what needs to be done the most, and we'll help however we can."

Brian's eyes softened as he slumped down into a chair. Someone on the phone spoke up.

"Who's there? What the hell is going on, Brian?" The voice asked.

James grinned maliciously. "Oh, hey strange voice on the phone! My name is K—"

James' voice was suddenly muffled by Tom's hand over his mouth.

"My name is Tom. I have with me James and Derek. We just came to the Center to see what we can do to help. Hopefully, we can get some semblance of order going on to help Brian with what is happening," Tom explained.

"Right. I think getting everyone on the same page is the first step," Brian said. He stood, putting his hands on the table, his voice steady with determination. "We should prioritize the list of tasks that need to be done. Once we have a clear order, it'll speed up the process of mobilizing people to help others as they arrive at the Center." Brian took a deep, slow breath—seemingly letting out some of the tension he'd been holding on to. "We can use the gym. There's a basketball court where we can gather everyone and try to address as many people as possible."

"You've done this before?" Tom asked.

"Well, there's never been a fucking apocalypse before, but this isn't my first crisis. So, yes, I've worked with panicking people before, and I know what I'm doing. I've got a laundry list as long as my fucking arm to get ready and could really use some help with that," Brian answered, looking down at the conference room phone.

"Brian, we'll be sending people to you as well. Please help them find a place, and we'll also try to send over any supplies we can get our hands on. No promises, but we'll do what we can," the voice on the phone said before hanging up.

"Who was that?" Tom asked.

"Oh? Him? That was the mayor. I happen to be friends with him, so I put in a call to see if I could figure out what's going on. He wasn't too much help," Brian sighed. "But I'm definitely glad you all showed up. I have so many things to do that having you help talk to the people would take one of those off my plate."

"Well, looks like I'm up," James interjected, interlacing his fingers in front of himself and cracking them loudly. "Everyone knows I'm the diplomat of the group, so just point me at whoever needs a good talking to and—" He pointed a set of finger guns in front of him, mimed firing a round from each and blowing the smoke from his fingers. He leaned toward Brian, the back of his hand hiding his mouth for a stage-whisper. "We happen to have a very particular set of skills…" He waggled his eyebrows disconcertingly.

"Don't start that," Derek said. "Look, we'll do whatever we can to help, but the first thing people need to do is get over this sensibility of not killing monsters. They'll *kill* you, they won't feel bad about it, *and* they'll probably play with your corpse—*if* they don't just eat it. We've seen some pretty messed up shit today, and it's barely nine-thirty. So, unless people want to end up dead, we have to suck it up and start fighting back." Derek shook his head. "All of that is putting aside the fact that relying on someone else, even a mayor, for your supplies is a losing proposition. We need to be out there collecting everything that isn't nailed down, which—if I haven't made it clear—means fighting for everything we're going to need to survive."

Tom placed a hand on Derek's shoulder. The soldier nodded, letting out a breath of his own.

"If you could go ahead and start getting people ready to meet in the gym, we'd like to have a few minutes to look over our character sheets." Tom's voice was calm and steady. "We had a pretty eventful ride over here and need to see what we can do with our upgrades."

"I couldn't agree more. These monsters are throwing a wrench into everything, and people are still afraid to shoot at something for fear of getting sued. Also, upgrades?" Brian asked. "You guys already have upgrades?"

"That's what happens when you travel right now. No frequent flier miles, but the XP benefits are to die for… literally," James said.

"We definitely had to fight our way here. So, we just need to set a few things in order and get a slightly better handle on this new system," Tom said.

"Feel free to take this conference room for now, and I'll head down to start getting people arranged," Brian said.

And with that, he stood up and left the room to begin assigning orders to get people to the gym.

APOCALYPSE

"Alright, boys. Time to spend some points!" James said, rubbing his hands together.

Chapter 9

Introspection

Tom, Derek, and James settled into the plush office chairs around the conference table, the tension of battle still lingering as they prepared to review their latest achievements. Tom pulled up his notifications, feeling a surge of confidence that their recent kills would translate into valuable experience and levels. However, as the notifications began to flood his vision, he quickly realized there were far too many to sift through individually.

Taking a moment to think, Tom considered the tutorial messages and wondered just how much filtering he could do on the System notifications. He focused his thoughts, mentally requesting a simplified overview of his party's progress. Almost instantly, most of the notifications disappeared, replaced by a single prompt that neatly summarized the combat results, including the total experience gained and any notable achievements.

Relieved by the streamlined display, Tom glanced at Derek and James and explained what he had done so they could have the same reduction of information. Now, with a clear view of their progress, they could plan their next move with a renewed sense of purpose.

Combat:

Your party has killed 65 goblins between levels 3 and 6. Your party has been awarded 32,500 XP. Your share of the experience is 10,834 XP.

Tom felt a rush of elation as he reviewed the summary. The amount of XP gained was substantial—more than enough for leveling up. Encouraged by the progress, he eagerly glanced at the remaining prompts, curiosity piqued by what additional rewards or information might be waiting. With renewed enthusiasm, Tom began to go through each prompt, carefully reviewing the details to make the most of his newfound gains.

Skill Acquired: Swords

You have acquired the skill: Swords. You have shown that you can hold a blade. Pointy end toward the bad guy. Level up this skill to become more proficient in the use of this weapon.

APOCALYPSE

<table>
<tr><td>Current skill level: 1
Bonus damage with swords: +3%</td></tr>
</table>

Level Up
You have earned enough XP to advance to the next level. You are now level 6! Continue to work hard and push yourself to gain more XP to continue to level up. You receive 10 Attribute Points to distribute as you see fit.

Level Up
You have earned enough XP to advance to the next level. You are now level 7! Continue to work hard and push yourself to gain more XP to continue to level up. You receive 10 Attribute Points to distribute as you see fit.

Twenty Attribute Points was a lot to spend all at once, but in the grand scheme of things, it still felt like a drop in the bucket compared to what he might need down the line. Tom pondered his options, weighing how best to distribute the points for maximum impact. He wondered what would happen if he dumped them all into one attribute—would he become incredibly strong if he maxed out Strength, or lightning fast if he focused on Dexterity?

Reflecting on the battles so far, Tom was tempted to pour all the points into Strength and Dexterity to boost his combat effectiveness. However, he reminded himself that goblins were just the beginning, and the prompts hadn't indicated that they were the only creatures he would face. Stronger and more varied enemies with unique abilities could be on the horizon.

Considering the broader challenges ahead, Tom decided on a more balanced approach. He allocated five points into Intelligence to enhance his magic capabilities, and another five into Endurance to help him sustain longer fights with his greatsword. He also put five points into Strength to make the sword feel even lighter, despite the boost from his tattoo. Finally, he invested five points into Charisma, recalling that the book he had absorbed emphasized the importance of this attribute.

With his decisions made, Tom pulled up his character sheet, eager to see the effects of his newly distributed points.

Tom Harris	
Race: Human	**Class:** Warlock
Level: 7	**Total XP:** 21,334
XP To Next Level: 6,666	**HP:** 150/150
MP: 200/200	**SP:** 200/200
Attributes:	**Unused Attributes Points:** 0
Strength: 20	**Constitution:** 15
Dexterity: 15	**Endurance:** 20
Intelligence: 20	**Wisdom:** 15
Charisma: 20	**Luck:** 15

Non-Combat Skills:	
Inspect	**Level:** 1 **Rank:** Beginner
Combat Skills:	
Vehicular Homicide	**Level:** 3 **Rank:** Beginner
Swords	**Level:** 1 **Rank:** Beginner
Spells:	
Eldritch Blast	**Level:** 1 **Rank:** Beginner
Dark Ball	**Level:** 1 **Rank:** Beginner
Dark Healing	**Level:** 1 **Rank:** Beginner
Tattoos:	
Tattoo of Brute Strength	

"You guys should've gotten Class choices, right? For the amount of XP we earned?" Tom asked, looking up from his character sheet.

Both James and Derek nodded, still looking at screens he couldn't see.

"Derek, have you selected your Class yet?" Tom asked again. This time, Derek looked up at him.

"I was just about to. Why?"

"I wanted to try something, and I'm concerned that once you take your Class, it might not work on you," Tom explained. "I got a spell called *Dark Healing*, and I want to give it a shot. I bet it won't work if you become a cleric. I'm sure you're not fully recovered from that blast yet, so I want to see if I can help—and get a chance to practice casting a spell. I didn't want to try it until I had time to test how magic works. No sense in getting us hurt—or worse—because I was curious about magic or accidentally caused an explosion because I didn't understand something."

"Wait, blowing up is a possibility with magic?" James asked, now frightened and looking up from his screens.

"No idea. It's completely new to me. Pretty much anything could happen," Tom replied nonchalantly, hoping to get a rise out of James.

Derek nodded in agreement, and Tom made his way over to where Derek was sitting. Extending a hand toward him, Tom concentrated on the steps that had been etched into his mind when he learned the spell. He focused on channeling his mana, guiding it through his body and out to his hand. With the energy flowing steadily, Tom uttered the incantation for *Dark Healing*, feeling the spell activate as he directed its power toward Derek.

"Uthos manista. Morthit malistrom."

A bright, purple-colored energy left Tom's hand and enveloped Derek in a glow that surrounded his entire body. Derek's eyes became concerned, but he relaxed after a moment of being enveloped in the glowing light. His shoulders slumped, and he extended his leg out several times. When the light left him, he stood up and hopped on the leg that had been hurt.

"That feels pretty great!" Derek said, looking up at Tom. "This magic stuff is awesome! That would have taken days or weeks of recovery normally."

"Awesome!" Tom smiled. "And your HP is back to full?"

"Yeah! I can't wait to be able to do that, too," Derek said excitedly.

"I'm worried it won't work on me," Tom replied, looking slightly concerned and dejected. "But I have my own healing spell, so I should be able to take care of myself for now."

"I guess we'll have to test it out once I choose my Class," Derek said.

Nodding in agreement, Tom walked back over to sit down. He wanted to see how to get some more skills, but wasn't sure what to do to get them. In every game he had played, skills had been a big part of dealing more damage. He decided he would go to the vending machine to see if it offered any clues.

Before he could do that, though, a portal opened in front of James, similar to the one that had opened for him when he had selected Warlock for his Class, but this one was a vibrant green mixed with swirls of yellow. A book floated out and into James' hands. It was a brown tome with silver lettering etched into it.

"Is that your Ranger Class book?" Tom asked, eyeing the book with excitement.

"It is!" James exclaimed. "The Kama Sutra!"

Tom made a face that showed he was not amused, even though inside, he wanted to chuckle.

"Oh, come on," James said indignantly. "That was hilarious. And you should see the look on your face!"

James sat down to consume his book as well. The same process occurred for him, and he stared with a blank expression before blinking rapidly.

"Sweet! Now I get XP for dickshots!" James suddenly exclaimed, doing a little fistpump in the air before appearing to continue reading over his notifications.

Rolling his eyes, Tom ignored him, taking a moment instead to look at his Inventory. There were now twenty-two common Monster Cores in one of the slots. That meant that the others were given to James and Derek. Tom was glad that they would now be able to purchase their own equipment, and he could focus on his. He didn't mind paying for items for them; they were his friends, after all. Something about everyone having their own currency and being able to buy his own equipment, though, meant that he could splurge a little more on some nice items. Besides, there might be some skills he could get from the machine as well.

Thinking about this reminded him that he was going to have to give some kind of speech about what they had discovered so far about the Grand System. Deciding that the vending machines would be a big part of it, he made a decision.

"We need to find a vending machine and buy some items to show to the people we're going to be speaking to," Tom said to Derek and James. They both looked up at him. "If we keep the cans, we can show them how to open them, so they know what to expect. I'm sure there's a machine here somewhere since there's a lot of office space."

"Sure, retailers always put vending machines in offices," Derek replied. "And I like the idea of showing them the items and how to activate them. Seeing the effect for the first time is quite an experience. It would be good to try not to scare them."

"Where's the fun in that? You should toss it at someone and tell them to open it," James grinned maniacally. "The look on their face would be priceless!"

"As funny as that might be, it would be better not to make anyone's panic or anxiety worse than this apocalypse already has." Tom rolled his eyes but couldn't help picturing someone falling out of their chair as though they had just opened a joke can of peanut brittle with springy snakes inside.

"Are we really calling it an apocalypse already?" Derek asked.

"Seems like it. It's a global effect that ended the lives of who knows how many people, and likely will end far more, due simply to the fact that humanity has existed in a state of peace for so long, that they just don't know what to do with something that immediately acts with violence toward them," Tom replied, snapping out of his thoughts.

"True. I hate the thought of what's happening. That there's nothing we can do to stop it but adapt," Derek said remorsefully. "Maybe the governments can do something?"

"The governments are probably just trying to stop the bleeding. Rallying the military will only do so much, as they will have to choose places to wipe free of monsters and then sit and protect them. Because the notifications said that the monsters are appearing because of the mana being released, that means random spawns," Tom explained. "So, they can't go out and just wipe all the monsters out and everything goes back to normal. They have to be ready at a moment's notice to eradicate a monster that might appear in the area they cleared and are protecting."

"I wonder if using mana in that area would cause monsters to stop appearing there," James randomly mused, staring at a screen only he could see.

"That was quite possibly the most intelligent question you have ever asked," Derek said, looking stunned.

"Fuck you very much," James said in return, still not looking away from whatever he was reading.

"That's something to consider. If there was a way to use up the mana in an area, that would likely mean monsters couldn't appear there, making it safer," Tom pondered the thought. "We'll have to look into that once we get more people safe and figure out how to guide them to becoming more self-sufficient."

"Well, alright then. Let's go find a vending machine, get some new equipment, and get ready to try to help the people here!" Tom said, standing up and turning toward the door.

Chapter 10

Training

"Hey Tom, did you ever Inspect your sword?" James asked. "That thing has to have better stats than the starter weapons, right?"

"Honestly, I forgot. I haven't gotten used to being able to do that yet. I'll do it now," Tom replied.

Pulling his sword from his Inventory, Tom activated the Inspect ability on it.

Item: Black-Steel Greatsword	
The Black-Steel Greatsword is a formidable weapon forged from a rare black-steel alloy. Renowned for its lighter weight and increased durability, this two-handed sword is capable of delivering devastating blows that can cleave through armor and bone alike. The blade's dark, polished surface absorbs light, giving it a menacing appearance on the battlefield. The greatsword's edge is incredibly sharp, and the weapon is well-balanced despite its size, allowing skilled warriors to wield it with surprising agility, making it a fearsome choice for any combatant who seeks to overpower their enemies with brute force.	
Item Type:	Weapon, Slashing
Durability:	150/150
Attack Damage:	18-25
Item Quality:	Well-Crafted
Item Rarity:	Uncommon
Sword Skill: Cleave	
This skill allows the user to slice at multiple opponents simultaneously with an additional 50% power at the cost of 25 Stamina.	

"It's definitely better than the starter equipment. It even has a skill I had been activating and didn't know. That explains why those strikes were so much more powerful than I'd expected," Tom replied excitedly. "Though, it doesn't exactly feel like it's suited to a Warlock Class."

"I'm guessing that weapons will become more specialized as you level. At least it has more power," Derek offered. "Only time and more experience will tell, though."

"Let's just see what we can get with our new Monster Cores," James said, rubbing his hands together.

James stepped up and put his hand on the machine.

"Class recognized. Ranger. Adjusting available options."

The machine once again had rows that pulled back inside and then were replaced with new ones that had cans with more colorful labels and images.

"Damn." James shook his head sadly. "No bazooka. That's probably a higher-level kind of thing then." He kept perusing through the melee options, his shoulders slumping when he got to the end.

"What's wrong?" Tom asked.

James sighed. "No chainsaw, either." He threw his hands up in defeat. "I mean, I don't even need it attached to my wrist. I'm cool with holding it. It's not like I'm asking for the world here…" He looked through the cans again, stopping briefly on a display of katanas. "Hmm… No. Being a ranged weapon fighter," James said thoughtfully, looking at the items in the vending machine, "I think another handgun so that I don't need to reload as often and some axes are the best bets."

"But *chainsaws* are fine for ranged Damage Dealers?" Tom raised an eyebrow.

James turned, meeting Tom's gaze with a deadly serious expression. "Chainsaws are *always* fine." After an uncomfortably long moment of unnerving eye contact, Tom nodded. James mouthed the word 'always' one last time and turned back to the machine, continuing with his commentary as though he'd never been interrupted. "Also, some armor would probably be a good idea at this point. Though, I'm not sure how much I can get until we go out and kill some more monsters."

Tom guessed that the System had given James only about twenty coins based on the amount he received versus what the battle log said their party had killed. With the prices of items being slightly higher, but on average about five coins each for equipment of this level, they should be able to get a few good items each.

Looking over his shoulder, Tom watched as James bought another can with a picture of a handgun on it, though this one seemed to be different than the Glock he had bought before, and a can displaying axes that resembled hatchets. Grabbing the items, which cost fifteen cores, James was about to open the first can.

"No! Wait to open those until we get to the training for the new people. We want everyone to see us open them so they can be ready for what happens," Derek blurted out, reaching out and placing a hand on top of James' to stop him from cracking open the first can.

"Oh yeah, sorry. I just got excited about cracking open a cold one with the boys," James said sheepishly.

"You mean loot?" Derek asked.

James frowned. "And… what did I say?"

"…Nevermind. I'd also suggest that instead of armor, for now you buy more ammo and magazines, James," Derek said. "If you're going to be anything like I was in basic, you're going to run out faster than you hope, and it's better to be prepared now."

"Sounds similar to why my last girlfriend broke up with me," James muttered *almost* under his breath.

"...What?" Derek blinked.

"What?" James' head snapped up. "I didn't say anything."

"Right... So the magazines are so you aren't stopping after seventeen shots to reload. Load them out of battle and put them in your Inventory so you can just grab one, insert, and keep firing. If we keep a can of ammo unopened, it will give the people a chance to see what happens when opened. I feel like there will be a pretty big rush on buying guns so that people don't have to get up close and personal with monsters."

"People really don't want to get swords, spears, and axes?" Tom asked.

"Of course not. It's fun in video games, but in a world where we have assault rifles to kill so many enemies at once with little harm to ourselves? They're going to opt for the latter." Derek seemed to pause in thought. "I mean, if this whole Grand System incentivized archaic weapons and de-incentivized modern weapons of war, I think things would be different—but I'm not seeing that sort of bias. Maybe something can crop up at higher levels, but so far..." he shrugged. "We haven't gone to war with hand-to-hand combat for some time now for a reason. It's simple human nature and survival tactics. We might have been killers in the past, and some still go hunting, but we've lived in a peaceful society long enough that people are not going to be ready to take a life. Even if it's trying to kill them first. They'll need to see some atrocities before that can happen. Even then, many won't be able to do it."

This was a sobering thought. The average person experienced very little actual violence. They had all heard about it on the news, and it seemed so prevalent because of the mass availability of the media on the internet and social media, but how many times had they actually felt the effects of true violence in their lives? On the playground as kids? In video games and movies where everything was fantasized and exaggerated? Tom couldn't remember the last time he had actually been in a fight before today.

Tom had been present for a killing one time in his life, but even that was abnormal. It had been in a convenience store, run by an older couple who had poured their life into the small gas station stop. A man had run in while Tom was getting a drink from the fridge. He had demanded money from the register, and when the husband had told him no, the man had shot him.

The wife had screamed and thrown herself at the assailant, who shot her, too. The would-be robber had panicked. He had lost control in the moment—not wanting to hurt anyone, just looking for some quick cash to get his next high— and he'd pulled the trigger.

He had bolted out the door after the second shot, not taking a single dollar from the store in his haste. Tom had watched the couple bleed out, unable to do anything but call 911 for help. He hadn't even been able to jump in to try to save them for fear of being hurt himself. He had cowered behind one of the shelves holding bags of chips until the man had left the store. Counseling had been the only way for him to get over that moment enough to return to work in the office.

Shaking himself from these thoughts, Tom was determined to help the survivors here do better than he had then. Derek purchased a few items and placed the cans in his Inventory before letting Tom take his turn.

Tom placed his hand on the machine and the options changed again for his Class. As he stared at the items in the machine, trying to decide what to get, he noticed one of the cans had the image of a book on it. Examining it closer, the machine spoke.

"Skill books can be purchased and read to learn new skills. Make a selection to gain new abilities."

The text on the can read *Summon Demonic Creature*.

"Does it have other skills?" Tom asked aloud.

As he said this, the machine shifted again to show two more skill book options. Tom decided he would buy all three and see what he could learn. Placing the Monster Cores in the machine and making the selections, the cans were dispensed, and he pulled them out and opened them.

Holding the three leather-bound tomes, he read the covers and then opened the first one. As he did, he felt the same familiar flow of knowledge he had from the Class book, and his mind was filled with the knowledge of how to use the skill. As the pages turned faster and faster, the words seemed to leap from the page and flow into his eyes.

The back cover slammed shut when the pages finished, and the book disintegrated. A prompt appeared in his vision.

New Skill: Summon Demonic Creature

This skill grants the Warlock the ability to summon a demonic creature from the depths of the infernal realms to serve in battle. The summoned demon will fight alongside the Warlock, following commands and unleashing its dark powers against enemies. As the skill level increases, the Warlock gains the ability to summon more powerful and fearsome demons.

Mechanics:

- **Demon Power Scaling:** Higher skill levels unlock access to stronger demons with greater combat abilities and unique traits.
- **Control Requirement:** Maintaining control over summoned demons requires the Warlock to have sufficient Charisma. The more powerful the demon, the higher the Charisma required to keep the demon under control.
- **Failure to Control:** If the Warlock's Charisma is insufficient, the summoned demon may rebel, potentially turning against the Warlock or escaping back to the infernal realms.

APOCALYPSE

Note: Use this skill wisely, as the strength of the summoned demon can become a double-edged sword if not properly controlled.
Skill casting cost: 50 mana
Duration: 1 hour
Cooldown: 30 seconds

He swayed slightly, feeling a little light headed, but quickly recovered. He decided to open the other two books as well and received similar prompts for these skills.

New Skill: Fear

This skill allows the Warlock to instill overwhelming fear in a target of their choice, causing them to falter, flee, or become paralyzed with terror. The intensity and duration of the fear inflicted are directly influenced by the Warlock's Charisma. As the Warlock levels up this skill, the number of affected targets increases, making it a powerful tool for crowd control and disrupting enemy formations.
 	
Mechanics:
 	
    • **Fear Effect:** Targets affected by Fear experience a range of debilitating effects, such as reduced attack power, slower movement speed, or temporary loss of control.
    • **Charisma Dependency:** The effectiveness and severity of the Fear effect are determined by the Warlock's Charisma. Higher Charisma results in stronger fear responses from targets, increasing the likelihood of paralysis or panic.
    • **Multiple Targets:** As the skill level increases, the Warlock gains the ability to affect additional targets simultaneously, expanding the scope of this potent control ability.
 	
Note: The success rate and severity of Fear depend on the Warlock's Charisma relative to the Willpower or Mental Resistance of the targets. Use strategically to control the battlefield and turn the tide in your favor.

Skill casting cost: 25 mana
Duration: 5 mins
Cooldown: 10 mins

New Skill: Corruption
Corruption grants the Warlock the power to weaken the abilities of a chosen target by inflicting a debilitating debuff. As the skill levels up, the potency of the debuff increases, and the Warlock gains the ability to affect multiple targets simultaneously. The effectiveness of Corruption depends on the Warlock's Charisma; the greater the difference between the Warlock's Charisma and the target's, the more severe the weakening effect. **Mechanics:** • **Debuff Effect:** Corruption reduces the target's combat effectiveness by lowering their key attributes such as Strength, Defense, Speed, or Magic Power, depending on the type of enemy. • **Charisma Dependency:** For Corruption to be effective, the Warlock's Charisma must be higher than that of the target. The greater the disparity in Charisma, the stronger and longer-lasting the debuff. • **Multiple Targets:** As the skill levels up, the Warlock gains the ability to apply Corruption to additional targets, spreading the weakening effect across a wider range of enemies. **Note:** Corruption is most effective against enemies with significantly lower Charisma than the Warlock. Use this skill strategically to cripple key opponents and turn the tide of battle in your favor.
Skill casting cost: 75 mana
Duration: 2 hours
Cooldown: 6 hours

"Tom? We need to head to the gym," Derek reminded him.

"Right. Sorry. Got a little excited there about these skill books. Alright, let's get going."

When they arrived, they were surprised at how many people were there. Metal bleachers had been set up on one side and reached almost all the way from one end of the room to the other. Tom had been expecting more of a weight room than an actual regulation-sized basketball court. There must have been almost five hundred people crammed into the seating.

A microphone had been set up on a stand at half-court with a couple of speakers on either side for them to give their speech. Brian stood in the middle of the circle, waiting for them and talking to another man in a suit. He noticed them and waved them over.

APOCALYPSE

"Lads! Glad you're here. It's time to talk to the people we have here. Everyone is gathered except the security that's protecting the perimeter, and we'll update them after your training," Brian said.

"Who are all these people?" Tom asked.

"Mostly the people who worked for companies renting office space in the building and those nearby," Brian replied. "A few are survivors who came here as you did."

"And none of them have any idea what they're doing?" Derek asked.

"I wouldn't say that. This isn't the 1970s. I'm sure many of them are figuring it out. We do live in a pretty advanced society, technologically speaking. We've got smart phones and self-checkout systems, but it's always nice to have someone who seems to know what they're doing guide you through something new," Brian said. "Remember that this has been a traumatic experience for them. They're scared and just looking for something to hold onto that is steady. Try to be patient and understanding."

Taking a deep breath, Tom stepped up to the microphone.

"H-hello, everyone. My name is Tom. I'm a software engineer who works on... well, *worked* on, I guess now—video game development. These are my friends Derek and James. They worked with me and we've been able to use some of that knowledge to begin learning what to do with this new reality we find ourselves being a part of."

A hand went up in the middle of the crowd.

"Um... yes? You with your hand up."

A middle-aged woman stood up. "Do you know how to stop this and make things go back to normal?" She asked.

"Uh, no. We don't have the ability to make that kind of change. At least not right now; and certainly not alone. I believe that the road to the kind of power you're talking about—the ability to take back control of our collective destiny as a society—has already been laid out in front of us," Tom replied. "This is a lot bigger than just us. It's a global issue that affects everyone at once. We're just here to try to help you all adapt a little better."

"I don't want to adapt. I was happy living my life before. I want to go back to that," The same lady replied, seeming to get irritated at the answer.

Some murmurs of agreement began to spread through the crowd. James pushed past Tom and took the mic from the stand.

"Well, that's too fucking bad. You're stuck now. You've got two options. Buck up or die," James said to the crowd.

A wave of confusion and anger began to run through the crowd at this pronouncement. Brian looked pale and started to move as though he was going to intercede. Derek put a hand up to delay him as he stepped forward to speak.

"You all think that this is just some kind of inconvenience that's going to go away like a cold? Do you think that we can just wish it all away? Well, you're wrong. Our world has been fundamentally changed in a way we didn't even think was physically possible a few hours ago. It defies our understanding of science. But we are *humans*. Apex predators who have adapted to every situation that the world has ever thrown at us," Derek's voice carried with it that strange militaristic authority that battle-hardened warriors possessed. "The ice age, earthquakes, tornados, tsunamis, hurricanes, plagues, and pandemics. We can overcome this too if we work to adapt to what we have. We can even thrive again if we put our minds to it. Now, listen to Tom because he's going to begin to explain what you fuckers need to do to stay alive."

Handing the mic back to Tom, Derek nodded once, then stood behind him, trying to look menacing to the crowd. Everyone in the room had gone silent at Derek's declaration.

James leaned forward, already mean-mugging the audience in the wake of his earlier outburst. He whispered only loud enough for Tom and Derek to hear. "I feel like I already summed all that up." He made a face as though weighing Derek's speech before giving a surreptitious thumbs up. "But not bad."

"Thanks, James. That was... interesting." Tom glanced toward Derek. "And thank you, Derek. I think you summed things up well." He turned back to the crowd. "As for everyone in this room? My good friend James here might be a bit rough around the edges, but he isn't wrong. This is a new paradigm we find ourselves thrown into. We can't change it. At least not without understanding it more. So, what we need to do first is try to stay alive," Tom said. "By a show of hands, how many of you completed the tutorial the Grand System offered?"

At least three hundred hands were raised.

"Of those of you with your hands raised, how many of you felt like you understood at least a small bit of what those prompts said based on video game knowledge?" Tom asked.

Some of the hands went down. Most of them remained up, though.

"That's great news! We can work with that," Tom said. "Have any of you used the System to *do* anything so far?"

Half of the hands went down.

"Okay. Still a good number. I was really worried we were going to end up with a crowd of people who had no idea what was happening," Tom said. "Have any of you fought off or killed creatures that have been appearing?"

Most of the hands went down this time.

"Okay. That is still alright. I didn't expect there to be as many people in that group," Tom said. "Does anyone feel like they would be able to help with training others, or feel comfortable working with people to learn more about what's involved?"

Only two hands stayed up at this request.

"Cool! Can the two of you come down here to join me? I think we can use your help in explaining this to others later," Tom said.

The two who had raised their hands moved down from their seats. Looking at them as they moved, Tom noticed he recognized one of them.

"Kevin?" Tom asked into the mic.

"You bet your sweet ass it is!" Kevin called back.

"Hurry up, dude! We wondered what had happened to you!" Tom said.

Most of the crowd turned to look at Kevin, not sure what this meant for the meeting they were having.

APOCALYPSE

"Now, for the rest of you. The first thing we need to explain is our new way of operating. You've all seen the screens that appear in your vision," Tom began. "As most of you have already discovered, you can control them with your mind. You can also organize them and set the information you receive to only be what you want so you aren't overwhelmed."

With that, Tom spent the next several hours reviewing everything that he, Derek, James, and Kevin knew about using the Grand System—things they had learned from experience, things they guessed at from their knowledge of creating video game software, and things they still didn't understand. They fielded questions from the audience and did the best they could to answer them as truthfully as they could.

The other man who had raised his hand was named Jay Beraz. He was not a software developer but had spent some time working in IT and was a gamer who had been able to make most of the associations they had, if only from the amount of time he had spent playing video games.

The entire crowd had been completely in awe of the process of the cans. Tom, Derek, and James all brought out different cans and opened all but potions to show them what they did.

James held up two of the cans in the air that held ammo for his weapon, riling up the crowd. Like Stone Cold Steve Austin, he enthusiastically smashed one of the cans against his head, which only served to send him half tumbling to the side. Shaking his head, he held the can up once more to the jeers of the crowd. One can disappeared into his Inventory as he reached for the tab of the other. Ripping it open, he raised it above his head, mouth wide as ammo spilled out. The rounds landed in his mouth and overflowed onto the ground around him. He straightened abruptly, one of the rounds clutched firmly in his teeth, to the claps around him.

Holding his hands out and patting the air, James calmed the crowd. He then took the round from his mouth and held it out like a stubby wand. He took the microphone from Tom, who was actively shaking his head at the man's antics. James made a sound like a vacuum cleaner as he triggered the Inventory System, making all of the rounds on the ground disappear into his Inventory.

James flourished his hand like a magician, crossing his arm across his body before taking a deep bow to the claps and hoots of the crowd.

"Say what you will about that crazy bastard," Derek didn't even have to whisper into Tom's ear with the adulation of the crowd. "But he probably just did more for this group than a month of therapy."

Tom nodded. *There hasn't been a lot to smile about since the integration.* He looked around at all the faces, feeling the weight of responsibility on his shoulders. He sighed. *And all of this is only the beginning.*

After the demonstration, they told everyone to take a ten-minute break, and then they would reconvene to begin working more closely with them. Tom walked over to Brian and motioned for the rest of the guys to also come over.

"Do you know how many people there are here?" Tom asked Brian.

"About five hundred, give or take," Brian replied.

"Okay, that's what I guessed as well. I want to divide them up into groups that each of us can take to walk them through the tutorial if they haven't finished it and try to answer questions. This'll give us a better way of helping them as a whole, I think," Tom said.

"Why don't we just teach everyone at once and have the rest of us just move through the crowd to answer questions? That way, they all get the same training," Jay asked.

Jay was a little bit older than the others—probably mid-forties—with a goatee. He carried himself with an air of confidence that showed he wasn't afraid to do what had to be done. He was not the typical person who was now confused and scared of what might happen.

"Jay, was it?" Tom asked.

"You can call me that," Jay replied. He took Tom's hand in a thick-fingered grasp, his eyes suddenly gaining a steely glint. "Just don't call me late for dinner."

"It's a pleasure to meet you." Tom said, chuckling as they clasped hands. "I wish it could have been under different circumstances."

"Not sure I'd agree. Not much for people normally. I usually find those I like the best in situations that try a normal person. So far, I like what I see in you. Time will tell if that opinion changes or not, though," Jay said, a more solemn look on his face.

"Straightforward and honest. I like that in people, too," Tom said. "I also like the idea of giving everyone the same training, but different people will be in different places in understanding and capability. I'd rather not bore the majority with the tutorial stuff, since it's just panning through pop-ups. Most people should have understood that if they ever touched a phone. That'll mostly leave the older crowd to walk through that. So, we should divide them up into groups, and each of us should take a group to help. If there's a question that everyone should hear, please say it out loud so that it can be answered for everyone."

With everyone in agreement, they went back to await the return of the rest of the crowd and began to divide into groups based on their understanding of the System.

Chapter 11

Hop In

After a few more hours in the gym, everyone had successfully completed the tutorial and received instruction on a variety of essential topics, including Classes, weapons, forming parties, skills, XP, leveling, basic magic, and how to balance a party for the best chance of survival. However, as the hours passed, people began to grow cranky, and the need for food became increasingly urgent.

While some supplies had been brought to the Center, they were far from sufficient to feed five hundred people for an extended period. It was clear that they needed to find a sustainable solution to address the growing food shortage.

"What about the vending machines? Can't we get food from them?" Brian asked. "I mean, they *are* vending machines after all."

Tom, Derek, James, Jay, and Kevin all looked at each other for a moment, sharing a sheepish exchange.

"Wait, you mean, you didn't even check if they have food?" Brian replied, closing his eyes for a moment as he took in a deep breath.

"We were busy, alright," James replied in a slightly angry tone. "You haven't had little green monsters trying to blow you up yet."

"It's fine," Tom interjected, trying to keep the peace. "We can go look to see what's available. But that costs Monster Cores. We need more options."

"What about hunting?" Jay offered.

"Where are they supposed to go hunting?" James interrupted. "I'm not eating a fucking goblin."

"Well, if you'd give me a moment, I'd explain it to you, jackass," Jay retorted, anger rising at being interrupted. "Goblins ain't the only thing that this new mana infusion brought here, and I don't want to eat something that could give Sandra Bernhard a run for the ugly trophy either. I saw wolves on my way to the Center, which means there are likely many other forms of life out there as well. I figure we get some of these big trucks and SUVs and head outside the city or into some parks to see what's out there. An exploratory mission. See if we can't find a way to get some kind of food system going."

"And farming?" Tom asked.

"That's going to be a bit tougher. My original thought would be to put it on the roof, but it's pointed. So, we may need to get creative about trying to remove part of it to open it up to sunlight and rain. We need to get dirt in here and get it up to the higher levels."

James gestured at the building and its people. "At least we got fertilizer covered, if it comes to it."

"Funny thing, that." Jay raised an eyebrow. "Why do you suppose we haven't done that kind of thing as a modern society before now?"

James shrugged. "Not sure. Maybe no one thought of it. I'm a pretty smart guy, you know."

"Smart *ass*, more like." Jay scowled.

James only pointed a finger at him, nodding in confirmation.

Jay sighed. "Human waste contains human pathogens, kid. Unless this new magic stuff can fix that—and I'm not saying it can't, but otherwise we're out of luck there. There *is* some good news, at least. The electricity is still working for now, but it won't stay that way. We should do it while we can use the elevators," Jay explained.

"Brian, can you get some people to work on that? It's not going to be easy, but if we can get it started, then we can hopefully begin to grow some food," Tom said, turning to look over at him.

"You'll want to make some kind of boxes to hold the dirt in. Like a flower box but really fucking big. See if anyone has any knowledge about growing plants. They should be able to get a skill and work the plants better," Jay said.

"I'll see what I can do to find people who have experience and get others to help with moving the dirt," Brian said. "Can you see about helping to set up a perimeter around the building? We should be able to dig up the medians and other grassy places for dirt, but we need to be sure the people doing the work are safe. Check in with the security team and get their help with clearing the area."

"We'll do a sweep before we move out. We just need to get our hands on a bigger vehicle. Something that can run things over," Tom said.

"We have a company vehicle I can give you the keys to. It's a Tahoe. Not like we're going to need it anymore," Brian offered. "It was used as a security vehicle—cattle guard and everything—so it'll likely suit your needs well."

"Perfect! Let's go get it," Tom replied, excited at the prospect of seeing the new vehicle.

"No problem." Brian smiled. "Follow me and I'll take you guys to check out your new ride."

After assigning some of the staff to oversee the farming project and evaluate potential recruits, Brian led the team to inspect the SUV. The vehicle was nearly perfect for their scouting needs: a large black SUV equipped with a sturdy cattle guard on the front, metal cage coverings protecting the taillights, a light bar mounted on the roof, and oversized off-road tires. The SUV had been lifted slightly to accommodate the larger tires, enhancing its rugged appearance. It looked tough, practical, and more than capable of handling whatever challenges they might encounter on the road.

"Oh, ho, ho, ho! That'll do nicely," Jay said, rubbing his hands together.

"Calm your tits, Jay. *I'm* driving," Tom said.

"And *you're* riding bitch," James whispered in Jay's ear, having slipped up behind the big man.

"What? Why?" Jay jumped, turning and putting his hands on his hips.

"Because I'm the one with the *Vehicular Manslaughter* skill that gives me extra damage when I run over shit," Tom replied, grinning and grabbing the keys dangling in Brian's hand.

"I bet if you let me drive it, I could get it too," Jay retorted. "Won't know unless we try."

"We can try that later. For now, we need to do as much damage as we can so we get as many kills as we can. You'll get XP, I promise. We'll add you to the party," Tom said, not looking back as he walked to the Tahoe.

"Ugh! Fine... but let the record show it should have been me," Jay called after him, annoyed. "Fucker," he added under his breath.

James leaned into Tom and whispered, "I like him… Can we keep him?"

"Yeah, we can keep him," Tom groaned, rolling his eyes and stopping before he got to the vehicle, remembering the new team members and their lack of equipment. "But Kevin, Jay. We need to get you some gear. And to do that, we need to do a little goblin hunting."

Everyone smiled at that. Thinking about the party and then about Jay and Kevin, Tom sent them each a party invite. They accepted, and now all of their HP bars showed on the left side of Tom's vision.

"Before you go out there, let's get the other two at least a weapon. The security team has been pooling their cores in order to organize themselves better. I had their supervisor in your training, and he's been working to get them operating more efficiently. We can spare some Monster Cores to get a weapon for them," Brian added.

"Excellent!" Kevin exclaimed.

"They have cores already?" Tom asked.

"They do now. After your little show of force, they shot anything that wasn't human. You really made them look bad." Brian smiled at him.

"Sorry, that wasn't our intention," Tom replied.

"It's fine. They needed a good kick in the arse to shape up," Brian said, dismissing his apology.

"Have you two thought about your Classes yet?" Tom asked, turning to Kevin and Jay.

"Sure have," Kevin said, flexing one modest bicep. "Barbarian!"

They all stared at him for a moment. Kevin was a little on the thin side and a bit lankier than the figure one normally thought of as a Barbarian. But he had been known to have a bit of a temper, so those who knew him only stared for a moment before shrugging.

"You guys are okay with that? Beanpole over there is going to be a Barbarian?" Jay asked. As the only one in the party who didn't know Kevin, he was a little concerned.

"Look, his Attribute Points will buff him up. I'm sure he'll be okay once we get things rolling. Besides, it's always nice to have someone willing to run in and cause a scene while we execute a plan of attack," Derek said.

"If you guys say so. I think I'm going to go with Rogue. It'll suit my needs well and will help the team. Always nice to have someone do a little stabby-stabby in the back while the enemy is distracted," Jay said, his face splitting into a maniacal smile.

James nodded sagely. "Rogues do it from behind."

Without looking back, Jay extended a fist, which James bumped with an equivalent level of nonchalance.

At that moment, the door to the parking garage burst open and a woman with bright purple hair came striding out of the door. She wore ripped, black jeans with a black leather jacket over a black tank top and a metal chain around her neck. She walked with purpose toward the party, a swagger to her steps.

"Hold on just a minute, you sons of bitches," the woman yelled as she marched toward them. "I want in on this little party you have going on and I'm not taking no for an answer."

"And just who the fuck are you, lady?" Jay asked, crossing his arms, a look of mistrust on his face.

"I'm your worst fucking nightmare if you try to stop me, bub," the woman said, walking right up to Jay and pointing a finger into his chest.

"Calm down, little sister—" was all Jay got out, raising his hands placatingly before she started in again.

"Don't you patronize me. I'll kick your ass," She began, her anger rising at being spoken to like that.

"Hold on, hold on, hold everything!" Tom interjected, putting his hands out and in between them.

"Look, we're pretty much full up on the team right now. We could include you, but you would need to be looking to pick a Class we need to complement the team. What Class were you considering taking?" Tom asked.

"Bard," the woman said with a tone of finality that dared anyone to question her choice.

"So, you're a whore?" Jay asked.

The woman reeled on him and stomped on his foot, then kneed him in the crotch. Jay first danced on one foot, crying out before he wheezed and fell onto the floor, grabbing his family jewels.

"No, asshat. I'm a *performer*. I was the lead singer for a local band that performed in the bars around downtown Dallas before the shit hit the fan. Figured I could continue what I know by being a Support Class and still get to use my voice. I'm Kiera, by the way," the woman, Kiera, introduced herself, looking over at Tom after glaring down at the writhing Jay. "I'm guessing none of you were looking to be a Bard?"

Everyone shook their heads in silence. James even covered his own family jewels out of fear.

Kiera sniffed. "Now, can we get this show on the road?"

"One sec," Tom said, holding up one finger then turning to the rest of the team. "Anyone that isn't Jay have a problem with the lady joining us? I think a Bard would be great."

They all looked over his shoulder at Kiera, who smiled warmly as she crossed her arms over her chest and turned her body back and forth, and then they looked back at Tom. Everyone looked a little afraid, shaking their heads.

Everyone except James. Tom looked at him, clearly asking his opinion on the matter.

"What?" James shrugged. "You kidding me? She's a badass. What's not to like?"

Kiera's fiery gaze shifted to the man, burning with approval. To his credit, James only flinched slightly, offering a shaky smile in return.

James turned his back to the group, but Tom still caught him pulling a tampon out of his Inventory and glancing between it and Kiera thoughtfully before shaking his head and making the toiletry disappear.

Tom rubbed his temples.

"Then it's settled. Welcome to the team, Kiera. We were about to go get some gear so we could head out to level everyone to five to be able to select Classes," Tom explained, holding his arms out in what he hoped was a welcoming gesture. "Then we need to go explore and see if we can find some game to hunt."

"Badass. Let's go," Kiera said, smiling even wider that her antics had worked.

Tom extended a party invite to Kiera, and she accepted. Heading back into the building, Brian led them first to the security office to grab some Monster Cores, then to the vending machine in the cafeteria. Jay was given some daggers and a short sword. Kiera chose a crossbow and bolts after talking with Derek about what she had experience with, and Kevin...

Kevin chose a greataxe.

He could lift it but was absolutely *not* able to wield it properly. He would be putting all his points into Strength at first. Fortunately, there wasn't a window for Kevin to hang out of, so he was along mostly for the ride and XP. He looked a little dejected at first after being told he would be a ride-along but perked up at the prospect of getting points for coming with them and then being able to contribute later.

"Why the hell did you choose a crossbow? Guns would be better," James said.

"I'm a better shot with the crossbow. Used to shoot with my grandad out on his property when I would visit," Kiera said. "I won some competitions too. We'd go hunting every year, and he taught me how to use one. I'd prefer a rifle, but they are too expensive right now."

"You used to go hunting?" Jay asked.

"Yup. I was pretty good at it, too. Grandad used to live through the winters on his kills, so we went out a lot. Shot my first deer at twelve." She tapped her sternum with two fingers. "Right through the heart."

"Badass. I wish I had someone that had taken me hunting. It always looked so fun," James said.

"It's not. It's boring as shit. Sitting there for hours on end, just waiting for something to come by. But Grandad used to tell me stories about the war he fought in, and we bonded. So, I have fond memories of the time," Kiera said, seemingly remembering the time she spent with him and smiling to herself. "He had a fake deer target he used to set up in the field behind his house that we would practice on. That thing had so many holes in it by the time I was done."

With everyone now armed and ready, the party headed back out to the garage.

"Tom is driving. I'll be in the passenger seat. Jay, you take the driver's side rear, Kiera the passenger rear. James will stand in the sunroof and fire from above," Derek said, explaining the strategy to the team.

"Why don't I stand in the sunroof?" Kiera asked, beginning to take her 'I'm going to get my way' stance.

"Because you need to be able to reload without all the wind in your face," Derek explained, not fazed by her attitude this time. "And the major benefits of a crossbow is its silence and the ability to recover and reuse your ammunition. Which we can't do with a drive-by." He pointed at the SUV. "You'll need to pick your shots carefully if we're in a position where we can't recover the bolts or you'll be wasting cores unnecessarily."

She nodded in acceptance with a silent oh forming on her lips.

"We'll move out and try to kill a good number of goblins before we return. Ranged fighters, try not to engage unless you have a clear shot. No sense in getting a group of them chasing us when Tom running them down will still get us XP. Conserve ammunition for when you need to back up one of the melee fighters," Derek continued, laying out a clear strategy for each of them to follow.

James and Kiera nodded in understanding.

"Besides, it'll take Kiera a half hour to reload that crossbow," Jay added, chuckling and elbowing James in the side playfully.

A whoosh of air escaped him as the stock of the crossbow slammed into his stomach.

"Oh, sorry. Didn't see you there," Kiera said, not missing a beat as she swung the crossbow onto her shoulder with its strap and briskly walked past him. "This weapon is a little unwieldy sometimes." Kiera's face was a picture of innocence as she smiled at the hunched-over Jay.

"But you just got it," Jay wheezed.

"And I'm still not used to it," Kiera smiled at him as she walked backward.

"Remember, this is also a scouting mission. We need to see what we can find out there and report back. We don't need any heroes. Everyone comes back safe. Am I clear?" Derek asked.

Everyone nodded curtly, grasping the gravity of what he was saying, and not questioning Derek's tone as he fell back into his military background and organization habits. Tom looked at him and was immediately grateful to have run into him at the office. He sure as hell didn't know how to organize people like this. This kind of knowledge only came from being in a position where you were first taught, and then placed in a position to lead people in a rigid and strict form.

Tom had been brought up in a home where academics had been the predominant path. Prizing grades over athleticism or strength. So, he'd worked hard to get the best grades possible. Then, he got a scholarship to college and graduated with honors. Straight away, he got a job at a software development company in the DFW area that made school management software. After a few years there, while he worked to get his master's degree, he left and joined up with Underdark, where he met James, Derek, and Kevin.

"Alright, everyone ready?" Derek called, snapping Tom out of his thoughts.

They nodded again.

"Then hop in! It's time to MOVE OUT!"

He smiled as he heard the groans from every single person in their party.

Chapter 12

Scouting Fun

Driving down the streets of Dallas with the windows down, looking for a fight might have been a typical college night out for some, but it was a whole new experience for the ragtag band of people in the vehicle. Tom felt like he was in a mobster movie where he and his crew were looking to shake someone down. James seemed to agree.

"You come to me?" James shouted, his voice thick with an Italian accent. The wind tried and failed to sweep away his words. "On the day of my daughter's wedding?" He stood in the middle of the vehicle with the upper half of his body sticking out of the sunroof, scanning the area for any threats.

A small whistling noise caught James' attention just before a small rock hit him in the head.

"BASTARDO! *Motha*-fucker! Chi cazzo credi di essere?" He wailed, dropping down into the car.

"What happened?" Derek started, looking around in every direction for something.

"One of the Families' must've sent an Enforcer," James cried, his Italian accent not slipping in the slightest. A small bit of blood started to run down from his scalp and between his fingers.

"You speak Italian?" Kiera's voice was thready with fear or excitement, Tom couldn't tell.

"What?" James blinked, his accent gone in an instant. "What are you talking about, lady? I just got my shit busted by a rock." He paused for a moment, a look of grudging respect crossing his face. "Good aim." He rolled the last words strangely.

Kiera shared a look with Tom.

"Just…" He shook his head.

Looking back to James, seeing the blood on the left side of his head, Derek cast a healing spell on James and looked to Jay.

"Jay! Your side! Be ready!" Derek ordered.

Jay grunted and then looked carefully out the window. Seeing movement, he turned back to the others.

"They're coming from the left and slightly behind us. Can we turn around to get at them?"

Turning to look, Derek saw where they were coming from.

"Make a U-turn at this street and let's see if we can hit any of them with the vehicle first," Derek pointed ahead to the next signal light that was hanging on by a single wire.

"On it!" Tom replied, placing both hands on the wheel, readying himself.

Pulling to the right of the street at the intersection and then turning the vehicle as tightly as he could, Tom performed a U-turn and almost struck a vehicle parked on the side of the road, stopping to avoid a collision in their new vehicle.

The goblins saw this and began to increase their speed toward them. Whooping and yelling at the top of their lungs in what looked like an attempt to get themselves into a frenzy, they charged at the party full tilt, ready to meet their new challengers.

"Hey, look, is that goblin-Rambo?" James asked, pointing at the group approaching them.

Derek squinted hard as he looked closer at each of the goblins coming toward them. His eyes widened suddenly. "Shit, that's not Rambo—that's a bandolier of explosives!"

James rose to his knees, staring out at the goblin with a stony expression. "Goblin-fuckin' Rambo," he growled. "My Nemesis. We meet again."

James aimed his gun at the approaching goblin when Kiera slapped his arm, knocking it down and away.

"Are you a damned moron? Just going to shoot through the windshield? AKA—the thing separating us from the cannibal goblins?"

James scratched the top of his head, embarrassed. "Right. Sorry about that. I got excited."

Tom hit the gas pedal and rushed at the goblins before the explosives-goblin could finish pulling one of the objects from its death-sashes free.

The goblins with melee weapons raised them to stab the SUV and were rewarded with a cattle guard to the face and tire marks on their body. The first goblin's face practically exploded on impact with the metal grill, as the bones in its face were shoved through the rest of its skull and out the back of its head. Their weapons bounced off the metal of the car, shattering the crude weapons. The Tahoe rocked back and forth as the small bodies were crushed under its immense weight.

"This is way easier than in my car!" Tom cried in elation, a smile plastered on his face.

Kiera looked like she was going to be sick.

"I'm not so sure I can handle this," Kiera said.

"Oh, come on. It's just like hunting or fishing. You catch 'em, and then you gotta gut 'em!" Jay said, looking back at the devastation they had wrought, grinning.

"Hey, no fair," James groaned in protest, still shaking off the blow to his head. "That's my line..."

Kiera held her head out the window and retched, vomit streaming down the side of the vehicle and eating away at the clear coat of the paint.

"What's the matter, princess? Can't stomach the violence?" Jay teased her.

"I'm not sure if it says more about me that I'm not doing so well, or more about you that it's not bothering you," Kiera replied, wiping her mouth with the back of her hand and glaring daggers at Jay.

"It's okay if you can't handle it. We can find another place for you," Jay mocked.

Kiera pursed her lips and began to turn bright red. Her anger boiled over at his words.

"I'll show you who can't handle it, you stupid motherfucker!" Kiera shouted.

And with that, she shot up out of her seat and through the sunroof. Turning to point the crossbow behind the vehicle, she took aim and fired a bolt backward. It soared through the air and embedded itself to the feathers in a goblin's skull—the only remaining one that the vehicle had missed running over.

She slammed herself back down into the vehicle and began angrily reloading the crossbow. Jay sat still with his eyes wide in shock and disbelief. Silence reigned in the SUV for a moment before Kiera spoke.

"Want to place bets where the next one's going to go?" Kiera said threateningly, her eyes tracking across Jay's body before seeming to find a likely candidate for her ire.

Jay crossed his legs, hunching onto himself uncomfortably.

"Hmmph." Kiera studiously ignored the man as she seemed to break some kind of record reloading and arming her crossbow.

Tom continued on and took a right at the next intersection, so as not to backtrack to the Center, and kept driving for a few moments when he noticed there was a group of people making a left off a street a few lights ahead of them. They were running toward their vehicle, panic written on all their faces. The men and women were clearly running for their lives. Some of them were carrying children.

As they saw the vehicle moving, they began to scream for help, begging the party to come to their aid. Just as everyone was beginning to wonder what was chasing them, a large creature turned the corner.

Its skin was a greenish-grey color along with long, oily, thin, stringy hair that came down from its head to about the middle of its back. Black-banded tattoos wrapped around its upper arms, and it wore nothing but a loin cloth. Carrying a giant wooden club in its hand, lazily dragging on the ground behind it, the creature had to stand at least twelve feet tall with long, lanky arms and legs, and it looked like it wasn't very well fed.

"What the actual fuck is that?!" James shouted, staring out the windshield as Tom brought the car to a halt.

"It's an ogre..." Derek said, looking at it in awe.

"How the hell do you know that?" Jay asked, unable to take his eyes off the monstrosity in front of them.

"I used Identify on it," Derek replied, also not able to look away.

"So, what do we do?" Kiera asked, looking at Jay, then Derek, then Tom, who were all staring at the creature with unblinking eyes.

No one answered.

"Oh, come on. They did less staring in Jurassic Park. Wake up and let's figure out what to do!" Kiera shoved each of them in the arm as she spoke loudly.

"I say we fuck it's day up!" Kevin called from the backseat, hefting his axe menacingly.

"It's gigantic. It's not like a goblin," Kiera replied.

"The bigger they are, the harder they fall! Cut its legs out from under it and it'll topple. Easy peasy," Kevin said as he began to climb over the seat.

"He's right," Tom said with a mixture of fear and determination. He turned, looking at Derek. "We can't leave these people, there are fucking children in there!"

"Fine. Put it in park, take the keys so one of these lunatics doesn't steal our ride, and let's roll. Except you, Kevin. You stay in the car until you can carry that fucking axe you chose," Derek decided.

Nodding, and pouting in Kevin's case, everyone who could jumped out of the vehicle and gathered in front of the Tahoe.

"So, what's the plan?" Jay asked.

"Tom and myself will get its attention. James, you make it mad by shooting it. Kiera, aim for the eyes. Jay, try to get behind it and cut its Achilles tendons," Derek called out to each of them in turn. "Don't try to be a hero! Stay safe, stay alive, and call out moves or openings as you see them. Teamwork is the goal."

"Let's do this shit," James said in a deep voice while holding up both handguns menacingly.

Moving out from in front of the vehicle, the first of the people running down the street began to pass them. Some looked over their shoulders at the fools moving *toward* the monster, but most were too shocked to even try to look around. The monster was fixated on a woman carrying one child and leading two others near the back of the pack to notice the party moving toward them.

"James! Move right and start firing up at it! Get its attention off that family!" Derek yelled.

"On it!" James called back as he jogged to the right and aimed at the creature.

"Kiera, stand ready! Don't fire until you are sure you have a shot! That crossbow takes way too long to reload to fire too soon!" Derek called out to her.

"You got it!" Kiera answered back.

"Jay! Get gone!" Tom called over to him, making sure he knew they had the center.

Jay just nodded and sprinted off to the left to try to get behind the creature.

"I CAN WIELD IIIIIIIIIIITTTTTTT!" came a bellow from Kevin that made even the panicking people turn and move out of his way.

The ogre looked up from its chase at the yell. Seeing the party that was advancing toward it instead of fleeing, it paused in confusion.

"Fucking Kevin!" Derek growled as he stood helplessly watching his friend rush toward the ogre far faster than he'd ever seen the man run.

"I'm going to try something, so... sorry in advance if it doesn't pan out," Tom called out to the team.

With that, he began to cast a spell. Greenish energy formed in his hand, and it crackled and spat like a fire burning up wood that was too wet. He uttered the magical phrase and then pushed his hand forward at the ogre's head.

A green fireball shot from his outstretched hand and hit the ogre in the face. Its hair caught fire and began to burn. The ogre started dancing around, dropping its club, and swatting at its head in an attempt to put out the fire. Gunshots sounded from the right as James opened fire at it as well.

The beast put its arms up in front of its face to block the bullets and began to growl angrily. When all the hair had burnt up and the fire was out, it reached down and picked up its club off the ground and charged at them, letting out its own roar of anger.

"Split! Try to keep its attention though!" Derek called out, sprinting to one side of the ogre as it charged.

Everyone changed course to either side of the street and moved to stay out of its path. The sudden shift in movement confused the ogre again as it couldn't decide who to chase. It didn't take long for it to decide to chase after Tom, who had shot it with the spell. It raised its massive club to smash him.

Derek raced forward as Tom rolled across the ground to get out of the way of the strike. The club hit with a thunderous force that cracked the sidewalk, leaving a major indentation. Derek got to the creature just after it struck and lashed out with his mace at the ogre's knee.

Buckling under the force of the blow, the ogre was forced to one knee as it howled in pain. Unfortunately, Derek had struck the back of the ogre's knee, and so now the mace was firmly held in the crease of its leg. It reached out to grab Derek, who let go of the mace and danced backward.

Tom had pulled his greatsword from his Inventory and lunged forward, stabbing the ogre in the side while it was looking at Derek. Another wail of pain erupted from the ogre as it swung its other arm out instinctively at Tom. Unable to react in time, Tom was sent flying backward, his sword still embedded in the ogre's side. He landed on the ground and bounced as he continued his trip, coming to a stop when he rolled into another vehicle on the street.

Jay suddenly appeared behind the beast and used his shortsword to chop at its Achilles, which was laid out before him on the kneeling leg. There was an audible snapping sound as the tendon released back up into the ogre's leg and blood fountained out of the wound. The screams of the ogre reached a new crescendo as it let loose a sound that was now almost deafening. As it turned its head back to see what had injured it, there was a twang from behind the group.

A bolt sprouted from the eye of the ogre and the screaming suddenly stopped. Its body went slack, and it began to slump to the ground.

"Tom!" Derek yelled as he ran over to him.

Tom was just starting to try to roll over. A purplish light began to surround him as Derek got closer.

"I said don't be a fucking hero, you moron!" Derek chastised him.

"I had it covered," Tom groaned out, then coughed as blood came out of his mouth. "Besides, you all needed the distraction, and I can heal myself."

"Are you alright now? You're coughing up blood!" Derek fussed over him, looking down at the red fluid on Tom's hands and shirt.

"Yeah, HP shows I'm fully healed. Just had some leftovers from before I cast *Dark Healing* that had to come out," Tom replied in a rasp, his throat now raw.

Derek let out a relieved sigh.

"If its head had just been lowered, I could have cut it off!" Kevin said from behind them.

The party laughed.

"I'm sure you would have. Good on you for distracting it with that yell," Tom coughed out as he stood up.

As they were talking, some of the fleeing bystanders began to come over to them and thank them.

"Look," Tom said to the people as he put his hands on his hips to catch his breath and recover, "tell everyone that if they go down this street two blocks and then turn left, they will run into the Trammel Crow Center where there are others waiting. They can help you and fill you all in on what is going on."

They continued to try to thank the party until they were ushered off to head to the Center with promises that the party would watch the rear and make sure no monsters followed them. They also let them know they had killed any monsters they had seen on the way there. Relief was visible on all the bystanders' faces as they turned to walk down the street toward the Center.

"We did good there. What the hell was that spell you used?" James asked Tom.

"Oh, it was *Eldritch Blast*," Tom replied as he smiled.

"Seriously?! That was fucking badass," James crooned over the spell.

"I know, right? I can't wait to use it again," Tom said excitedly.

Just as he said this, another roar sounded from further down the street in the city. This time, from around the corner came *two* of the ogres.

"Well, shit," Tom said.

Chapter 13

Ogres and Skills

"You just had to say it, didn't ya?" Jay asked, slapping his hand to his face.

"Are we sure we can handle two of them?" Kiera asked, her voice showing her concern after the last battle. "We had some trouble with the first one."

"We don't have much of a choice," Derek offered, readying his shield and picking up his mace from the dead ogre's body.

"I've got a few more tricks up my sleeve," Tom said, retrieving his own weapon from the ogre's side. "Let's handle these mostly the same as the other. I'll help keep them off of us."

"And get slapped across the room again?" Jay asked.

"Not this time. I'm using my trump card," Tom replied, giving Jay an annoyed look. "We have to make sure they don't hurt anyone."

"Bastard's already got a trump card," Jay growled, but readied up gamely enough.

Everyone moved into position again and Jay took off, disappearing down a side street. Tom activated his tattoos as he rolled his neck, feeling a few vertebrae crack in the motion. The familiar feeling of strength flowed over him, and he charged toward the first ogre. Seeing something this small coming right for him gave the ogre a moment of pause. That was all Tom needed.

He activated his new skill *Fear*. Tom felt his consciousness expand outward as he focused on the ogre. He could hear his heartbeat pounding in his ears, the world feeling quieter around him. Tom felt another presence as his mind brushed against the ogre's. The creature, which had just begun to lift its club after shaking off a brief hesitation, suddenly stopped again, frozen under the weight of Tom's influence.

Its eyes suddenly grew wider at the sight of Tom, and it began to back up, first one step, then another.

"LEEEERROOOOYYY JEEEEEEEEENKINNNNNS!" came a shout from the right as Kevin came running in, straight at the ogre that was backing up.

The ogre physically recoiled in fear at the sight of Kevin, who proceeded to run straight at its leg, and waving the greataxe, swung at its knee, severing it with one blow. Toppling to the side now that one of its legs could no longer support it, the ogre crashed to the ground, screaming in agony as blood gushed from its wound.

Reaching down to grab at Kevin, the other ogre barely missed him as he dodged out of the way. Not watching Tom, the ogre paid for this with an *Eldritch*

Blast to the face, which proceeded to set its hair on fire. It flailed wildly about as the fire burned its skin. Derek bashed its knee from the side this time and it went down. However, when it went down, it flung its arm out and managed to hit Derek on its fall.

Derek barely raised his shield in time to take the impact, but he was still sent flying backward and into a building, where he crashed to the ground.

Kevin saw the whole thing happen and went absolutely berserk. Swinging his axe around in wide arcs, he first took off the arm of the ogre that he had already taken the leg from, and then slit its throat with a second swing, using the momentum of the axe to continue the attacks. The ogre died with a look of abject terror on its face.

Tom had not been idle either, and when he heard gunshots firing at the second ogre, he raced over to it with his greatsword. Placing its arms over its face to protect from the gunshots, the ogre couldn't see Tom as he approached. Swinging his greatsword down in an overhand chop across the ogre's arms, Tom severed both arms at once, midway up the forearms.

Howling in pain and frustration, the ogre tried to stand up again but collapsed when it put weight on the knee that Derek had bashed. As it dropped to one knee again, blood still spewing out of its severed arms, a crossbow bolt erupted from its eye as well. It fell over dead, joining its fellow ogres.

Tom rushed over to Derek, who was already getting up.

"Are *you* okay this time?" Tom asked.

"Sure, I'm the Cleric, remember? I can heal myself too," Derek replied, groaning as he stood up shakily.

"What a relief. But Kevin… What the hell man? How were you able to do that?" Tom asked.

"Oh, easy—I just put all my points I got from leveling up in the goblin and the first ogre fights into Strength. Didn't take long," Kevin replied. "I already knew where they were going to need to go, so I just dumped them all in."

"Does that mean you have a Class now?" Tom asked.

"Not yet. I just slammed the points in for the fight," Kevin replied, leaning on his greataxe.

"But what about that berserker rage just now?" James asked.

"What are you talking about?" Kevin said, clearly confused.

James just looked around, his hands out to his side.

Tom shrugged. "Now you know how the rest of us feel."

James considered that statement a moment and nodded. "Fair enough, yeah."

"It's probably for the best. It would be good to get back to the Center before we choose Classes," Tom said. "That goes for the rest of you as well. Wait until we return."

Everyone nodded, showing they understood.

"That skill of yours is pretty powerful, Tom," Derek said, stretching his now-healed back.

"Well, it's Charisma based. I'm pretty sure those ogres have a really low Charisma, and that makes it work better on them. At least, that's my working theory," Tom explained, thinking about how ugly they had been.

"I'm glad it did! That gave us the opening we needed to win that fight," Derek said, clapping Tom on the back.

"You guys didn't give me a chance to get in on that one," Jay complained, walking back over to the rest of the group.

"Sorry, Jay. But like my family says on Thanksgiving, if you wait to get in line for the buffet, you'll miss the stuffing," Tom joked, smiling at Jay.

"I hate missing the stuffing," Kiera chirped.

Jay, who had been drinking from a bottle of water, suddenly spit it out, coughing and choking. He looked at Kiera, his eyes wide.

"What?" Kiera frowned. "Don't look at me like that. You're the one that missed out. Try harder next time," Kiera continued, not letting up.

"I didn't exactly see you giving a lot of help. Shooting off that crossbow once the beasts were already down," Jay smirked as he thought he found a point to get back with.

"At least I got two kill shots. Better than the alternative of just sitting on your ass and watching," Kiera replied.

"Oh yeah?" Jay growled. "Well, maybe next time I'll remember to bring plenty of *stuffi*—"

"Get a room, you two. We get it, you love each other," James jeered from off to the side of the group, reloading his magazines.

Kiera glared daggers at James. She turned bright red and stormed off to the car. The others laughed and then began to head back to the Tahoe. On the way back, James saw a pigeon sitting on top of a street sign and pointed his gun at it. Firing off a round, the bird exploded in a shower of feathers, blood, and bird parts. Checking his Inventory, he was shocked to see a Common Monster Core showed up from the kill.

"You guys! You aren't going to believe this, but I just shot a pigeon off that sign, and it gave me a Monster Core!" James called to the group.

"What? No way. Common fauna never give off loot like that in games," Tom said in disbelief. "It should only be the main monsters that are giving cores. Unless of course, they are monsters brought here with the mana as well."

Seeing another pigeon a short distance off, James fired at it as well. Again, he was rewarded with a Monster Core in his Inventory.

"Now I know it's happening. I just watched it appear in my Inventory," James said again.

Tom watched a bird in flight and reached up, casting *Eldritch Blast* at it. The bird burst into greenish flames and fell to the ground. Sure enough, a Monster Core appeared in his Inventory as well.

"Well, I'll be damned," Tom gasped. "He's right. Time to kill us some birds, people!"

"But not bird-people!" James clarified, ignoring the looks people gave him.

APOCALYPSE

With that, the party began to point out birds while James, Tom, and occasionally Kiera fired at them. They had killed about fifty birds in total before a System message appeared in all their visions.

<table>
<tr><td align="center">System Update:</td></tr>
<tr><td>We apologize for any inconvenience this may have caused, but the Grand System has informed us of a glitch where local Earth wildlife was incorrectly awarding Monster Cores. Monster Cores are intended to be granted only by creatures classified as monsters. This issue has now been resolved, and these creatures will no longer drop Monster Cores. However, since this was an error on the part of the System development team, all players who received cores due to this glitch will be allowed to keep them. Thank you for your understanding.
~ The Grand System Administrators</td></tr>
</table>

The prompt had a golden border, adorned with swirling filigree, and sparkled subtly in the background. Clearly, this was an important message. It also hinted at the existence of beings actively working on the System, even referring to themselves as Administrators.

Tom's curiosity was immediately piqued. As a former system admin himself, he wanted to know more about how this worked. Unfortunately, there was no way for him to currently uncover more information; but it was definitely something to pursue in the future.

Dismissing the thought for now, Tom and the others returned to the vehicle. They drove around for about another hour, encountering several more groups of goblins and one pack of wolves. These were the first wolves anyone had seen, except for Jay. The goblins were relatively easy to deal with; they practically threw themselves at the Tahoe, unaware of the danger it posed. The wolves, however, were a different story. They quickly darted out of the street, keeping a cautious distance from the SUV, never allowing it to get too close.

<table>
<tr><td colspan="2" align="center">Wolf</td></tr>
<tr><td colspan="2">Wolves are agile and cunning predators known for their pack mentality and keen hunting instincts. They possess a strong sense of smell, acute hearing, and swift movements, making them formidable opponents in the wild. Wolves are often encountered in forests, mountainous regions, and other natural habitats where they hunt for prey.</td></tr>
<tr><td align="center">HP:</td><td align="center">85/85</td></tr>
<tr><td align="center">MP:</td><td align="center">0/0</td></tr>
<tr><td align="center">SP:</td><td align="center">150/150</td></tr>
</table>

Attacks:	Bite, Claw, Howl

James and Kiera fired at them, and James managed to take one down, but the rest quickly wised up to their tactics and took cover behind nearby cars.

Everyone looked at each other inside of the vehicle.

Derek sighed. "We *could* use the meat."

"And the pelts," Kiera agreed.

Tom gave Jay a deadpan expression. "Weren't you mentioning gutting things earlier?" He glanced at the man's knives. "Now's your shot."

"Aww man," Jay moaned.

Kiera snorted a laugh at his torment, giving Tom a thumbs up.

With no other options, the team exited the vehicle and took up positions: Derek covering the front with his shield, Kevin guarding the rear with his greataxe, James and Kiera in the middle, and Jay and Tom flanking on either side.

These wolves were clearly smarter than the average predator. They began to circle the team as they moved in closer. Having discussed the plan of attack in the Tahoe, the party was ready and waiting for the first to attack. It came from the side first, charging toward Jay. Kiera fired a crossbow over his shoulder, and it hit the wolf in the left front shoulder.

It whined as it tried to pull back, but with the bolt in its shoulder joint, was too slow. Jay gave the wolf a shortsword to the side for its effort. The move left him exposed, however. Another wolf moved in to take advantage. Unfortunately for the creature, James was ready and fired. It took one shot to the back and then one to the head before it died.

Another wolf charged Kevin, not wanting to tangle with the shield, and was promptly cut in half as Kevin swung his axe through the air as it leaped for him. Becoming more cautious, the wolves started to look for a way to escape. The party didn't let them get one as they pressed their attack and moved to hunt the wolves instead.

Turning to run, one was shot down by James, and another took a bolt to the back of the head from Kiera. That one was an especially gruesome death as the bolt came out through the inside of its mouth, spraying the ground with shattered skull fragments, blood, and brain matter. Perhaps mercifully, the destruction of the canine's brain stem instantly killed it before it could choke to death on its own blood running down the back of its throat.

Derek leaped in front of a fleeing wolf, slamming it with his shield to halt its momentum before bringing his mace down on its head with deadly force. The crunching sound as the mace's flanges struck the top of its skull echoed off the surrounding buildings. The impact was so powerful that the wolf's head was driven into the pavement, causing it to bite its tongue off.

Tom surprised one of the wolves that had tried to escape but had been cut off by Jay. It turned to run but found its path blocked as Tom jumped out from behind an abandoned vehicle.

Slicing out with his greatsword, he managed to cut off one of the legs of the beast. It growled at him and made one final attempt to bite Tom. Jamming his sword into its mouth, the blade stabbed into the back of the wolf's throat, killing it when the blade severed its spine.

Seizing the moment while Tom was distracted, another wolf lunged from behind the impaled one, its jaws wide open. Tom's eyes snapped wide as he yanked at his sword, but he was too late. The beast crashed into him, sinking its teeth deep into his shoulder.

A sharp cry tore from Tom as the fangs ripped through flesh, sending a wave of pain through his body.

The creature wrenched its head back and forth, shredding his muscles. Despite the agony, Tom had managed to form the pattern for a spell with his other hand just before the bite.

Gritting his teeth against the searing pain, he shouted, "Uthas per mishtu!"

A ball of dark purple light erupted from his hand, which he placed on the wolf's belly, and rocketed the creature off him. This, of course, ripped open his wound even further, but it did manage to kill the wolf by blowing a hole in its abdomen, and all its internals fell out.

Lying on the ground in pain, Tom cast *Dark Healing* on himself, feeling his shoulder begin to knit back together. He watched in fascination as the torn muscles and tendons reconnected and finally the skin mending itself as if nothing had harmed him. Though he had to cast the spell a couple more times, it was truly amazing how quickly it could heal such severe injuries. Looking at his mana, he saw he was running low after the spells; but before discovering magic, an injury like this would have left him out of commission for months, and likely left him with a permanent limp if he was lucky.

The last of the wolves were finally put down, and smiles spread across everyone's faces. This had been a successful hunt. The wolves were quickly, albeit terribly, harvested by Jay with notes from Kiera, and the meat stored in their inventories.

It was time to return to the Center to check on the survivors and assess their gains from this excursion. With the numbers they had now, they should be able to get everyone in the party both Classes and gear. They were really starting to resemble a true adventuring party.

Chapter 14

Adventuring Party

Making their way back to the Center proved uneventful. Monsters were still spawning in the area, but it appeared as though they were either learning about the danger the team posed, or there were less spawns within the general vicinity of the Center. Either way, this meant that safety was increasing for the people that had found their way to this little haven. On their return, they also found three more groups of people.

The first group of survivors had been huddled in a movie theater, and when they heard the vehicle going by, they had run out to see if they could get help. Tom assured them that they had cleared the path to the Trammel Crow Center and gave them directions to get there.

They found a second, larger group of people holed up in a hotel. The manager on duty had locked the doors, but goblins had managed to break the glass. James commented again on the desire for more secure doors, and the team had to admit that, though the glass doors had been nice in the normal world, in this new and much more dangerous reality, it was a major flaw.

After several people had died trying to hold the goblins back, the rest of them had managed to get some of the furniture in the way of the doors so the goblins couldn't get in again. The team had to yell at the survivors behind the wall of couches, chairs, and tables to get their attention and assure them it was safe to come out. When they finally were able to leave, many of them had wounds and bloody clothes from their fight with the creatures that had attacked them.

They had been amazed at the magic used when Tom and Derek helped to heal them. Tom explained that everything they knew could be explained when they reached the Center and encouraged them to quickly start heading there. Thanking them profusely for their aid, the group hurried off in the direction of safety.

Lastly, they came upon a mother holding the hands of what looked to be twin boys, wandering the streets aimlessly. She had a glazed-over look in her eyes, tears making tracks in the dirt that coated her cheeks. Sobbing loudly, the children were sure to attract unwanted attention.

When Tom pulled up next to them, the children instinctively hid behind their mother, who continued to stare off into the distance, her gaze vacant as she walked forward without blinking.

Derek got out of the vehicle and stood in front of her. Tears began streaming down her face again, but she remained unresponsive to everything around her. Derek gently shook her shoulders, finally getting her to look at him. She began to mumble something incoherent, and when asked what she was saying, her face crumpled, and she broke down, crying uncontrollably.

"My baby! I left my baby! They took her! We couldn't stop them!" she screamed suddenly and sank to her knees weeping.

The young boys tried to comfort her, but they appeared to be about four years old and just cried while they tried to hug their mother, unable to articulate anything past their fear and sadness. Derek placed the woman and children in the back of the Tahoe, trying to assure the boys that they were safe now, and Kiera crawled over the seats to comfort her.

There are two sides to apocalypse movies that no one puts much focus on. This was one of them. The trauma of the inevitable loss and tough decisions that must be made so that others can survive. The other was the number of bodies that littered the streets.

On just about every sidewalk, street, and intersection, the death toll could be seen. Most of the corpses were mutilated or cut to pieces by goblins. Some were half-eaten by wolves or other animals. It wasn't just adults either. Teenagers, kids, and even some turned-over strollers with blood-stained blankets could be seen on their drive through the city. The sight was heart wrenching and stomach turning all at the same time.

Flies were beginning to be attracted to the corpses, buzzing around and fighting for a place to land on the bodies, where they would inevitably lay their eggs and maggots would eat away at the flesh as well. They were starting to smell from sitting out in the sun, blood and bodily fluids mixing on the ground around them. They hadn't begun to bloat yet, but that was only a matter of time.

No one was going to be out here cleaning up the streets. They were too busy trying to survive. Scavengers were the best hope for that to happen. The party couldn't even loot the bodies because money had become worthless in the blink of an eye. Humans didn't typically carry weapons because they lived in a peaceful society with laws and police to do the dirty work of handling criminals. Still, this was Texas, so there might be a gun on a person here or there, but the risk of getting out of their vehicle while patrolling, on the off chance someone was carrying one, was not worth it.

Convenience stores or grocery stores would be worth raiding soon. But that would take a team of people to pull off and multiple vehicles for the number of people they needed to provide for now. Their Inventories could be used to store a lot of the food, but they would still need many people to get all the supplies.

The party drove by many more buildings, not sure how many of them might hold other survivors. Windows and doors had been shattered by the raiding goblins and other monsters, glass littering the ground as they had attempted to attack people trying to hole up inside for protection.

Tom also considered the fact that soon there would be an issue of gasoline for vehicles. The power grid would fail eventually, and everything would become dark. If they got enough people together, they might be able to get some kind of system working for a building or two, but that was going to be a while out. Maybe they could craft something similar to gasoline?

"Demon-diesel? Magicoline?" James muttered quietly from the back, staring out as they passed a gas station.

But he still heard it. A tingle ran up Tom's spine. "James?"

"Hmm?" James replied.

"I need you to tell me the truth." Tom had angled the rearview mirror so he could look the man in his eyes… sort of. "Are you reading my mind?"

James just stared back at Tom unnervingly.

Sighing, Tom fixed the rearview, muttering under his breath, "You're so fucking *weird* sometimes."

Tom pushed James' Jamesism to the side for a moment as he kept thinking about their situation. Crafting seemed to be a big deal since there was a whole page dedicated to it in the tutorial. That would be something he would need to investigate later. For now, they just needed to get back to the Center.

They arrived around twenty minutes later. The security team had been busy putting barriers in place around the building, and they had a guard posted at a drive-in point waiting for them. He noticed them coming and recognized their vehicle, a smile coming to his face as he walked over to the driver's side window.

"Hey guys, welcome back. Seems like you had an eventful time," the guard said, looking at the vehicle with its new goblin decor.

"We did pretty well. Did the other survivors make it here? We were expecting about three waves of them, plus another group soon after we left earlier," Tom replied, putting an arm on the window as he spoke to the guard.

"They did. They are inside being taken care of. Brian wants to see you too, by the way. You can find him in the conference room again," the guard said.

Tom nodded, and they pulled into the parking garage and parked the Tahoe near the building entrance. Piling out of the car, Kiera helped the mother into the building while James and Jay both took a kid. James had put one of the children on his back and was galloping around like a horse, making neighing noises while the little boy laughed and kicked his legs. Who knew James would be the one good with kids?

Making their way to the conference room after passing off the children and their mother to others in the building, they found Brian sitting and waiting. There were ten chairs in the conference room, and with the addition of all the new party members, the room was becoming quite full.

"Welcome back. I see you've sent more people our way. I am glad to see you're the kind of person who helps others," Brian sighed, putting his hands together and leaning on his elbows. "But we are in a position where we are not going to have enough provisions."

"We can't just leave people out there to be killed," Tom replied, feeling his gut knot up at the thought of being told he had to stop helping people.

"No," Brian agreed tiredly. "We can't. But we *are* going to need more supplies. So, I'm going to need you to go back out soon and see what you can find. Raid grocery stores first. Food is the number one priority," Brian said, standing up to pace around the room. "We need to be able to help these people until we can provide for ourselves. And that is going to be a good while. So, try to focus on non-perishable items."

"We got wolf meat we can hand off for now," Jay interjected.

"Fine, but I still need you to hit up the stores," Brian replied, looking slightly horrified at the prospect of having wolf meat thrust upon him.

"We can do that. We just need to stop, settle our team on Classes, then gear them up for the fights to come," Tom said.

"Understood. Now, there is another matter we need to discuss," Brian began. "I've talked to some of the others here and we think this is a good time to look at starting a Guild so we can see about getting some of the other bonuses. We want your team to lead the Guild."

Tom was a little shocked at the news. When he thought about it though, it made sense why they would ask them. He had been the one helping all the others and giving them advice. Though sometimes it felt more like orders.

"I have one condition if we consider that," Tom said, crossing his arms over his chest.

"And what is that?" Brian asked.

"You have to be the Guild Administrator," Tom replied, holding up a hand to forestall any arguments. "I'm more a lead-from-the-front kind of guy, and so is my team. Which isn't a bad trait for a Guild Leader," he admitted, but gestured at the center they were in. "But logistics and organization aren't my strong suit."

Brian was quiet for a long moment before answering. "Fine. I've been doing the job anyway; I might as well get some benefit from it by being a member of the only group of people I've met that I think could survive this fucking hellscape."

"Okay. If you agree, then we will consider it. I can't give you an answer right now because I need to confer with my party first," Tom said, gesturing to the other people in the room.

"That is understandable. I'll leave you all here to use the conference room however you need. Feel free to call for me if you need something. For now, I need to get to work on setting up some management systems for this place. We need to organize people into what they are going to be good at," Brian said. Nodding to the rest of the group, he turned and left the conference room.

"Okay, guys, I want you to be thinking about that possibility now. But first, we need to get everyone their Classes," Tom said, standing at the head of the table. "Everyone should be able to pick theirs. You are going to get a portal that opens and gives you a book. When you read the book, it's going to fill your mind with information about your Class. It's going to hurt. Sorry in advance, but it goes away after a little bit. Are all three of you still set on the Classes you picked before?"

Jay, Kiera, and Kevin nodded.

"Alright then, let's get going. We also need to get gear from the vending machine and then go out and get those supplies. I'd also advise that anyone who hasn't already assigned their Attribute Points, not do that until they read the book. Kevin, I know you threw a bunch at Strength and that was a pretty safe bet, but I'm guessing Constitution is going to be a big deal for you as well. You all need to read that book. I can give you some advice on where to put your stat points—

at least in the beginning. But you need to be sure of your decisions because I'm not always going to have the answers," Tom said, looking at each of them in turn.

Kiera, Jay, and Kevin each focused on their screens, reviewing the notifications they had received during the outing. Tom, James, and Derek followed suit, checking their own messages while the others made their selections. It turned out that the ogres, being much tougher than the goblins, dropped Uncommon Monster Cores. From what they could recall, these uncommon cores were worth ten times as much as the common ones. Each of them received one for every ogre they had dealt damage to. Unfortunately, Jay only received one, but the others were ready to help him get more equipment if he needed it.

Kevin was the first to make his selection. He seemed dead set on Barbarian. A red portal opened for him, and the leather-bound book was also bright red with orange inlaid lettering.

Jay and Kiera opened their portals next. Kiera's was a bright purple color along with the book, and Jay's was a grey color like that of a rain cloud. All three of the party members began to read their books and all three clearly got the same headaches everyone else had from making their selections.

However, Kevin underwent a dramatic transformation after reading his book. His body began to shift and undulate as if worms or snakes were writhing beneath his skin. Suddenly, his muscles swelled to about three times their previous size. Kevin began grunting with his teeth gritted so tight the others worried he was going to crack them as he changed. No longer resembling a twig with a head, he now looked like a bodybuilder, with muscles bulging from every part of his body. His shirt ripped apart, and his pants strained, threatening to burst at any moment.

His toes poked through the ends of his shoes, and he appeared to have grown about six inches taller in a matter of moments. The watch he had been wearing had burst from his wrist with such force that it was now embedded in the wall next to him.

For his part, Kevin took one look down at himself, held one hand up, and yelled, "I HAVE THE POWER!"

"Holy shit, dude!" James gasped. "You are JACKED!"

"It's part of the Barbarian package. I get a boost to Strength if I don't take any beginner skills except Rage," Kevin explained, flexing his new muscles like a bodybuilder in a competition. "There were a few I would've liked to have, but the Strength boost seems like the best option for the beginning."

"So, you're saying that if we all boost our Strength, we will begin to look like that?" Kiera asked, concern evident on her face.

"No," Kevin chuckled. "This is a special feature called Barbarian Build. It's not necessarily a direct representation of my Strength attribute, but it *is* intimidating. Though my Strength is fairly high now with the bonuses and Attribute Points I put there."

Kiera sagged in relief. "I *really* don't want to look like a roided-out Amazonian woman just because I added one too many points to the Strength attribute."

"You didn't forget to add points to Constitution, did you? Don't need you being a glass cannon," Derek asked, eyeing Kevin closely.

"Don't worry, I put points there too. Can't go dying on you all," Kevin replied.

Jay and Kiera didn't undergo any noticeable changes. They had each chosen less physically driven Classes, focusing on skills that would be useful in battle or espionage. With their Classes selected, the crew headed to the vending machine in the cafeteria to get new equipment, skill books, and spells tailored to their roles. The selection available was much better suited to their needs, and they each picked out gear that would enhance their abilities.

Jay was up first for the vending machine.

"What do you think you need for your equipment?" Tom asked.

Placing his hand on the machine, it transformed, presenting options tailored to his Rogue Class. He carefully browsed through the available items, taking a long moment to think before finally speaking.

"I like the kama and chain option. Lets me hit something and use them as a thrown weapon with a retrieval factor. You know, the old wrap around a leg and trip someone tactic," Jay answered, still staring at the machine. "Looks like three cores for that."

Taking out the cores, he put them in one at a time and selected "F-7" for the kamas.

Item: Kamas and Chain	
The Kamas and Chain is a versatile weapon designed for both close and mid-range combat. This set includes two razor-sharp kamas, each attached to a durable chain, allowing for a combination of slashing, entangling, and disarming techniques. The kamas themselves are crafted from high-quality steel, ensuring they retain their sharp edge even after prolonged use. The chains are lightweight but incredibly strong, enabling the user to swing the kamas with precision and force. The Kamas and Chain weapon set is particularly favored by those who value agility and adaptability in battle. The chains can be used to extend the reach of the kamas, trip opponents, or even retrieve the weapons if thrown. This weapon is ideal for warriors who prefer a fluid combat style, allowing for swift transitions between offense and defense.	
Item Type:	Weapon, Slashing
Durability:	100/100
Attack Damage:	12-15
Item Quality:	Average
Item Rarity:	Common

"Leather armor is also a must. Need something to protect me, while being able to move," Jay said.

Leather armor was also three common cores as basic gear, and he purchased it as well.

Item: Leather Armor Set (Cuirass, Bracers, Greaves, Tassets, Boots)

This set of leather armor is crafted from high-quality, treated leather designed to provide both flexibility and protection. The set includes:

- **Cuirass:** A fitted leather chest piece that offers solid protection of the torso while allowing for ease of movement. It is reinforced with additional layers over vital areas to absorb and deflect blows.

- **Bracers:** Sturdy leather bracers that shield the forearms from attacks. They are lightweight, providing protection without sacrificing dexterity.

- **Greaves:** Leather greaves that protect the lower legs, reinforced to guard against cuts and blunt force. They are designed to fit snugly, ensuring they do not impede mobility.

- **Tassets:** Leather tassets hang from the waist, providing additional protection to the upper legs and hips. They are crafted to allow for free movement while covering vital areas.

- **Boots:** Durable leather boots that protect the feet and ankles, reinforced to provide stability and support. They are designed for comfort during long journeys and battles.

This leather armor set is ideal for those who prefer a balance between protection and mobility, making it suitable for Rogues, Rangers, and other agile combatants. The armor is lightweight, allowing for quick movements in combat, while still providing adequate protection against attacks.

Item Type:	Armor
Durability:	200/200
Defense:	+75
Item Quality:	Average
Item Rarity:	Common

"I already have daggers and a shortsword that work for now. So, I think I need some throwing knives to keep my distance," Jay mentioned as he equipped the gear.

"Sounds like you have this handled. Have you used throwing knives before?" Tom asked.

APOCALYPSE

"We used to set up a target in the backyard when I was a teenager, and we would throw knives and hatchets at it for fun. I have pretty good aim from all the hours of doing that. Though it has been a little while. I'll have to practice a little to bring back the muscle memory," Jay replied.

Item: Throwing Knives	
Throwing Knives are precision-crafted blades designed for ranged combat. Balanced for accuracy and distance, these knives are perfect for silent and swift attacks. Each knife is made from tempered steel, ensuring durability and sharpness, with a sleek design that minimizes air resistance for smooth flight. The knives are small and lightweight, making them easy to carry in large quantities and ideal for quick, successive throws. Their pointed tips and sharpened edges are crafted for penetration, capable of striking vital points with deadly precision. Throwing Knives are favored by assassins, Rogues, and any combatant who values stealth and agility. They can be used to take down enemies from a distance or as a surprise attack in close quarters, making them a versatile and essential tool in any arsenal.	
Item Type:	Weapon, Projectile
Durability:	50/50
Attack Damage:	5-8
Quantity	10
Item Quality:	Average
Item Rarity:	Common

Stepping back from the machine, Kiera took a turn next. Placing her hand on the machine, it readjusted to show options for her Bard Class.

"I really want that rifle. But it's thirty cores. While I *could* get it, I wouldn't get much else," Kiera resigned to herself. "An instrument would help with my abilities as well."

"So, like a guitar?" Tom asked.

"I was considering that. It would work well, but I just saw something else I think would be really cool," Kiera said, eyeing a can on the right side of the machine.

She placed an uncommon core in the slot, and the screen showed she had ten credits. Selecting "B-4," a can fell into the retrieval slot, and she pulled it out and opened it. After the smoke cleared, there was a beautiful cherry wood lute in her hands.

Item: Lute
The Lute is a beautifully crafted instrument made from rich, polished cherry wood. Known for its warm, resonant tones, this lute is designed to produce clear, melodious music that can enchant and inspire. The body of the lute is expertly shaped for optimal sound projection, and the smooth, rounded neck allows for comfortable playing. The lute features finely tuned strings that respond well to both gentle and vigorous strumming, making it suitable for a wide range of musical styles. The cherry wood gives the instrument a distinctive reddish hue, adding to its aesthetic appeal. This lute is ideal for Bards and musicians who seek an instrument that not only sounds exquisite but also adds a touch of elegance to their performances. Whether used in battle to buff allies or in a peaceful setting to entertain and soothe, the Lute is a versatile and cherished companion for any musical adventurer.

Item Type:	Accessory
Durability:	100/100
Item Quality:	Well-Crafted
Item Rarity:	Uncommon

"A lute?" Tom asked.

"It feels right. A nostalgic instrument for a Bard who would sing in taverns to a crowd of townsfolk and adventurers for tips to make their living. I don't know, it just feels more poetic than the guitar," Kiera said.

"Can you even play a lute?" Tom asked, looking at her with concern.

"I sure can. It's something that I picked up at a renaissance fair one time and learned to play," Kiera replied, cradling the new instrument in her arms.

"Hey, by all means. I loved when players did that in our gaming sessions, so a lute fits well," Tom said.

"I want some kind of weapon as well. What type of blade should I get as a Bard? Maybe a shortsword? I'm not sure I'm going to be much good with a heavier weapon," Kiera asked.

"Try the Rapier," Derek offered, pointing at a sword with a handguard and a thin blade.

"Oh! That looks like something better for me. Stabby-stabby!" Kiera said, getting excited.

The machine showed she had five credits left and asked if she wanted to make another purchase or receive five cores back. Selecting the "A-1" option, a can was dispensed.

Item: Rapier
The Rapier is a slender, sharply pointed sword designed for agility and precision in combat. Its narrow blade is optimized for thrusting attacks, making it an ideal weapon for duels and quick strikes. Crafted from high-quality steel, the blade is both durable and flexible, allowing for swift movements. The hilt of the Rapier is intricately designed, featuring a protective guard that curves around the hand, providing both style and defense. The lightweight nature of the rapier ensures that it can be wielded with speed and finesse, allowing the user to parry and strike with remarkable accuracy. Favored by fencers, duelists, and any combatant who values skill and precision over brute strength, the Rapier is a weapon that turns combat into an art form. Its design allows for fluid movements and sharp, controlled strikes, making it a deadly and sophisticated choice in battle.

Item Type:	Weapon, Piercing
Durability:	100/100
Attack Damage:	12-15
Item Quality:	Average
Item Rarity:	Common

"I also liked Jay's idea of having some kind of armor for protection, but I need to be able to move as well. So, leather armor it is," Kiera said.

"Maybe these pelts could be crafted into armor?" Jay offered.

"Do *you* know how to do that?" Kiera asked, annoyed at the prospect that he would recommend that to her. "And are you saying because I'm a woman I should be able to make clothes?"

Jay stared at her in stunned silence for a moment before trying to backpedal, "...I, uh, I just meant... I don't know how to... no, what I mean is..."

"Leave him alone, Kiera. We can look into the idea of getting those crafted if someone here knows anything about leatherwork," Tom chuckled as he tried to diffuse the moment.

Placing three cores in the machine, she selected the leather armor as well.

"How many cores do you have left?" Derek asked.

"I have thirteen cores left," Kiera said.

Without saying a word, Derek pointed at an item in the "G-8" spot on the far-right side of the machine. Kiera's face lit up as she looked at it and immediately put in twelve of her remaining cores for the selection. The can was dispensed, and after opening it and the smoke had cleared, she was holding a black pump-action shotgun.

"Damn," James bemoaned. "Looks like Derek found the ladies' G-spot." He slapped Jay on the shoulder as he stage-whispered, "It's 'G-8,' by the way, you know—just in case."

Jay shook his head and rolled his eyes, but Kiera was either not paying attention, or simply didn't care to respond to James' crass commentary.

"Hehehehehehe... This is gonna be fun," She chuckled maniacally.

Item: Shotgun
The Pump-Action Shotgun is a versatile and powerful firearm designed for close to mid-range combat. Known for its reliability and ease of use, this shotgun features a sliding pump mechanism that cycles the ammo, ejecting spent shells and chambering the next round with a simple motion. This design allows for rapid follow-up shots, making it ideal for situations where stopping power is essential. Chambered for 12 gauge shotgun shells, the Pump-Action Shotgun excels in delivering devastating firepower with each pull of the trigger. The wide spread of pellets ensures a high hit probability, especially in close-quarters combat, while the ability to load slugs provides precision for longer-range engagements. The shotgun is equipped with a durable stock and a smooth, ergonomic grip, providing stability and control during intense situations. Its robust construction and straightforward operation make it a favored choice for hunters, law enforcement, and combatants who need a reliable weapon that can deliver substantial damage quickly.

Item Type:	Weapon, Ranged - Limited
Durability:	150/150
Attack Damage:	15-25
Item Quality:	Average
Item Rarity:	Common

After purchasing several boxes of shells, she moved away from the machine. With Kiera stepping back, Kevin moved up to the machine.

"Do we even need to ask?" Jay asked.

"Probably not," Kevin said, touching the machine and watching the options change.

He placed two uncommon cores in the machine and selected "A-4." A can was dispensed, and he opened it. A huge greataxe was in his hand with curves in all the right places. It was a beautiful piece of craftsmanship that looked to have a dwarven design to it. The haft was made of tigerwood with dark stripes inlaid in the wood and a leather-bound handle.

Item: Barbarian Greataxe
The Barbarian Greataxe is a massive two-handed weapon, forged for brutal strength and devastating power. Crafted from reinforced steel, its broad, double-edged blade is designed to cleave through armor and bone with terrifying efficiency. The weight of the axe demands a wielder of great strength, but in the hands of a skilled Barbarian, it becomes an instrument of utter devastation. The long, sturdy haft is wrapped in leather for a secure grip, allowing the wielder to channel their rage into powerful, sweeping strikes. The Barbarian Greataxe is not a weapon of finesse; it is built for raw, unrelenting force,

capable of ending fights with a single, crushing blow. Perfect for those who embrace the fury of combat, this greataxe amplifies the Barbarian's natural power, making each strike an unstoppable force on the battlefield.
The design of this axe comes from a dwarven background and was integrated into the System after Borin the Great used a similar weapon to defeat the Balrix while defending his home single-handedly on a bridge over a bottomless pit.

Item Type:	Weapon, Slashing
Durability:	300/300
Attack Damage:	28-36
Item Quality:	Well-Crafted
Item Rarity:	Uncommon

Selecting "B-7" next, another can fell into the retrieval bin, and when he opened it, a leather loincloth was in his hands.

"You're not seriously going to wear that, are you?" Tom asked.

"Of course I am. Barbarians get a bonus to defense for wearing almost nothing," Kevin said confidently.

"Just like my ex-wife," Jay quipped.

Off to the side, James choked on one of those small cartons of chocolate milk they handed out in schools that he'd found somewhere.

"What happens when the wind blows? We can't be distracted by your junk every time we are fighting and you're running around killing things," Tom said with disgust at the thought.

Kevin looked the loincloth over and then held up the bottom of it.

"Look, undercarriage holding. No one has to stare at my dangle-downs while I'm fighting," Kevin explained, showing him the loincloth closer.

"Unless we *really* want to," Jay waggled his eyebrows suggestively.

"Gross," Kiera gagged.

Item: Barbarian Loincloth

This Barbarian Loincloth was developed in response to the notorious exploits of Darin the Annihilator, whose unconventional battle tactics involved repeatedly flashing his opponents, causing them to vomit and lose focus during combat. To prevent further "incidents," this loincloth was designed to maintain the Barbarian's fierce and intimidating presence while ensuring more… appropriate coverage.
Crafted from durable, flexible materials, the Barbarian Loincloth offers freedom of movement without sacrificing modesty. It is reinforced with strong stitching to withstand the rigors of battle, ensuring that it stays in place even during the most intense skirmishes. This item serves as both a practical piece of clothing and a humorous reminder of Darin's legacy, blending functionality with the Barbarian's wild and untamed spirit.

Item Type:	Clothing
Durability:	100/100
Defense:	+0

Item Quality:	Average
Item Rarity:	Common

"I'm sure you could wear a T-shirt or something else," Tom said.

"And hide away this bitchin' bod?" Kevin replied, proudly flexing his new muscles. "Thanks, but no thanks."

"Here, Brian. Give this to the security team so they have an additional weapon. Repayment for the cores they gave us earlier," Kevin said, pulling out his previous axe and giving it to Brian.

Brian accepted it and almost dropped it from the weight.

"Thanks. I'm sure they will be pleased to have this gigantic paperweight," Brian said sarcastically as he looked around for someone to pass the heavy object off to.

Stepping back and smiling, Kevin made way for Derek to get a turn. Placing his hand on the machine, it once again changed options for him.

"Geez. These items get more expensive as they get better, don't they?" Derek said.

"That's sort of how the economy works, yeah," Tom scoffed. "How much for what you need?"

"I want better armor since I'm tanking. But it's twenty-eight cores," Derek said. "I guess it can't be helped."

He pulled out cores, counted them as he dropped them into the machine, and selected the heavier armor. What came out of the can was a combination of leather and plate. It wasn't full plate, as that was unwieldy, but it did have metal plates covering the most vital areas over the leather armor, making him much more durable than most everyone else.

Item: Half-Plate Armor Set (Cuirass, Bracers, Greaves, Tassets, Boots)

Half-Plate Armor is a robust and versatile set of protective gear, mixing metal and leather components for greater flexibility. Each piece is crafted from hardened steel to provide additional protection without the full restrictions of heavier plate armor. This armor set includes:

- **Cuirass:** The centerpiece of the armor, this steel chest plate protects the torso, featuring reinforced segments that guard vital areas while allowing for flexibility in movement.

- **Bracers:** These armguards shield the forearms, offering protection during combat while maintaining the dexterity needed for wielding weapons.

- **Greaves:** Protecting the lower legs, these steel greaves are designed to deflect blows and resist damage from weapons and rough terrain.

- **Tassets:** Hanging from the waist, the tassets cover the upper legs and hips, providing additional protection without restricting movement.

- **Boots:** While being primarily made of leather, there is steel crafted into these boots, reinforced for durability and offering protection to the feet and ankles, while providing flexibility in combat.

The Half-Plate Armor is ideal for warriors who require solid protection on the battlefield but prefer to avoid the weight and movement restriction of full-plate armor. Its design offers a balance between coverage and mobility, making it a popular choice among knights, fighters, and other heavily armed adventurers.

Item Type:	Armor
Durability:	400/400
Defense:	+150
Item Quality:	Average
Item Rarity:	Common

"That will definitely come in handy when on the front lines," Tom said.

"Yeah, I am getting some other abilities from my Class, so this is definitely my biggest concern right now," Derek replied. "That about taps me out. You're up, James."

"It's a little unfair that it gives him Cores for barely damaging a monster we had to *kill* right?" Kiera asked, teasing James.

"Don't hate me cuz I'm beautiful," James said, not even turning around.

"That's definitely not why we hate you," Jay said sardonically.

Touching the screen, James looked at his options.

"Oh! I think it's time to upgrade the guns."

"—Already did that," Kevin quipped, flexing his biceps.

James paused, turning to the Barbarian with a wink. "Nice." James put in two uncommon cores and selected option "B-2" twice. The cans dispensed, and when he opened them, he held two Sig Sauer 1911 .45 caliber handguns. "These will do nicely." Handing over his Glocks, James said, "Brian, give these to security as well. I'm sure they can use them to defend the building."

"Everyone just *loves* hand-me-downs," Brian said, putting them in his Inventory to take to the security team. "But guns will always be useful."

"Let's see, steel throwing axes would be more durable than my current ones, but I haven't used them much. Maybe something slightly different?" James said, pondering the options. "I know!"

Putting fifteen more cores into the machine, he selected "C-2," took out the can and opened it. When the smoke cleared, James was holding an Uzi.

"Really? *That's* what you wanted?" Derek asked, looking at him with a glare.

"Why not? It's badass and has a much higher rate of fire than my handguns," James replied, the smile never leaving his face.

"And eats up ammo like a game of hungry, hungry hippos," Derek said, giving up. "But whatever floats your boat, I guess."

Item: Uzi	
The Uzi is a compact, fully automatic submachine gun designed by Israeli army officer Uziel Gal in the late 1940s. Originally used in the military, this firearm is highly favored for its rapid rate of fire and versatility in combat. Capable of a firing rate of 600 rounds per minute, it is accurate up to a range of 200 yards in its semi-automatic mode. Utilizing 9mm rounds, the Uzi is capable of delivering a high volume of fire with precision. It utilizes a blowback design, where the energy from the combustion of the powder in the round blows the bolt back and expels the spent shell. The Uzi is equipped with a detachable box magazine, typically holding 25 to 32 rounds, though larger capacity magazines are available for purchase from vending machines.	
Item Type:	Weapon, Ranged
Durability:	150/150
Attack Damage:	8-10
Item Quality:	Average
Item Rarity:	Common

James also chose leather armor to give him a little more protection than just his street clothes. Using almost all his cores, he also got ammunition and magazines for the 1911s.

Tom took the most time to choose. There were so many options for him. He currently liked the way his build was going with the greatsword, so he decided to go with chain armor, metal bracers and greaves for defense, and some spell books.

He learned the spell *Dark Weapon Flame,* which would give him the ability to light his weapons ablaze with a dark purple fire that dealt both additional fire and darkness damage when striking an opponent. He also picked up the spell *Doppelganger,* which allowed him to make a copy of himself that couldn't do damage but would throw off an opponent, as well as *Lightning Strike,* which sent a bolt of lightning out to an enemy and had a chance of recasting to another target one time.

"Can't you just learn spells from being a Warlock?" Jay asked him when he saw his selections.

"They would have to be granted by my patron. I figured a little extra firepower for something that can be bought from the machine would do some good," Tom replied.

APOCALYPSE

Brian came back to the cafeteria after taking the weapons they had given him to the security team.

"I have more news that you are absolutely going to want to hear. I think we need to go to the conference room first, though." Brian's face was granite. "You're going to want to be sitting down for this one."

He turned and strode from the room as the adventurers looked at each other, worry casting a pall over the room.

Chapter 15

Guild

Tom, Derek, James, Kevin, Jay, and Kiera all walked into the conference room fully decked out in their new adventuring gear and ready to go. Sitting down at the table, the party waited patiently for Brian to tell them the news.

"One of the groups of survivors that you helped and sent back here has some very interesting information for us," Brian began, pausing for dramatic effect. "They claim they have found a Dungeon."

Everyone in the room perked up at this. Anyone who played video games knew a Dungeon was the ultimate find. It offered an opportunity to fight monsters in a way that would pay out loot at the end while offering a challenge that was usually unique from the rest of the gameplay. That one was found so early into the Grand System's integration meant they were very likely to be the first to explore it. Tom, Derek, James, and Kevin all knew this usually meant extra loot.

Their excitement was tempered by the fact that a Dungeon meant extra danger as well. While fighting monsters was dangerous, Dungeons meant traps, puzzles, and many other factors, all while being essentially trapped inside without an easy path of escape. In games, however, the payouts were usually worth the added risk.

Dungeons were often created with a bonus for people who completed it for the first time. It could be later farmed for more loot, but it was never as good. Despite the risks, the party was eager to hear more about this new find.

"I don't have a lot of details, but it was supposedly in the movie theater you rescued people from. We don't normally have basements here in Texas, but one of the survivors said there was a door that was marked as Dungeon, and when he opened it, there was a set of stairs leading down," Brian continued. "No one went inside, so we have no idea what to expect, but we assume something is in there that will be worth exploring, and you all are the only ones I would remotely trust at this point to come back alive."

"We would love to take a look," Tom said, his excitement showing through his attempt at professionalism. "Do you want us to make the supply run first, then go to the Dungeon?"

"That would be preferable, yes. While we are not low on supplies yet, I'd hate for us to get to that point, and there are a lot of people to feed," Brian replied.

"Don't worry about it. We will get the supplies first," Tom assured him.

"Thank you for understanding. Now, if you would like to get going, you can move your asses as soon as you are ready," Brian said, trying to give Tom a hard time.

Preparing to head out, the party met up with another team from the security guards. One man with a clean-shaven head, leather armor, and an assault rifle walked up to the team and stuck his hand out in greeting.

"I'm TJ, it's nice to meet you all," the man said.

"Good to meet you, TJ. I'm Tom," Tom said, taking the offered hand and shaking it firmly. "That is a nice weapon you got there. Did you get it from the vending machine?"

"What? This old thing? I'm just kidding, I did!" TJ said excitedly, tipping the weapon in Tom's direction as he pretended to have just noticed it was in his hands. "We've been watching the perimeter, and there have been plenty of goblins looking to come to the building. We've been weeding them out, though, so there have been less and less coming, but we were able to get quite a few Monster Cores before they started avoiding the Center."

"I'm glad to hear they are starting to notice our presence and choosing not to come here. If we can keep it up, we can hopefully make it an area of safety," Tom said, feeling a sense of relief at the progress. "Are you all joining us on the outing?"

"We are. There are going to be a lot of supplies needed, so Brian thought we could join with another vehicle to provide additional transport space," TJ said. "Plus, more people means more security. And we figure we can learn a thing or two from you all. You've already taught us so much."

"Aww, it wasn't that much," Tom said bashfully. "We just put a few things together that any gamer should have been able to know. Also, cargo space shouldn't be an issue. We should all be using our Inventories. If that fills up, then we can use the vehicles."

"Well… that makes a lot more sense. Hadn't thought about that. We'll be happy to help however we can. And don't be so modest. You guys have some pretty cool insights into the System. Like the Inventory thing. We would have been trying to load groceries into the back of a car if you hadn't said something," TJ replied genuinely.

"Well, we're happy we could help. We all want to live through this." Tom beamed as he felt a sense of peace at the thought of so many working together. "We know it's not going back to the way things used to be, so we need to stick together to find a way to make a new version of this world." Tom looked TJ over again and couldn't help but comment. "It still baffles me a little bit that they are offering us guns, but the armor we use is leather and metal instead of something like Kevlar," Tom speculated.

"Oh, that's simple," TJ said, stepping up to offer a reason. "Kevlar is designed to stop *bullets*. The force from bullets is very different from that of a sword, spear, or other sharp object. So, it doesn't offer the same kind of protection that leather or metal does. While bullets are available as projectile weapons and offered because they were popular on Earth, Kevlar is likely not—because of the type of weapons monsters have. While it will protect against some slashing damage, anything piercing or stabbing will break the fibers because bullets flatten upon impact and end up more as blunt-force damage than a knife tip. Or at least that's my working theory."

"You have a lot of time to think, don't you? I don't have much experience with Kevlar *or* bullet-proof vests," Tom admitted.

"I used to be a police officer before being hired into private security for the Trammel Crow Center," TJ offered. "We have some bullet-proof vests in the security office if we need them, but it's not a great option against puncturing attacks."

"Makes sense to me. Should we head out now?" Tom said.

"Time to hop in the Goblin Slayer 2.0," James said.

"Ha! I like that. Goblin Slayer 2.0 it is," Tom said.

A System prompt showed up unexpectedly in Tom's vision.

Name your Vehicle?	
Would you like to name the Tahoe Goblin Slayer 2.0?	
Yes	*No*

Tom stopped walking, staring at the message.

"What's up, Tom?" Derek asked, looking back at him.

"The System just asked if I wanted to change the name of the vehicle," Tom said, slightly confused at the prompt. He moved over to the car and activated Inspect on it.

Item: Chevy Tahoe
The Chevy Tahoe is a full-size SUV known for its rugged durability, spacious interior, and powerful performance. Designed to handle both on-road and off-road conditions, the Tahoe is equipped with a V8 engine, providing extra horsepower and torque for towing, hauling, and navigating challenging terrains. The Tahoe features a variable seating arrangement with room for up to eight passengers, making it ideal for families, large groups, or those needing extra cargo space. Its advanced suspension system ensures a smooth ride. With its combination of power, comfort, and reliability, the Chevy Tahoe is a popular choice for those seeking a capable SUV that can handle a wide range of driving conditions, from city streets to rugged trails.

Name:	{Undefined}
Item Type:	Vehicle, Weapon - Upgradeable

APOCALYPSE

Durability:	95,428/100,000
Attack:	42-75
Item Quality:	Well-Crafted
Item Rarity:	Rare
Upgradeable:	Yes
Item Level:	6
Item XP:	16,425
XP to Next Level:	4,575
Item Skill: Upgraded Armor	
This skill allows for upgrading the armor on the vehicle as it levels.	

"The Tahoe can level up?!" Tom exclaimed.

"It *what*?" Derek gasped suddenly.

"Inspect it." Tom waved frantically at the Tahoe.

Derek did, and his eyes went wide.

"How is this possible?" Derek asked in amazement.

"I have no idea. Maybe it has something to do with it being used in tandem with my *Vehicular Manslaughter* skill?" Tom pondered.

"Your *what*?!" TJ asked incredulously.

"Yeah, it's a skill I got for running over so many goblins with my car," Tom said dismissively as he thought about the implications of the stats.

TJ looked at Tom with a mixture of horror and awe.

"I'm not sure whether to be horrified or impressed." He held up a hand. "No. Wait. I'm both," TJ admitted. "Why did you decide to run them over? That seems like a terrible way to deal with anyone."

"Look, I just panicked the first time. We were on I-75 and there were people being slaughtered by goblins and I just stepped on the gas after we jumped in the car to get away. Then I saw it was working really well so I just kept going. Now it's kind of second nature to run the little bastards over," Tom said, chuckling a little at the thought of killing the goblins after what they did. "They killed children for fuck's sake."

TJ stopped, and his expression softened. He seemed to grasp that this wasn't the old world, where horrors like this were just stories on the news that you discussed with your family while condemning the perpetrator. Everything had changed now. Goblins would just as soon kill you and fuck your corpse as follow the laws of society that humans had set up.

Brian came out through the parking garage door.

"Did you have a chance to talk about the Guild offer yet?" Brian asked.

"Yes, we talked about it, and everyone agreed it seems like the right thing to do. And we also collectively agreed that we want you to help run things before we just go letting anyone into the Guild," Tom said.

"Very good. We can begin as soon as you get the Guild set up," Brian replied, smiling at Tom.

"I need ten willing members. There's six of us and one of you. Who are the others?" Tom asked.

"That would be us, sir," TJ interjected.

"How many of you?" Tom asked.

"Five, sir," TJ replied.

"No more of all the *sirs*. I'm not your boss. I'm some guy barely holding on like the rest of you. Just call me Tom," Tom replied, feeling embarrassed about being addressed so formally.

"Sure thing, Tom," TJ said.

"Right. Then we just need a place to claim, which I guess is the Center, and a name," Tom said, pausing and thinking. "Anyone got any thoughts on a name?"

"Battleshits!" James called out.

"Anyone but *James*," Tom clarified, facepalming.

James made a pouting face and pretended to be upset as he put his hands in his pockets and kicked an imaginary rock.

"Anyone," Tom said when no one answered. "Just throw them out till we hear one we like."

"Rumble Maggots?"

"Battlehearts?"

"Chaos Wielders?"

James was practically vibrating, the palms of both hands were pressed together and squeezed between his knees as a small, nearly imperceptible squeal emitted from the depths of his chest.

"Electric Vagabonds?"

"Super Legion?"

"Venom Sharks?"

James' squeal was reaching a concerning pitch as the group glanced at him out of the corner of their eyes.

"Fire Wolves?"

"Phobic Knights?"

"Lightning Shadows?"

"PIRATES OF BALLZ DEEP," James' voice exploded out of himself as he sat there panting.

Seven heads turned his way.

"*James*." Tom scowled. "What. The. *Actual*. Fu—"

"Nutty Squirrel Gang? What about I'd Mana Tap That?" James raised an eyebrow.

Kiera stood to her feet, cracking her knuckles.

"Beta Tested Your Girlfriend?" James offered.

Kiera scowled. Jay slid his chair back as he also stood up, casually rotating his shoulder.

"Ten Inches, Unbuffed?" James' eyes were wide now as he stood, taking a step back from the table. He clapped a hand over his mouth as Derek threw down his napkin and stood as well. "Sorry Baby, I'm On Cooldown!" James' muffled voice came from behind his hand.

Jay began taking off his belt and Kiera was slipping off her shoes and taking pins out of her hair. Derek was the first to lunge for the man, narrowly missing as James jumped onto a nearby table.

"IT HURTS WHEN I PVP!" James shouted while being tackled from behind by Jay, who began thoroughly and neatly hog-tying the man with his belt, while Derek casually handed Kiera a balled up sock he'd just removed from his combat boot.

"I CRIT MY PAAAANTS! Mmmmppfff," James moaned one last time as Kierra stood up, dusted off her hands and froze.

"Vanguard?"

Tom blinked. "Wait, what was that last one?"

"Vanguard," Kiera said again.

"I like that one. Okay, we will go with Vanguard, we will claim this center as our base, and we have more than ten members," Tom said, pulling up his character sheet and going to the Guild tab. There he found only a single option available: Form Guild.

"Aw man," James pouted, his voice still muffled somewhere on the ground nearby.

Mentally clicking the button, the option for the name appeared. Tom input "Vanguard" into the field. Next was the invitation list. He sent an invitation to everyone present, and all of them accepted. Last was the field for the Guild Building Location. Tom looked at a map of downtown Dallas and found the Trammel Crow Center. Selecting it, Brian received a notification stating that someone was trying to claim the building as a Guild location as he was the one placed in charge of the building.

Brian mentally clicked approve, and the Guild was created. The outside of the building gained banners at the entrance, the four corners of the building, and a flag at the top, which all unfurled showing a white shield with a black sword crossed over it on a red background.

Congratulations!

You have formed a Guild. You will need to make selections for Guild Leaders before any benefits can be given out. Once you have done so, all steps will be complete for creating the Guild.

<table>
<tr><td align="center">Special Reward:</td></tr>
<tr><td align="center">For being one of the first 500 Guilds created on Earth, you will be awarded one special upgrade. Please refer to the Guild tab to select from available upgrades.</td></tr>
</table>

Special Reward? That was very interesting. They had been fast to act on this, with it only being day one of the apocalypse, but one of the first five hundred in the entire world? Not wanting to look a gift horse in the mouth, Tom decided he would look at the options later. He did, however, pull up the Guild tab and found he was already the leader, so he added Brian as the Guild Administrator and gave him access to almost everything that he had the power to do.

"Make sure everything runs smoothly and begin screening people. We can look at adding them when we get back from the supply run," Tom said, turning to Brian after dismissing his screens. "Looking at the time, we are likely going to need to wait on the Dungeon until tomorrow."

"Sounds good. I'll handle things here, Tom," Brian said, turning to go back into the building.

"Alright everybody, let's load up and move out! We've got supplies to get and people to protect. Stay formed up and have people watching all sides. I don't need any surprise attacks on what should be a simple mission," Derek yelled out as they headed to the vehicles.

Tom remembered one more thing and pulled up the message about naming the Tahoe. He selected "Yes" for Goblin Slayer 2.0 and the prompt disappeared.

"Time to see if we can help this vehicle live up to its name on the way!" Tom said, turning on the Goblin Slayer 2.0.

Jay was indifferently dragging James' subdued body toward the car.

"What do we do about this?" Jay tilted his head toward their vaudevillianesque companion.

Kiera paused before shrugging. "Trunk Monkey?"

Jay smiled.

The group drove away to the music of James' struggling body and muffled voice echoing from the back of the Tahoe.

Chapter 16

Off to Find a Dungeon

"Groceries acquired," James said in a mock AI voice.

"Grocery carrier has arrived," Jay's mechanical voice followed on James' heels as he looked like he was trying to carry everything in all in one trip.

"Bro," James whispered out of the side of his mouth. "Why didn't you just use your Inven—"

"Ready to roll out!" Jay interrupted, his eyes held open too wide.

"That's not even Proto—"

"We require more minerals!" Jay shouted, grabbing more groceries and setting off at a run.

"Hey!" James shouted, chasing after the man. "Get back here and do it right!"

"My life for Aiur!" Jay's voice trailed off as they headed toward the room the Center was using as storage.

The grocery run went off without a hitch, and the team efficiently used their Inventories to stock up on non-perishable canned goods. They grabbed everything they thought they might need, from paper plates to plasticware, and cleared out all the toilet paper in the store, including the supply in the back. With their haul secured, the new Guild members drove back to the center, leaving most of the store bare. As they returned, a group of people was waiting to greet them and quickly helped unload the groceries into a storeroom as the members retrieved items from their Inventories. There was a brief interruption due to Jay and James' antics, but everyone seemed to take it in stride.

"It's the least we can do since you are putting your life on the line to get these for us," said an older gentleman who helped in the storing process.

Given the time it took for the first run, the team made two additional trips to gather as many supplies as possible from other stores. Brian reasoned that the longer they waited, the more likely it was that others would take the food first. So, they decided to stock up while the panic was still fresh, ensuring they secured as many goods as they could before supplies ran out.

With a solid initial stock of supplies, everyone prepared to bed down for the night. Since the Trammel Crow Center was an office space, there were no beds readily available for everyone. Fortunately, Brian had arranged for a large number of blankets and pillows to be sent over from a nearby hotel, ensuring everyone had something to sleep on.

Using the bedding provided, people found places to rest for the night. In a building this large, it wasn't difficult to find a spot to be alone or to stay with family and friends. Tom and his party decided to settle in the conference room for the night.

"You know we are going to have to find a way to build up fortifications for this place, right?" Derek asked, lying back with his hands behind his head as he stared at the ceiling.

"Yeah, if it's going to stay as the Guild base. We might be able to find somewhere else, but it's a pretty good option for now," Tom replied. "I wonder if there's going to be a way to power a building of this size once the power grid fails."

"No idea. With magic, there might be any number of possibilities," Derek said.

"I would think that there could be a way to collect mana and use it to power things," Jay added. "I've read about it in books. Mana collectors that feed power to generators."

"And were these in textbooks or in novels, Jay?" Derek asked.

There was no response.

"So, it was a work of fiction. There's no telling how this form of magic might actually work. I like the thought, but without some clue to go off of, we're sunk on that point for now," Derek said.

"Yeah, but surely we can find some people to help figure it out. I'm sure glad we have Brian to help with all of that. He is an absolute boon for this Guild," Tom said.

"I agree. And I could listen to that man speak all day long," James said. "His voice is sweet nectar to my ears, and I think I have a real man-crush."

"Why do you have to make everything weird?" Kiera asked.

"It's just who he is. You get used to it. It's almost endearing now," Tom said, joking back.

"Love you too, Tom," James said, making a heart with his hands in the air.

Kiera sighed as she rolled over and covered herself with her blankets. "Men are so fucking weird."

"You just don't understand the rich and complex male bond," Jay said.

"Nor do I care to, if it means putting up with that," Kiera replied.

"You two make a cute couple," James said.

"SHUT THE FUCK UP!" both Jay and Kiera said in unison.

"The ladies doth protest too much, methinks," James continued.

The guys all laughed together, sharing the first real moment of forgetting that the world had become a giant shithole. For a brief time, they managed to push the horrors of the day out of their minds, focusing instead on being with friends and simply existing in that moment. It was hard to believe that just that morning, their lives had been turned upside down. The routine day they had anticipated had been completely derailed, sweeping them into this new reality. It felt like something that had happened years ago, yet it was only that same morning.

Witnessing so many horrors in such a short time made it feel as though the day had stretched on for an eternity. Tom felt as though he had aged years in just one day. He had made tough decisions, risked his life, and committed acts of violence in the name of survival. What would be the next moral line he would have to cross to ensure that he and his friends saw the next sunrise? Would the world continue to descend into this nightmarish reality, or was there a glimmer of hope for a new form of peace that could restore some semblance of normalcy?

Existential crisis was settling into Tom's mind as he began to think of all the things he would have normally been doing at this time. All the creature comforts he had come to love in his free time at home. The world seemed to pass before his very eyes in a way he was completely powerless to control, and not for the first time since this world had made a complete left turn, Tom found himself wishing none of this had happened.

Tom thought back to all the times he had felt truly overwhelmed at work. How he had let off steam by playing a video game in which he had killed creatures like goblins. Here, he had not only just killed them, but run them down in cold blood to ensure that he survived. Why had he been able to simply ignore the fact that he was annihilating a species that was considered a blight on the land in those games but felt like he was committing genocide when he was faced with the same reality?

"Hey, Tom?" James asked.

"Yeah, James?" Tom replied.

"Sorry if I'm a bit of an ass sometimes," James said. "I just have all these intrusive thoughts, and I can't control them sometimes. I guess what I'm trying to say is—thanks for still being my friend."

"Hey, you don't have to think like that. You're my friend and there is nothing that could change that," Tom said.

James reached out for a hug, which Tom accepted. After the first few seconds, Tom tried to pull back, but James held on, his hand slowly sliding down Tom's back toward his ass.

Tom's blow to the man's floating ribs put an end to further explorations.

"Sorry…" James gasped. "The intrusive thoughts won."

And with that, they all went to sleep for the night, each completely exhausted from the day's events.

The next morning, the party woke early, eager to locate the new Dungeon. Excited to see what awaited them, everyone quickly geared up and headed to the Goblin Slayer 2.0. By the time Tom finally arrived, the rest of the group was already standing by the Tahoe, ready to hit the road. Their anticipation was palpable as they prepared to embark on the day's adventure.

"Sorry," Tom said, truly apologetic for how long it took him to get to the garage. "I had to meet with Brian about some of the new people that would be helpful to the Guild. This is going to get pretty rough if I need to be the one that approves everyone that can join."

"Can we trust Brian to pick the right people for certain jobs?" Derek asked.

"I don't see why not," Tom said.

"Then give him the authority he needs to make some of those decisions so that we can work on the things that we need to address," Derek replied.

"That does make sense. Fine," Tom said, pulling up his menu and giving Brian the ability to approve new members to the Guild. "There, now Brian can make those changes himself and we don't have to approve them."

"Although, how well do we actually know Brian and his motives?" Derek asked.

"We know him fucking well enough that I don't have to make these fucking decisions!" Tom replied, getting seriously angry about all the second-guessing going on.

"Haha! I was only joking Tom," Derek teased. "Cool down a bit and everything will be alright."

"Okay. Sorry, this is just a lot of pressure now, and I'm ready to delegate as much of it as possible," Tom said.

"I get it. Heavy is the head that wears the crown," Derek said.

The team loaded up in the Goblin Slayer 2.0 and pulled out of the garage. As they drove down the road, they encountered a group of goblins attempting to block their path. Without hesitation, Tom accelerated and plowed right through them. Kevin, Derek, and Jay leaned out of the windows, slicing at any goblins that the vehicle missed, as if they were mounted on horseback. James stood through the sunroof, aiming behind them to shoot any stragglers that still moved. However, he needn't have worried. With the *Vehicular Manslaughter* skill leveling up, the goblins stood no chance—Tom did more than enough damage to ensure every one of them was crushed under the vehicle's wheels.

"I'm beginning to hate this tactic," Derek said, climbing back into the window. "I think I got goblin in my mouth last time."

"No wonder they seemed to like you so much," Jay retorted.

Derek scowled, though it was Kiera who snorted a laugh. When everyone turned toward her, however, her face was serenely innocent.

Reaching the movie theater where the survivors had been holed up, the party exited the vehicle and cautiously approached the entrance. The doors creaked on their hinges, now stained with dried blood, as Tom slowly pulled them open. Inside, the lobby was a monument to the chaos of integration. The queue line stanchions had been toppled in the panic as people had desperately fled from whatever had attacked them, leaving the place in complete disarray.

Popcorn was scattered across the movie-reel-themed carpet, adding to the disarray. One of the red soda machines, known for offering nearly a hundred different flavors, had been tipped onto its side. The door to the ticket sales counter was broken open, and a woman lay dead on the counter. Two arrows were lodged in her chest and her throat was slit as though she had been trying to back away from something—likely goblins. Several other bodies were strewn across the lobby, with one more lying behind the concessions counter, adding to the grim scene.

APOCALYPSE

There were no goblin bodies to be found, so these people must have either panicked, or the goblins had cleaned up after themselves—which seemed unlikely based on their previous behavior. Arrows stuck out of the walls as often as they did bodies, and one man was still standing upright, a spear driven through his body just below the rib cage, pinning him to the wall.

Moving further inside, there was a rustle as something turned and fled down the hall and into one of the theaters.

"Looks like we have a bit of a mess to clean up before getting to the Dungeon," Derek said.

"Time to try out some of our new gear," Jay said as he moved off from the group to survey ahead.

Two entrances to the theater stood on either side of a set of trash cans with the text 'Thank you for cleaning up' printed on the lids. The team split, with Kevin at the front of one team and Derek at the front of the other. James and Tom went with Derek; Kiera and Jay went with Kevin. All had weapons ready and waited for the doors to open. Derek silently counted down from three by holding his fingers up. When he reached zero, they breached the doors and ran in yelling.

The goblins must have been warned by a comrade and were crouched low in the rows of chairs, attempting to avoid detection. Some fired arrows, while others hurled rocks and spears at the party.

Derek easily deflected the attacks with his shield, and Kevin had no trouble blocking the worst of the projectiles with his axe. Stones simply bounced off him, seemingly unnoticed. Most surprising of all was that the goblins' crude arrows had no effect on him; when one struck, it splintered and bounced away as if his skin were armor itself.

Realizing that their projectiles were useless, the goblins began to panic. They scrambled over one another in a desperate attempt to reach the exit, only to discover that it was blocked by the other half of the party, who had approached from an angle they hadn't noticed.

What followed was a massacre. The goblins stood no chance against the overwhelming might of the party. Swords, axes, and maces tore through them, ending their lives without allowing them to inflict even a single point of damage.

"Well, that was fun," James commented.

"Thanks for not shooting anyone," Kevin said, goblin blood dripping from his body.

"Don't mention it. I figured the axes were the way to go this time," James responded, cleaning blood off the weapons.

Kiera flicked her rapier to the side, causing all the blood to fly from the blade. "We do appreciate it. Awfully thoughtful of you not to deafen us with the indoors sound of gunfire."

"Anything for a lady. That goes for you too, Kiera," James replied without looking over.

Jay laughed, doubling over with a full-belly chortle, while the others could practically hear the steam coming off Kiera as she dove at James and tackled him to the floor, punching him in the face. The rest of the party pulled her off and held her back. Tears now blurred Jay's vision and he had to sit to keep himself from falling as he continued to laugh.

Once everyone had calmed down, and James had taken a potion for the beating Kiera had given him, they left the theater and continued down the hall in search of the Dungeon door. They eventually found it at the end of the hall, tucked into a corner behind a support pillar. The door looked like all the others, but instead of a pull handle, it had an ornately designed brass doorknob with the crest of a droplet centered on a shield, and vines curling around the edges.

Tom reached out and grasped the doorknob. A prompt appeared in his vision.

Warning!

The Dungeon of the Bloody Baron is a notorious and perilous Dungeon known for its gruesome history and deadly challenges. Once the lair of a ruthless warlord known as the Bloody Baron, this Dungeon is now a labyrinth of traps, dark magic, and bloodthirsty creatures. Those who enter must be prepared to face relentless adversaries and navigate through a maze of treacherous corridors dripping with the echoes of past battles.

Dungeon Difficulty: Common

Recommended Level: 5+

Objective: Defeat the Bloody Baron

Current parties in the Dungeon: 0

Current completions of the Dungeon: 0

Recommended Party Composition: A balanced party of melee fighters, ranged attackers, magic users, and healers is essential to navigate the Dungeon's challenges and defeat the Bloody Baron.

Enter?

| *Yes* | *No* |

"Everyone ready?" Tom looked back to the party and asked.

The entire team smiled and nodded.

"Then let's do this shit!" Tom said and opened the door.

Chapter 17

Dungeon of the Bloody Baron

Glowing with a dim light, the door swung open, showing a staircase leading down under the theater.

"Spooky, eh?" James said.

No one responded. They didn't even look back at him. All eyes were on the staircase leading down.

"You scared?" Jay asked Tom.

"Not really. Mostly excited. I've dreamt of this for so long. Hell, I *designed* games like this, but never thought I'd get to experience it myself," Tom replied. "It's a bit unnerving thinking about all the possibilities, but that same thought is making me so excited that I'm finding it hard to move. I feel like if I do, this dream will end."

Tom stared down into the depths and then, with his breath held in, took a single step through the doorway. He had expected something to happen when he stepped into the stairwell, but nothing did. The wall this door was attached to was clearly an external wall of the building, so the door had to be some kind of portal.

Since nothing happened, he continued down the stairs. They descended further than a typical staircase for a single-story building, but not quite as far as one would expect for a full second story. Once everyone was inside the Dungeon, the door behind them shut firmly, the sound echoing through the halls causing them to flinch. When they turned to look back, the door had vanished.

The interior of the Dungeon was made entirely of stone, as though it was some medieval manor or castle. At the base of the stairs, a red runner stretched the entire length of the hallway in front of them. Tom realized that the only reason this Dungeon didn't look like every castle he had ever seen in TV shows was the absence of windows.

Torches lined the walls every fifteen to twenty feet, providing just enough light to see by. The party advanced in single file down the narrow hall. When they reached the end, the corridor branched into a T-junction, leading both left and right.

"Any thoughts on where to go?" Tom asked.

"Some people say that might makes right," James said, pointing to the right-hand turn. "But I say right is right."

"...Isn't that the same thing?" Tom asked, scratching his head.

"Do you mean right is the right answer? Or that right is literally just right like the name suggests?" Jay asked.

"I dunno. I just thought it would help to stay right," James replied.

"*Stay right,*" Jay clarified, "as in not being wrong, or is it more of an Aristotle's Law of Identity kind of thi—"

"Right, it is," Tom said, pinching the bridge of his nose and chuckling slightly.

Turning to the right, they proceeded into the now much wider hallway. The group could move almost four abreast in this direction, and the carpet was much wider to cover most of the floor as well.

Suits of armor lined both sides of the hallway, each holding a spear in an attention position. The group paused to examine the armor, noticing that many of the suits were covered in rust—but not the typical kind. This rust was a deep maroon color, almost as if the armor had been coated in blood before the rust set in.

"Wait, I've seen this before," James said and promptly kicked over one of the suits of armor, causing muted clanging sounds as the metal bounced on the carpet.

Falling to pieces, the suit pieces scattered near the base while the helmet rolled a bit before coming to a stop.

"Hmm… well, that's a good sign," James said.

"What's a good sign? That the entire damn place knows we're here?" Jay asked.

"No. That it didn't come to life when I kicked it. Have you never experienced animated armor before? It's like a classic mob," James said.

"He's right. Any one of these could come to life to attack us," Derek said.

Tom reached down to pick up one of the armored gauntlets. He tried to place it in his Inventory but received a warning prompt.

Error:
This piece of armor belongs to the Dungeon of the Bloody Baron and cannot be taken.

"Well, that would have been too easy," Tom said.

"What would've?" James asked.

"I tried to add it to my Inventory. Figured we could use the armor somewhere, but it appears we can't take it," Tom said.

"Bummer," Jay said.

As the group continued down the hallway, James and Kevin took it upon themselves to gleefully knock over the suits of armor—James handling one side while Kevin took the other. Halfway down the corridor, rather than falling to pieces on the floor, two suits of armor stumbled off their pedestals before righting themselves and leveling their spears at the party. Realizing the difference in sounds, the party turned and drew their weapons. As they did, the sounds of two more suits of armor moving into position sounded from the direction they had been heading.

APOCALYPSE

Tom used Inspect on one of them.

Blood-Rusted Animated Armor	
Blood-Rusted Animated Armor is a formidable and eerie construct, animated by dark magic and fueled by the lingering hatred of fallen warriors. These suits of armor, stained with the blood of countless battles and rusted from years of neglect, serve as relentless guardians to the Bloody Baron in this cursed Dungeon. They move with an unnatural grace despite their corroded appearance, driven by a singular purpose: to destroy any intruder who dares to cross their path.	
HP	550/550
MP	0/0
SP	500/500
Attacks:	Can wield weapons, Iron Resilience, Rusted Strike

"Shit. James was right," Tom called out mournfully. "Now he's gonna gloat. There's nothing inside, so we're gonna have to hack these things to pieces."

"Got it. Let's slice and dice!" James said.

"Kiera, you aren't going to be much use fighting with that thing," Tom called out, pointing at her crossbow. "Got anything to help?"

"Sure do," Kiera replied as she pulled her lute out of storage and began to play it. She sang a song about hope and heroes. A song about better days and the light that lives on in everyone through their connection to each other.

Buff Received:
Kiera has played the Song of Hope. For the next 5 mins, your attacks deal 10% more damage.

"Hell yeah!" Jay exclaimed. "That's the stuff, little sister."

Pulling out his kamas, Jay readied himself to provide support. From the rear, one of the armored figures lunged with its spear, but Kevin quickly swiped it away with his axe. Without losing momentum, he swung it back around, bringing its head crashing into the chest of the metal armor. The blade bit deep, cutting nearly seventy-five percent of the way through the thick plating.

"Too bad you don't have a body in there," Kevin said as he smiled, pulled his fist back, and punched the helmet off the armor.

Dropping the spear, the armor moved around as though it couldn't see, waving its hands through the air and trying to find the helmet.

"Neat!" Kevin said. "Hey guys, knock the helmets off. It's hilarious."

Not needing to be told twice, Tom engaged the armor in front of him, swiping at it with his sword. The armor stepped back and Derek moved forward, deftly blocking a spear thrust with his shield at an angle, causing the spear to slide harmlessly to the side. Continuing his momentum, Derek swung his mace at the helmet, sending it flying off. Just like the other armor, the figure dropped its spear and began fumbling around for the helmet, resembling a cartoon character searching for its lost head.

"This feels like it's going to be too easy," Tom said, swinging his sword at the head of the other armor in front of them and knocking it off too.

"Don't get too confident. I nearly split one in two, and it didn't even slow down. We need to figure out how to stop them for good," Kevin called out.

He had just knocked off the last helmet still on one of the armors when Derek then reached down and, with his mace, smashed the helmet he had knocked off earlier, pounding it repeatedly until it was nearly flat. As soon as the helmet was destroyed, the suit of armor it belonged to collapsed into pieces and stopped moving.

"Looks like it's the helmets," Derek said. "Smash or damage them enough and it's over."

Jay took the helmet he was holding and jammed the tip of one of his kamas into it several times. The corresponding armor also fell apart and stopped moving.

Smiling wickedly, Kevin took his axe, and with a powerful downward swing, cut the remaining rear armor's helmet in half. Its body died as well. The last remaining armor was dispatched by Derek with his mace.

"Cool. Now we know the trick," Derek said. "Let's keep going."

The party made their way down the hallway, battling each suit of armor that sprang to life. They smashed, cut, or stabbed the helmets to put an end to them. By the time they reached the first set of doors, they had destroyed several dozen suits of armor, leaving the hallway littered with pieces they wished they could take with them. When they finally arrived at a massive pair of wooden doors, the party paused and stared.

However, it wasn't the doors that demanded their attention, but rather, what was standing next to them.

It was a vending machine.

"Well, I'll be damned. They got these in here too?" James said excitedly.

It looked a lot like the one in the Guild building but had some different options. There were a few basic weapons, some armor, and a couple of potions, but what stood out most were the items they had never seen before in the vending machines outside the Dungeon. These new options piqued their curiosity.

"What's a 'safe space?'" Jay asked.

"It's more than likely an item that can be used in a Dungeon to provide a space to sleep or rest and recover," Tom explained. "Some Dungeons in games are really big and can take days to explore, so a safe space would offer protection for rest and recovery from injuries or time to recover mana and stamina."

"There are also rations, waterskins, and an escape coin," Kiera said, trying to understand some of them.

"Rations might be an option for the people in the Guild building," Kevin offered.

"Maybe if everyone was out killing monsters. But only a handful of us are doing that right now. So we could afford to feed ourselves, but five hundred people with—let's be generous and say—thirty people out killing monsters? The math doesn't math there," Derek replied.

Looking at the prices, Tom was sure he had more than enough to buy one of each to see what they did. Taking out some Monster Cores, he purchased a safe space, rations, waterskin, and an escape coin.

When he had the cans in his hands, he looked them over. Turning the safe space can over first, Tom found a warning label.

"Do not open this can until ready to use," Tom read the warning aloud. "This is a one-time use item and can only be activated in a room that has been cleared of monsters. Cannot be used if hostile creatures are nearby."

Pulling the tabs on the rations and waterskin, the rations appeared as small paper-wrapped bundles of beef jerky. The waterskin was just what it said—a waterskin filled with clean drinking water. Looking at the last can, it appeared to be the most unique. It also had a warning label but appeared to be something that could be opened immediately.

"Escape Coin, an item to be used in the direst of situations," Tom read out loud. "When you crush the coin in your hand, you will be transported out of the Dungeon to its entrance."

"Well, that seems handy," Derek commented.

"Not able to be used during boss fights," Tom continued. "Cannot be used by the dead."

"Ominous," Kiera commented.

"What about undead? Or living dead?" James asked.

Everyone looked at him in confusion.

"Just curious," James replied. "I mean, what if I wanted to change factions?" He looked around at the different expressions on everyone's faces. "Well, I didn't mean right *now*," he finished defensively.

Tom popped the top on the last can, and a small coin that appeared to be made of sandstone appeared in his hand. Turning it over, he admired the intricate work of the etching that was done around the outside of the coin. He used Inspect on the coin to see if it offered any more information.

Escape Coin:

The Escape Coin is a powerful tool designed for emergencies, offering a swift escape from perilous situations within a Dungeon. When crushed in your hand, the coin activates a teleportation spell that instantly transports you to the Dungeon's entrance, allowing for a quick retreat from danger.

Usage:

- To use, simply crush the Escape Coin in your hand. This will trigger the teleportation effect, removing you from the Dungeon and placing you safely at the entrance.

Warnings:

- **Not Usable During Boss Fights:** The Escape Coin cannot be activated during encounters with Dungeon bosses. Plan your escape carefully.
- **Cannot Be Used by the Dead:** The coin is ineffective if you are already dead. It can only be used by living adventurers.

Note: Keep this coin close for critical moments when escape is the only option. Use it wisely to avoid losing valuable progress and to save your life when all else fails.

So, nothing new. He turned it over again in his hand.

"I think everyone should buy one of these just in case. Open it and put it in your Inventory," Tom said to the team.

They complied, recognizing the wisdom in the plan. After storing the coins, they felt a bit more secure, knowing they had an escape option if needed. James also bought a potion to replace the one he had used on his face, ensuring he was fully prepared for whatever lay ahead.

After making sure that they had all the items they needed, the party moved back to the giant doors. Huge pieces of iron-banded wood with hardly-noticeable seams. Rings as big around as a man's head hung from the doors as handles. The edges of the doors had ornate carvings on them of battles fought by men on horseback and slaying beasts in forests.

"Do you think they are compensating for something?" James asked, looking up at how tall the doors were.

"You really think someone with a tiny dick just wakes up and says, 'You know what would make me feel like more of a man? Huge fucking doors.' Is that truly what you are asking here?" Jay said.

James just looked at Jay, unblinking.

"Of *course* you do," Jay threw up his hands. "More likely he would have a big sword he couldn't carry around."

"Guess we need to open them," Derek said.

They grabbed the handles and began to pull on the doors. The doors were super heavy. It took three of them on each handle to get them to open all the way. Swinging outward on hinges that creaked and protested the entire way, the doors slowly opened.

Inside the room was a banquet hall with the tables pushed to the sides, leaving a wide-open space. At the head of the room were three seats. In the leftmost chair sat a man in his early twenties, holding a sword that appeared to be about six feet long and eighteen inches wide. He looked up at them with a wide smile and addressed them warmly.

"Hello, subjects. Have you come to play with me?"

Chapter 18

The Bloody Prince

"Subjects?" Tom questioned.

"Why, yes. You are in my Kingdom, after all," the young man said.

"So, you are the Bloody Baron?" Derek asked.

"No, well not yet. The baron is my father. Though we don't really like the name Bloody Baron, regardless of how apt the name may be," the young man replied, seeming at ease with an armed party of adventurers in his presence.

"Ah, so that makes you…" Tom asked, trailing off.

"Forgive me. Where are my manners?" the man said, placing the point of his sword down on the stone floor and standing up. "I am the baron's son, Prince Henry."

"Prince?" Tom asked.

"Yes, Prince Henry," the man replied, puffing out his chest and striking a regal pose.

"But… your dad is a baron… Wouldn't that make you…" Tom tried to continue.

"Baronlet?" James offered.

"Barontini?" Jay suggested.

"I'M A PRINCE, DAMN YOU! SHOW SOME RESPECT!" Henry screamed at them, his previous demeanor gone.

"Fine, fine, hakuna your tatas, dude," Tom said, putting his hands out placatingly. "I was just slightly confused, that's all."

"Well, being as you *are* merely lowly peasants, I guess I can forgive your lack of etiquette. But don't let it happen again," Henry said, lifting his sword and pointing it at them.

"See what I mean?" Jay said, leaning over to James. "*That's* the kind of thing someone would use for compensation."

"WHAT DID YOU SAY?" the prince yelled.

"Nothing, I said nothing," Jay tried to back pedal.

"He said you must be compensating for something with such a big sword," James called back.

"And what, pray tell, would I be *compensating* for?" the prince asked, a sneer appearing on his face.

"Usually, it's your tiny penis," James said mildly. "Although, sometimes it could be an inability to please your lover, and in rare cases, it's because you can't get it up," James said. "So, which is it, milord? Teeny peenie, hot dog in a hallway, or a limp bizkit situation?"

The prince reddened to the point where it almost looked like steam might come out of his ears. He clenched his fist around the sword, his other hand balled tightly at his side.

"You *dare* to discuss my sexual prowess and call into question the Royal Dangle-Downs?" The prince seethed through clenched teeth.

James leaned toward Jay. "Did… Did you get the feeling that he somehow capitalized that last bit?"

"You felt that too, eh?" Jay replied in confirmation.

Suddenly, the prince's muscles began to bulge, and he raised the sword over his head with one hand.

"You will pay for the words that have spilled from your vile lips with your life! I am Prince Henry! Master of this domain! Champion of my father's realm! Undefeated in a hundred battles! Slayer of monsters!" the prince yelled in a voice that had now dropped an octave. "Taste my blade, you vile cur!"

The prince launched himself from the dais, hurtling toward the party with blinding speed. They barely had time to react, scrambling out of the way as he swung his massive sword, carving a deep furrow into the stone floor where they had stood just moments before.

"You really had to go and make the dude mad?" Tom asked.

"He is the mini-boss. Isn't it obvious, dude?" James replied.

Jay paused to eye the prince with a critical eye before nodding, his words suggestive. "Definitely a *mini-boss.*"

James simply held out a fist, though due to the space between them, Jay bumped the air with his own by way of reply.

Thinking it over, it made a lot of sense that this was the mini-boss. The baron was likely the final boss, and this guy was just a pretender. It seemed he was designed to lose his temper at anything short of the sincerest flattery, making him prone to flying off the handle.

"That… actually makes sense," Tom replied. "So, what's the play?"

"I don't know. Fuck him up?" James said, pulling his guns out and firing.

The bullets seemed to bounce harmlessly off the prince's back. Tom and Derek quickly moved in to engage. Derek took the full force of a powerful blow on his shield, which drove him down to a knee as he struggled to keep from being crushed. Meanwhile, Tom swung his sword at the prince, but it struck with a resounding clang and bounced off.

"Is he wearing fucking metal armor under his clothes?!" Tom asked in surprise, trying to keep his teeth from rattling out of his head.

Kevin ran in bellowing and shoulder-checked the prince, knocking him off Derek.

"Thanks, Kevin!" Derek said, rising to his feet.

Rolling with the blow, the prince came back to his feet and charged at Kevin. He grabbed him and tossed him against the back wall as if he were a stuffed toy. Swinging his arm out to the side, he also caught Derek across his shield, which he had brought up to protect against the blow, and sent him flying back into the tables that were against the wall.

Stabbing out this time, Tom aimed the tip of his greatsword at the prince, but it merely glanced off the prince's side as he turned to face him. The prince retaliated with a powerful uppercut, sending Tom sprawling onto his back. As the prince looked around, his eyes locked onto Kiera, who had been singing her Song of Hope.

"The hope of tomorrooooow! Oh shiiiiit! He's coming after meeeeee! Someone stop him pleeeeeease!" Kiera sang, changing the lyrics of the song as her eyes grew wide, trying not to lose concentration on casting the spell.

As he charged her, Jay jumped in front of Kiera to try to stop the prince. Jay was no match for the prince's strength. Plowing through Jay's poor attempts at blocking them, the prince barreled right through Jay and into Kiera as well.

Both were sent flying backward, crashing into a table that shattered under their combined weight and the force of the fall.

James fired several shots, aiming at the back of the prince's head, but the bullets simply bounced off. The prince turned to locate their source, his lips curling into an evil, predatory grin as he spotted James standing there with a defiant look on his face. Without hesitation, the prince charged at him.

James tried to dodge to the side and nearly made it, but the prince managed to grab his foot as he dove. Yanking James back, the prince held him up, jammed his sword into the ground to free both hands, and delivered a brutal punch to James' face. James was lifted off the ground, then slammed down hard onto the floor. The prince casually walked over and placed a boot on James' stomach before stomping down with force. Blood spurted from James' mouth as he was crushed under the prince's weight.

The rest of his team were hurrying to get to their feet, but they still weren't sure what to do. Kevin recovered first and reached James, grappling the prince in a bear hug from behind.

"How about a suplex?!" Kevin bellowed as he picked the prince up and bent over backward. Slamming the prince into the stone floor headfirst, the prince winced but turned and pulled himself free of Kevin's grasp. He lashed out with a couple of punches and Kevin went down.

"Nothing seems to hurt this motherfucker!" Kiera called out.

A kama whipped out, and the chain attached to it wrapped tightly around the prince's neck. The prince grabbed the chain, and for a moment, he and Jay engaged in a fierce tug of war. It was clear that Jay was on the verge of losing, but then Tom jumped onto the chain as well, adding his strength to the struggle, helping to even the odds.

With an extra grunt, the prince raged even harder and pulled back and to the right on the chain. Tom and Jay began to swing in that direction, until they hit the wall on the other side of the room, and collapsed in a pile. Turning back to James, the Prince smiled down at him.

James' face was a wreck. One of his eyes was swollen shut, he was missing a front tooth, and his nose was clearly broken, with blood streaming from both nostrils. Despite his injuries, he raised his gun, locking eyes with the prince. Then, with a defiant smirk, he lowered his aim and pointed the gun directly between the prince's legs.

"Don't worry bro, my girl says the big ones hurt anyways," James said and pulled the trigger, firing a shot right at the prince's crotch.

The prince's eyes went wide as the bullet penetrated his clothes and blood began to pour out from the wound he received.

"CHEEEEEEOOOOOOOWWWWWWWEEEEEEE!" the prince wailed in pain as he grabbed at his groin.

Everyone in the room froze.

"GO FOR THE WILLY!" Derek shouted.

And with that, the entire party sprang into action, charging at the prince with a singular, brutal intent. Kamas, swords, maces, knives, axes, feet, and even a chair were wielded with fierce determination, all aimed at reducing the prince's privates to a pulp. The team went to extreme lengths, repeatedly, to ensure that the prince would never have the option of fathering children. Their assault was relentless, turning his manhood into something fit only for bolognese sauce.

When they had all had their fill of beating the prince's meat, Tom set it on fire with an *Eldritch Blast*.

"Take that, you son of a bitch!" James said, spitting on the prince's corpse.

"Who knew that the prince's ding dong was the weak spot?" Kiera asked.

"Looks like James knew," Derek said. "Not only did you tease him about it, but you shot him there first."

"Mere coincidences," James said, drinking a potion. "I simply made fun of him to get the fight started because I knew you all were just going to talk it out forever. Then I only shot him in the dick because I was pissed at getting beaten up so badly. Figured if he was so hurt by insults about his bald-headed giggle stick, that shooting him in the beef whistle was likely to be something he would hate just as much. I had no idea that his knob goblin was going to be his weak spot. I just wanted to knock him in the old blue-veined custard chucker simply because he was a bit of a Dallas Dangler himself."

"Whatever the case is, we pulled through. But we can't have a close call like that again. We need a sounder strategy for attacks than just running at the guy full tilt. We took our numbers for granted and fell apart there," Derek said. "Next time we might not be so lucky."

"Derek's right. We can think of a better way," Tom said.

With that, they sat down on the floor of the room to recover and plan their strategies.

After about an hour of resting, they got up and left the room. The only way out was back down the hall and to a passage to the left. Clearly, this wasn't a very large Dungeon, but that was perfectly fine with Tom. He needed to get back to the Center to finish setting some things up and making sure the people had everything they needed. But the thrill of exploring and fighting in a real Dungeon was too enticing, and he knew he had to see it through to the end.

The other direction had the same type of armors guarding them, and the team took them out in the same way. They reached the other end of the hall, and there was no vending machine this time. Just an even larger set of doors decorated in the same way as the last.

"I guess we should go in and say hello," Tom said, smiling at Derek.

Chapter 19

The Bloody Baron

Pulling open the doors, the party walked inside. They were met with what was clearly a grand throne room. Once again, at the end of the room were three chairs. One huge throne was in the center of the raised end of the hall, with two smaller thrones set slightly behind and to the sides. They were all wingback chairs with elegant gold filigree decorating them. Sitting in the largest of the chairs was an older gentleman sporting a grey beard.

To the right and behind him was a woman who looked to be about the same age. She was elegant in her gown and held the posture of someone important. The third chair was empty.

"Guessing it's pretty obvious who this is…" Tom said.

"Mommy and daddy knobjob," James said.

"Let's try not to anger them so quickly," Derek said.

"Why not?" James said.

"Have you seen what's lining the walls?" Derek returned.

Turning to look at the walls, James noticed the suits of armor. Ten on each side. Each holding spears while their helmets followed the party as they entered the throne room. Squeaking as the heads turned, bits of dark rust fell off in a shower as they moved.

"Halt!" the man called to the party. "Who are you and why do you disturb us? We called for no one to enter."

His voice sounded hoarse, as though it hadn't been used in a long time, the wear of age creeping in. Yet, commanding them was still no issue for him; he exuded an air of authority that demanded obedience, a result of having wielded power for a very long time.

"We do apologize for the intrusion, Baron. We merely wished to complete the Dungeon," Tom called back.

"What Dungeon? These are our hallowed halls. The barony of Unifold. You have no business here," the baron replied.

"Are you the Bloody Baron?" Tom asked.

"…what did you call me?" the man asked, his voice dropping in volume.

"The Bloody Baron," Tom said again.

"How *dare* you throw those accusations at me here in my own hall!" the baron spat in a voice barely above a whisper, yet it carried through the room as if propelled by magic. "I will not have you besmirch my name and stand idly by. GUARDS! Arrest them!"

With that, the suits of armor began to stir, slowly stepping down from their pedestals. The creaking sound grew louder as more of the armors came to life, the screeching of metal scraping against each other becoming an unbearable noise, like nails on a chalkboard. As the painful noises filled the room, the woman standing behind the baron rose to her feet and began to chant something in a low, ominous tone.

"What the fuck is that?" James said, turning to look at the woman.

"Shit, she's casting something. Can you hit her?" Tom asked.

"Let's find out," James said, raising a gun and firing at her.

The bullet went wide, traveling to the left of the baron's wife. James fired again and again, struggling to hit his mark. He was too far away and lacked the experience to make such a long-distance shot, but one bullet finally got lucky and headed straight for her abdomen. However, it was stopped by a glowing blue barrier that materialized in front of her just as the bullet got close.

"Apparently not. She's got a shield," James said back.

Finishing the casting, the woman raised her hands into the air and blood began to flow from between the pieces of armor. As the red fluid oozed out from every crevice and ran down the armor like a macabre oil, the suits of armor moved faster and faster as the screeching sounds eased and then stopped.

"Fuck! She just gave those suits a bloody lube job!" Jay called.

The armor now moved with a grace that none of the other suits had before.

"Guess it's time to get angry," Kevin said.

Hunching over, Kevin gripped his axe, his eyes burning with intensity. He began to let out a low, rumbling bellow that gradually rose in volume. Within moments, he was roaring at the top of his lungs, his skin glowing with a faint red light as his fury built.

"Is Kevin going super saiyan?" James asked.

"IT'S TIME TO RAGE!" Kevin called out.

Bursting forward with more speed than he had ever shown before, Kevin sliced through the suits of armor as if he were harvesting wheat. Kiera once again strummed her lute and sang her song, boosting their attack power. Tom cast *Lightning Strike* at the nearest suit of armor, and the electricity leaped from one suit to another, its conductivity allowing the spell to hit multiple targets. Although the attack didn't cause much damage, it had a stunning effect; each suit froze in place, their limbs sticking out like a cartoon character after a shock. This gave the others a perfect opening to strike.

Derek followed the path of the lightning, skillfully striking the helmets from the suits of armor. Kevin, driven by a seemingly unstoppable force, leaped in front of Derek, moving like a man possessed. His mouth began to froth as though he was losing control, and it seemed the only thing keeping him from completely going off the rails was the destruction of the armor. The rest of the party wisely backed away as Kevin tore the suits apart limb by limb, smashing the pieces with relentless fury.

Tom turned to the baron and his wife. "I guess he's got those covered," he said.

APOCALYPSE

The pair looked at Kevin and the destruction he was wreaking with utter disdain, their expressions souring as if they had caught a whiff of something foul and couldn't be bothered to figure out what it was.

"So, you brought a beast with you. That won't help you in this endeavor!" the baron said as he rose from the throne and drew his sword.

Charging forward, the baron moved to strike at Tom.

Derek stepped in front of him, bringing his shield up to block the blow. Seizing the opportunity, Tom moved to attack while the baron's sword was engaged with the shield, but the baron deftly twisted, slipping off the shield and raising his sword just in time to parry Tom's greatsword.

The baroness began casting another spell and sent a ball of fire hurtling toward Jay and Kiera. They quickly rolled out of the way, avoiding the fiery attack. Splitting up to force the baroness to divide her focus, the duo ran to either side, attempting to close in on her. However, she responded with a powerful force attack, simultaneously striking both of them and sending them crashing into the walls.

"What am I, chopped liver?" James asked.

"You are no threat. Go back to the gutters you came from, you miserable whelp," the baroness said.

"Ohhhhh, hell nah!" James yelled. "No one calls me 'no threat' and lives to tell about it!"

Pulling out both 1911s, James aimed them at the baroness, who smirked, dismissing his attempt as futile. But before she could react, James shifted his aim to the baron, firing off a shot. The baroness' smirk vanished as her eyes widened in shock—the baron doubled over in pain, clutching his crotch where the bullet had struck.

"Headshot!" James exclaimed.

Blood began pouring out from between the baron's fingers as he held his family jewels with an expression of true pain and horror.

"NOOOOOOOOOOOOOOOOOOO!" screamed the baroness.

Beginning to chant anew, the baroness' voice deepened into a throaty, menacing tone that seemed to rise from the pits of hell itself. James fired at her, but her shield held firm. Jay and Kiera launched their own attacks, but they too were thwarted by the barrier she had erected. Kiera pressed her rapier hard against the blue barrier, but the point couldn't penetrate. Jay slashed at it with his kamas, but no matter how forcefully he struck, the blades failed to break through the barrier.

The baroness' chant rose to a new crescendo as she raised her hands to the ceiling and threw her head back, finishing the final words of her incantation. Her eyes glowed with a sinister red light, and she turned back to the party with a malicious grin. Extending one hand, she began to beckon something unseen. Suddenly, Kevin walked past the party toward the baroness, his eyes now glowing the same eerie red as hers. Without warning, he turned and bellowed at the group, his voice filled with an unnatural, echoing fury.

"Fucking shit," Derek said.

All hell broke loose after that. Kevin, now a raging force of nature, turned on his comrades, attacking them with a fury that couldn't be contained. Derek quickly jumped in front of him, using his shield to block Kevin's relentless onslaught, trying desperately to protect the others from his frenzied attacks.

"Get the baroness! I'll hold him as long as I can!" Derek yelled to the rest of the party as he was driven back step by step under the force of the strikes.

Kevin was on the verge of overwhelming Derek, and they knew they had to stop the spell before it was too late. The entire party charged the baroness in unison, slamming their weapons against the shield with every ounce of strength they could muster. In a moment of frustration and determination, Tom remembered to activate his tattoo. With a yell, he brought his greatsword down in an overhand strike, using both hands and putting all his strength into the blow as it crashed against the shield.

Cracks began to form and spread across the barrier under the force of Tom's attack. The baroness' eyes widened in fear as she began to step backward, only to find herself trapped against the wall. Desperately, she started casting another spell, the words of power tumbling from her lips as quickly as she could articulate them. But Tom didn't give her the chance to finish. With another powerful overhand strike, he brought his greatsword down, shattering the shield and releasing a concussive force that sent the entire team flying backward and crushed the baroness against the wall.

Rolling backward and trying to get to their feet as quickly as possible, the team stared at the place where the baroness stood.

Her head had slammed into the wall with such force that her skull had fractured, sending a grotesque spray of blood splattering against the surface. She wobbled for a moment, her eyes rolling back as she stood frozen in place. Then, as death claimed her, she slumped to the floor, leaving a bloody streak down the wall where her head had slid.

The baron cried out in despair from his fetal position on the floor, still unable to stand. Meanwhile, Kevin's eyes returned to normal, the red glow fading from his skin. He glanced at Derek's shield, realizing with shock that he had nearly split it in half with his frenzied blows.

Falling to the floor backward, Kevin placed his hands over his mouth in horror as he began to apologize profusely for what he had done.

"Oh shit! No! What have I done!" Kevin said. "I'm so sorry, Derek. I never meant to attack you."

"You were under a spell. *You* didn't do anything. Besides, I'm fine," Derek said, panting heavily and simply relieved to be safe from the onslaught. "But you owe me a new shield."

James walked over to the baron, lying on the floor and sobbing uncontrollably.

"You sad sack of shit. You aren't even deserving of that title Bloody Baron. It was your wife that did all the work," James said, holding up his gun and aiming it at the baron's head.

He fired two shots, and the baron lay still.

Chapter 20

A Grand Warning

Slumping with relief, the team paused to recover from the fight.

"So, the whole time, the baron was covering for the baroness," Tom said. "She was involved with some kind of blood magic, it appears. Hence the title."

"Looks that way," Derek said. "I can't exactly blame the guy for protecting his wife, but seriously dude, she could take control of people!"

"Right?! If Kevin had been a little stronger, we would have been in serious trouble," Tom replied.

"I'm sorry again, guys. Especially Derek. I didn't mean to attack you," Kevin said sheepishly.

"Don't worry about it, bro. It wasn't you. You were being controlled. All good," Derek said, reassuring Kevin.

"I still feel like…" Kevin began but trailed off as a light shone from the end of the room where the thrones were located.

The baron's throne began to transform before their eyes. Slowly morphing, the chair shifted into a box shape, its glow intensifying with each passing moment. The light grew so bright that the party had to shield their eyes. Finally, with a soft popping sound, the transformation was complete, and the light abruptly winked out, leaving behind the newly formed object.

Standing in place of the throne was a vending machine.

"Seriously? We kick the Dungeon boss' ass and we have to *buy* something?" James asked. "What a crock of shit. I don't know what twat-waffle designed this fucking system, but if I find them, I'm gonna introduce them to Chip and Dale here."

"You named your guns Chip and Dale?" Jay asked.

"Of course I did. Because they destroy deez nuts and they sexy as hell! Get it?" James said and began laughing uncontrollably.

While James was laughing, a prompt appeared in all of their visions.

> **Dungeon Complete!**
>
> ---
>
> **Congratulations!**
>
> You are the first to complete the Dungeon of the Bloody Baron!
>
> **Reward:**
>
> As a reward for this remarkable feat, a special prize awaits you. At the end of every Dungeon, a vending machine will appear, allowing each party member to select one item for free. However, because you were the first to clear this Dungeon, each of you may choose **two items**.
>
> **Item Selection:**
>
> Item selections will be curated to your Classes. Unlike standard vending machine purchases, customization of the selection is not available.
>
> **Continue to fight hard, strive for excellence, and greater rewards will follow.**

"Ohhhh… so we don't have to pay to use this one. Well, never mind then on the chestnut chucking," James said.

"For fuck's sake, James, quit talking about people's nether regions and just go pick something from the machine," Derek said.

"Alright, alright, don't get your panties in a wad, Mom. I'm going," James replied, getting annoyed. "Now let's see, what should I get?"

Peering into the machine, the party noticed that some of the items were similar to those available in other machines. Weapons and armor resembling what they already had were among the options. However, this time the machine also offered something new: jewelry. Cans containing rings, pendants, bracelets, earrings, and more were available, adding a surprising variety to the selection.

James scratched his head, trying to figure out how to work the machine.

"Put your hand on the screen, dumbass!" Derek called.

Feeling embarrassed for not thinking of that before, James put his hand on the machine and it changed out the options to fit his Ranger Class.

"Ah! I know what I need!" James said and made a selection. Then he made the same selection again.

"What did you get?" Kiera asked as she walked up behind him.

Holding the cans up, James opened them one at a time and held out his prizes after the smoke had cleared.

"Red-dot sights!" he said, beaming with pride. "These babies should increase my accuracy."

Tom took one and Inspected the item.

Item: Ranger's Red-Dot Sight
The Ranger's Red-Dot Sight is an advanced piece of optical equipment designed to improve a Ranger's accuracy in the field. When equipped, this sight increases the user's accuracy by 25%, allowing for precise, rapid targeting. The red dot projected onto the lens provides a clear aiming point, ensuring that even fast-moving or distant targets can be easily tracked and shot. This sight is crafted for durability, able to withstand harsh environmental conditions while maintaining its precision alignment. Designed for use with ranged weapons such as bows, handguns, and rifles, the Ranger's Red-Dot Sight is an invaluable tool for any Ranger looking to enhance their marksmanship and maximize their effectiveness in combat.

Item Type:	Accessory
Durability:	250/250
Item Quality:	Well-Crafted
Item Rarity:	Uncommon

"You didn't want anything else?" Tom asked.

"Why would I want something else when I can use these babies to kill more monsters to get more loot?" James questioned back.

He did, however, turn back to the machine and try to get another prize.

"Both purchases for user 'James' have been used. Please change users before attempting to make an additional purchase. Once all other members of the party have made their selections, the options in the machine will be reset and users may make purchases as normal." the machine said in its female, automated voice.

"Worth a shot," James said as he stepped back to let someone else choose.

Kiera stepped up and put her hand on the screen. Making two selections, she stepped back with her prizes.

"What'd ya get?" Jay asked.

She held one of the cans up to his face to let him see the image and promptly opened the can mere inches from his face, causing the smoke to blast him from point-blank range. Coughing and sputtering, Jay reeled backward and almost fell over.

"I got a Ring of Spell Storage and a rifle," Kiera said, smiling from ear to ear at Jay's discomfort.

Item: Ring of Spell Storage	
The Ring of Spell Storage is a finely crafted magical ring with the ability to store a single spell at a time. Once a spell is cast into the ring, it remains stored and ready for instant use. The stored spell can be instantly released, allowing the user to unleash its power without the need for preparation, somatic or verbal conditions. This ring is especially valuable for spellcasters who want to have a powerful spell ready in reserve. The ability to store and use a spell at will provides strategic advantages, making the Ring of Spell Storage a coveted item among magic users.	
Item Type:	Acessory
Durability:	500/500
Item Quality:	Well-Crafted
Item Rarity:	Uncommon

Item: .30-06 Bolt Action Winchester XPR Pro	
The Winchester XPR Pro is a precision-engineered bolt-action rifle designed for accuracy and reliability. Utilizing .30-06 ammunition, this rifle offers the perfect balance of power and performance, making it ideal for long distance attacks. The XPR Pro features a black polymer stock with a textured grip, providing a secure hold. The barrel is finished with a matte blue coloration to make it tough and non-reflective. Equipped with an M.O.A. trigger system and a robust bolt-action system, the XPR Pro is built to withstand the elements and deliver consistent accuracy shot after shot. Accessories such as scopes, bipods, and slings can be purchased from vending machines.	
Item Type:	Weapon, Ranged
Durability:	500/500
Attack:	50-75 Damage
Item Quality:	Well-Crafted
Item Rarity:	Uncommon

"So, this thing is basically the treasure chest at the end of the Dungeons?" Tom asked.

"Looks that way. In some games, the Dungeon will have a chest that just gives a set number of items that the party has to divvy up between themselves. In other cases, it will allow each member to open the chest and give either specific

APOCALYPSE

or random items out to each party member," Derek explained at the confused looks on Kiera and Jay's faces.

"Oh, I see. So, when we finish a hard task or quest, we might just pick from a vending machine instead of finding a treasure chest?" Kiera asked.

"That seems to be the gist of it right now," Derek confirmed. "But only time will tell if that happens in every case."

Jay stepped up and got a Cape of Stealth and Ninjato of Bleeding.

Item: Cape of Stealth	
The Cape of Stealth is a finely woven cloak imbued with magic that enhances the wearer's ability to blend into their surroundings. When worn, it increases the effectiveness of the user's Stealth by 20%, making it easier to move undetected or hide in plain sight. The cloak's fabric subtly shifts to mimic the colors and textures of the environment, aiding in camouflage. Perfect for Rogues, scouts, or anyone needing an extra edge in stealth operations. ***Note*** Works best with dull non-fluorescent colors and in less than full light.	
Item Type:	Accessory
Durability:	1500/1500
Item Quality:	Well-Crafted
Item Rarity:	Uncommon

Item: Ninjato of Bleeding	
The Ninjato of Bleeding is a deadly blade designed for silent, precise strikes. Enchanted with dark magic, this weapon inflicts a bleeding effect on any enemy struck, causing wounds that are slow to clot and steadily drain the victim's health over time. Each cut from the Ninjato weakens the enemy, making it harder for them to recover. Ideal for assassins and stealth fighters, the Ninjato of Bleeding turns every strike into a potential death sentence.	
Item Type:	Weapon, Slashing
Durability:	500/500
Attack:	18-28 Damage
Item Quality:	Well-Crafted
Item Rarity:	Uncommon

Derek obtained a Ring of Cure Wounds and a Helm of Clarity.

Item: Ring of Cure Wounds	
The Ring of Cure Wounds is a magical item imbued with healing magic. When activated, it casts the spell Cure Wounds, instantly restoring 50 HP to the wearer or a designated target. The ring holds three charges, allowing it to be used up to three times per day. The charges replenish every 24 hours, making this ring an invaluable tool for those who find themselves in frequent combat situations.	
Item Type:	Accessory
Durability:	500/500
Item Quality:	Well-Crafted
Item Rarity:	Uncommon

Item: Helm of Clarity	
The Helm of Clarity is a finely crafted helmet imbued with powerful enchantments that heighten the wearer's perception. When worn, it sharpens the user's senses, allowing them to notice subtle details and react more swiftly to threats. This increased perception grants an advantage in combat, helping the wearer anticipate enemy movements, detect hidden foes, and make more precise strikes. The Helm of Clarity is especially valued by tacticians and Warriors who rely on keen awareness to outmaneuver their opponents.	
Item Type:	Armor
Durability:	1500/1500
Defense:	+50
Item Quality:	Well-Crafted
Item Rarity:	Uncommon

Kevin selected the Pendant of Might and the Belt of Constitution.

Item: Pendant of Might	
The Pendant of Might is a powerful amulet imbued with the essence of strength. When worn, it increases the wearer's Strength attribute by +8, enhancing physical power and allowing for more formidable attacks and greater feats of endurance. This pendant is highly sought after by Warriors	

and Barbarians looking to gain an edge in battle, making it a prized possession for anyone looking to dominate their foes with raw power.	
Item Type:	Accessory
Durability:	250/250
Item Quality:	Well-Crafted
Item Rarity:	Uncommon

Item: Belt of Constitution	
The Belt of Constitution is a sturdy, enchanted accessory designed to bolster the wearer's vitality. When worn, it increases the wearer's Constitution attribute by +7, enhancing their overall endurance, resistance to damage, and ability to withstand harsh conditions. This belt is highly prized by adventurers who need to endure long battles and survive in hostile environments.	
Item Type:	Accessory
Durability:	200/200
Item Quality:	Well-Crafted
Item Rarity:	Uncommon

Finally, Tom stepped up. Placing his hand on the screen, he perused the items available and purchased the Charismatic Pendant and a Tome of Summon Familiar.

Item: Charismatic Pendant	
The Charismatic Pendant is an elegantly crafted amulet imbued with enchantments that enhance the wearer's natural charm and influence potential. When worn, it increases the wearer's Charisma attribute by +8, making them more persuasive, likable, and compelling in social interactions. This pendant is a prized accessory for leaders, diplomats, and merchants, while also offering boosts to powers utilized by Warlocks.	
Item Type:	Accessory
Durability:	500/500
Item Quality:	Well-Crafted
Item Rarity:	Uncommon

The tome fascinated Tom. He had always loved animals, and the idea of having a companion in this new world brought him a sense of comfort and excitement. He imagined himself running alongside a wolf or puma into battle, or playfully sparring with them during their downtime, finding joy in the companionship and the bond they would share.

Reading the instructions, Tom learned that the tome was a single-use item that would summon a familiar to bond with its user. Commanding the familiar was as simple as invoking the bond and giving it a direct order. Seeing no downside, Tom opened the book and recited the incantation inscribed within. Instinctively, he raised his hand, palm down, sensing that this was the correct action to take.

A symbol resembling a distorted ampersand within a circle and glowing with red light appeared on the ground beneath his hand. As he finished the incantation, the symbol flashed brightly, and the book snapped shut in his hands before disintegrating.

A beam of light erupted from the floor, shooting up to the ceiling and shining brightly for five seconds. Everyone shielded their eyes from the intense light. When it finally faded, a small creature stood in the circle. It looked like a bizarre fusion of an insect, a lizard, and a goblin. Long, antelope-like horns protruded straight up from its head, while pointed ears jutted out to either side. Its mouth was filled with needle-like teeth, spines lined its back, and a long, whip-like tail extended behind it. Its legs resembled a cross between a frog and a grasshopper, giving the creature a strange, unsettling appearance.

"What the fucking hell is that ugly piece of shit?""James asked.

Inspecting the creature, Tom groaned slightly at what he saw.

Quasit
The Quasit is a tiny demonic creature known for its ability to shapeshift into any creature of similar size. Typically, Quasits have an evil alignment, which gives them a distasteful and malicious disposition. However, through the power of the bond with your patron, this particular Quasit has been transitioned to a neutral alignment, tempering its naturally malevolent tendencies. Despite its small size, the Quasit remains a resourceful companion, capable of aiding in both reconnaissance and mischief.

HP:	20/20
MP:	300/300
SP:	150/150
Level:	1
Name:	No Name Given Yet

Skills:	Shapeshift, Stealth, Poison Immunity, Darkvision
XP:	0
XP to Next Level:	1000
Bonded to:	Tom Harris

"It's a… demon?" Tom questioned.

"What kind of demon?" Derek asked.

"There are *kinds* of demons?" Jay said.

"Sure, there are lots of kinds. Not as many small ones like this, but still some," Derek replied.

"It says it's a Quasit," Tom said. "And it looks like I need to name it."

"A Whatsit?" James frowned.

"Shut up!" everyone said simultaneously.

"Geeze, tough crowd." James pouted.

"Yes, name good," the creature said, staring up at Tom.

Everyone jumped back at once.

"Did that fucking thing just talk?" James said in a fast, hushed tone while he grabbed Tom by the shoulders and placed him between himself and the Quasit.

"Sure as shit did!" Jay replied, unable to take his eyes off the small being.

"Awe… it's kinda cute. If you can get past the needle teeth and sideways blinking eyes," Kiera said, though she too was hiding behind Tom.

The Quasit wagged its tail at being called cute.

"Yes, me cute! Like lady. Lady be friend?" the Quasit asked.

"Awww… how adorable," Kiera said, coming out from behind Tom and kneeling in front of the creature.

Moving closer to Kiera, the Quasit wrung its hands together nervously as it stared up at her.

"Don't worry, I won't hurt you, little guy. We can be friends. Here, would you like some jerky?" Kiera asked, reaching into her storage and pulling out a piece to hand to the creature.

Reaching out its head tentatively, it sniffed the jerky, then grabbed it out of Kiera's hands as it stepped back quickly to stay out of reach. It sniffed the meat some more, then licked it. Taking a big bite of the meat, it ran over to Kiera and began to snuggle up against her as it devoured the jerky.

"There, see, it's good, isn't it?" Kiera said as she patted the creature on the head behind its horns.

"I'll have to think of a name for it. For now, let's head back. We've been in this Dungeon for a long time," Tom said.

"Gnob Goblin," James suggested.

Jay nodded. "Dangle Demon."

Tom glared at the two as they continued their *helpful* dialogue.

Nodding in agreement, the others watched as Kiera scooped up the Quasit. With their new companion in tow, the party turned to leave the room. As they walked back down the hall, they eventually reached the spot where they had originally entered. Where there had been only a stone wall before, a door had reappeared, with the word "Dungeon" now visible on the placard above it.

Next to the door was a stone pedestal that had an angled, flat surface on top. Tom stopped and stared at it, feeling a tugging sensation coming from it.

"What is it, Tom?" Derek asked.

"Hold on. I need to do something," Tom said, reaching out his hand.

Touching the flat surface of the pedestal, a blue light shone from his hand. When the light winked out, there was an engraved image of Azroc on the pedestal, winking and giving a thumbs up.

"What the hell? Is that Azroc?" James asked.

"Yup. Had to place his symbol at the end of the Dungeon. Which is apparently just him giving a thumbs up," Tom said.

Quest Complete: Complete a Dungeon
You have completed a Dungeon and placed Azroc's mark at the end to show you do these tasks in his name.
Rewards: •   +500 XP •   1 Permanent Buff
Please choose one of the following as your reward: •   Attack Boost - Adds a 5% bonus to your attack power. •   Defense Boost - Adds a 5% bonus to your defense. •   Charisma Boost - Adds a 5% bonus to interactions requiring a Charisma check.

Not hesitating, Tom selected the Charisma Boost skill and closed out the quest prompt. As he did, Tom felt a stinging pain from his tattoo as it began to change, and noticed when he checked his Character Sheet that the bonus had indeed been added.

Leaving the Dungeon, the team headed straight for the front door and made their way toward their vehicle. However, before they could reach it, a window appeared in the sky once again, emerging from the obelisks that had been silent since the initial introduction to the Grand System.

The same androgynous alien as before stood on the screen and spoke to them again.

"People of Earth, I address you now to inform you of a new threat that has been detected. A fleet of space pirates has been identified, and it appears they have plotted a course directly toward your planet. Their estimated time of arrival is approximately one year. Although we have dispatched military fleets to

intercept them, the pirates have a significant head start. As a result, they will likely reach you about a week before our forces can arrive," the voice said.

"You are advised to train and level up as much as possible to prepare for this impending threat. The pirates will be intent on plundering your planet's resources and valuables. We urge you to stand strong and defend yourselves until our forces can arrive to assist. We hope you can stand against them until backup arrives."

With that, the screen disappeared, and a cacophony of sound could be heard across the city as people began to panic.

Chapter 21

Reality

To say the drive back to the Guild building was awkward and silent would be an understatement. The only noise in the vehicle was the noise of the Quasit munching on more jerky. Everyone else simply sat in silence and thought about what this newest announcement meant. The Quasit had been happy in Kiera's arms until she had stopped petting it. Now it moved up to the shoulder of the driver's seat to be near Tom.

"You sure do like that jerky. Maybe that's what I should name you. Jerky," Tom said, both trying to look at the Quasit and keep his eyes on the road to avoid stalled cars and bodies.

"Jer-ky," The Quasit said, testing the name. "Yes, Jerky. Me like."

"Alright, then, Jerky it is," Tom said, reaching up to pat the Quasit on the head and scratch it behind the ears. He wasn't sure why he did that, but it's what people did with pets. Besides, he didn't know what else to do and Jerky seemed to enjoy it.

Arriving at the Center a short while later, the team piled out of the car and raced to the conference room that had become a sort of base of operations in the building. Brian was already waiting for them.

"Well, this is a fucking delightful surprise now, isn't it?" Brian asked. "We've been in the apocalypse for two goddamned days and now we have to worry about our planet being invaded by… space pirates!"

"Yeah, not exactly ideal. But maybe we can find a way to protect ourselves. We have a whole year, and look at what we've accomplished so far," Tom said.

"These are a species of beings that can travel the galaxy and invade planets to plunder them. What hope can we possibly have of fighting them off?" Brian asked.

"I'm not sure yet, but a couple of days ago I wouldn't have thought about fighting off a mugger with a gun, and today I led a team into an actual Dungeon where we killed magical suits of armor and a fucking blood mage," Tom replied. "I feel a strong sense that we need to give this a try and see if we can make weapons and defenses that can take them on. We can use magic now, for fuck's sake!"

Brian paused at Tom's words, absorbing the realization that their world had fundamentally changed. They were no longer bound by the limitations of the old world and now had access to a form of technology that had once seemed impossible. With this new reality, there might just be ways to figure out how to defend themselves.

"Okay. I'm willing to give it a shot, but there are a few people I need you to meet," Brian said.

"Great, let's do it," Tom said.

Brian led the group out of the conference room and down the hall to a small set of offices. Inside the office area was another small conference room with a group of people sitting inside and talking amongst themselves. Bursting into the conference room, Brian stared at everyone, disturbing the meeting, and causing all eyes to turn in his direction.

"Hello, all. I have some people that you all need to meet," Brian began. "This is Tom. He is the leader of the Guild."

The people at the table either nodded or waved.

"Tom, these are the people I think will be most beneficial in our Guild if we accept them," Brian said.

"Now hold on a moment. Who said we wanted to join a Guild?" an older gentleman sitting at the head of the table asked.

"This is the man that saved your lives and has been repelling the goblins outside the building, along with supplying our security force with items and information about this blasted system that we are all interfacing with now," Brian said, looking at the man. "Besides, there are too many benefits from being in a Guild for you not to want to join."

"And who is this?" Tom asked.

"This is Harold. He's an engineer. Worked with large-scale machines for factories," Brian said, gesturing toward Harold.

"It's a pleasure to meet you, Harold," Tom said, nodding to the man.

"Well, I for one would be happy to join the Guild," a woman said, sitting to Harold's right.

"This is Charlene. She was the head chef at Dakota's Steakhouse here in Dallas," Brian said.

"Chef, you say," Tom said, now very interested.

"Indeed. I figured I could offer my assistance here in getting things running for the people of the Guild. There is a kitchen with a full cafeteria here, so we wouldn't need to work too hard to get something up and running to keep people fed. Provided you are willing to keep us defended," Charlene said.

"Can you cook a wolf?" James interrupted.

"I can cook anything," Clarlene challenged.

"Yeah, dumbass," Jay slapped James on the arm. "She can cook anything with nipples."

"*Charlene,*" Tom interrupted the two, "you would be a welcome addition to the team. If there is ever anything that you need, you can always come ask and we will do whatever we can to make it happen," Tom said.

"Thank you, Tom. I will definitely keep that in mind. I'm glad to add my skills to the cause," Charlene replied.

The others in the room were introduced to Tom and his team one by one. Jim, a pawnbroker; Paul, an architect; Steve, a tailor; Andrea, who grew up on a farm where her family had supplied vegetables to a grocery store chain; Rebecca, a doctor; and Mark, a mechanic.

"Wow, if we could find a plumber and an electrician we would be set," Tom commented.

"That is on my list of people I'm searching for. I'm sure we will eventually come across someone. Or rather, I hope so, and I assume you will help bring more people in," Brian said.

Next, Tom introduced his whole team. Jerky hopped up onto the table and introduced himself, much to the chagrin of everyone at the table.

"Me, Jerky," Jerky said, bowing slightly on the table.

"What the fuck is that thing?" Mark asked.

"Jerky? He's my Familiar," Tom said. "He's a Quasit."

"He's ugly as sin is what he is," Mark said, still shying away from the little creature.

Jerky looked at him, then shapeshifted into the form of a puppy sitting on the table.

"What the damn hell?!" Harold cried from the head of the table.

"This better? Not ugly?" Jerky said.

"It can fucking change shape?" Mark asked.

"Yup. And become invisible, apparently," Tom said.

Just as he said that, Jerky became completely invisible. Several people at the table stood up, backing away while the others rolled their chairs back as far as they would go. Jerky reappeared a few seconds later, still in puppy form, sitting on the table wagging his tail, tongue lolling out of his mouth with a grin on his face.

"That just ain't right," Mark said.

"Look, can we get back to the topic at hand?" Brian asked.

"This thing doesn't upset you?" Mark asked.

"I mean, it doesn't exactly give me the warm fuzzies, but after watching Tom and his crew run over goblins like he was trying out for the college bowling team, it's pretty far down on my list of disturbing things for the day," Brian responded. "Besides, Tom said it was his Familiar. I trust Tom. With my life."

Jerky picked this moment to lift his leg and begin licking himself on the table for everyone to see. Everyone watched for a moment, too stunned to say anything.

"Dude, Jerky," Tom said. "Come on man, not here in front of everybody."

Jerky looked up to see everyone staring, his tongue still halfway out of his mouth as he was about to go in for another lick. Smiling, he lowered his leg and hopped off the table to sit at Tom's feet.

"Anyways, as I was saying. We would like to ask you to join the Guild. In exchange for your services, we will provide you with protection, opportunities to level up, and any items that you need that we can acquire," Brian said, panning across the room. "Each of you has a unique skill set that will come in handy in this new world, and banding together will only make us stronger. Money no longer means anything as the economy will have completely crashed. The only thing that matters now is trying to survive and doing what we can to prepare for this new attack we've been warned about."

Everyone in the room sat quietly, deep in thought. Tom understood their hesitation; they were being asked to completely shift their mindset in just two days. They used to work for money, which bought them the things they wanted or needed. Now, they faced the challenge of simply surviving long enough to find a new sense of normalcy. The satisfaction of earning a living had been ripped away in an instant, replaced by the harsh reality that money was now worthless in this new world.

On top of all that, they were now responsible for an infrastructure that required them to manage others who would join in helping with the projects that could ensure their survival or bring about their downfall. It was a worrisome prospect, and they weren't given much of a choice in the matter.

"What if we say no?" Harold asked.

"Then we will be happy to say adieu to you and let you go on your merry way out in the world to wherever you would like," Brian replied.

"So, you are saying that we either help you or we fuck off?" Harold asked.

"I'm saying if you help us, we will spend our resources to help you in return. If you do not want to help us, we cannot afford to spend our resources to help you in return, so in an effort to maximize our resources we will absolutely show you the door," Brian said with a smile on his face.

Tom was immediately happy in that moment that he'd found Brian. He was worth more than his weight in gold… well, Monster Cores, now.

"That doesn't seem very fair," Harold replied.

"What isn't *fair*, sir, is that you intend to keep sitting around here without contributing and expect us to feed you, house you, clothe you, check on your health, and put our lives on the line to ensure you stay safe without offering us anything in return for our trouble," Brian said, the smile leaving his face. "I'm sorry that we cannot afford to just hand out free goodies to anyone who needs them, but we will not be running a charity in this current state of affairs. We are still not one hundred percent sure how we are going to continue to survive, but we are doing our damnedest to find a solution to every problem that comes up, and if you do not want to be a part of that solution, then we need to drop your deadweight. One thing we *are* sure of is that there will be an economy, and that economy will center around Monster Cores. If *you* want to be paid in Monster Cores for your contribution to our efforts, so that you can eat and have a place to sleep, I suggest you get with the program." He pointed toward the door. "Otherwise, you can get your ass out there and get Monster Cores the *hard* way."

Harold's eyes were wide after this rant. He really seemed to have not considered the bigger picture. As though he was only thinking about his current predicament and not the fact that there were other things involved in making sure that they had the best chance of surviving.

Everyone around the table was silent. Deep in thought. Finally, Jim spoke up.

"How do I fit into this plan?" Jim asked.

"You, sir, have experience in trading. You know how much things are worth and how to get a deal on them. Eventually, this world is going to consist of Guilds because it's the only obvious solution to banding together. We will need to trade with those Guilds, and you will be a vital part of that process," Brian replied.

"We also found that the Dungeon vending machines have rations that might be a viable option for food and likely trade," Tom added.

"Then I'm in. I'll do whatever I can to help," Jim said.

"The same goes for me," Rebecca said. "I've already been helping to treat people, may as well continue."

One by one, everyone else in the room agreed until it was only Harold left. He didn't appear to even be paying attention, simply taking in all the information about the situation they were truly in.

"Harold?" Tom asked, watching as he jumped slightly at being called out. He softened his voice, "I know what you're going through. This is all a shock, and you weren't ready for it. But you have to know that it *did* happen. This is all real, and we are stuck in this situation. It doesn't have to be the end though. We can build something great here and take care of each other if we work together. And you have my word I will step up to help you with anything you need. All we ask is for your expertise as well."

Tears began to fall down Harold's face as he looked up at Tom.

"My wife… My wife, Susan, was killed while we were trying to get here. I couldn't stop it. I tried to get to her, but the crowds pushed me back. By the time I could get through…" he trailed off.

Tom knelt in front of Harold and put a hand on his shoulder.

"I'm so sorry, Harold. I saw some terrible things happen as well. Children cut down right in front of my eyes. Men and women slaughtered. I don't want to see that happen to anyone else," Tom said. "The only way we can stop that is if we work together."

Harold began to weep openly now. "I had thought this couldn't be real. This couldn't actually be happening. We had been married for twenty-eight years. I loved her so much. I was just going to wake up and this would all be a bad dream," Harold continued through his sobs.

More people began to tear up thinking of the devastation that had happened or the loved ones they had lost. The reality of what they faced sank in harder than they had expected.

"You have to grieve, Harold. You cannot just bear the weight of this and continue on, or it will break you. Take the time you need to grieve. We will help you until then. Brian will check in with you in a day or two to see how you are doing and we can decide where we go from there," Tom said.

Harold nodded, placing his head in his hands, continuing to cry. Standing up, Tom turned to Brian.

"Let me know what he says in a day or two. It won't hurt us to wait just a bit longer," Tom said.

APOCALYPSE

Brian nodded and the party left the conference room, hearts heavy with the burden of the new reality they faced.

Chapter 22

Chicks and Hot Rods

The following day, Tom woke up earlier than most of the others and left to go to the cafeteria. Charlene was hard at work, already training some of the other survivors in the kitchen area. Grabbing a cup of coffee, he headed over to one of the tables and sat down. As he thought about what had happened over the past few days, he decided to check in on his character sheet. He had taken to looking at it before he went to bed each night but still felt like he had been neglecting the strategy aspect of how he should be developing himself.

Tom Harris	
Race: Human	**Class:** Warlock
Level: 12	**Total XP:** 74,650
XP To Next Level: 12,850	**HP:** 200/200
MP: 250/250	**SP:** 250/250
Attributes:	**Unused Attributes Points:** 0
Strength: 25	**Constitution:** 20
Dexterity: 20	**Endurance:** 25
Intelligence: 25	**Wisdom:** 20
Charisma: 35	**Luck:** 20
Non-Combat Skills:	
Inspect	**Level: 2 Rank:** Beginner
Combat Skills:	
Vehicular Homicide	**Level: 6 Rank:** Beginner
Swords	**Level: 4 Rank:** Beginner

APOCALYPSE

Summon Demonic Creature	**Level:** 1 **Rank:** Beginner
Fear	**Level:** 1 **Rank:** Beginner
Corruption	**Level:** 1 **Rank:** Beginner
Spells:	
Eldritch Blast	**Level:** 1 **Rank:** Beginner
Dark Ball	**Level:** 1 **Rank:** Beginner
Dark Healing	**Level:** 1 **Rank:** Beginner
Lightning Strike	**Level:** 3 **Rank:** Beginner
Doppelganger	**Level:** 1 **Rank:** Beginner
Dark Flame Weapon	**Level:** 1 **Rank:** Beginner
Tattoos:	Tattoo of Brute Strength

Jerky hopped up onto the table and sat down to watch Tom as he was thinking. Looking at the Quasit, he suddenly realized he had been completely forgetting to use his spell to summon creatures as well. Deciding that now was as good a time as any, he sat his coffee down, turned around, and began to cast *Summon Demonic Creature.*

Dark purple lights engulfed his hands as he began to pronounce guttural words that felt wrong in his mouth. His vision turned red for a second, then a portal opened on the ground, and a small creature hopped out of it.

Appearing to have bird-like legs, a pointed head with rows of teeth, a pink tongue lolling out of its mouth, drool dripping onto the ground, and its body resembling an upside-down Dorito chip, this creature was a strange and unsettling sight.

"What the actual fuck is that thing?" Tom wondered aloud, feeling very uneasy at seeing it. He Inspected it to get a better idea of what he was dealing with.

Abyssal Chicken
The Abyssal Chicken is one of the most diminutive demons from the abyssal plane, but don't let its size deceive you. This tiny, malevolent creature is extremely aggressive, attacking almost anything that crosses its path. Armed with unnaturally sharp teeth and claws, the Abyssal Chicken is an ironically fierce fighter, capable of inflicting significant damage despite its small stature. In addition to its combat capabilities, the Abyssal Chicken can fly/glide short distances using its distinct wing flaps. This allows it to close the gap between

itself and the enemy quickly. Although not the most powerful of the demon creatures, its usage cannot be discounted.

HP:	10/10
MP:	0/0
SP:	100/100
Level:	5
Attack:	Bite, Claw

"Wing flaps? I don't see any wing flaps."

Just as Tom said this aloud, the Abyssal Chicken let out a terrifying squawk, its sound unnervingly deep—an octave lower than that of a normal chicken. The pointed part of its body began to peel apart from the top, revealing grotesque wing flaps that it excitedly lifted up and down, looking a bit like a pair of leather pants flapping the legs. The creature's disturbing display only added to its unnerving presence.

"Buk-buk-buk BAGAAAAAAAAWK!" the Abyssal Chicken screamed and then took off around the cafeteria.

Tom watched in horror as the creature began chasing people around, trying to bite or scratch them. It became even more fearsome when it leaped onto a table and then jumped into the air, flapping its horrifying skin flaps with all its might, trying to stay aloft. It was hard to call what it was doing actual flight. It was more like falling… without style. And unfortunately, it's awkward—whatever mode of transportation that was—had it heading straight for the kitchen.

Tom jumped up to try to stop the demon's movement but couldn't get close enough before it sailed through the service window into the preparation area. Screams erupted from the back as people tried to get away from it. Dishes crashed to the floor and broke, pans made loud clanging noises as they were tossed to the ground. It ran across the counters and the stoves, appearing unaffected by the fires as it chased people around the room.

"No, no, no, no, no, STOP!" Tom yelled, and surprisingly, the horrifying chicken seemed to hear him and turned to look at him. It cocked its head to one side in confusion.

"SIT!" Tom yelled at the obscene creature, and in another shocking move, it obeyed, squatting down. Right on a stove fire that burned beneath it.

Charlene and two other women were backed into a corner where the demon was working to keep them corralled, leaning against the counter with Charlene's arms out protectively across the other two. They stared at Tom with wide horrified eyes, breathing heavily.

"Come!" Tom called to the beast. Again, it obeyed, hopping off the counter and walking over to the door to leave.

175

Once it was back out in the cafeteria area, it looked up at Tom expectantly. For the first time, Tom noticed it didn't have any eyes to look at him with. Wondering for a moment how it could see, he recovered quickly and pointed toward the hall.

"Go, we need to move out of here. You've caused enough trouble, you little shit," Tom said.

Finally getting up enough courage, Charlene called to him. "Is that… thing yours?" she said, still clearly shaken.

"Ummm… Yes. It's a spell I have, to summon a creature," Tom said, not wanting to use the word demon right now. "Sorry about that. I didn't know what was going to happen and didn't think it would go ballistic. Jerky here was so calm when I summoned him, I didn't stop to think about what might happen."

Relief swept over Charlene as she put her hand over her chest and closed her eyes, breathing out a huge sigh. "Oh, thank God. I was sure we were about to die there. Please, just don't summon any more creatures in the cafeteria or kitchen. It's probably not sanitary, anyway."

"Yes, ma'am. I will *not* be doing that again," Tom replied.

"Good, because if you do, I'm making you the same kind of food they give Russian prisoners for a month," Charlene said, clearly meaning business.

Tom chuckled for a moment, but that died when he noticed Charlene was not laughing with him.

"Oh shit, you're serious. Yes, ma'am, I swear it will never happen again," Tom said.

Charlene nodded sharply then went back into the kitchen area to continue prepping and clean up the new mess she had.

Tom turned around to see where the Abyssal Chicken had gone and didn't see it. Then he heard a yell from the hallway.

"Fuck!" Tom yelled and raced out into the hall. There he saw a man backed into a corner at the end of the hall and the chicken looking at him with drool dripping from his mouth. It hissed at the man, who had fallen to the ground and was trying to protect his face with his arms and hands.

"Get back here, you little monster!" Tom yelled at it.

The creature turned to him, seeming somehow disappointed, and walked back to Tom. The man rolled to his knees and crawled away as fast as he could down the turn in the hall. Tom glared at the creature in anger with his arms crossed. Seeming oblivious to his fuming, the chicken just stared up at him and waited.

Facepalming, Tom motioned to the chicken. "Come on, let's just go to the parking garage where you likely can't scare anyone else."

With that, they made their way out of the building. Once in the parking garage, Tom decided to inspect the Tahoe as well to see what progress it had made.

Item: Chevy Tahoe
The Chevy Tahoe is a full-size SUV known for its rugged durability, spacious interior, and powerful performance. Designed to handle both on-road and off-road conditions, the Tahoe is equipped with a V8 engine, providing extra horsepower and torque for towing, hauling, and navigating challenging terrains. The Tahoe features a variable seating arrangement with room for up to eight passengers, making it ideal for families, large groups, or those needing extra cargo space. Its advanced suspension system ensures a smooth ride. With its combination of power, comfort, and reliability, the Chevy Tahoe is a popular choice for those seeking a capable SUV that can handle a wide range of driving conditions, from city streets to rugged trails.

Name:	Goblin Slayer 2.0
Item Type:	Vehicle, Weapon - Upgradeable
Durability:	115,687/120,000
Attack:	45-78
Item Quality:	Well-Crafted
Item Rarity:	Rare
Upgradeable:	Yes
Item Level:	8
Item XP:	29,450
XP to Next Level:	6,550
Item Skill: Upgraded Armor	
This skill allows for upgrading the armor on the vehicle as it levels.	

"Awesome! It's already better than it was before," Tom said to the chicken and Jerky.

Noticing that there was another tab at the top of the screen, Tom selected upgrades and found that there was a long list of options that could be added to the vehicle. Scrolling through the list, there were some items that were greyed out and showed they needed other requirements first, but the list was so long that Tom was really getting excited about upgrading the vehicle.

APOCALYPSE

<table>
<tr><td colspan="1" align="center">**Goblin Slayer 2.0 Upgrades**</td></tr>
<tr><td align="center">Available Upgrades: 2</td></tr>
</table>

Please select from the following options to upgrade your Chevy Tahoe:

- Reinforced brush guard
- Lift kit (height in inches):
    - 1 in.
    - 2 in. *must purchase 1 in.
    - 3 in. *must purchase 2 in.
    - 4 in. *must purchase 3 in.
    - 5 in. *must purchase 4 in.
    - 6 in. *must purchase 5 in.
- Increase tire size (one upgrade point per in.)
- Bumper upgrades:
    - Front bumper spikes
    - Increased cattle guard size
    - Reinforced rear bumper
    - Oil slick dispenser
    - Smoke screen deployment
- HID headlights
- Light bar upgrade
- Roll cage
- Armor:
    - Reinforced driver door
        - Armor-plated driver door *must purchase reinforced driver door
    - Reinforced driver rear door
        - Armor-plated rear driver door *must purchase reinforced rear driver door
    - Reinforced passenger door
        - Armor-plated passenger door *must purchase reinforced passenger door
    - Reinforced rear passenger door
        - Armor-plated rear passenger door *must purchase reinforced rear passenger door
    - Reinforced tailgate
        - Armor-plated tailgate *must purchase reinforced tailgate
    - Reinforced front end
        - Armor-plated front end *must purchase reinforced front end
- Glass:
    - Bulletproof glass windshield
    - Bulletproof glass driver window
    - Bulletproof glass passenger window

<table>
<tr><td>○</td><td>Bulletproof glass driver rear window</td></tr>
<tr><td>○</td><td>Bulletproof glass passenger rear window</td></tr>
<tr><td>○</td><td>Bulletproof glass driver third-row window</td></tr>
<tr><td>○</td><td>Bulletproof glass passenger third-row window</td></tr>
<tr><td>○</td><td>Bulletproof glass tailgate window</td></tr>
<tr><td>○</td><td>Bulletproof glass sunroof</td></tr>
</table>

- Roof-mounted Gatling gun *must purchase full armor plating *must purchase full bulletproof windows
- Performance exhaust
- …

The list went on and on and on for options to upgrade the GS2. Scrolling through the options, Tom began to feel overwhelmed. He did, however, notice a few items that would make his current use of the vehicle better. He selected the reinforced brush guard and the front bumper spikes.

The bumper glowed and large conical spikes began to appear out of the metal of the cattle guard until they protruded about eight inches. The underside of the vehicle also began to glow as metal formed over the undercarriage, creating a protective cover to ensure that nothing could get stuck in the components below.

Wanting to take it out right then, Tom grabbed the handle to open the door but realized it would be bad to go out alone, remembering the ogre encounters. Shoulders slumping, Tom turned back to look at his summons. Jerky was now riding the Abyssal Chicken as it tried to buck him off like some kind of demonic rodeo.

Staring at the sight far longer than he thought he should have, Tom finally spoke to the pair, "Can you two please stop? We need to figure out what this nightmare poultry is capable of."

A thought occurred to Tom as he was looking at the knee-high monstrosity. Tom began chanting again and cast *Summon Demonic Creature*. As he finished casting, another Abyssal Chicken exited the portal on the floor.

"Ooooooohhh… This could be fun," Tom said, remembering a video game in which villagers highly advised the hero not to attack the chickens.

This meant that he could summon five chickens right off the bat. Then waiting for his mana to regenerate, he could summon more. He took out his phone and watched his mana, timing how long it took to return one point. It took about two point seven seconds to return one point of mana. Tom did some math and found it would take him a little over eleven and a half minutes to get all his mana back. That meant he could summon five sets of five chickens before the first ones would disappear, giving him roughly twenty-five chickens at any given time if he wanted to focus fully on his summons.

The thought of twenty-five of these monsters descending on his enemies went through his mind and he chuckled at the idea. With that fun thought in mind,

APOCALYPSE

Tom cast *Summon Demonic Creature* once more. This time, however, the portal that appeared was larger than the one that had let out the Abyssal Chickens.

A single green hand with black claws reached out of the portal as the creature began to drag itself out. As its head poked out, a grotesquely disfigured face that looked like a cross between a mole and a dog showed, with long pointed ears that stuck straight out to the sides. It had teeth similar to a dog, but its body was shaped more like a bear. The creature sat down on its haunches and waited expectantly for Tom to do or say something.

"I'm really not sure about this skill anymore. These are some fugly-ass creatures that it keeps sending. And it's not even consistent. How am I supposed to have a chicken army if it gives me this…"Tom said, pausing at the end and realizing he needed to Inspect the creature.

Dretch
The Dretch is a lowly and wretched demon from the Abyss, often considered one of the weaker forms of demonic entities. Despite their limited intelligence and pitiful status among demons, Dretches are dangerous in large numbers. They are squat, misshapen creatures with a bloated, fat body covered in pustules and coarse hair. Their limbs are short but powerful, ending in sharp claws that they use to tear at their enemies.

Dretches are known for their foul stench, which can sicken those who come too close. While they lack the cunning of more powerful demons, they make up for it with a relentless, animalistic ferocity. These creatures are often summoned in hordes to overwhelm foes, using sheer numbers to drag down even the most formidable opponents. In combat, Dretches are driven by fear and instinct, attacking anything in their path with mindless aggression.	
HP:	50/50
MP:	0/0
SP:	150/150
Level:	5
Attacks:	Bite, Claw, Abyssal Fart Cloud

Abyssal Fart Cloud:
Dretches can release a noxious gas cloud from their anus that extends out for 10 ft. in all directions. This gas is poisonous.

"Are you kidding me? The System gave me what is essentially my grandpa after taco night at the nursing home?" Tom asked.

"I didn't think your grandpa would be that ugly," a voice came from behind Tom, and he turned to see Brian walking up to him.

"You never met my grandpa," Tom laughed. "But what brings you down here?"

"We have a message from another Guild in the area, and they're asking to meet with you. I think we should go and try to be as kind as possible. We could use allies right now," Brian replied.

"Okay. Let's go meet them. I'm sure we can find a way to get along," Tom said.

Chapter 23

Rivals Turned Friends

Walking back through the building with two Abyssal Chickens, one Dretch, and a Quasit was quite the entourage for all the survivors to see. Along the way through the building, Tom was joined by his party members, who were curious about the situation as well.

"So where are we meeting the other Guild, Brian?" Tom asked.

"We are to meet outside the building across the street. There was a cafe there before all this apocalypse shit happened," Brian replied.

"Anything else we know about them?" Derek asked.

"I get the distinct feeling that the leader of the Guild didn't want to meet with us but that some of their people were pushing for it. So I would advise to hear them out, consider what they have to say, and be as cordial as possible," Brian said, looking back suddenly at the demons. "Is there any way to not have your new friends with us? Monsters being the big issue with this new world we find ourselves in and all."

Stopping mid-stride, Tom looked back at them. He hadn't considered if he could dismiss them. He thought about the skill, which didn't give him any new information. So he just looked at them and spoke.

"You are dismissed. Return to where you came from."

With that, portals opened on the ground and the creatures went back inside.

"Apparently, I can," Tom said.

"Excellent! And the other little friend?" Brian gestured to Jerky.

"Oh, no, he's here all the time. Can't send him away, but he can turn himself invisible. Jerky, I need you to stay invisible while we talk to this other group of people, okay?" Tom said, looking down at the Quasit.

"Jerky invisible. Okay!" Jerky said happily and then vanished from sight.

Tom felt the Quasit climb up and sit on his shoulder, so at least he knew where he was.

"Where did he go?" Brian asked.

"He's here on my shoulder. Shouldn't be a problem. He's much more agreeable than the other summons," Tom replied.

"Alright," Brian said, still a bit apprehensive. "I guess we should get moving, then."

They continued out to the front of the building, where there were security guards posted twenty-four hours a day. Saluting as the team passed, Tom felt guilty at not remembering their names. Walking across the street, there was a man sitting at one of the tables wearing camo pants, a vest with so many pockets filled with stuff that Tom was sure it weighed at least ten pounds, and a white t-shirt with a cowboy hat. Even in Texas, this getup was weird. Not the hat, but the rest of it.

Standing up as they approached, the man stared intently at Tom. Tom, for his part, extended his hand to shake. The other man just stared down at it and then back up at Tom.

"Hello, I'm Tom of the Guild Vanguard. It's nice to meet you," Tom said, still awkwardly holding his hand out.

Squinting at Tom, and still not shaking his hand, the man continued to eye Tom down until he finally spoke.

"Name's Joe," the man said in a low, almost raspy sort of voice.

"Well, Joe, how can we help you today? I heard you wanted to meet with us," Tom said.

Again, there was a long pause. Joe took a toothpick from his pocket and put it in the corner of his mouth as he continued to stare at Tom with a look that showed he did not want to be there.

"I really didn't. It's some of the people in my Guild that wanted me to reach out. I knew this goddamned day would come, but no one wanted to listen to old Joe," Joe said.

"What do you mean you knew this day would come? You knew aliens would invade and turn our lives into a video game?" James asked.

"No, dumbass. I knew that the apocalypse was coming, and I was prepared. That's why they follow me," Joe replied.

"Oh, so you're one of those preppers," Tom said.

"I am. And it has served me well so far. I was *ready* while most others were caught with their pants down. I have food, shelter, guns, ammo, and a whole lot more to live on. Some of them laughed at me for what I did. But I'm the one laughing now," Joe said, staring even harder at Tom. "What about you? Were you ready, boy?"

"Well, not like that, no. But we managed to adapt pretty well so far," Tom replied.

"Ah, so you were one of those non-believer sissies. Well, that's too bad. But I'm here because my friends think we could benefit from an alliance. I think you got too many people to look after and it's gonna drag you down. I only formed my Guild with enough to get the basic benefits from the System. You got so many people you're gonna constantly run out of resources. You'll see," Joe said, derision clear in his voice.

Tom really wanted to give this guy a piece of his mind about how he treated people. Then he remembered what Brian had said and tried to push down his feelings.

"So, what is it you're hoping to gain from this meeting?" Tom asked.

"An alliance of sorts. I'd hope that if either of us was in trouble we could rely on each other for a little backup," Joe said.

"I don't see why not. We do want to try to help people out. If you need us, we will be happy to help."

APOCALYPSE

"Good, good, that's great," Joe said in a way that immediately made Tom uneasy.

"Because, you see, we got this little problem with some monsters around our building and we'd really like to get a little help in getting rid of them," Joe said.

"Ah, I see," Tom said, feeling like he was getting more of the truth behind their meeting than before. "What kind of monster problem?"

"Some kind of flying lizard. Been a real nuisance to us over the past day as they began to swoop in to attack as we tried to leave the building," Joe explained.

"And you can't just shoot it down?" Tom asked.

"We have been. But we can't seem to get them under control. There are too many and they're pretty fast. With more bodies, we could clear them out better. I notice you don't have any monsters roaming around here anymore," Joe said.

"No, we have been out daily killing as many creatures as we can find, going further and further out to try to keep a safe perimeter. So far, it appears to be working," Tom said.

"We are trying to do the same, but there aren't enough of us," Joe said, a bit exasperated.

"Why don't you join up with us, then? We could use someone who was prepared for an apocalypse to help us out here," Tom offered.

"Too many people. That's the problem, boy, you won't be able to extend your resources to so many people," Joe replied. "I can't risk running out of supplies since this is the new way of life."

"But you also can't replenish your supplies on your own," Tom said.

"That's where you're wrong. But I don't want to go down that path, giving away all my secrets," Joe retorted.

"Fine, whatever. Keep your secrets. We will see if we can help," Tom agreed reluctantly.

"'Preciate it, boy. And if we can return the favor later, just let us know," Joe said in return.

"It would be nice to just join Guilds together, but if that isn't an option, I guess I'll have Brian keep you on the list of people to call if shit hits the fan," Tom said.

"Boy, we are already standing in a brown-splattered room with human-shaped silhouettes from where the shit flinging at the fan hit us. All we are doing now is trying to clean the walls off with a single square of toilet paper," Joe replied.

"Well, that was very... descriptive," Tom replied.

"And it's only gonna get worse, mark my words," Joe said.

"Yeah, we know... the space pirates and all. That's why I want us to work together," Tom said, feeling like he was beginning to talk to someone only willing to listen to themselves.

"Space pirates are the least of your concerns," Joe said. "You need to be worried about the *people* who are going to get desperate enough to try to kill you for what you have."

"Space pirates are definitely the biggest part of my worry. I know how to handle things here on earth. It's beings who can travel across entire galaxies and will come here with weapons likely far behind our capabilities that worry me most," Tom replied.

Joe paused as if thinking about this fact for the first time. He stayed quiet for a long moment before he spoke.

"Still don't think that I can join up with you. I have a stockpile specifically rationed out for the number of people I have with me," Joe replied.

"We are working on growing our own crops as we speak and have professionals looking into most other options as well. If you, as a survivalist, joined us, then we would be that much better for it. I'm not asking you to share your goods, just your knowledge," Tom countered.

"So, if I join you, I get to keep all my goods?" Joe asked.

"Certainly. And we can even help you out if you need something," Tom said. "You may find that being part of the larger group has its own benefits."

Joe stared at Tom, trying to decide if he was telling the truth or not.

"Help me with the lizard problem, and you got yourself a deal. I was gettin' tired of havin' to make all the decisions, anyhow," Joe replied. "But I get to keep all my items. Better not be hearin' you go back on your word a few days down the road."

"We've never made anyone give up any items. In fact, we tend to hand down our old items when we get new ones. You might end up with new gear," Tom said, feeling a sense of relief come over him that he wasn't going to have to continue dealing with this man as an opponent.

"Well, alright then. Let's get going so we can bring everything over," Joe said.

Tom and his party followed Joe back to his base while Brian went back to the Center. They arrived a few blocks away at a small diner that Joe had apparently claimed as their Guild building. To say that they had a little lizard problem was an understatement. There were hundreds of the little things.

Small reptiles looking like anoles, but ten times bigger with wings on their backs, nearly covered the building. As the team approached, all their eyes went straight to them. Freezing on the spot, the party didn't move any closer as they waited to see what the lizards would do. Tom Inspected one of them.

<table>
<tr><td align="center">Sky Scale</td></tr>
<tr><td>The Sky Scale is a species of small, agile flying lizards known for their tendency to congregate in large numbers. These creatures are covered in iridescent scales that shimmer in the sunlight, making them both beautiful and dangerous. Despite their small size, Sky Scales can be formidable when attacking in swarms, using their sharp claws and teeth to overwhelm larger foes.</td></tr>
</table>

APOCALYPSE

<table>
<tr><td colspan="2">Sky Scales are highly social creatures, rarely seen alone, and often travel in flocks that move in synchronized patterns through the sky. Their presence is usually heralded by the sound of rustling wings and high-pitched screeches. Although they prefer to avoid conflict, when threatened or provoked, they can become a terrifying force of nature, descending en masse to protect their territory or drive away intruders. Their coordinated attacks and sheer numbers make them a threat that should not be underestimated.</td></tr>
<tr><td>HP:</td><td>5/5</td></tr>
<tr><td>MP:</td><td>0/0</td></tr>
<tr><td>SP:</td><td>100/100</td></tr>
<tr><td>Level:</td><td>3</td></tr>
<tr><td>Attack:</td><td>Bite, Claw</td></tr>
</table>

"They appear to be really weak, but there are so many of them that it's going to be a bit of a problem," Tom said.

"Does anyone have any big AOE spells?" Derek asked.

"Big what?" Joe asked.

"AOE, it means area of effect. It's a spell that targets a specific area instead of just one specific enemy," Derek explained.

"Oh, well then, no, I ain't got nothin' like that," Joe replied.

"That's alright. Anyone else?" Derek asked.

Everyone stopped to look at their skills. Tom checked on his spells as well.

<table>
<tr><td colspan="2" align="center">Eldritch Blast</td></tr>
<tr><td colspan="2">Eldritch Blast is a spell that allows the caster to summon and hurl a green fireball of Eldritch energy at their target. When invoked, the Warlock channels arcane power into a swirling sphere of green flame, which is then launched with a forceful blast toward the enemy. Upon impact, the fireball explodes, dealing significant force damage infused with the chaotic energy of the Eldritch planes.

The green flames of this Eldritch Blast are not only visually striking but also burn with an unnatural heat, searing the target with both physical and mystical energy. As the Warlock's mastery over this spell increases, the intensity and size of the fireball will be enhanced, allowing for multiple blasts and increased destructive power.</td></tr>
<tr><td>Cost:</td><td>20 MP</td></tr>
<tr><td>Damage:</td><td>15-22 Damage</td></tr>
<tr><td>Cast Time:</td><td>2 Seconds</td></tr>
</table>

Cooldown:	N/A

Dark Ball

Dark Ball is a malevolent spell that conjures a sphere of pure darkness, infused with destructive shadow energy. When cast, the caster hurls a ball of concentrated shadow at a target, which explodes upon impact, dealing dark damage. The dark energy within the ball corrupts whatever it touches, draining the life force of the target and leaving a lingering aura of dread.

As the caster's proficiency with Dark Ball increases, the potency of the spell intensifies, allowing for greater damage and a wider area of effect. The spell is particularly effective against light-based creatures or enemies susceptible to dark magic, making it a favored tool in the arsenal of those who walk the path of shadows.

Cost:	20 MP
Damage:	18-24 Damage
Casting Time:	2 Seconds
Cooldown:	N/A

Dark Healing

Dark Healing is a spell that channels the power of darkness to restore health to the caster. Unlike traditional healing spells, Dark Healing draws upon shadow energy to mend the user's body. This spell can only be cast on those with a dark-aligned Class, lest it cause harm instead of healing.

As the caster's mastery of Dark Healing increases, the amount of health restored grows, making it a powerful tool for dark-aligned Classes.

Cost:	25 MP
HP Restored:	50 HP
Casting Time:	3 Seconds
Cooldown:	N/A

Dark Weapon Flame

Dark Weapon Flame is a spell that engulfs the caster's weapon in black flames, imbuing it with the essence of darkness and fire. The weapon's blade becomes wreathed in a flickering black fire that adds additional darkness and fire damage with each strike.

The dark energy infused in the flames allows the weapon to penetrate defenses more effectively, making it particularly effective against creatures vulnerable to darkness or fire. As the caster's proficiency with this spell increases, the intensity and duration of the flame will be enhanced.

Cost:	15 MP
Damage:	10-15 Darkness & Fire Damage
Casting Time:	1 Second
Cooldown:	N/A

Doppelganger

Doppelganger is an illusion spell that creates a perfect duplicate of the caster, mirroring their exact movements and actions. The doppelganger appears identical to the caster in every way, making it difficult for enemies to discern which is the real threat. However, the doppelganger is purely an illusion and cannot deal any damage.

This spell is often used to confuse and distract opponents, drawing their attacks away from the caster and buying precious time in battle. As the caster's mastery of Doppelganger increases, the illusion becomes more convincing, with even the most perceptive enemies struggling to identify the decoy.

Cost:	50 MP
Casting Time:	5 Seconds
Duration:	5 Minutes
Cooldown:	15 Minutes

Lightning Strike

Lightning Strike is a potent spell that conjures a bolt of lightning, striking a targeted enemy with electrifying force. The bolt deals electric damage upon impact, with a chance to chain to a secondary target, recasting itself from the original target to another nearby enemy. This cascading effect can continue as long as there are additional targets within range, and the caster has the mana to continue the casting, making Lightning Strike devastating in clustered combat situations.

The spell's power and the chance of recasting to another target increase with the caster's proficiency, allowing for greater control and more extensive damage across multiple foes.

Cost:	25 MP
Damage:	22-30 Damage
Casting Time:	2 Seconds
Cooldown:	N/A

"Just murder-chickens," Tom sighed.

"I have taunt. Which would just make them all attack me, but I'm not sure how that will help in this situation except to make me die faster," Kevin said.

"Hang on a second. Kevin, you just got the Belt of Constitution, right?" Tom asked.

"I did," Kevin replied.

"And does rage increase your defense along with your ability to have extra-high defense when you aren't wearing armor?" Tom continued.

Kevin paused to check his skills before replying. "Yes, it does."

"Do you think it would be enough to shrug off most of those attacks? They seem pretty small," Tom asked.

"I'm not so sure. There are a lot of them to whittle down my defenses," Kevin said.

"Well, then I'm not sure there is anything for it. We are just going to have to do the best we can with what we have. I can summon some fodder for us for the time being, and then we have to just try to kill as many as we can," Tom said.

Casting *Summon Demonic Familiar* four times, Tom summoned three Abyssal Chickens and one Dretch. Seeing the Dretch reminded him that it had an AOE gas attack.

"Chickens, it's lunch time, go get you some lizard snacks. Dretch, you need to go in there and use your Abyssal Fart Cloud to try to poison as many of those lizards as you can. Is that something you can do multiple times in a row?" Tom asked.

The Dretch nodded its head.

"Great! Time to get in there and cut the abyssal cheese. Do you need me to pull your finger or anything?" Tom joked.

The Dretch looked at him, confused, then turned and plodded off after the chickens, who had needed no second urging to find a snack.

The lizards turned their attention to the demons headed their way and began to hiss in warning from their perches as they drew closer. As the chickens showed no signs of slowing down, the lizards jumped off the building, spread their wings, and began to fly toward the creatures daring to invade their territory.

As they took flight, Tom was reminded of the nature documentaries of bats flying out of a cave at night. They flew erratically and started to dive-bomb the demons. The chickens were having a heyday grabbing the lizards out of the sky and eating them as they flew by. The Dretch was swatting them down and would then grunt as it let out a noxious green cloud from its ass. It was thick-like fog rolling in, and any lizards that got caught in its billows would crash to the ground choking.

This wasn't going to last, though, because the demons were being slowly picked apart by the mass of lizards.

"If you have spells, use them now!" Tom called, readying his *Eldritch Blast*. He fired it off at one of the lizards and several others caught on fire with it as it went down. Having little mana left, he cast *Dark Weapon Flame* and moved in to start swinging. Kevin activated rage and went in to start attacking as well. The rest of the team either followed in or fired at the targets from a distance.

The lizards began to swarm all the melee combatants, biting and scratching at them. The weapons were just too big and the targets too small. The team had to retreat.

"FALL BACK!" Tom called to everyone.

Everyone began to make a run for it. The lizards persisted and tried to swoop in to continue the attack as the team ran for cover.

Chapter 24

Tiny Fuckers

"Well, that was a fucking disaster," James so eloquently offered.

"Yeah, yeah, yeah. We fucking saw it, okay," Tom said, annoyed at how poorly that plan had gone.

"Your fucking fart-bear was doing better than the rest of us. Man, that thing was *ugly*. It probably has to sneak up on a glass of water to get a drink. It didn't get hit with an ugly stick—the whole fucking tree fell on it," James continued.

"We get it; it's as ugly as sin. But it was fairly effective," Tom replied.

"Compared to us, anyway," Derek said.

"Apparently, AOE spells aren't so common at lower ranks? I would have thought one of us would have one by now," Jay said.

"Clearly, we didn't choose the right Class or path or something," Derek replied.

"I'm guessing a wizard would have something to help with this, but we don't have one of those," Tom said.

"I have AOE spells; they just pretty much all target team members," Kiera said.

"Yeah, that will be helpful later, but not here," Derek said. "It's okay, we just need a different strategy."

The team was panting heavily after running several blocks. After about a block and a half, the lizards gave up the chase and returned to the diner. Running an extra block just to be sure they weren't still being followed had seemed like the best option. Tom and Derek began to heal the others. Starting to feel lightheaded and have an ache behind his eyes, Tom had to stop and rest from his lack of mana.

Derek was able to heal all of the neutral and light aligned people present, and sighs of relief escaped them as they felt their wounds close and the pain dissipate. The team sat on the sidewalk as they recovered. Tom noticed a blinking icon in the corner of his vision and opened it to see what the message was about.

Pact Update:
You have completed both of your first quests to upgrade your pact. Kill monsters and send their souls to Azroc 100 of 100. Kill a Boss-level monster 1 of 1. New powers are ready for you to choose. Summon Azroc to get your reward.

"Well, I guess there's no time like the present," Tom said aloud.

"No time like the present for what?" Derek inquired.

"Time to summon Azroc again and get a new power," Tom replied.

"Oh, I like that guy! Let's get that son of a bitch on this side!" James interjected.

Tom found a rock on the ground and used it to mark out the summoning circle on the asphalt. He ensured it was on the ground this time, not a wall. After the summoning circle was complete and he chanted the ritual again, the circle lit up, and a portal opened on the ground. As before, Azroc began to rise out of the ground in his typical "I'm a badass" pose.

Some of the others were a bit skeptical of what was going on, having not seen the ritual before.

"What the fuck are you doing? Summoning more demons? You don't know what powers you're dealing with! This seems evil," Joe said.

"Nah, he's just my patron. It's how I get my powers. We've met before. A bit of an asshole sometimes, but he's cool," Tom replied.

"You summon demons to get your powers?" Jay asked, concern in his voice as well.

"I don't really think Azroc is a demon. Just some super powerful entity from another realm," Tom said.

"I'm totally digging the vibes. This would have made a badass metal song," Kiera added. "Rising from the portal at the beckoning of their call, the master showed his favor by giving power to them all!"

"Kinda catchy," James said at the lyric Kiera sang.

As Azroc finished ascending from the portal, he looked around at the group.

"Ah, I see you shitbags learned from the last encounter. Well done not putting me on a wall again," Azroc said. "Though that does mean I don't get to hurt anyone. That's kind of a bummer."

"Yeah, sorry about that last time. There wasn't a space big enough on the floor, and we didn't know how the whole summoning thing worked," Tom said.

"That was the only reason I let you off with a warning. You dickholes can *read*, so it should have been pretty obvious that summonings are intricately detailed affairs. One wrong move, and you could summon something else entirely that might chew you up and swallow you like a cheap whore on a night out," Azroc said. "I see you completed the quests. Well done. I have gained power from the souls you sent, so I shall increase your power as well."

Joe pushed to the front to see Azroc.

"Can you give me powers?" Joe asked.

"No, you didn't choose the path of the Warlock. So, I cannot help you," Azroc answered.

"Well, if that ain't a pile of chicken shit," Joe said.

"Come on, shit for brains. You had a chance to choose this sort of power, and you chose something stupid. Don't blame me for your fucking choices. Next time, read through the list, and don't just pick the first thing that seems macho, asshat," Azroc said as he slowly turned to face Joe. "Your ego is the thing that will get you killed in this world. Stop being such a prick and listen to the people trying to help you instead of spending all your time being a fuck-for-brains know-it-all, you little cunt fart. Now go back to sucking at your whore mother's saggy deflated teat before I get upset."

Everyone was stunned into silence. Joe stood there, his mouth agape, trying to understand what had just happened. He finally collected himself and became angry.

"Now listen here, you…" Joe began but was cut off completely when Azroc turned to him, eyes now glowing bright red.

"I highly suggest you keep your next words to yourself, you fucking cockholster, or I'll turn you inside out just to see if we can make you prettier," Azroc said.

Joe's eyes were wide with fear as Azroc leaned in closer to his face. He almost appeared to grow in size, towering over Joe, who looked like he was about to wet himself.

"I don't know what kind of a pompous asshat you think you are, but you're nothing but a cum stain on my boot. So go back to your miserable shit stain of a life and let me do my business," Azroc continued.

Jerky appeared on Azroc's shoulder, flipped Joe the bird, and then turned and hopped over to Tom's shoulder.

Joe only nodded and started to back away.

"And who is this little fella? I like him. He's spunky," Azroc said, reaching out and scratching jerky behind the horns.

"This is Jerky, he's my Quasit familiar," Tom replied.

"Well, you got a good one. Keep him around. Some Familiars are so stupid they would be better off left where they were. So, where were we? Ah, yes! Your powers," Azroc said, turning back to Tom and brightening. "Now, since you finished the quest, you can choose one of these powers to help you."

A notification appeared in Tom's vision.

Pact of the Tattoo Upgrade:

You have completed a quest for Azroc. Due to your continued service, Azroc has rewarded you with an additional power. Choose one of the following:

- Tattoo of Dexterity - This tattoo will allow you to move faster for 1 hour. Your speed will be increased by 50% at the cost of 20 mana.

- Tattoo of Scrying - This tattoo will allow you to see anything within 5 miles of your current position if you have seen it before. Scrying costs 20 mana per use and cannot be used to see underground.

- Tattoo of Life Absorption - This tattoo will allow you to sap the energy of creatures nearby. This will target all enemies within a 60-foot radius of you and leech away their HP. Activation of this tattoo costs 50 mana and lasts for 40 seconds.

"Shit… these are all great. I want all of them!" Tom said, excited at seeing them and sad that he could only pick one.

"I know, right?! You take care of me, and I'll take care of you. Now, what's it gonna be?" Azroc asked with a knowing wink.

"You knew which one I would need, didn't you?" Tom asked.

"Of course not. These are all *randomly* generated powers," Azroc said. Tom raised an eyebrow but the Patron was adamant. "That's my story, and I'm sticking to it."

Tom eyed him suspiciously, then decided not to look the gift horse in the mouth. He selected the Tattoo of Life Absorption. Needle pricks began to burn on his chest over his heart as a new tattoo was inscribed with black ink. He pulled the collar of his shirt out to see it finishing the design. Another intricate tribal symbol where the outer lines all seemed to flow into a central power design. Gritting his teeth against the pain, Tom sighed with relief when the tattoo was complete.

"Excellent choice. The Tattoo of Scrying was a face tattoo, so not sure how people on your planet would have reacted to that," Azroc said. "But I think you made a good choice. This can be activated to help in a fight as well as keep you alive in desperate situations. Your health can't be more than one hundred percent full, so if you are low on mana or stamina, it will fill those instead. Unfortunately, if you are totally full, then the energy is just lost. Also, bear in mind it can only target enemies, so none of that fruity stealing life from plants or animals around you bullshit. Unless, of course, you attack something, and it can fight back."

"Alright, I think that's fair. Thanks for the new power, Azroc," Tom said.

"You're welcome. I'm glad you are grateful. You wouldn't believe how many dumbasses are out there complaining about the powers they get," Azroc said. "Ungrateful bastards. I go out of my way to help someone, and all they can do is fucking whine about it. Spoiled little shit stains. I have half a mind to smite them so hard there's nothing but an ashy DNA smear where they used to be. And speaking of DNA smears, Joe, go fuck yourself. The best part of you ran down your mother's leg." The patron straightened a non-existent tie around his neck primly. "Alright, time for your next request."

<table>
<tr><td align="center">New Requests:</td></tr>
<tr><td>Your Dark Patron, Azroc, has sent his requests to you. Complete the following tasks to receive further powers and gifts.

•   Kill 1000 monsters and send their souls to Azroc.
•   Claim a site of power in the name of Azroc.</td></tr>
</table>

"A site of power? What the hell is that?" Tom asked.

"You'll know it when you see it. I can't give you any more information than that. Even someone as powerful as I am is bound by the fucking rules of the Grand System," Azroc replied. "You either play by the System's rules, or you don't play at all, if you catch my drift."

Tom nodded.

"Excellent! Most of my protégés have been nothing but absolute idiots who want nothing more than to further their own stupid agendas. Warlock is definitely the number one choice of assholes when it comes to Class selection," Azroc said. "If I didn't need the power, I'd find new and creative ways to fuck each and every one of them over repeatedly. Thanks for not being a big pile of dickweed, Tom."

"Um… You're welcome?" Tom said, unsure how to respond.

"Alright, time for me to head back. I'll see you shit stains later. Oh, and one more thing," Azroc said, turning to Joe. "If I find out you did something to my Warlock, I'll make sure you end up nothing more than a stain on a bukkake rug, you fucking jizz dumpster. Am I clear?"

Joe nodded vigorously.

"Good. Alright, I look forward to our next meeting, Tom. Don't take too long to finish those requests," Azroc said with a wave as he descended back into the portal.

The light winked out, and the party looked at each other momentarily.

"I think it's time to go pay those tiny fuckers another visit," Tom said.

The party turned back to go to the diner. On the way, Tom explained what his new tattoo did, and the rest of the party was excited to see it in action. Agreeing that this should be a perfect tactic to handle the lizard problem, the team decided that Kevin should stand next to Tom and activate his taunt ability to draw as many of the lizards in as he could. This would allow Tom to activate his new tattoo and drain their life away.

When they could see the diner, Tom, who had borrowed Derek's shield, and Kevin strode forward. Making sure that Jerky stayed with Kiera, Tom took in a deep breath and let it out. Hisses came from the lizards again as they warned them about getting too close.

"Alright, you cocky little bastards, it's time for a rematch," Kevin said. "Your mothers were nothing more than cum gargling dumpster sluts!"

"Hmm, channeling Azroc I see..." James said, adjusting an imaginary monocle while studiously examining the Barbarian's word usage. "A bold choice."

"Quite," Jay retorted, sipping from an imaginary cup of tea, his pinky held at an exquisite angle. "Let us see how it works out for him."

At these words, Kevin emitted a red glow that moved out in all directions. The lizards reacted immediately, becoming increasingly agitated as they began leaping into the air to fly toward the two men. Tom waited until they were within striking range and raised the shield to block the first wave.

Multiple resounding pings rang out from the first of the lizards hitting the shield. Behind the first wave, the others saw the tactic, pulled up and down to avoid it, and began to latch onto Kevin and Tom. Letting out a massive roar, Kevin activated his rage and started grabbing lizards, stomping on them, and punching them out of the air in an attempt to kill as many as possible around him in a frenzy of motion.

"This really fucking hurts!" Tom yelled. "Note to self: bring eye protection next time."

Activating his new tattoo, Tom felt a rush of power come back into him as his life went from sixty-five percent from all the bites and scratches up to one hundred percent in a matter of seconds. Next, his mana bar was filled, followed by the stamina bar that had dropped from the exertion of holding the shield up. Soon, all his bars were full, and the energy began to be lost to the ether, but he could still see his health bar flickering down a tiny bit and immediately back up to full. His tattoo began to burn from absorbing so much life force from the hundreds of lizards around him. After forty seconds, the tattoo released its power, and steam began to rise from under Tom's shirt.

The vast majority of the lizards lay dead at Tom's feet, and the other members of the party were picking off the rest. Slumping to the ground, Tom rested on his knees with the shield out in front of his legs, panting heavily.

"Great job, Tom," Kiera said, coming over to put a hand on his shoulder. "Kinda regretting my Bard decision after seeing some of the things you can do."

Tom laughed at that, and Kiera chuckled as well. "I think you're perfect as a Bard. Your buffs are a big part of the team dynamic."

"That's true. I am pretty awesome, aren't I?" Kiera said mockingly.

Once all the lizards were cleaned up, Joe went inside the diner to tell the others what they had decided. Nine other people exited with Joe and seemed excited to be joining forces with the new Guild.

"I gotta go pack up the supplies. Most of it will fit in my Inventory, so I'll only be a minute," Joe said as he returned inside.

"Don't mind him," an older woman said to the group. "He's a bit of a hard ass, but he's just trying to survive in this world. I'm Susan, by the way."

"Nice to meet you, Susan. I'm Tom, the leader of the Vanguard Guild," Tom said, shaking her hand.

"We are so glad you agreed to let us join. There just weren't enough of us to get any sort of self-sustained system off the ground. Despite what Joe thinks, having more people to help actually makes things easier because they can share the load," Susan said.

"We couldn't agree more. Welcome to Vanguard. We will head out for the Guild building as soon as Joe is back. I think you'll find it nicer than this diner. We just need to work on getting beds set up for everyone," Tom said.

"Oh, I think we can help with that. Carl here is a carpenter, and we can look at finding some mattresses from hotels or a mattress store in the area," Susan said.

"Susan, I think we are going to be great friends," Tom said with a big smile.

Chapter 25

Uneasy Peace

Level Up!
You have earned enough XP to advance to the next level. You have reached levels 13, 14, & 15! Continue to work hard and push yourself to gain more XP to continue to level up. You receive 30 Attribute Points to distribute as you see fit.

As Tom walked back to the Center, he reflected on how much he used to enjoy spending time alone in his room—escaping the world's harsh realities with a good video game or a show on TV. It was his way of decompressing, letting the day's worries melt away, if only for a while. But now, free time was a rare luxury. With a Guild to run and people constantly looking to him for solutions, moments of solitude had become almost nonexistent.

Even though Brian seemed to have a handle on most of the day-to-day affairs, he still needed to make critical decisions and help protect the group. Most people in the Guild weren't fighters; hell, *he* wasn't really a fighter himself. He just happened to have a better understanding of the game-like mechanics that the Grand System used. Sometimes, it felt like he had been in the right place at the right time—or maybe he had just made a few strange, risky decisions that ended up working in his favor.

"Why the fuck did this stupid System have to come here? Why couldn't they have just left our planet alone and let us continue to exist?" Tom thought to himself.

It wasn't worth dwelling on those thoughts—there was only despair and anger down that path, which wouldn't help him move forward. Tom decided to focus on something productive: allocating his points. With thirty points to distribute, he had a good opportunity to make some large movements with his attributes. After reviewing his character sheet, Tom decided to invest ten points each into Charisma, Intelligence, and Wisdom. Spells and skills had proven invaluable, and he wanted to be able to use them more effectively. Satisfied with his choices, Tom looked over his character sheet again, feeling confident with his choices.

Tom Harris	
Race: Human	**Class:** Warlock
Level: 15	**Total XP:** 138,940
XP To Next Level: 15,560	**HP:** 200/200
MP: 350/350	**SP:** 250/250
Attributes:	**Unused Attributes Points:** 0
Strength: 25	**Constitution:** 20
Dexterity: 20	**Endurance:** 25
Intelligence: 35	**Wisdom:** 30
Charisma: 45	**Luck:** 20
Non-Combat Skills:	
Inspect	**Level:** 3 **Rank:** Beginner
Combat Skills:	
Vehicular Homicide	**Level:** 6 **Rank:** Beginner
Swords	**Level:** 4 **Rank:** Beginner
Summon Demonic Creature	**Level:** 2 **Rank:** Beginner
Fear	**Level:** 1 **Rank:** Beginner
Corruption	**Level:** 1 **Rank:** Beginner
Spells:	
Eldritch Blast	**Level:** 1 **Rank:** Beginner
Dark Ball	**Level:** 1 **Rank:** Beginner
Dark Healing	**Level:** 2 **Rank:** Beginner
Lightning Strike	**Level:** 3 **Rank:** Beginner
Doppelganger	**Level:** 1 **Rank:** Beginner
Dark Flame Weapon	**Level:** 1 **Rank:** Beginner

Tattoos:	Tattoo of Brute Strength
Tattoo of Life Absorption	

Before he could get much further, the Center came into view, and Brian was standing right out front with TJ, waiting for them to return.

"I see your trip was successful," Brian said.

"Eventually," Tom replied. "We nearly had our asses handed to us by a bunch of tiny lizards. It really drives home that we don't currently have a lot of crowd-control options."

"We might be able to do something about that," TJ offered. "We've been thinking about what we would do if a mob came to the Center and tried to steal our stuff."

"A mob like torches and pitchforks? Or a mob like mobiles from the video game term sometimes meaning moving enemies?" James asked.

"Mob, as in torches and pitchforks… I didn't know the other was a thing. Anyway, we have been gathering some supplies from nearby pawn shops and gun stores. We have a veritable armory now, and with that comes some incendiary devices," TJ said with a knowing look.

"You mean… *grenades*?" James' voice squealed with ecstatic enthusiasm as he ran up to TJ and made grabby-hands toward the man.

"All in favor of James never getting explosives, say aye," Derek said.

Everyone in the area said "aye." Even the security guards back at the doors chimed in their agreement.

"What the hell? I don't even know you guys," James said, pointing at a group of men off to the side wearing tactical gear and carrying automatic rifles.

"Yeah, well, we know you. No explosives, buddy," one of the men said.

"Don't you think that grenades are a bit much on the force side for people?" Kiera asked.

"We have gas to use first, but if that doesn't disperse them, or we are dealing with adventurers who have been leveling up, we may not have a choice," TJ replied.

"As a side note, I have made TJ the head of security, which the Guild calls Defense Captain, so he has an official position within the Guild. I still need to find someone for our General," Brian interjected.

"Derek," Tom replied without hesitating.

"What? Me? Why me?" Derek said.

"You have the most combat experience of anyone I know, so you're the man for the job. Besides, I have to be able to trust a general," Tom said. "No one I can think of that I'd trust with that job more."

"Hey?!" James said incredulously.

Tom just stared at James with an unflinching look.

"Alright, alright… I get it. I just wanted you to say you trusted me, too," James said.

"I do trust you—to get us both into and out of a bar fight in any city you care to name," Tom said. "Just not with all our troops."

James' lower lip began to tremble as he wiped a tear from his eye. "You *do* love me!"

"I will be looking for other positions to place the rest of your team, but if you would look through the titles as well and find spots that best suit them, that would help me out a lot," Brian said.

"Anyway," TJ cleared his throat, trying to regain control of the conversation. "Returning to the topic of defence, we have tactics for handling those, and we can give you some of the explosives if you need them."

"That would be great! I appreciate your efforts, TJ," Tom said.

"Lastly, we have some reports from some of our scouts that another group of people is sending some emissaries here to try to meet with us. They should be here within the hour," TJ said.

"We have scouts?" Tom asked.

"Of course. We needed some people who were going to be willing to look ahead at what was going on and make sure the area was safe and secure in case of an attack. So, we are finding people who wanted to be Rangers and helping train them on survival techniques so that they would be effective in their Class," TJ replied.

"That's awesome! I'm so glad you guys are in charge of these logistics," Tom said.

"We're doing our best. We appreciate you coming in and giving us some footing to go on. And we truly appreciate the things you've done protecting people. We're just doing our best to help as well," TJ said.

"Do we know what to expect from these people coming to visit?" Jay asked.

"Not really. We've been told they are fairly well-equipped, though, similar to you all," TJ said.

"So, likely adventurers. Not sure how that will go," Tom said, thinking about the situation.

"Agreed. That's why we're happy you're back already. We could use the backup in case diplomacy goes sideways," TJ said.

"And we are emphasizing that we do not want diplomacy to go sideways," Brian said, looking pointedly at James.

"What? Why is everyone looking at me?" James said.

"Oh, I don't know. Does insulting a certain young ruler in a Dungeon about his unmentionables ring any bells?" Kiera said.

"That douche canoe had it coming," James said.

"Be that as it may, we don't want to incite anything out here with people that will be living so close to us," Brian said. "So, you will be keeping your mouth shut and letting us handle the negotiations."

"Fine. Sounds boring anyway," James said.

"Indeed. Just how we like it. Nice and boring," Brian said.

"Whatever. You guys are no fun," James said.

"If your idea of fun is getting the shit beat out of us by a roided out Royal, then count me out," Jay said.

"Well, *that* part wasn't fun. But did you see his face when we all jumped to attack his hoo-ha? Priceless," James said.

The team waited with TJ and Brian out front of the building to receive the visitors. After about another half hour of waiting, they could be seen walking up the road. There were three people: one wore heavy armor similar to Derek's but with a red cross on the breastplate and a greatsword across his back; another wore a long, brown leather trench coat, a brown leather cowboy hat, and revolvers at his hips; and the last was a female wearing all black. She seemed the most unassuming of the team, appearing to only carry a single katana on her hip.

No smiles were exchanged except from James, who waved at them as they approached. The woman, who appeared to be the leader based on her giving directions for them to stop, sneered at James as he waved.

"Who is in charge here?" the woman called to them from a safe distance.

The man in armor crossed his arms over his chest, and the man in the trench coat held one of his revolvers in his hand.

"I guess that's me," Tom said, holding a hand up and taking a single step forward.

The woman looked him up and down incredulously.

"You? Seriously?" she asked.

Tom looked to either side of him, and Brian and TJ just shrugged.

"Ummm. Yes. I am the Guild leader. Is there something I can do for you?" Tom asked.

"We were sent here to check out the competition," the woman said.

"Competition? We're all on the same team as humans, aren't we?" Tom asked.

"No. We aren't," the woman said. "There are the strong, and there are the weak. In this new world, the weak won't survive. This is an opportunity for evolution to take its next step and weed out those who should've never existed. Society created a generation of weak people. This is nature's way of resetting."

"That's a pretty morbid and heartless outlook on this situation where banding together seems like the best way to survive, especially with the new space pirates threat," Tom said.

"You have a bit of a point. But not the whole picture," the woman said. "The *strong* need to band together. The weak can be left out, which is why we're here. Your Guild appears to have strong members. You've made progress where many others have not."

"Well, I guess I'm a little confused about your definition of strong. Not everyone here is physically strong or able to fight well. Those that are protect the others. We have plenty of people who can't wield a sword or fire guns well, but they have other strengths. Those strengths they contribute to the Guild, and all of them working together, is what makes us advance," Tom said.

The woman regarded Tom momentarily, seeming to mull over his words.

"I don't agree," she said finally. "But I am here to offer anyone in your Guild with strength the opportunity to join our Guild. We will eventually be the strongest one around, and we will be able to stand against anything that comes."

Tom looked at his party and the others standing around him. Every one of them shook their heads when he looked at them.

"I don't think that anyone here wants to leave. But we could form a Guild alliance. I'm Tom, and this is the Guild Vanguard," Tom said.

The woman frowned, appearing disappointed that her offer had not been taken up. She looked around again at everyone assembled and then back at Tom.

"Fine. If that's how you feel, then a tentative alliance would be acceptable for now. I'm Shandra, of the Guild Stormcrusher. Know that we will be the Guild on top," Shandra said.

Tom paused and looked at Shandra, an idea forming. Why he had never thought of this before made Tom feel a little stupid. He used Inspect on Shandra to see what he could find out.

<table>
<tr><td align="center">Error:</td></tr>
<tr><td align="center">Inspect Failed:</td></tr>
<tr><td align="center">Due to System-enforced encryption protocols, inspection of another individual's character data is prohibited. Personal information is classified and accessible only to the owner or authorized parties.</td></tr>
</table>

Seriously? That was dumb. But it couldn't be helped, he supposed. They really needed to find out more about these "System Rules."

"That's fine with us. We don't want to be on top. We just want to provide safety for humanity," Tom replied.

Shandra sneered again at this, disgust clearly written on her face.

"You're *pathetic*, but you may yet have your uses," Shandra said. "Come on, Shane, Griff. This was a waste of time. If any of you change your mind, you can find us at the Reunion Tower. For now, we'll be keeping an eye on the town from there."

With that, they turned and left. After they had walked a fair distance off, the Guild turned to each other, sharing concerned looks.

"That doesn't bode well for us," Brian said.

"There are always people like that in the world. Bullies that think that might makes right. It's like fucking high school all over again," Tom said.

"I had a very different experience than you in high school," TJ said.

Tom stopped and looked TJ over, observing all his muscles. "I'm sure you did," Tom said.

Jerky appeared on Tom's shoulder and blew a raspberry at TJ.

"Oh, come on, Jerky. We like TJ. Don't be like that," Tom said.

"Jerky sorry," Jerky said, looking ashamed.

"That's alright, little buddy," TJ said. "I understand you're just standing up for Tom. I'm glad he has a friend like you."

APOCALYPSE

"IT'S COMING! RUN! MONSTER!" a man screamed as he ran from around a corner.

"Connor?! What is it? What kind of monster? Goblins? Ogres? Wolves?" TJ asked, grabbing the man by the collar as he tried to run by. "Where's the rest of your team?"

"They're dead! All dead! We couldn't stop it!" Connor began crying as he gripped TJ.

"What monster could do that? We are now stronger than most individual monsters around us, and the odd ones that aren't, we've been able to defeat using better tactics," TJ said.

A roar sounded from straight ahead down the street. It was loud and long and sounded big. Around the corner came a creature straight out of a nightmare. Arms long like an orangutan's, with jagged protrusions from its elbows, horns growing out of its head, standing about twenty feet tall, green-grey skin, nothing but a loin cloth that didn't entirely cover its swinging bits, teeth protruding from its lower jaw like tusks, and carrying a tree trunk for a club, the monster lumbered into view. Tom inspected it to try to get more information.

Troll Fiend (Region Boss)	
Trolls are monstrous creatures with terrifying regenerative abilities. Standing taller than an average troll, the Troll Fiend is a hulking, grotesque beast with coarse, matted hair, and teeth that protrude from his mouth, giving it a horrific appearance. Its skin is thick and rough, covered in scars from battles that healed within moments due to its incredible regeneration. This creature's regenerative abilities are nearly unmatched, allowing it to rapidly heal from even the most grievous of wounds. Limbs that are severed can regrow in minutes, and damage that would be fatal to other creatures barely slows the Troll Fiend down. This regeneration makes the Troll Fiend an incredibly difficult opponent to kill, as conventional attacks are quickly undone by its healing factor. The Troll Fiend's resilience is only matched by its ferocity. It charges into battle with relentless aggression, using its brute strength and razor-sharp claws to tear through foes. Despite its fearsome power, the Troll Fiend is not without weakness—fire and acid can slow or even halt its regenerative abilities, making these the most effective means of combating this otherwise unstoppable beast.	
HP:	3500/3500
MP:	100/100
SP:	5000/5000
Level:	28
Abilities:	Demonic Troll Regeneration

Attack:	Bite, Claw, Stomp

"Well… fuck," was all Tom could think to say.

Chapter 26

Trolling Around & A Joyride

"FIRE! WE NEED FIRE! Derek called to everyone around. "TJ! Get those explosives! I'm not sure we have anyone that can dish out enough fire magic yet to make a difference!"

"On it!" TJ called back.

"Everyone else, lay down cover fire while we work on keeping it busy!" Derek continued.

"What about your Eldritch Blast?" Derek asked.

"I think we need something a bit… bigger," Tom replied.

The security guards all rushed to get behind the concrete barricades that had been put in place in front of the building, and braced behind them to aim at the Troll Fiend.

"Fire as we move in!" Derek yelled. "Party members spread out; don't give it one big target to hit! Try to take it apart, but remember—Trolls regenerate! We need time for TJ to get back!"

Tom summoned a creature to fight with them, and an Abyssal Chicken appeared from the portal.

"Well, maybe it can be a distraction," Tom said, looking at the beast. "Go attack!" he told the chicken.

Taking off running, the chicken ran straight at the troll as if it had no fear, mouth open and screeching at it in fury. Suppression fire came from behind, firing at the troll. The bullets struck the monster and opened holes in its skin, for all the good they did. Its skin started regenerating almost immediately and within moments, it was like nothing had taken place.

"Eat lead, motherfucker!" James yelled, firing at the monster but aiming at the giant dong swinging between its legs like a grandfather clock.

Roaring in fury at the small amount of pain it was feeling, the troll took a step forward and then paused. Seeming to suddenly notice the chicken running at it, it smiled and reached down to grab it. Scooping it up from the ground, it pulled it up to its face. For its part, the Abyssal Chicken fought and bit its fingers the entire way up, trying in vain to harm the troll. Up it went, tilting its head back until it dropped the chicken into its mouth and began chewing.

"Well… all we did was feed it," Jay said. "Everything really does love chicken."

"Let's get in there, guys! We have to keep it away from the Guild building!" Tom called.

Moving to intercept the troll, the team spread out to encircle the monster. As the troll took another step toward the Center, Tom stepped in front of it and used his skill *Fear*. Looking down at Tom, the monster moved its hand as though it was going to strike him, then paused. Its expression changed from one of anger to concern as it continued to stare at Tom.

"BOO!" Tom yelled up at it.

Flailing its arms slightly, the monster took a single step back, away from Tom.

"Boo? Really? Come on, man, this isn't a toddler!" Kiera yelled at Tom.

"Hey! It worked, didn't it?" Tom called, not taking his eyes off the slightly fearful beast.

Kiera had also set herself up behind the barricades, pulled her rifle out, and taken aim. Firing a shot off, the troll's left eye exploded, and it screamed as it reached up to grab it. Not wasting any more time, Tom cast *Dark Weapon Flame*, activated his Strength Tattoo, and moved forward to strike.

Tom slashed horizontally across the Troll's body, his greatsword cutting deep into its lower abdomen. The blade tore through the creature's flesh, releasing a nauseating stench of rot and burning tissue. As the troll's intestines spilled out, severed and gushing fluids, a torrent of foul matter splashed onto Tom, who was standing directly in its path. The heat and steam rising from the fresh wound made the grotesque scene even more unbearable.

Hearing the sounds of people retching behind him, Tom scrunched his face up, trying not to get it in his eyes. He continued his swing, aiming for another horizontal cut, but the troll had backed up, causing Tom to miss. The slippery offal on the ground sent him crashing to the floor and as he struggled to regain his footing, the troll stepped forward and kicked him, sending him flying. He landed twenty yards away, groaning in pain as he clutched his side.

Derek shouted at the beast right after it kicked Tom, then charged past it, smashing his mace into its knee. With a sickening crunch, the joint buckled inward at a grotesque angle, forcing the troll down. Despite the injury, the troll's regenerative abilities were already at work, and the knee began knitting itself back together almost immediately. The troll let out a roar of pain and made a clumsy attempt to strike at Derek as it fell. Its swing went wild, missing its mark as Derek continued to move.

"Nobody gets to kick Tom like that and get away with it except *me!* Die, you giant pile of shit!" James yelled as he shot at the troll.

The bullets did little to damage the monster, and the holes were immediately healed again, but James was on a direct collision course with the beast on the opposite side of Derek. Placing his guns back in his storage and pulling out his hand axes, James leaped into the air and came down, bringing both axes down on the wrist of the troll that was attached to the hand resting on the ground.

Chopping through the wrist, the axes clanged against the ground behind the troll's arm as the monster began to topple over after losing its anchor point. Roaring again, the beast landed on its face, unable to stop itself after swinging at Derek.

APOCALYPSE

Taking full advantage of the downed opponent, Jay and Kevin rushed in. Jay silently, and Kevin yelling at the top of his lungs, invoking his rage.

Leaping onto the beast's back, Jay drove both kamas into the sides of the troll's neck, ripping backward to draw the blades through the meat, opening large gashes. Kevin began hacking away at the troll's side like a housing development company through a rainforest. Soon, the monster lay in two pieces on the ground from a combination of Tom's strike and Kevin's relentless attacks. The monster's arms began to slow down, then they stopped moving.

Jay pulled out his weapons and jumped off its back.

"Not so tough. Regenerative somewhat, but nothing we couldn't handle," Jay said.

Suddenly, a finger twitched as the body pieces moved closer together. Backing away in horror, the party stared as the beast began to knit itself back together. Everything came together except the cut Tom had made in the stomach. It started to stand and roared at the people around it.

"You've got to be fucking kidding me!" Jay yelled at it.

Walking up next to Jay, Tom looked at him, still holding his side. "What did you expect? It's a Troll, after all."

"I didn't expect it to regenerate from those kinds of wounds!" Jay yelled indignantly.

"Anything but fire. That's why we need the explosives or molotovs," Tom said as he stepped up to the beast again.

This time, he used his *Corruption* skill on the beast. Then, as the creature swung at him, he danced backward and sliced at its wrist, once again severing it with his sword. Howling with rage and pain, the troll held its arm against its chest.

"It shouldn't be as powerful, and the regeneration should be lessened now. We need to keep it busy!" Tom called.

The team once again moved into position and began to attack it from all sides, not letting it focus on any one person. Arms or legs hit several of them as they got too close, but it was whittled down again. Just as before, though, it regenerated from all the attacks, though slightly slower than before and not its left hand.

Tom cast *Eldritch Blast* at its face, and it danced around, trying to put the green flames out. They didn't last long as the spell was not very powerful, but its face did not heal from the burns.

"HERE!" TJ yelled from behind them as he ran up with a package in his hands.

"Grenades?" Tom asked.

"C4, actually. If you can get it onto its body, I have the trigger here," TJ motioned at the button in his hand.

"Where the fuck did you get C4?!" Tom cried.

"The backroom of a gun store. I don't really think they were supposed to have it, but I figured… no rules anymore, right?" TJ replied.

Tom smiled an evil grin. "Yeah, no rules. And I bet I can do better than get it onto its body."

Summoning another demon, he was unfortunately met with a Dretch. "That's not what I fucking need," Tom said and cast the summons again. This time, an Abyssal Chicken popped out. "Perfect."

Tom took the C4 and held it up in front of the chicken.

"Now, I need you to take this in your mouth and go to the troll. Let him grab you. We'll do the rest," Tom said to the chicken.

It cocked its head to one side, then took the package in its mouth and began to run furiously at the troll.

"Are you doing what I think you're doing?" Kiera called.

"Depends on what you think I'm doing," Tom replied, not looking back at her.

The chicken ran up and kicked the troll in the shin. Looking down at it, slightly confused, it smiled when it noticed that it was another chicken. It reached down, picked it up, and held it over its mouth. Once again, it dropped it, seeming quite pleased.

"NOW!" Tom yelled, and TJ pushed the trigger.

The head of the troll exploded out in a rain of gore, covering everyone nearby.

"Yuck! I got some in my mouth!" James called out from where he had been, closer to the monster than the others.

Falling first to its knees, then flat out, the troll's body lay lifeless on the ground, not regenerating.

Regional Boss Defeated!

You and your guild have defeated the Regional Boss {Troll Fiend}!
The next ranked creature will now replace it as Regional Boss!

"Alright, everyone, nice job. Time to hit the showers," Tom called, wiping troll brain out of his eyes.

"You aren't even going to worry about that message?!" Kiera shouted at him.

"It's not even the worst thing to happen to me today," Tom said nonchalantly as he walked back toward the Guild building.

Trudging inside, the Guild members all hit the bathrooms and cleaned up from the fight. Tom and Derek spent some time at the entrance, healing anyone who was hurt, but it was primarily minor injuries. Their numbers had prevented the troll from being able to single out any one person and cause too much damage.

After getting cleaned up, the party met in the main lobby.

"Here ya go, Jay," Tom said, tossing keys to him.

"What's this for?" Jay asked, confused.

"You wanted to take the Goblin Slayer 2.0 out for a spin, didn't you?" Tom replied.

APOCALYPSE

Jay's eyes lit up like a serial flasher finding a new park.

"Really?! Oh man, let's go!" Jay said, already running toward the parking garage.

"You probably should have kept working on your skill," Derek said.

"Yeah, but this way, I don't have to get him a Christmas present," Tom joked.

A short time later, the team loaded into the vehicle and set off to scout the area. Jay, cackling with glee, drove out onto the main streets, revving the engine as he screeched out of the garage in a wild slide. It took them a few blocks of driving, but they eventually found what they were looking for—goblins. With true murderous joy, Jay slammed on the gas, plowing through the ugly creatures without hesitation. One goblin got impaled on the new cattle guard spikes and was dragged along for about half a mile before Tom had Jay stop so he could remove it. The goblin had apparently died screaming, the spike gruesomely lodged through its mouth and out the back, creating a macabre scene, as if it had tried to eat the spike but had gone too far.

Hopping back in, the team passed a mattress store.

"Hey, stop here, Jay. I wanna go look in that store," Tom said.

"Okay, but I get to drive back, too," Jay said.

"Alright," Tom said, chuckling.

Hopping out of the car, the team moved to the entrance and had to break the glass on the door to get inside.

"Looks like the apocalypse happened before this place opened. No one seems to have been here at all yet," Derek pointed out.

"Kinda weird not seeing all the fluorescent lights on these mattresses. I've never been in one of these stores after they closed," Kevin said, looking around, placing a hand on the bed, and pressing down to test out the firmness.

"I had a thought. We have been bringing things back but not really using this Inventory System like we could," Tom said. "I want to see what it can actually do."

Reaching out, Tom touched one of the mattresses and thought about adding it to his Inventory. He got a prompt in return.

This action cannot be performed:
This item is too large to fit in your Inventory.

"Well, that's too bad. I was hoping we could bring some back for the people in the Center," Tom said.

"What about memory foam mattresses?" Derek asked.

"Aren't those the same size?" Tom asked in return.

"When they're open, sure. But they come compressed in a much smaller box. I bought one a year or so ago for my bed, and it was rolled up pretty small compared to its full size," Derek replied.

"Let's go check the back. They likely have a stockpile of them for selling," Tom said, getting excited.

Moving on to the warehouse area at the back of the building, the team found the shelves where they kept the mattresses.

"There must be a couple hundred of these different types of memory foam mattresses. Let's see if this works," Tom said, reaching a hand out to touch one of the boxes.

Thinking about adding it to his Inventory, the item disappeared and showed as an item in his Inventory.

"HA! It worked! We need to get all of these in our Inventories and take them back to the Center," Tom told them.

For the next half hour, the team began to take all the memory foam mattress boxes off the shelves and add them to their Inventories. Finding that each one of them could carry about thirty memory foam mattresses before they were rejected, they were able to take one hundred and eighty mattresses between them and set aside the rest to come back and get. Unlike some of the smaller items, they didn't appear to stack in the Inventory. Which Tom felt made some sense due to the size of the items.

"We need to tell people about this and send them out for more runs. And these should go a long way toward having a better night's sleep!" Tom said.

With that, the team hopped back into the GS2 and returned to drop off the mattresses. Brian assured them that they would set up some for the team and pass the rest around as fairly as possible. They were able to grab the rest before heading back out on patrol again. Jay gleefully drove around until the sun began to set.

The radio they took with them to communicate with the Guild building, another courtesy of TJ and his team, went off.

"Home base to GS2, home base to GS2, come in GS2," the radio called.

"GS2 here, go ahead," Tom replied.

"There has been a break-in at home base. We need you back here pronto."

Chapter 27

Theft

Arriving at the Guild building, the party poured out of the GS2, leaving the doors open in their haste to enter and find out what had happened. As they got to the main lobby, Brian was already there waiting for them, a large crowd of people standing around with worried faces.

"What the hell happened?" Tom blurted out, unable to control his curiosity and panic.

"It really isn't that bad. People are blowing this way out of proportion, but someone broke into the Guild building and stole part of our food supply. We can always recover it; they didn't cause any major damage, and everyone is safe," Brian explained.

"How did they get in?" Derek asked.

"Looks like they just walked in the front door," TJ offered.

"And we just let them?" Derek asked again.

"We don't have a policy in place to check everyone. We don't have a system that says this person is part of the Guild or not, and we haven't been just barring people from entering," TJ replied.

"Sounds like we need to go ahead and make that a priority," Tom said.

"We already have," Brian stated. "As we speak, we are looking at the options for identifying Guild members and non-Guild members. Almost everyone within the building has now been interviewed, and nearly one hundred percent of them are willing to join the Guild and contribute. The outliers are being talked to specifically about their plans so that we can make sure we know who is with us and who is not. I did look at the Guild tab and found some interesting things about building options, but we should discuss that privately."

"Okay. Then can we move this meeting to the conference room? Bring anyone you feel should be included in this meeting to help make decisions," Tom said.

"Very good. We have also moved your items out of the conference room, so don't be alarmed that they aren't there. We have individual rooms set up for you now," Brian assured them.

"Thank you, Brian. I appreciate you looking out for us," Tom said.

Moving to the elevators to go upstairs, the entire building suddenly lost power.

"Damn. We knew this would happen, but we had hoped to be further along when it did. But nothing can be done about it at the moment. To the stairs!" Brian directed.

"Further along with what?" Tom asked.

"Well, we had Harold working on a new prototype item. He was able to buy some schematics from the vending machine that pertained to a Profession he obtained so he could begin making things," Brian said.

"Wait, a Profession? What is that?" Tom asked.

"Apparently, it's like a Class but has to do with jobs you perform related to things like crafting. Harold became an Engineer, as he had been in the former world, because he continually implemented new things in the building and built machines," Brian replied.

"I wonder why none of us have Professions?" Jay asked.

"Likely because we have been spending all of our time running around fighting and putting out fires, so we can't perform jobs. Warrior is a Class, not a Profession," Derek offered.

"So, Professions also play a role in what happens in a vending machine?" Tom asked.

"That appears to be the case," Brian replied.

"Will the machines still work with the power out?" Kiera interjected.

"We have been looking at the machines, and there doesn't appear to be any power cords attached, so we see no reason they should stop working, but I will have someone go check it out," Brian said.

"Back to the issue at hand, what project was Harold working on?" Tom asked, attempting to get the group back on track.

"That isn't really the matter at hand, but okay. It's a mana battery of sorts that will feed into a power generator for the building. It has to be connected to mana collectors that can be placed on the building, but it should allow us to get the power back up and running even though the power grid has given out," Brian explained.

"So, like how solar power works in collecting energy and storing it in a battery to power things in a house?" Kevin asked.

"Exactly, but the generator has to be able to allow for the conversion of mana to electricity," Brian said.

"That's amazing!" Tom exclaimed. "I hope he's fairly close."

"It's likely to take a while—probably another month. But we have others who are getting Crafting Professions that will be going to work with him on the project as a top priority. The conversion is the part we are unsure about, but Harold feels like he can make it work," Brian said.

The party arrived at the conference room and sat down. Fortunately, the room was located along the exterior wall of the building and had windows that they could use for light.

"While we wait for the others to get here, let's look at the building options in the Guild menu really fast, as there are a few options I think we should consider," Brian began once they had all been seated.

Pulling up the Guild menu, Tom noticed several tabs along the right side of the screen. Selecting the one that said "Building," Tom was greeted with a blueprint-style drawing of the Trammel Crow Center with information about what was on various floors.

"If you're on that screen, you will notice that there are several drop-downs on the left side of the building menu that are filled with options. These appear to be upgrade options we can purchase with the Guild Points or GP. GP is at the top of the page, and we already have a fair number. Plus, we still have the free Guild reward for being an early Guild former," Brian began. "In the drop-down marked security, there is an option for doors; in the sub-menu for the doors, there is the option for coiling doors. These are those roll-up doors that are used in many shopping centers to secure an opening. I would advise we use the free reward on this if possible."

"There are so many options in these menus. How can you be sure we shouldn't use it for something else?" Tom asked.

"Because now that the power is out, security is going to be our main concern, and if those are on the first floor entrances, we can be protected from not only intruders but monsters," Brian explained.

That did make a lot of sense to Tom. He looked through a few more menus and then, feeling completely overwhelmed by the sheer number of choices, decided to trust Brian and selected the coiling doors.

"Done. I have no idea how that works, but I used the freebie on the doors," Tom said.

"Thank you, Tom. I appreciate your willingness to trust me," Brian said.

"Why do we have so many Guild Points? It looks like we already have almost a thousand of them," Tom asked.

"It appears to be primarily based on the size of the Guild and overall level of happiness, based on what I can tell from the other screens and the tiny bit of information I could get from the System helper," Brian replied. "Having nearly five hundred people willing to join the Guild and put in work, and the basic consensus being that they are as happy as they can be given the circumstances, means we are getting a lot of points. I'm sure their happiness will change because, right now, they are mostly happy you saved them or aren't on the front lines. Now that power has gone out, I expect a drop in happiness."

"Yeah, that's going to be true. Hopefully, Harold can get the generator going so we can improve their lives again," Tom said.

"I'm sure he will. Until then, we can still have meals because the stoves and ovens are gas, and that will keep running for a while yet. Oh, and here are a few other people we can rely on," Brian said, looking at the door to the conference room and gesturing for the people there to enter.

"Joe and Andrea, you know already; the other person here is Chris. Chris has shown a desire to help your team with clearing the area. He has some military experience, just like Derek, and should be a fine option for forming another adventurer team. We need to get someone in place who can be here more often to help train up more of a militia," Brian explained. "Since we met with Shandra, I have felt we need more people who can help with defense and focusing on leveling up so we can be prepared for anything that happens with the rival we seem to have now."

"An excellent idea. I have been wanting to do that but haven't had time yet to help train anyone," Tom said.

"And Joe and Andrea here are working together on the farming topic. Andrea has set up some great planting boxes, and Joe actually had a large supply of seeds we can grow to help begin to expand our farms," Brian explained.

"Yeah, I was hoarding those, knowing the apocalypse was coming and all," Joe said. "But I figure now that we are here, there isn't much use in keeping them. Besides, we will get more seeds if they grow for the farms. We will eventually have to move everything outside, as we won't always have enough room here, but the upper floors should do for now if we can remove more of the roof. That being said, we need to make an area for trees, so we can have some more fruits."

"The variety of seeds Joe had massively changed our trajectory. We can now focus on growing things and gaining more seeds rather than having to go out and hunt for them," Andrea added.

"What happened to my stuff is mine, Joe?" Tom asked.

"Well, ya know… I thought about it and realized that I didn't want to grow all this shit by myself. So, I thought Andrea could use it more effectively," Joe said, rubbing the back of his neck in embarrassment.

"This is excellent! I know it'll take time to grow these things, and we'll have to find food until then, but I think being here already means that we're further ahead than we could've been," Tom said.

"We definitely are. We should be able to move forward with these plans to be prepared for most situations," Brian said.

"That's wonderful to hear. It takes a big weight off my mind. Now, Chris, let's go over some things so that you can be the most effective teacher you can be," Tom said.

Tom spent a long period of time with Chris and his party, everyone giving input on things that could be used to create effective fighters and teams. Then, everyone went about their business as usual, with plans being put into place to allow daily life to progress in this new world.

Over the next few days, Tom worked with Chris to help train up several teams that could be used as adventuring teams, as well as hunting teams that could roam the surrounding area looking for monsters. Part of the training was going over a primer on the local Dungeon. After about a week of training, Chris came to Tom with several teams he thought were ready to go out independently. After evaluating them, Tom and his team agreed that they should be good to go out on their own.

There were three teams: Alpha, Bravo, and Charlie. Tom's team was designated Leader, and Chris' team was designated Omega, with the Alpha, Bravo, and Charlie teams able to go out on patrol, which left Tom and his team with the opportunity to look at something different. They had been doing well and found they could grow reasonably consistently. Tom pulled up his character sheet to see how he was progressing.

APOCALYPSE

Tom Harris	
Race: Human	**Class:** Warlock
Level: 22	**Total XP:** 502,450
XP To Next Level: 27,550	**HP:** 300/300
MP: 450/450	**SP:** 250/250
Attributes:	**Unused Attributes Points:** 0
Strength: 35	**Constitution:** 30
Dexterity: 30	**Endurance:** 25
Intelligence: 45	**Wisdom:** 40
Charisma: 65	**Luck:** 20
Non-Combat Skills:	
Inspect	**Level:** 6 **Rank:** Beginner
Combat Skills:	
Vehicular Homicide	**Level:** 12 **Rank:** Novice
Swords	**Level:** 10 **Rank:** Novice
Summon Demonic Creature	**Level:** 9 **Rank:** Beginner
Fear	**Level:** 5 **Rank:** Beginner
Corruption	**Level:** 5 **Rank:** Beginner
Spells:	
Eldritch Blast	**Level:** 5 **Rank:** Beginner
Dark Ball	**Level:** 3 **Rank:** Beginner
Dark Healing	**Level:** 4 **Rank:** Beginner
Lightning Strike	**Level:** 5 **Rank:** Beginner
Doppelganger	**Level:** 1 **Rank:** Beginner
Dark Flame Weapon	**Level:** 3 **Rank:** Beginner
Tattoos:	Tattoo of Brute Strength
Tattoo of Life Absorption	

"Why don't we set our sights on Dungeons?" Derek offered. "In games, they were always the best way to farm for resources."

"That seems like a good idea. But we only know where the one is right now," Tom said.

"Yeah, but I could go in for more dickshots," James said, pulling out a handgun and looking through the sights.

Rolling his eyes, Jay looked at them and offered, "Is there no way to track where they are? We should be able to find a way to detect them. Or maybe some other Guild in the area has seen some."

"I guess I could reach out to Shandra and see if her team has any leads," Tom said.

"Ugh, that bitch never wants to help. You tried to talk to her a couple of times since that one meeting where she basically threatened us, and she was a stuck-up cunt," Kiera said.

"Yeah, but it's the only option we have right now other than praying we blindly stumble into one," Tom countered.

"I know. I just hate her," Kiera said.

"Our teams are already running the Dungeon we do know of," Derek said. "They are getting acclimated to tougher opponents and team strategies, and they can get some gear. I don't see why running it at least three times a week per team isn't doable."

"Sure, let's start with that and see if we come up with anything else," Tom agreed.

Chapter 28

A Pet for James

Heading out for the day, the team hopped into the GS2 and drove around town to patrol the area and look for signs of new Dungeons. While the party was out, they came across their usual quarry of a few invading goblins, trying to find food or things to steal, and dispatched them easily. Running them over was nearly impossible now without getting out and chasing them. They seemed to be learning about the vehicles, and so would run onto the sidewalks or scurry into buildings. The team had developed patterns to corral the little green monsters and could still gain some XP for the GS2.

Needing to move further and further away from the Guild building to find monsters meant that the teams were finally making progress in creating a safe zone around their new home. There were still the occasional random monster spawns that could potentially threaten the non-adventuring members, but the Guild had adjusted to dealing with these incursions to the point they rarely gave them any trouble.

On today's outing, the team encountered a lone wolf walking across the road in town. The wolf stopped to sniff a completely rotten corpse and then thought better of trying to eat it. Moving around, it saw the GS2 and paused, staring at it with suspicion.

"Stop the car!" James said excitedly.

"What is it, James?" Tom said, bringing the GS2 to a stop in the middle of the street.

"That wolf. I think it's finally time I got a pet!" James said.

"Really, you think you need a pet, and you chose a wolf? Can't we get you something that fits the pet description better, like a dog or a girlfriend?" Jay said, followed quickly by an "OW!" as Kiera smacked him on the back of the head.

"Women are *queens*, not pets!" she growled.

"It was a joke, little sister. Come on," Jay played.

"I don't care if it was a joke. You treat women with respect!" Kiera replied.

"Yes, ma'am....OW! WHAT WAS THAT FOR?" Jay cried out again.

"Don't call me ma'am! It makes me feel old," Kiera replied.

"It's a term of respect... We're Southerners, for Christ's sake!" Jay retorted.

"Don't care. Don't call me ma'am! EVER!" Kiera replied.

"Duly noted..." Jay replied, wincing and rubbing the back of his head.

"I don't mean I just want to make friends with it and have it follow me home... Well, that *is* what I want, but I mean it's a Ranger skill. I can have an animal companion," James informed the group. "We just haven't seen wolves for a while, so I was waiting for the right time."

"Well, if you think that's what you want, then go ahead. It's taming time!" Tom said and gestured to the wolf.

James got out of the vehicle and began to walk toward the wolf. Noticing his approach, the wolf began to back up and growl at him. Unfortunately for the wolf, it had made its way up onto the sidewalk and was backing into the entrance of a building with nowhere to go. It backed through the doors of the building with walls on either side and bristled as it growled, the hairs on its neck and back standing on end.

"Nice puppy. I just wanna be friends. I have treats. You want a belly rub…" James began but couldn't finish as the wolf leaped at him with its mouth open wide.

"AHHHHH! OH GOD! NO! SO MANY TEETH! OW! FUCKING CUNT SHARTS THAT HURTS!" James began screaming as he wrestled with the wolf.

"Should we go help him?" Kevin asked.

"Nah, he's got this. It's just a wolf. It shouldn't be able to kill him at this point," Tom said, smiling slightly at James' predicament.

Rolling around on the ground, James and the wolf continued to fight to gain the upper hand. The wolf growled, and James spat out a string of profanities that would make a sailor blush. Eventually, they rolled past the building's second set of doors, and the pair were hidden from sight.

More rustling and swearing came from inside the building, and then a scream came from the building that was far worse than anything they had heard.

"Okay, I think we should go check on him now," Tom said, realizing they might have been mistaken in letting him handle this alone.

Stepping out of the car, the team moved toward the doors.

"Stay the fuck out!" James yelled from inside. "I got this, so just fuck off until I'm done! Now where were we, you shit biscuit?"

More growling, snarling, and grunts came from inside the building for about another thirty seconds. Then two gunshots went off, and everything went silent. Standing there anxiously now, the team just waited. Long minutes passed while they simply stared at the door, trying to determine if they should go in to check on him.

Just as Tom was about to make the executive decision to go see what had happened, the door began to open. First, the wolf appeared, which made everyone take a step back, preparing their weapons. They stopped when James appeared right after it, holding the door open. James looked mostly okay, but his clothes and armor were torn, and there was a giant blood stain covering his crotch area.

"What the fuck happened?!" Tom questioned, more than a little concern in his voice. "Your pants are covered in blood in a very unfortunate spot!"

"I missed," was all James said as he walked to the GS2, opened the trunk, and motioned for the wolf to hop in. It did.

Shocked by what they saw, the party ran over to the vehicle. They all began asking questions simultaneously, trying to get answers.

"I don't want to talk about it. Suffice to say that potions can help grow back body parts," James said, not meeting any of their eyes.

Stunned to silence, everyone looked at James, down to his crotch, then back to his face—realization setting in. Kiera burst out laughing. The others began to feel a bit queasy.

"Can we just fucking go!" James yelled.

"BAHAHAHAHAHAHAHAHAHA!" Kiera continued. "I'm sorry—HAHAHAHAHA—I don't mean to laugh, but—HAHAHAHAHAHAHA!"

"Yeah, hahaha, fuck you too," James said.

Everyone piled into the GS2 and continued their patrol. The wolf was sitting in the trunk, its head leaning over the last row. It panted as it stared at the party.

"So, are you going to introduce us to your new friend?" Derek asked, a huge smile pasted on his face.

James let out an exasperated sigh. "Fine. Everyone, this is Squirrel. Squirrel, this is Kiera, Jay, Kevin, Derek, and Tom," James said, pointing at each person in turn. "They are family. We treat them like such."

"Squirrel?" Jay asked. "Because he likes chasing them?"

"No," James replied. "Because he likes nuts… and not the kind that grows on trees."

The entire car burst into a fit of laughter at this. They drove on and continued to find monsters to kill over the rest of the day, ending with stopping at the Dungeon to make a run through it again. Squirrel was actually a big help in defeating the Bloody Prince in record time because when James snapped his fingers, the wolf darted straight at the man and grabbed onto his crotch with his teeth.

The girlish scream that came from the prince's mouth as he rolled around on the ground, trying unsuccessfully to dislodge the canine from his dangle-downs, made for a hilarious scene. Distracting the sub-boss enough that he couldn't even transform into his berserk form, the poor bastard was put out of his misery quickly and efficiently.

Squirrel attempted to similarly latch onto the baron's wife during the boss fight.

"No, Squirrel! No nuts there! The other one!" James had to yell at the poor wolf.

It nonetheless bit the woman in the crotch, which actually threw off her concentration, and her spells began to backfire on her, causing her to die from mana backlash.

"Well… huh… that *did* work," was all James could manage to say at the end of the fight. "Who's a good boy? You're a good boy!"

Loving the praise, the wolf let James rustle his fur and scratch him all over as he panted, his mouth open in what looked like a smile. He even howled at the praise.

"So, this is what we really have to look forward to?" Derek asked.

"Oh, come on, they're perfect for each other. Dickhead and his pet, cockgobbler," Jay said.

The pair had a good laugh at that. Finishing up, the team moved to the vending machine that appeared at the throne. Kevin stepped up first and put his hand on the machine.

"What the fuck?" Kevin said, staring at the options in the machine.

"What is it?" Tom asked.

"I don't think these are the right options for me," Kevin replied.

Moving to the glass to look inside, sure enough, the items in the machine seemed to be spells and staves that had magic attacks tied to them. Usually, the machine was filled with two-handed weapons and Strength or Constitution buffing items. This time, there were a lot of items designed to boost his Intelligence or Wisdom.

Typing out the item number for one of the items in the machine as his reward for completing the Dungeon, Kevin bought one of the Staves of Fireball. It dispensed out, and he opened the can. Sure enough, a wooden staff with a red gem on the top appeared in his hand when the smoke cleared.

"It says I can't use this with my Class," Kevin said after looking at a screen only he could see.

"What the hell is going on?" Tom said, moving forward to put his hand on the machine.

Resting his hand on the screen, the options began to change. Holy symbols and heavy armor with light magic options started to appear.

"Now, I know I can't use this shit. I'm a fucking Warlock," Tom said. "This is like Cleric or Paladin gear. I can't even heal them because my powers are dark-aligned. What's the deal?"

Completely confused, the party could do nothing but stare at the machine, unable to understand. These machines had always worked perfectly and distributed the items they needed to grow in their Classes. A message suddenly appeared in every display all at once.

System-Wide Message:

Attention all users: Unmanned virtual storefronts, commonly known as vending machines, have begun malfunctioning. Admins are currently investigating the issue to ensure no further incidents or fatalities occur due to the incorrect dispensing of equipment. We apologize for any inconvenience and urge all users to exercise caution when making purchases until the issue is resolved.

"Further incidents or *fatalities?* As in, people have been dying from purchasing the wrong equipment?!" Tom said incredulously.

The message had come in a prompt bordered with bright red coloration and exclamation marks inside triangles at each corner of the border. Clearly, it was an important message. Moments later, another message popped into their view. As with the last one, it could not be minimized until it was read.

<table>
<tr><td>

Planetwide Quest – Destroy the Corruption:

You have been offered a quest to eliminate the corruption that has infected the vending machines on Earth and restore order to the world. A creature with the ability to corrupt mana-powered devices has emerged and infiltrated the central vending system. Your task is to travel to the Grand Canyon, where the central vending machine hub is located, and destroy the source of the corruption. Completing this quest will help restore functionality to the vending machines and prevent further chaos.

Rewards:

- 20,000 XP
- Rare Monster Core
- Restoration of the vending machine system

</td></tr>
</table>

"A quest?!" Derek asked.

"I didn't even know the System gave out quests. We haven't gotten any before now," Tom said.

"This must be a really big deal. I wonder if quests will become a thing now that this has happened?" Jay wondered.

"Quite frankly, it doesn't fucking matter," James said.

"What do you mean?" Kiera asked.

"This was on everyone's displays, right? So that means that everyone in the damned world saw it, and now they are all going to be out for twenty thousand fucking XP plus killing a monster," James said.

"Shit," Kevin swore.

"Well, all we can do is try to go find out what we can do. Seems like killing the creature is the best option regardless of the reward. We need to get our access to gear back, or we are all fucked," Tom said.

Nodding, everyone agreed it was the best option.

"So, we need to head back and tell Brian and TJ what we need to do and come up with a plan while we are gone," Derek said. "And before we go, let's try to see if we can get items that'll help each other. Tom, I'll take a look at your items since they might be for me."

Chapter 29

Party Prep

Heading back to the Guild building, the team pondered the implications of the worldwide message and quest. Not being sure how many people had survived the initial System integration, but trying to compare the number of people they had encountered in Dallas as a standard to go on, was starting to give Tom a headache.

"How many people in the Dallas area do you figure are alive out of the number that used to be here?" Tom asked.

"Figuring just for downtown Dallas, there were roughly fifteen thousand people that lived here, and then the commuters from the suburbs and other cities, with employment the way it has been, I figure one hundred and forty thousand is a good estimate. Though not everyone that worked downtown would have been here since some worked late shifts and what have you. I figure you can make it a nice round one hundred thousand people. Having seen another group out there, I'd guess there are maybe three to five thousand still alive, depending on how many were able to band together to fight. Why?" Derek asked.

"I was just thinking about how many people would be trying to make it to the Grand Canyon for the quest all at once. I'm not trying to be competitive for the prize, but I bet others will be, and that means a fight. Not to mention the fight with whatever is corrupting the vending machines," Tom replied.

"That does complicate things," Derek said, putting his hand on his chin. "There's really nothing for it. We just have to go there and see what can be done. At this point in time, we could not go and hope someone else does it, but there is always the chance that everyone else in the world does the same thing. It's a low chance, but still a chance. So, we have to go."

"We should ask Shandra to join us for the trip with some of her people," Jay piped up.

"Ugh… not that bitch. I do *not* want to travel with her," Kiera said.

"I know, but she's built a group of people who are grinding, so we stand a better chance of success by teaming up with her people," Jay pointed out.

"Jay has a point," Tom said. "I'll reach out to her and see if we can't team up for the trip and the fight. Don't worry, Kiera, we'll take the GS2, and she will have to have her own vehicle, so we technically travel separately."

"Really wish we could still fly there," Kevin said.

"Me too, but there's no way to know if we could even find a plane at this rate, so we have to use what we know works," Derek pointed out. "Not to mention a pilot."

"I know, I know. I was just sayin'," Kevin replied.

"It'd also be a good idea for us to take at least one more person with us," Derek recommended.

"Why? Our party has been doing fine so far," Tom said.

"Sure, but we have a max party size of eight and seven seatbelts in the GS2. We should definitely take advantage of at least one extra person for some extra firepower. I was thinking of Cliff from the Beta team," Derek said.

"He's the wizard, right?" Tom asked.

"Yes. His spell power could come in handy if things get hairy," Derek said.

"What about DeeDee? From the Alpha team," Kiera said. "Kinda tired of the sausage party I keep getting drug along on. And she's a Druid, so extra heals along with spells."

"That's not a bad option," Derek agreed.

"There's also Melvin from the Alpha team. A Paladin. So, heals and a Tank," Jay said.

"I can't stand that self-righteous prick," James said. "Always telling me I have a potty mouth. Well, fuck you very much, *Melvin.* Fuckity fucking fuck fuck!"

"I don't think Melvin will fit in with the team dynamic," Tom said, trying not to laugh looking into the rearview mirror at James.

"So, then we need to decide on Cliff or DeeDee," Kiera said.

"I actually want to change my vote to DeeDee as well," Derek said. "She could take some of the pressure off of me so I can tank more. As far as I know, Cliff has no healing spells, so he's pure DPS."

"Well, it sounds like we need to let Chris know we need to borrow her for a bit. I'm sure someone can fill in for her," Tom said.

A short time later, the GS2 pulled into the parking garage and parked next to the Guild building. Entering the building, TJ was in the lobby, reviewing some security plans with another man Tom didn't immediately recognize.

"Hey, TJ, have you seen Chris around? We need to talk with him about that message everyone got," Tom said, walking over to him and shaking his hand in greeting.

"I can find him. Do you want him to meet you somewhere?" TJ asked.

"Sure, send him to the cafeteria. Feeling a bit hungry, so we're gonna hit up the food since we've been out most of the day," Tom replied.

"I'll send him over. You guys have a good... what the fuck is that?!" TJ said, immediately becoming alert. He drew a pistol from a holster at his side and pointed at the wolf that had walked into the building.

"That's just Squirrel," Tom said quickly, putting himself in front of the gun. "That's James' Familiar. Gonna need you to spread the word about that, too. Forgot to mention it with all the frenzy of this new quest."

TJ eyed the wolf suspiciously but put his gun away when the wolf sat and cocked its head curiously at him.

"Alright, but I *really* need to know these things before you get here. You could radio it in, you know," TJ said.

"Radio died. You got a way to charge them yet?" Tom asked.

"We have a battery that we can charge with a solar panel. Give me your radio," TJ said, holding out his hand.

Tom placed the radio in his hand, and TJ gave him another one.

"There, now let me go get Chris and pass the message around about… Squirrel?" TJ asked.

"Don't ask. Not a good joke," Derek said.

"It's fucking hilarious," James said.

TJ stood there with one eyebrow cocked.

"Ugh… he calls him Squirrel because he likes nuts,' Derek said exasperatedly.

"And not the kind that grows on trees!" James said excitedly, pointing at the giant bloodstain on his pants.

"Oh, dear God! You okay? That looks like a lot of blood!" TJ asked, becoming panicked.

"He's fine. We found out that potions can regrow body parts," Tom said. "At least some of them, anyway. Can you pass that along to Rebecca? I really need something to eat."

"Yeah… sure. I'll pass those messages along," TJ backed away before he could hear anything else.

Turning toward the cafeteria, the team walked through the hallways, greeting people as they passed. Everyone seemed to be contributing in some way, and Tom felt a growing sense of community with each encounter. He was grateful that nearly everyone was willing to pitch in to improve their situation, reinforcing the bond among them all.

Standing in line at the cafeteria, each member of the team ordered lunchroom-style and went to sit at the tables.

"It's nice to be back in the building," Kiera said. "You guys start to stink after a while in that car and all the fighting."

"Psshhh, you're no basket of roses yourself, miss thing," Jay retorted. "Do you even still have deodorant? We could go try to find you some. Make it a grand quest."

"I absolutely have deodorant, and compared to you pigs, I smell like the perfume counters at the mall," Kiera countered.

"You mean really strong, and everyone tries to rush past without making eye contact?" Kevin commented, getting a round of laughs from the others.

"Hey, Tom, you wanted to see me?" Chris said, walking up to the table.

"Yeah, hi Chris, how's it going?" Tom asked politely.

"Oh, not too bad. Staying busy like always," Chris replied with a smile.

"Glad to hear it. Look, we need to ask to borrow someone for that quest that I'm sure you saw the System message for," Tom explained.

"Yeah, I saw it. You guys are going out there?" Chris asked.

"We think it's the best option. We're sure plenty of other people will, too, but there's the tiniest of chances that no one takes it seriously, and they don't go. We have to make sure the quest gets completed so we have access to the right gear again," Tom said.

"Yeah, that makes sense. You think the other teams are up to protecting everyone?" Chris asked.

"They have to be. There's always the chance one day we never come back," Derek added.

Chris looked uneasy at this statement.

"Look, Chris, we have faith in your training and believe you can keep everyone safe here while we're gone. We just need to borrow DeeDee to try to make the most of our party slots and increase our survivability chances," Tom said, trying to reassure the man.

"Okay. Losing DeeDee will be a bit of a blow to the team, but we have a Cleric we can replace her with. I'd rather you guys be sure you come back. Do you want to take another person? Make the full eight party members?" Chris asked.

"We thought about that, and we don't have the room in the GS2, so we think seven is the max we can do right now with James getting a pet," Tom replied.

"James got a pet?" Chris said.

Squirrel got up, walked over to Chris, and nudged him in the crotch. Chris pulled back, concern written on his face.

"This is Squirrel. He uh… likes nuts," Tom said.

"I can see that," Chris said. "He's tame?"

"Eh." James waffled a hand back and forth uncertainly.

"Alright. Well, I'll get DeeDee for you. I'll send her here to meet up with you for now," Chris said, backing away, hands covering his privates.

"See ya later, Chris. And thanks for everything you're doing!" Tom called after him.

Continuing with their meal, the team spoke about what they thought they might encounter on the trip until a woman approached their table. She was a shorter individual with dark brown hair pulled up in a bun, freckles across her face, and glasses. She smiled at them as she approached. She carried a whip on her hip and wore leather armor.

"Hi, guys! I'm DeeDee! Chris said you wanted to see me?" DeeDee said with a bright smile.

"Hey, DeeDee. Yeah, we wanted to see if you wanted to come with us out to the Grand Canyon, where we are going to be seeing what we can do to help complete that quest that was in the message everyone got," Tom explained.

"Oh," DeeDee said, her smile faltering a bit.

"Something wrong?" Derek asked.

"Well, I just wasn't sure about leaving my husband. Can he come too?" DeeDee said.

"We don't have enough room in the GS2 for two more people. So, unless you have some other form of transport, I'm not sure we can take both of you," Tom said. "Who is your husband?"

"His name is Graham. He's on the same team I am. He's a Warrior, though," DeeDee replied.

"Hmm. Let me look at something really fast," Tom said, pulling up his menus.

Flipping through, Tom found the menu he was looking for: the upgrade screen for the GS2. Scrolling through the hundreds of options, he found what he was looking for. Extend cargo space. Seeing he had precisely one upgrade point, he looked up at DeeDee.

"I have a way you can both go, but someone will have to ride in the trunk with Squirrel," Tom said to her.

"A squirrel shouldn't take up much space. I can ride with it," DeeDee said.

"No, not *a* squirrel, *with* Squirrel," Tom said, pointing at the wolf lying at James' feet.

DeeDee gasped audibly as she saw Squirrel. "OH MY GOSH, HE'S SO CUTE!" She squealed as she ran over to hug him. "I love dogs!"

For his part, Squirrel looked up at her and licked her face, seeming to enjoy the attention.

"Well, I guess that means we can take you both. I bet Graham will be a good addition to the team," Tom said, selecting the "Extend Cargo Space" option for the upgrades.

Tom radioed over to Chris and let him know they needed Graham, too, and Chris said that was fine. They had several backup Warriors, which was the most common Class selected. DeeDee continued to sit on the floor with Squirrel and rubbed his belly as he turned over for more attention, closing his eyes contentedly.

"Should have known a Druid would like animals," Derek said, a smile forming as he watched the two.

"What do you mean?" Kevin asked.

"Druids are nature lovers. If someone chose that, they likely read the description about forming bonds with animals. I wonder what animal she can turn into?" Derek asked no one in particular.

"A bear," DeeDee answered.

"Really?! That could be extremely helpful," Derek replied.

"It is. That's why I chose it. Goblins basically pee themselves when they see me transform. It's hilarious," DeeDee said, never taking her eyes off Squirrel.

"Well, I can't wait to see that in combat," Derek said, really excited about it.

A short while later, a man walked into the cafeteria. The man was very light-skinned, with red hair and glasses. He wore heavy armor, though, and carried a twin-headed battle axe with a huge blade in one hand and a metal coffin shield in the other.

"Wow, he looks like a badass, doesn't he?" James said.

"That is definitely someone I would want on our team. But just because he has good equipment doesn't mean he can fight," Derek said.

"Oh, Graham used to be a professional medieval fighter. We used to tour around the world, where he would compete in tournaments with others wearing medieval armor and fighting with weapons like these. He's quite good," DeeDee said, boasting about her husband and beaming at him.

The entire party stared at the man in a new light.

"Seriously? Where were you hiding him? We could have used him on our team from the start!" Kevin said.

"Oh, you guys were *fine*. Besides, we liked training the others as they came in and teaching them to fight with this kind of equipment," DeeDee said.

"You mean you fight, too?" Derek asked.

"Well, I learned from Graham while we were dating. Then, when we got married, we trained together while we were on the road," DeeDee explained. "It definitely deepened our bond."

"Are you overselling me again, DeeDee?" Graham asked as he smiled through his goatee at her.

"No, my love. I'm just telling people a little bit about us so we can get to know each other since we'll be working together," DeeDee said, smiling back up at him.

"Dude, if you're even half as good as I think you are, then you're going to be training us on the road, especially Kevin and me," Derek said. "We need to learn a little more about fighting."

"You got it! I'll teach you what I know. Happy to help make the team better," Graham agreed happily.

"Alright then, let's go grab some supplies, and we'll head out first thing in the morning for Arizona," Tom said.

Chapter 30

Road Trip

The following day, the team met back up at the parking garage, and Tom extended party invitations to DeeDee and Graham. Upon their first look at the now larger GS2, they noticed that the vehicle appeared to not only be longer, making it more of a Suburban than a Tahoe, but it was also slightly taller and broader, making the room inside more spacious for the passengers.

"Damn! I'm not touching people on both sides of me anymore. Though, the back row is still going to be a bit cramped," James commented on the inside, sitting in one of the captain chairs in the second row that had replaced the bench seat originally there.

Hopping back out of the vehicle and opening the tailgate, Squirrel hopped up into the far more spacious trunk and wagged his tail as he stood happily with his mouth open, tongue lolling out, staring at the team.

"Squirrel fits nicely, and there's room for someone else back here, too. These storage spaces are great, so we don't need to take equipment with us in the vehicle, which takes up space," James commented again.

"That's true. Going on vacation in the old world would have been so much easier with Inventories," Tom said.

"So would sneaking a bomb on a plane," Derek said absentmindedly.

"Man, you are *such* a downer," James said.

"Just thinking about the practicality," Derek said, looking at the inside of the vehicle.

"You could let us have the moment," James said.

"Or I could warn you of danger like I always do. Seems to help keep you alive pretty well," Derek said, looking directly at James.

"You have a point," James said.

Reaching up and scratching Squirrel behind the ears, DeeDee also looked into the trunk.

"I've brought along some blankets and pillows for the ride, so it should be quite comfy for me and this good boy here," DeeDee said.

Squirrel leaned into the affection and beamed with happiness.

"Hey, you're *my* pet, you little fucker," James teased Squirrel.

Squirrel gave James a look and then licked DeeDee's face as if to say "I like her better now."

"Fine, be that way. See if I give you any treats on the way," James said in mock offense.

"Everybody have water and food stocked?" Tom asked.

Everyone nodded.

"Good, then we can load up and start the journey. The drive used to be about fifteen hours, but with vehicles stalled on the road and other unknown dangers, I'd expect the journey to take several days," Tom said, getting the team's attention. "Brian was able to get us enough gas to get there and back, which Derek and I also have in storage. Does anyone need to use the bathroom before we go? Speak now or forever hold your pee."

No one moved, and several shook their heads.

"Alright, then load up, and let's move out!" Tom said.

"Shotgun!" Derek exclaimed, staring at James.

At Derek's shout, Kiera pulled out her literal shotgun from her Inventory and aimed it vaguely at the man, her expression deadpan. "Shotgun."

"Fuck," Derek frowned, taking his hand off the door handle.

"Stone cold killer, that one," James murmured as they crawled into the back.

"Tell me about it," Derek growled. Climbing into the vehicle, everyone got ready to depart. Graham had to sit in one of the captain's chairs because of his armor, but no one minded having him along as they would stop in the evenings for training sessions with him to help them fight better. Taking up defensive positions as they had been, with the exception of Graham also leaning out a window now, the team prepared to drive through the city.

As they exited the garage, a large group of people were waiting out front, with the security team standing guard. They all waved and called out their wishes for success in the mission. Some yelled their thanks for the efforts they had put in to keep them safe.

"Wow. Is this what celebrities feel like?" James asked.

"I don't think we're celebrities," Derek replied.

James stuck one hand out in the air and proceeded to do a princess wave to the crowd, blowing kisses with his other hand as they drove by.

"Is he always like this?" Graham asked, his southern drawl coming out a bit.

"You get used to it," Jay said.

Once clear of the crowd and the building, the team kept a vigilant eye out for any monsters as they drove through the downtown streets. The scene resembled something out of a warzone; downtown Dallas was nothing like it used to be. Trash littered the streets, and vehicles were left abandoned where their owners had fled. The Guild had managed to clear many of them out of the way, but some obstacles remained, forcing them to maneuver around vehicles that had been immobilized by accidents or other damage. The once bustling city now felt eerily quiet and desolate, a stark reminder of how much their world had changed.

Lifeless bodies still lay scattered throughout the city, some unavoidable as they drove through, having been run over multiple times. With no resources to properly handle the remains, scavengers had begun feeding on the corpses, making it common to see buzzards and coyotes gnawing on flesh and bones. The sight was a grim reminder of the harsh realities they now faced.

Finally reaching Highway 183, the team could pick up the pace slightly, but they were still far from reaching highway speeds. Abandoned vehicles littered the road, forcing them to navigate carefully and slowing their progress significantly compared to how things were before the apocalypse. Several times, they had to stop, exit the GS2, and physically move crashed vehicles that completely blocked their path.

As they traveled, the true extent of the devastation became painfully clear. Bodies, left exposed under the harsh sun, had begun to decompose. The stench of rot filled the air, with many corpses bloated from the gas build-up, some having burst from the pressure. Others had been partially consumed by scavengers, leaving behind only skeletal remains. The grim sights and smells emphasized the harsh new reality they were now living in.

"Feels like a zombie show out here. Hope none of them come back to life and start walking around trying to eat us," James commented.

"Is that a possibility?" DeeDee asked from the trunk, concern sounding in her voice.

"Honestly, if you had asked me two weeks ago, I would have said no way. But now… We haven't seen any indication it could happen, but magic makes impossible things possible. So just keep an eye out," Derek said. "I'm sure we can kill any zombies that pop up, though."

"Yeah! Sweet XP and fat loots!" James said excitedly.

"Seriously, dude? Is that all you think about now?" Jay asked.

"I mean, why not? We need to get stronger. Killing things is the best way to do that so far," James replied.

"But if they're zombies, those are someone's friends or kids or parents," DeeDee said.

"*Were*," James corrected. "Now they're loot bags!"

The collective eye roll at this comment was so strong it could practically be heard.

"I don't know if I could kill someone," DeeDee said.

"You might have to," Derek replied.

"What?!" DeeDee exclaimed.

"This world isn't like the one we lived in before. There will be people who survived who want to be the strongest or might even just like killing people. You'll have to be ready for that because it will be you or them," Derek said. "The police aren't going to come in and save you in this world. You'll be put in kill-or-be-killed situations eventually. I don't like having to tell you that, but it's the reality."

Silence reigned in the car for a long minute as this thought permeated the party.

"What did Shandra say, Tom?" Jay asked, trying to change the subject.

"She said they are also sending a team to investigate the quest. But she didn't want anything to do with working with us," Tom replied.

"What a bitch," Kiera commented.

"Well, what did you expect? It's who she is. We can't change that. We can just be as neighborly as possible and work to show them we are just trying to be good human beings in this new reality," Tom said.

"I expect people to be decent human beings and help when something big is on the line like this," Kiera replied.

"You wouldn't know a decent human being if I was sitting right next to you," Jay teased.

"If one were sitting right next to me, I could point them out. Too bad they aren't," Kiera shot back.

"Come on, you can do better than that," Jay said.

"Fine, you smelly sack of shit, if you want it, you can have it. You probably fucked your mom and cat-called your sister, you backwoods, vag-drying, old-ass dick carpet. I'd call you a cunt, but you lack the depth and warmth," Kiera said.

"*There* she is!" Jay said excitedly while chuckling.

"And you all talk to each other like this all the time?" DeeDee asked.

"Yup. Everyday." James smiled at her.

"The power of friendship," Graham said, forming an imaginary rainbow with his hands.

"Don't you go all My Little Pony on us, Graham," James said.

"Oh, come on, it's better than being known as the dick guy," Graham shot back, a big grin on his face.

"Hey! I'll have you know, I'm *not* the dick guy, I'm the *nuts* guy!" James retorted indignantly before pausing for a moment. "I like this guy. Can we keep him?" he asked, turning to Tom.

Tom laughed from the driver's seat. "You're gonna fit in great, Graham. DeeDee, you gotta let loose a little. It's the end of the world, after all."

"I'm good. You guys can keep at it. I don't feel comfortable using that kind of language," DeeDee replied.

"What a goody two shoes," Kiera said.

"Sorry, I just never was like that. But feel free to keep going. It is amusing," DeeDee said back.

Continuing down Highway 183 for quite some time, the team made steady progress until they encountered an impassable blockade. Cars were lined up across the highway in a way that clearly wasn't accidental. Spray-painted across several vehicles were the words "SURVIVORS MEET AT IRVING MALL," indicating a potential gathering point for those who had made it through the chaos.

"Think we should check it out?" Tom asked, looking at Derek.

"Might as well. They might need some help," Derek replied.

Turning off the freeway, they took the exit that led down to the mall. A path had been cleared straight to the parking lot. Once in the lot, they drove around until Graham called out.

"Someone just ducked into the Macy's. There are definitely people here."

Pulling over to the entrance, Tom brought the GS2 to a stop. They sat there for a moment, trying to decide what to do.

"Should we just go in?" Tom asked.

"I don't like that idea. There could be an ambush waiting," Derek replied.

"We could knock," James offered.

"Still gets us too close," Derek replied.

While discussing options, a man exited the building wearing what looked like chain armor and carrying a greataxe. He was a little over six feet tall and had red hair with a full beard. He walked to the edge of the sidewalk and stood there, looking at the party in the vehicle.

"Friend or foe?" the man called to them.

"Hopefully, friend," Tom called back. "What is going on here?"

"The fucking apocalypse, you twit," the man replied.

"I mean with the mall. Why are you all here?" Tom said.

"Not a bad place to hole up. We've been working to get people safe," he replied.

"I'm Tom. We're coming from Downtown Dallas. We're heading to the Grand Canyon to check out the quest and see what we can do," Tom told the man.

"I'm Kedron. Good to know people survived. We haven't seen many others. Was beginning to wonder if most of the world had died off," Kedron said.

"How many are here?" Tom asked.

"A little over thirty. We found that these department stores had many creature comforts we could use, so we moved here to make use of the facilities. These monsters have been a real bitch, though. Always showing up at inopportune times," Kedron replied.

"You form a Guild yet?" Derek asked from the passenger seat.

"No, haven't been able to get enough people to agree. You have one?" Kedron asked.

"We do. It's in the Trammel Crow Center back in Dallas. If you have transport, you could all head there and be welcomed to use the facilities we have there," Tom said.

"That would be most appreciated. But I'm not sure many would want to leave. Most of the survivors here had their spirits broken when this all started. They weren't ready to deal with such loss and horrors," Kedron said. "I'll bring it up to them, though. See if any want to head that way. You say you are headed to check out the quest?"

"We are. The vending machines acting up have been a huge disruption to survival. We need to see if there's something we can do," Tom replied.

"I have some people with me that want to do the same. Would you mind if we joined you?" Kedron asked.

"If you have transportation, you're welcome to come along. We just can't take anyone else with us in the GS2," Tom said.

"GS2?" Kedron questioned.

"Oh, right, the Goblin Slayer 2.0. It's what we call this vehicle," Tom replied.

Kedron chuckled at that. "So, you use this to slay goblins?" he asked, gesturing at the vehicle.

"Quite a few, actually," Tom said, smiling.

APOCALYPSE

"Hadn't thought to do that. But now it seems so obvious," Kedron said. "We have a vehicle, though not as nice as yours, and I'm sure the others could find some that would still run to take to Dallas. Let me go in and talk with them. You are welcome to come in for a time if you like."

Looking at Derek and then back, Tom replied, "I think we'll wait for you here. But we would love the additional help in finding out if we can complete the quest."

"Suit yourselves. I'll be back in a few minutes," Kedron said, turning to go back inside.

The team turned off the vehicle to conserve gas and stepped out to stretch their legs in the parking lot. About twenty minutes later, Kedron returned, accompanied by a group of four others: a large red-haired man, a shorter, portly balding man, a woman who appeared to be in her late fifties, and a towering man, around six foot six, with a well-built frame, dark hair, and a beard. All of them wore leather armor and carried various weapons, except for the woman, who was dressed in white garments and carried a staff.

They walked over to the team, and Kedron addressed them, "So, who's ready to go save the fucking world?"

Chapter 31

New Friends

"That was a badass intro!" James said excitedly.

"Don't mind him. He's an idiot," Derek said.

"I guess introductions are in order. I'm Tom, this is Derek and James, over there is Jay and Kiera. The loincloth is Kevin, and they are DeeDee and Graham," Tom said.

James opened the trunk and Squirrel hopped out, shaking his fur out and stretching.

"AH! A fucking wolf! Kill it!" the balding man exclaimed at seeing Squirrel.

"You moron, the wolf got out of their vehicle. Clearly, it's with them," the big, red-headed man said, slapping the balding man over the back of the head. "Don't mind him; he's crazy. I'm Bobby. The crazy one is Clay."

"This is Briana," Kedron said, gesturing at the female, "and the big guy is Austin."

"It's a pleasure to meet all of you. Are you all prepared for what we might be facing? This could be really dangerous, and there will be monsters along the way," Tom said.

"All of us have acted as the first line of defense here. We have been fighting off any monsters in the area, so we know what to expect," Kedron said as the others nodded behind him. "We've lost some friends. We know the risks."

"Alright. Then, let's get headed out. We don't have time to waste. Do you all have enough gas?" Tom asked.

"We've been siphoning out the other cars, so we have plenty for now," Kedron said. "Does the offer still stand to join your Guild? We would all be happy to be a part, if you'll have us."

"It does. You just have to be aware that everyone pulls their weight. We'll ask you to lend any skills you have to the Guild. But we're always looking for good people who can fight," Tom said.

Turning to Derek momentarily, Tom double-checked he was making the right call. Derek gave one curt nod, and Tom looked back to Kedron. His shoulders slumped as if a weight had been lifted.

"I'm happy to hear you say that. We all believe that the more people stick together, the more likely they are to survive. I've left some people here who are going to try to help others to your base. Those willing, anyway. Can't help anyone not willing to help themselves," Kedron replied, looking sad at saying it. "And don't worry, we aren't afraid of a little hard work."

Tom nodded. "Agreed, but you do feel bad. I know the feeling all too well."

Navigating to the Guild page, Tom extended an invitation to the Guild to all present. They all accepted.

"The others will be able to get an invite from Brian when they arrive. They just need to say that they met us here, and they should be accepted without issue," Tom said. "Now, what vehicle are you taking?"

"We have been using a sedan for the most part, but seeing your vehicle, I think we have something we will use instead," Kedron said.

With that, they walked off to a parking garage attached to the department store and drove out a few minutes later in a second-generation Hummer.

"Where the hell did you get *that?*" Derek asked as Kedron rolled down the window and smiled at them.

"It was just parked here in the garage. We've been doing Inventory of the vehicles here and which one's had keys. This one had the driver dead about twenty yards from it. They had clearly been running for the vehicle when something attacked them. We figure gobos got them. Keys were in their pocket," Kedron said. "You gave me the idea when you talked about running things over. It's not as maneuverable as the smaller car, but it's way more durable. Plus, we look pretty badass."

"It's *definitely* badass! If we see any goblins, be sure to run them down. It gives you a skill for killing things with it, and it seems to offer you the ability to upgrade the vehicle as well," Tom said.

"Fucking dope! I can't wait to run over some of those green bastards," Kedron said. "They… they took my brother. So, now I murder any of them I see. Those fuckers will pay!"

"I'm so sorry," Tom said.

"It's not your fault. And I appreciate you just being willing to take us in. We didn't know what we were going to do being stuck here. So, let's just hit the road and figure out what we can do with this quest. Twenty thousand XP is a lot to look forward to," Kedron replied.

With everyone back in the vehicles, the team headed for the highway once more. Kedron guided them around the barrier using a few side streets, and as they approached the on-ramp, the first set of goblins appeared. The creatures had constructed a crude barricade out of wooden sticks, blocking access to the highway. Huddled behind their makeshift defenses, the goblins jeered at the approaching vehicles in their chittering language. Tom pulled the GS2 up alongside the Hummer, and with a gesture that said "after you," he gave Kedron the lead.

Kedron grinned wickedly and revved the Hummer's engine. Releasing the brake, he roared forward, barreling toward the goblins' barricade. The goblins tried to pelt the vehicle with rocks and crude spears, but their expressions turned to terror as the Hummer smashed through the barricade, reducing it to splinters and painting the ground with their blood.

Tom and his team followed close behind, running over a few goblins that had tried to dive out of the way. One of the goblins met its end when Graham, leaning out of the side window, delivered a decapitating blow with his axe. There were no survivors. Pulling up next to the Hummer, Tom and his team saw Kedron's group high-fiving and cheering, celebrating their victory.

"Felt good?" Tom asked.

"We definitely should have done this sooner!" Kedron called. "That was fucking awesome!"

"Let's keep going for now. I'm sure there will be more chances for automotive assassination later," Tom said.

Continuing on, the teams drove for hours, taking Highway 183 over to 287 North. They pressed on until they reached Rhome, Texas, where they decided to pull off the highway for the night as darkness began to fall. Although they would have preferred to make more progress, the journey had been slow, with frequent stops to move abandoned vehicles blocking the road.

As they pulled into the small town, Derek pointed out a building on the outskirts that looked suitable for hunkering down for the night. The town appeared completely abandoned, devoid of almost all life. The only signs of movement came from wildlife scurrying away as they entered the parking lot. The eerie silence underscored the world's changes since the integration into the System.

"We should be able to stay here. It's likely only got one or two entrances and is fairly defensible, with easy access to the highway if we need to make a quick getaway," Derek said.

The building was a small credit union with very few windows. It left much to be desired in the way of comfort, but it would protect them from the elements and seemed to have been undisturbed so far, as the glass door was still intact.

"I'm guessing the vault is still closed, but we can still rest pretty easy knowing that the building is structurally sound," Derek added.

Derek smashed the glass door with his mace, leading the way into the credit union to scout the area and ensure they were alone. As he had anticipated, the building was completely deserted. With the coast clear, they decided to set up for the night, laying out some of the bedding they had brought with them behind the counters, near the securely closed vault door. The quiet, empty space offered a sense of safety, a rare comfort in recent days.

"We'll need to take watches—two at a time to ensure we stay awake—in three-hour shifts," Derek said.

"You sure seem to know what you're doing," Bobby commented. "Military guy?"

Derek nodded. "Couple tours in Afghanistan."

"Iraq," Bobby replied. "Good to see someone else with a good head on their shoulders."

"Bobby here has been our strategic coordinator. Without him, we would have died several times over," Kedron said, patting Bobby on the back.

"Just doing what I can to keep everyone safe," Bobby said humbly.

"You know, if we had some explosives, we could blow this bank vault wide open!" Clay said, looking at the vault door.

"And do what? Wipe our asses with the money?" Austin asked. "Shut up, you crazy fool. Money ain't worth shit anymore, and you just want to get your hands on some explosives."

"True. But I'd love to blow something up. It's really cathartic," Clay replied.

"So, Clay is a pyro. Neat!" James said. "We have some explosives back at the Guild building. Tom gave some to a chicken that we fed to a troll and watched its head explode."

"*Great...* Stupid made a crazy friend," Jay said, sighing loudly.

"I'm not stupid. I'm just easily excitable," James said, blowing a raspberry at Jay.

"And still five years old, apparently," Jay said.

"Ah, shove off, ya wanker. You're just no fun," James said in a mock British accent.

"Now, now, boys, you're both pretty. No need for a dick-measuring contest," Kiera said, reclining on one of the mattresses they had set out.

"Don't say the word dick around James. It gets him excited," Graham added.

"*I'm* not the one that gets"—he formed two fingers on each hand into quotes—"*excited.* But you might be careful of saying it around Squirrel," James said, giving his wolf a leery side eye as it lay on the mattress curled up next to Kiera.

Kedron and his team looked at James quizzically.

"It's a long story. We'll tell you once we're settled," Tom said.

The team spent another hour settling in, eating, and talking. James regaled them with the story of how he found Squirrel, adding some exaggerated heroism for effect. The lighthearted storytelling helped everyone relax, and they took the opportunity to get to know each other better, sharing stories and experiences.

"So, you seriously just ran out there and peed on the electric fence?" James asked, laughing hysterically.

"Damn straight! Jesse said I wouldn't, so I had to prove him wrong! Couldn't feel my dick for a week, but it was worth it!" Clay said.

"You are one crazy son of a bitch, Clay," James said.

Walking over to Kedron, Tom handed him one of the water bottles they had brought.

"Seems like our teams are meshing well," he commented.

"I'm just glad to see them letting their hair down a bit," Kedron said. "We've been stuck with a bunch of people who had no business being the ones that survived the first wave of monsters, but we just didn't feel like we could turn them away. Real party poopers when it came to getting anything done."

"I hear ya. We were fortunate enough to be in a place where, once we started putting in the work to help people, some Professionals stepped up and made some of the comforts of our old life available, and the others began to pitch in where they could. We also have a pretty great Guild Admin working on getting everything organized. That guy can work miracles," Tom said.

"Can't wait to be part of something more organized. Some of those people expected us to just do everything for them while they wallowed in their misery. I mean, really, people. It's the end of the fucking world. Buck up or die already," Kedron said. "But I just couldn't bring myself to do that. Just leave people to get killed."

"It's hard. We're so ingrained with the thought that every life matters because we lived in such a peaceful time, all things considered now," Tom said, shaking his head. "But we were soft. I still like to think there's a place for everyone, but with resources becoming more and more limited, I'm coming to believe that not everyone can be saved, even though I haven't been treating them like that yet."

"Right? You want to help anyone who comes along, but some of them just refuse to do anything, accept what is happening, and take action. They're frozen with indecision on things like violence, even when a monster is coming at them with a weapon. You throw yourself in front of the danger and tell yourself that they'll stand up and fight next time, but then they don't. They just stand behind you and cower. We lost one of our friends, Phil, because he was determined to save someone who had literally shit themselves when they had gotten cornered after throwing a woman in front of him to distract a group of goblins trying to kill them," Kedron said. "Phil was trying to fight off the goblins, but the other guy tripped him, thinking he could get away while they attacked Phil. He got dragged down too, though."

"Some people will do anything to save themselves," Tom said.

"Yeah, and it's fuckers like him that make me even angrier than the monsters. Someone willing to let another person die just for a chance at saving themselves," Kedron said.

"For now, though, all we can do is focus on us. Let the others deal with that. You told the others to leave them if they didn't want to go, right?" Tom asked.

"I did. I said enough was enough. We might not get another chance like this, so we have to take it. I hope everyone decides to go. I don't want the others to have to carry the burden of leaving someone behind. But I'm guessing they'll see reason when they realize that they will get left behind," Kedron said. "They're cowards at heart, so I think they'll go with them, even if begrudgingly."

"Yeah, I wouldn't want that either, but you can't carry all the weight. You gotta let some of that roll off your back. You didn't cause this. You're just as much a victim," Tom said.

"You're right. And I'm working on it. Just gonna take some time," Kedron said.

"Let's rest for tonight. Don't think about what's happening there, and let the others take care of that."

With that, they rejoined the others, sharing stories about what had happened since the screens first appeared in the sky. As the night wore on, they eventually settled in to rest, preparing to resume their journey in the morning.

APOCALYPSE

It was late into the night when a sharp kick to his side abruptly awakened Tom. He blinked groggily, trying to make sense of the situation as the darkness pressed in around him.

"Get up. You all are coming with us," a man said as a flashlight shone in Tom's face.

Tom looked up, blinking away sleep, and saw a gun barrel pointed at his face. He was roughly grabbed, his hands yanked behind his back as a man quickly handcuffed him. Without a word, the man led him outside, where some of the others were already sitting on the ground, their expressions a mix of fear and confusion.

"We want all your shit before you die. So don't hold out on us, ya hear?"

A man stepped out from behind a set of police cruisers that were sitting in the parking lot, blocking their vehicles from leaving.

Chapter 32

Dirty Cops

Lights swept across the ground like miniature spotlights, searching for a target as people moved around, their flashlights cutting through the darkness. The sound of gravel scraping against the pavement filled the air, a staccato rhythm created by the shifting of boots as the group was led to separate positions, far enough apart that they couldn't reach each other's bound hands.

After the men had gathered the entire group in front of the credit union building, Tom quickly scanned the area and counted about eight men, all dressed in police uniforms. It was clear they had managed to get the drop on them. Try as he might, Tom couldn't remember who was supposed to be on watch that night.

"It was Clay and James," Derek said when he saw the look on Tom's face.

Looking around, Tom didn't see Clay or James, though.

"Where are they?" Tom asked quietly.

"No clue. I haven't seen them. Don't look for them, though. We don't want them to know people are missing," Derek said.

"Quiet, you two! Just give us what we want, and we'll make this nice and easy. No more suffering in this shit hole of a world for you all. You can rest in peace," a man said, seeming to be the leader.

He was tall, at least six-four, with a cowboy hat and a star on his chest that said state trooper.

"Aren't you guys supposed to help people?" Tom asked. "You know, serve and protect and all. And how the hell did you get the drop on us?"

"That went out the window along with law and order when the fucking apocalypse happened, son," the trooper said. "And this here new System put in place gave us some very useful abilities. Like *Move Silently*, and a handy little spell called *Stasis* that helps keep you asleep. Doesn't *put* you to sleep, mind you. Shame that. But keeping someone asleep? That skill is solid gold. After that, it was just a matter of finding your vehicles parked here that weren't here before, and pulling up with our lights off. You stupid mother fuckers never saw us coming. And lastly, you dum-dums left the front doors unlocked."

Reading his badge, Tom could see that the man's last name was Carson. He sighed heavily, knowing James and Clay must have wandered off somewhere, which meant leaving the doors unlocked to get back in.

"So, why not change first? Why not wear street clothes?" Tom asked.

"Well, that's because this here badge puts people at ease. Everybody thinks the cops are there to save them. Then we swoop in, take what we need, and trim the fat, so to speak," Carson said, pointing to his head as if to show he was the brains behind the whole plan. "It's really efficient and has gotten us through some tough times. Plus, *we* are the ones with the guns. So, it gave us a starting advantage."

"This is Texas. You really think you're the only ones with guns?" Derek retorted.

"Well, no, not at all. But, again, the uniform kinda sells us as the good guys. So, it puts people off-guard at first. Makes the job a little easier. Thin blue line and all that crap," Carson said.

"Fucking dirty cops. I know your kind. You probably stopped people and let them off with a warning if they contributed to the 'police ball' or some shit like that," Kedron said.

"He's not a cop," Derek said.

"What?!" Kedron asked.

"How many troopers do you know with a neck tattoo?" Derek asked.

Carson, or the man pretending to be Carson, rubbed the tattoo on the side of his neck.

"Well, aren't we the observant one?" he asked, smiling deviously at Derek.

"So, what happened? You all find a cop and kill them, thinking you could impersonate them?" Derek asked.

"Not quite. We were in the town jail. Cops came in all panicked, and I managed to get one of them too close to the bars. Killed him and took the keys. Freed some friends of mine, and we formed a posse of sorts," the man said.

"So, who are you really?" Kedron asked.

"Doesn't really matter. You can just keep calling me Carson. Kinda fond of the name now," Carson said.

"What an asshole. Could have gone on your way, but I guess once a criminal, always a criminal," Bobby said.

"Maybe. But in this world and the last, you always gotta look out for numero uno, compadre. Otherwise, you get sucked into the system, and they treat you like trash," Carson said. "Fredericks! Go get the enforcement tools from the back of my cruiser. I think these guys are going to need a little persuasion to part with their gear."

The man, apparently Fredericks, ran to the back of one of the police vehicles and popped open the trunk. A minute later, he reappeared and handed Carson a rolled-up piece of canvas, which Carson spread out on the hood of the GS2. As the canvas unfurled, a chilling array of tools came into view: pliers, scalpels, bamboo shoots, a saw, and several other instruments that Tom couldn't name but instinctively recognized as torture devices.

"I'd like to think people can change. And we tried that for about a day. But in this new, fucked up world, it's even more kill or be killed than it was before."

"It was never kill or be killed before. There was order to how people lived," Tom said.

"Order? Was there *order* when I grew up in the projects and had to fight for my stuff? When the cops wouldn't come to help a boy who had his bike stolen? Or a kid finds his parents when they were cracked out of their minds just trying to make the world go away? No. We were left to fend for ourselves in a system that failed us," Carson said. "No one came to help us, so we did what we had to."

Carson stared at them for a long moment, daring them to question what he was saying. Daring anyone to tell him he was wrong.

"Now, who wants to go first? How about you, Mr. I-know-your-type. You seem like someone who will be tougher to break. Might as well start with you," Carson said. "Don't want to be tired when I get around to you later."

They roughly hauled Bobby up and dragged him away from the others. As they moved him, several people began to struggle against their handcuffs, but when all the so-called officers drew their weapons and pointed them at the group, the resistance quickly stopped. The threat of violence hung heavy in the air, silencing any further attempts to resist.

"Guys, don't, just don't. It'll be okay," Bobby said as they leaned him up against the side of the Hummer.

"If you lay a hand on him, I swear to God, I'll fucking kill you!" Kedron said, his anger rising.

"Oh, I don't think you're in any position to be making demands, son," Carson said.

And with no warning, he pulled his pistol and shot Kedron in the leg. Kedron yelled at the pain and fell over onto the ground.

"Anyone else have any objections? No? Alright then, let's get this party started," Carson said, turning back to Bobby.

Suddenly, a red dot illuminated the fake cop's uniform, right over his heart. A familiar voice carried out across the parking lot, thick with a southern drawl.

"Couldn't have said it better myself." James was leaning casually up against a decorative crenelation of the credit union. Somewhere, the man had found a cigar and was smoking it casually as he swung one leg back and forth over the edge of the building. "That, my friend, is a fifty-caliber sniper rifle aimed directly at that piece of black coal you call a heart." James puffed easily on the cigar, blowing a smoke ring into the air above him. "Bullshit, you might say. Never saw no sniper rifle in the vending machine, you might argue." James let his head fall casually to the side as he locked eyes with the man down below. "To which I would say: Ever been in a Dungeon? They got rewards in there you can't even imagine. Beat one and it gives you a little *something*—free of charge. Well, we got ourselves a cannon that kills shit stains like you by turning them into so much kibble." James flicked the cigar out in a lazy motion. As it spun, arcing its way to the ground, James casually rose to his feet. "So, how 'bout we—how did you put it?" He looked up for a moment as though trying to remember. He snapped his fingers. "That's right—get this party started? We can start by rearranging that ugly fucking face of yours."

The red dot slid up the man's body before centering itself on his forehead.

Carson's eyes were crossed, trying to look up at the dot that had moved toward his forehead. Shaking, he followed the dot back up toward the roof. Squinting, he seemed to have noticed what Tom had already seen.

APOCALYPSE

James was holding the 1911 with the red dot sight between his crooked elbow and was pointing it at the man as he spoke.

"You *mother* fucker!" Carson shouted. "That ain't no sniper rifle." He turned toward one of his men standing next to him. "Looks like we missed one. Jameson, go ahead and take care of him. Most of the loot is still fine," Carson said, turning to face James.

A man moved to point his gun at James, but before he could take aim, Squirrel suddenly rushed out from the side of the building and leaped onto the man, sinking his teeth into his face. The fake officer, who was clearly Jameson, let out a scream as the wolf tore into him.

Others moved to try and help Jameson, but a thunderous bellow from the opposite side grabbed their attention. Clay came charging out, wielding a sword in each hand, ready to engage.

"Time to die, motherfuckers!" Clay yelled as he stabbed and slashed at the men.

Carson moved to pull his pistol to aim at Clay but fell over, screaming and grabbing his crotch as a shot fired off from the roof.

"Dick shot!" James yelled as he jumped down from the roof.

Chaos erupted as people began to throw themselves at the impostor cops. Despite their hands being cuffed behind their backs, several members of the group jumped on top of their captors or charged into them to knock them down. Amid the melee, Clay continued his rampage, cutting down anyone wearing a uniform.

Derek, suddenly free from the handcuffs, punched one of the fake cops in the face. He quickly summoned his mace from his Inventory and brought it down with crushing force on the man's skull.

Nearby, Kiera screamed as she delivered a fierce kick to the face of one of the impersonators who had been knocked to the ground. Squirrel, ever the loyal companion, raced over and clamped down on the man's groin before standing protectively in front of Kiera, his first foe already lying dead.

From behind, green magic radiated as DeeDee summoned vines from the earth, which quickly wrapped around another cop's wrists, pinning his arms to his sides just as he aimed his gun at her. Graham, seizing the opportunity, sprinted over and delivered a powerful dropkick to the restrained officer's chest like a WWE wrestler. The sickening crunch of breaking bone echoed as the man's sternum cracked from the impact. Though winded from landing on his side, Graham quickly rolled over, got back to his feet, and began kicking the man repeatedly, ensuring he stayed down.

James sprinted around the chaotic scene, firing his gun at each of the officers he could find, aiming directly at their groins and shouting "dick shot!" after every round he fired. Meanwhile, Bobby was mercilessly stomping on Carson's chest as he lay on the ground, screaming in agony and clutching his crotch, desperately trying—and failing—to roll away from Bobby's relentless assault.

"You son of a bitch! I'm gonna make you regret the day you were born, you sick fuck!" Bobby yelled at the man on the ground as he continued to lay into him.

One by one, the criminals were killed, most meeting gruesome ends as the group fought with their hands still bound. Carson, however, still lay on the ground groaning in pain after the beating he had received. Bobby relentlessly kicked him in the sides, preventing him from even reaching for his gun. When Carson tried, Bobby stomped on his hand, breaking it, and then kicked the gun out of reach.

Once the scene finally calmed, James retrieved the keys from one of the dead officers and began unlocking everyone's handcuffs. Tom rubbed his wrists as he walked over to where Carson lay, his eyes narrowing as he approached.

"What the fuck happened to your cuffs?" he asked Derek.

"I put them in my Inventory. They are just like anything you can equip," Derek said.

"Seriously? We could have all had our hands free?!" Kiera yelled incredulously.

"I don't see why not, though you still did fine with them behind your back," Derek said.

Tom stomped over to Carson, still lying on the ground and now wheezing with blood running from his nose and into his mouth.

"Now, you sick son of a bitch, I think you should empty your Inventory before we kill you off," Tom said.

Carson, for his part, looked up angrily at Tom and spat at him.

"Go to hell," he said.

"Oh, I probably will, but not today. I think I'm going to enjoy this," Tom said. "You see, we don't need your stuff. So, what we do with you is no concern of mine. And since, as you said, all that went out the window with law and order, there is no jail to take criminals like you back to. And we can't just let you go. You'll just terrorize someone else. Because that's just what monsters like you do."

Tom stood up and pulled a potion from his Inventory, handing it to Kedron, who was clutching his leg from the gunshot wound. As Kedron drank the potion, the wound began to heal immediately, the torn flesh closing over in seconds. Once the healing was complete, Tom extended a hand and helped Kedron to his feet.

"He's all yours," Tom said and walked back inside the credit union.

A single gunshot echoed from the parking lot, and Tom knew exactly what it meant. He hadn't wanted to witness it, though. Despite everything, it still felt wrong to kill another human being, even someone as vile as Carson. But he also knew he couldn't let the man go. Some of the others quietly rejoined Tom, the weight of what had just happened settling heavily over them all.

"We should pack up and go. Find a place between towns to stay," Tom said.

"Alright," was all Derek said.

Everyone silently gathered their belongings, preparing to load up in the vehicles. They searched the bodies for the keys to the police vehicles, a necessary chore to clear the way for their escape. They also took the opportunity to loot everything they could from the cruisers, collecting handguns, ammunition, and several shotguns.

APOCALYPSE

Just as they were about to pull away, three more cop cars suddenly arrived. Six men, this time not in uniform, jumped out and immediately opened fire on their vehicles, forcing the group into another desperate fight.

"Cover fire, now, James!" Derek called.

James stood up through the sunroof as Derek opened it, aiming at the attackers and firing back. Suddenly, a blue light enveloped the Hummer next to them, and the bullets fired by the assailants began to bounce off some kind of barrier surrounding the vehicle.

Tom quickly reversed out of the parking spot, then slammed the vehicle into drive, ramming one of the cruisers as the people beside it dove out of the way to avoid being run over. Derek and Graham wasted no time—they jumped out of the moving car, weapons in hand and shields raised, advancing toward the disoriented officers. On the opposite side, Jay slid out of the door and ran along the vehicle's side, tossing a couple of throwing stars at the remaining cops.

The officers ducked behind their car doors to avoid being hit, giving Jay the opportunity to dash around one of the doors and stab an officer taking cover there with his ninjato. The man screamed as the wound began to bleed profusely, far worse than a normal stab wound, the extra bleeding effect taking hold.

Meanwhile, on the other side, another fake officer aimed his weapon through the open doors at Jay and began firing. Jay quickly ducked behind the rear door to avoid the bullets. In that instant, the Hummer roared forward, slamming the door shut on the officer, crushing him with brutal finality.

Seeing that all his comrades had been killed or were being killed, the last man's eyes went wide and he ducked into his car to try to flee. As he put the vehicle in reverse and started to leave, a shot rang out and hit him in the back of the head through the windshield. Four more shots rang out as the vehicle continued to reverse until it hit the sign for the credit union.

"Damn. Missed the dickshot," James said.

Chapter 33

Aftermath

"What was that light over the Hummer?" Tom asked Kedron as they stood beside the vehicles, watching out for more reinforcements.

"Oh, that was Briana. She's a Cleric and has a shielding spell. It puts up a shield that she can control the shape of. It's not super strong yet, but it'll stop most normal projectiles," Kedron said.

"That's handy. Hey, Derek, why don't you do that?" Tom asked.

"Because she must be a more caster-based Cleric, and I'm a Tank Cleric," Derek replied. "Depending on which God you chose, you get powers related to their specialties. We needed a Tank, so I chose a God with more melee powers."

"These specialties are tough to keep up with," Tom said.

"That's why people normally focus on their own Classes and what's good for them. I just happen to know more because I was in the group at work that specialized in game mechanics, so I know more about Classes. That doesn't mean it all applies here, but a lot of it has so far," Derek added.

"So now I can add murder to my resume," Austin said as he walked over. "My father was a cop. This kinda hits home. I heard stories about officers getting killed by criminals and not coming home, but it wasn't so real until now."

"Must be hard to deal with," Tom said.

"It is a little, but it's these kinds of people that I always worried about running into my dad. He always told us that someone had to stand in the gap to make sure that the rest of the people could be safe," Austin replied. "I was always so proud of the sacrifices he was willing to make. Though it never made the worry completely go away, we learned to live with the thoughts day by day."

"My uncle hated cops. Always trying to stop his moonshine runs," Clay said.

"Moonshining is illegal," Austin said.

"I'll tell ya what's illegal—the process the government had in place for making alcohol! Always telling you it's too strong, or you have to pay taxes, or it could be dangerous for people if it's not controlled. Bunch of power-happy fuckers," Clay continued. "A man should be allowed to drink whatever he wants and not have to pay an arm and a leg for it. Taxation is theft!"

"Think anymore will come?" Kedron said to Tom as Clay continued to rant about the government.

"Maybe, but this is a pretty small town. Likely not a ton of people in the jails like in a bigger city, and these guys likely got lucky. Think about how many others are stuck in prison and unable to get out, and there aren't people there to give them food or continue to take care of their needs," Tom replied.

"That is kind of a sucky thought. But these fuckers had it coming. I really don't like having to kill people, but threaten me and mine, and your ass is grass," Kedron replied. "Especially since that one fucker shot me in the fucking leg!"

"Yeah, that was a dick move," Tom agreed. "But I say we get out of dodge before we find out if more are coming. If they chase us, we can deal with them then."

"Okay. Let's head out, then," Kedron agreed.

After loading up, the team pulled out of the parking lot, heading back to the highway and continuing their journey north. It was still dark, and the frequent obstacles of abandoned cars on the road kept their progress slow. However, no other pursuers appeared, and with each passing mile, the group felt a growing sense of relief as they put more distance between themselves and the town.

In the car, Kiera pulled out a piece of jerky and gave it to Squirrel, praising him for coming to her aid. Meanwhile, Jerky appeared on Tom's shoulder, nuzzling against his head in a comforting gesture.

"And just where were you during all this, you little fucker? We could have used some invisible help there in getting keys or something," Tom asked.

"Jerky no want get killed. Jerky small. Jerky not good help. Jerky help show James where to hide," Jerky said.

"It's true. Jerky was the one who told us you all were in trouble," James said.

"That reminds me, wasn't it your turn on watch? If you had been there, you could have alerted us to those dirty bastards' approach!" Derek scolded.

"Clay and I were out back. We didn't know they were coming until we could hear their vehicles because they had their headlights off. The lights were all out, so we didn't see them coming. Once we did notice them, we decided to hang out and watch what happened. Not everyone we meet out here is gonna be a good guy, you know. If we had been inside, we might have been surprised with the rest of you," James said defensively.

"Or you could have at least seen them pulling up and woken us," Derek countered.

"Maybe, or we could have been captured with you and we'd all be dead now. Seems like it was actually lucky we weren't inside," James said, trying to brush it off.

Derek fumed, but couldn't come up with a retort to counter the logic. He stared holes into James.

"Look, it did work out. Only by literal luck, but it did. We can't fight amongst each other," Tom stepped in between the two to try to stop the argument. "And what was with that monolog?"

"That was to let Clay get into position," James replied.

"Next time, you stay on post. If we had been awake, they wouldn't have gotten the slip on us," Derek said, unable to think of anything else to scold James about.

"You're right, I'm sorry. We will keep a lookout next time," James said.

"You know what, no. There won't be a next time with the two of you. I'm not putting you both on the same watch. Crazy and ADHD clearly don't mix well. I guess I'm partly to blame. I put you two together because you seemed to hit it off so well," Derek said.

"Well, there you have it. Not my fault. I'm the Savior," James said.

"Oh, it's still totally your fault. But in this world of danger, I'll give you a small pass," Derek said.

"Yeah, dickweed, you really fucked up back there. Next time, I'm on watch with you, and you will pay attention," Kiera said. "Don't need you off picking fucking daisies or whatever. But thanks for coming to save us. I'll give you that one."

"And that was some pretty cool magic there, DeeDee," Jay said. "You had those vines all over that guy, and your hands were behind your back."

"Yeah, that was tough. I couldn't see the hand gestures, but it still worked. And my knight in shining armor also came to my rescue," DeeDee said, looking over from the back at Graham.

"Nobody messes with my wife. That asshole got exactly what was coming to him," Graham said.

"For next time, handcuffs are just items; you can put them in your Inventory. That's how I got my hands free so fast," Derek said.

"Seriously? You mean I could have cast my spells without being handcuffed? Wish I had thought of that," DeeDee said.

"Don't blame yourself. It was the heat of the moment, and you all did very well for the situation," Derek replied.

"Did you see Austin wailing on that one dude?" James said excitedly. "Fucking hilarious! He threw himself on top of the guy after Jay swept his feet out from under him and just started headbutting his face! Just WHAM, WHAM, WHAM! Totally brutal!"

"You weren't so bad yourself, dickshot," Tom said.

"Oh, that's totally your nickname now, dickshot," Jay said.

"I'll wear it with pride. Anyone can shoot someone in the chest; it takes a real marksman to blow someone's knob off," James said.

"Admit it, you were aiming for his chest and missed," Derek said.

"Was not! I was recapturing our bloody prince moment. Shoot 'em in the dick and ask questions later," James said.

"Look, for the last time, he couldn't have been a prince. His father was a baron," Derek said.

"I'm just going off what he called himself, a prince," James said.

"Bobby also turned into a bit of a monster on that Carson guy," Graham said. "That guy was messed up!"

"Well, he was about to be tortured. I'm sure he was just returning the favor for what Carson did to others before us," Tom said, looking in the rearview mirror.

"Probably. But still, that had to hurt, getting stomped in the chest so hard," Graham said, wincing at the thought.

APOCALYPSE

"Fucker had it coming," James said. "That sick son of a bitch deserved much worse than he got. Did Kedron shoot him with his own gun?"

"No, he had one on him. Pulled it out of his Inventory. It's a smart idea. We should all probably get weapons like that for when we're in a situation where we need another weapon," Derek said.

"Good call. Next time we stop somewhere, we need to see if we can find a vending machine to get them for everyone," Tom said.

"And this should also be a sobering moment for all of us," Derek spoke up so everyone could hear. "We've found a lot of 'friends' so far in this new reality, but not everyone we meet is gonna be a good guy. James was right, and we need to be more careful with our interactions."

Everyone paused, the words hitting home what they had just gone through.

"You're right, but for now, let's just focus on getting where we need to be," Tom added.

As they continued driving, the party chatted, occasionally having to stop and move abandoned vehicles out of the way. By the time the sun began to rise, they couldn't help but feel lucky to have survived. Each member knew how close they had come to dying; if the backup had arrived even a few minutes earlier, the fight might have ended differently. But no one mentioned it, content to be back on the road and move forward again.

As the teams reached Decatur, they noticed the city seemed more active and organized. The streets were cleaner, with fewer abandoned vehicles and debris, and people were out, working together to clean up the aftermath. They could see groups moving bodies to a burn pile on the edge of town, smoke rising in the distance—a sign that the community was taking steps to restore some semblance of order

"They really seem to have a system in place here for getting things cleared up," Derek commented.

"Yeah, I wonder if we can talk to someone about it?" Tom said.

Still somewhat reluctant to engage with others after the fake cop incident, the team decided it was worth investigating the town and possibly making some connections. They pulled off the highway and drove into Decatur. As they approached the edge of the city, they encountered a barricade with guards standing watch. The two men on duty were dressed in tactical gear, and one of them raised his hand, signaling the vehicles to stop. The team came to a halt, cautiously waiting to see how the encounter would unfold.

"State your business here," the man said without any preamble.

"We are just traveling on our way to the Grand Canyon to investigate the quest and were hoping to find somewhere to stop and rest for a bit," Tom said.

"You'll have to check in with the mayor, but we have some places you could stay. We just don't want any trouble here, ya hear?" the man replied.

"We definitely don't want trouble. We had enough of that last night in Rhome," Tom said.

"Yeah, we've heard reports of something going on there, so we have increased security to be sure no one tries anything. A few people came from there saying people were going missing. Know anything about that?" He asked.

"Probably the criminals disguised as cops in the town. They tried to take our stuff and were planning to kill us afterward, but we uh… stopped them," Tom said.

"You kill 'em?" the man said.

"Well, we, um…" Tom started to say.

"I'll take that as a yes. Nice job. We were worried they might make their way here. Glad to hear they likely won't," the guard said. "Head down this road and then park at the courthouse. Ya can't miss it. It's the big building, looks a bit like a castle. The mayor is there during business hours and he can help sort things out for you."

The guard stepped back as the other man moved the arm of a barrier gate up for the cars to pass through.

Just before they started moving, the man asked, "Hummer's with you, right?"

"Yeah, they're with us," Tom replied.

The guard gestured for them to proceed, stepping back to his post with a friendly smile. Tom released the brake and drove forward, heading down the street. As they moved through the town, they noticed people actively working—some were picking up trash, while others loaded the bodies of people and monsters onto trucks. Everyone seemed to have a job and carried it out without complaint.

Soon, the courthouse came into view, an impressive structure of tan-colored stone with a red-shingled roof. The building was adorned with turret-shaped structures along its exterior, giving it the appearance of a modern castle, except for the large clock tower that jutted from the top.

Finding a place to park near the courthouse, the teams got out of their vehicles and took in the sights of the town. People glanced at them briefly before returning to their activities. Women pushed strollers, others enjoyed brunch at a nearby café, and many other normal, everyday activities were happening around them, giving the town an oddly peaceful atmosphere despite the chaos beyond its borders.

"It's weird, right?" James asked.

"Yeah, it's weird. But it feels… normal?" Tom replied, unsure how to feel at that moment. "Why does normal feel weird?"

"Because normal isn't normal now," Derek said.

"Guess we should go in to speak with the mayor," Kedron said.

Turning to go inside, they were greeted by a man wearing a white suit and black string bow tie, holding the sides of his jacket with a big smile plastered on his face. He was the purest image of Southern hospitality personified.

"Welcome to Decatur, travelers. I hope you are in good spirits on this fine day!"

Chapter 34

Decaturville

"What in the Kentucky Fried hell is going on here?" James said.

"We don't see many visitors as of late. We are glad to welcome you to our city. What brings you to our humble abode today?" the man in the white suit asked with his Southern plantation accent.

"Uh… we're passing through on our way to check out the quest," Tom said. "Are you the mayor?"

"I most certainly am. Jeffery Stone is the name, and it is a pleasure to make your acquaintance," Jeffery said.

"Why do I suddenly want a mint julep?" Kiera asked.

"It's nice to meet you as well, sir," Tom said. "We're just looking to rest before we continue on our way."

"Well, you certainly have chosen the perfect stop on your journey. Decatur is a lovely town with historic roots that date all the way back to the Civil War," Jeffery said.

"Yeah, that sounds about right," Kiera commented.

"We have a rich history that celebrates the great state of Texas, along with that of the United States of America. We have many wonderful things to do and see here and are known for such famous people as Daniel Waggoner and Guinn 'Big Boy' Williams," Jeffery continued.

"Who?" Jay asked.

"Many families find Decatur to be a wonderful place to settle down and raise a family, and we have easy access to the DFW metroplex via Highway 287," the mayor went on, oblivious to the fact that no one seemed to understand any of his talking points.

"We boast such attractions as the LBJ National Grasslands, the Wise County Historical Museum, and the NRS Event Center," Jeffery said. "Tell me, fair travelers, from whence do you hail?"

"We're from Dallas," Tom said slowly, becoming more confused as Jeffery spoke.

"Well, I do declare. Dallas is a fine Texas city, indeed. We are so glad you decided to visit. I can show you to a place where you can rest your laurels for the night, and you can spend some time getting to know this fine city," Jeffery replied.

"Is this guy for real?" Kedron asked.

"I have no idea, but I feel like I should be fanning myself in a rocking chair on a wrap-around porch," Bobby said.

"Yeah, and I'll bring out the sweet tea," James added.

"If you would be so kind as to follow me, I will show you to your accommodations," Jeffery said, turning on his heels and walking down the sidewalk, not even waiting to see if the others followed.

Looking at each other first, shrugging, then hurrying to keep up, the group followed Jeffery, not seeing much other choice.

"As you can see, we work hard to keep this city clean and in order. We did experience a minor event that resulted in an influx of riff-raff recently, but the good people of Decatur endured and are now back on track to be a shining point in the great state of Texas," Jeffery continued as he walked, still holding the sides of his jacket as he beamed with pride at every statement.

"You call the apocalypse a minor event?" Jay asked in disbelief.

"My dear boy, there was no apocalypse. The Lord never came back, and therefore, this cannot possibly be the apocalypse," Jeffery said, finally responding to one of them.

"Ohhhh, you're one of those types. Yeah, that explains a lot," Jay said. "Pretty much explains all of it."

"I am quite sure I have no idea what you are referring to, but I assure you that no apocalypse has happened, and the recent events have been but a mere setback on the path to making Decatur as grand as any other city in these United States," Jeffery said, beaming with even more pride, which Tom had thought impossible until now.

"Yeah, this guy is crazy," James leaned in and said quietly to Kiera.

"I promise you, sir, I am not crazy. My mother had me tested," Jeffery said.

"So, how has Decatur fared with the Grand System integration?" Tom asked, trying to be more direct with the issues that had been happening.

"I do not believe I know what you are talking about. Life here has not changed one iota. We remain as we always have been," Jeffery asked.

"So, you're just pretending that you all don't have new abilities and can level up and gain XP?" Tom asked.

"Why, you sound like someone who wishes they lived in some of those children's video games. I never was a fan of those myself. I couldn't understand why someone would want to play in a fantasy world when they could interact with everything God placed on this earth," Jeffery said, pulling out a hanky to wipe his brow.

"Full-on loon," Kiera whispered to James.

"Here we are, the local inn. It has wonderful reviews on Yelp. We even allow pets, so your little puppy friend there can stay with you. I hope you find the stay to your liking, though I must apologize as our fair city is currently without power. There have been some disturbances that seem to be interfering with the Texas power grid, but never fear, for I, the Mayor, am working on getting it restored as quickly as possible," Jeffery said, indicating the building they had walked up to. "As you have been the first guests we have received in quite some time and there are plenty of vacancies, we will give you the penthouse suite on the top floor as an apology for the lack of comfortable air conditioning at this time. It should have plenty of space to accommodate your entire group."

Walking inside, Jeffery leaned on the counter with one elbow.

"Well, hello, Clarice. How are you this fine morning?"

"Hello, Mr. Mayor. It's a pleasure, as always, to see your shining face," Clarice replied.

"Indeed, the pleasure is all mine, I assure you. We need to book these fine people and their four-legged friend into the penthouse suite. They will be staying with us tonight. Please be sure they have everything they need," Jeffery said.

"It would be my pleasure. If you all would follow me right this way," Clarice said to the group.

"I will need to be heading back to the courthouse for some official Decatur business, but if you need anything, please let Clarice know and she will let me know if you need me," Jeffery said. "For now, I take my leave."

"If you'll follow me, please, I'll show you to your room," Clarice said, walking out from behind the counter with a key in her hand.

Following Clarice up the stairs, the group arrived at a set of double doors. Clarice unlocked them with a key and led them inside. The stateroom that greeted them was both elegant and luxurious, featuring a spacious living area filled with several couches and a leather fainting chair. An eighty-five-inch TV was mounted on the wall above a stone fireplace, creating a cozy yet modern focal point. Eight doors led off from the main living and dining area, each likely leading to private rooms. In the back corner of the room, there was a full kitchen with marble countertops and a fully stocked bar, adding to the opulent atmosphere.

"I hope you can enjoy your stay here. If you need anything at all, please be sure to let me know, and we will do whatever we can to ensure your stay here in Decatur is as wonderful as possible," Clarice said, then turned and left, closing the doors behind her.

Still in awe of the immaculate room, the teams wandered around the suite, claiming which rooms would be for which people. When they had settled slightly, they met back in the living area.

"This place is really fucking weird," James said.

"It's like everyone has been brainwashed or something," Kiera added.

"I'm guessing that the trauma of everything was too much for them, so they are trying to get a semblance of normalcy back in their lives," Derek said.

"You can't just ignore end-of-the-world events and just hope everything works out," Bobby said.

"True, but they seem to be doing okay," Tom said.

"If you count being completely delusional as okay," Kiera said. "And what's with Colonel Sanders and being the primmest version of a southern belle?"

"Yeah, that's not how any politician acts now," Jay said. "Really gave me the creeps the way he just ignored certain things to get out the vibes he wanted to portray."

"Look, we're just staying here one night, then we move on. We can handle this odd situation for that long. Think of it as a vacation from all the shit we've been dealing with," Tom said.

Squirrel found a fake plant in the corner of the room, relieved himself on it, then walked over and curled up at Kiera's feet.

"Seriously, dude? Inside?" James said.

Squirrel merely shifted his eyes to look up at James for a moment and then closed them as if he didn't have a care in the world.

Jerky appeared on the counter and sniffed the air. Turning his head back and forth, he took in the room and smiled.

"Jerky like. House good," he said.

"Sure, buddy. See, Jerky can see the good in it," Tom said.

"Still fucking weird," Jerky said.

"Really? Even you?" Tom said. "And I think you've been hanging out with James too much."

Jerky just shrugged and hopped off the counter to explore a room.

"We can still rest while keeping our guard up," Derek said. "It's one night, and this is a nice place."

"I wonder how they deal with monsters here?" Kedron asked.

"You saw them picking up the bodies. I'd guess in a similar way to us," Austin said.

A loud boom echoed from outside a moment later, catching everyone's attention. They all rushed to the nearest window to see what was happening. About a mile from the hotel, four ogres were wreaking havoc, smashing up vehicles parked on the street. The sight was alarming, the massive creatures causing chaos as they tore through the area.

"I guess we get to see how they deal with them," Briana said.

People began screaming and running in panic as the creatures continued their rampage through the downtown streets, leaving destruction in their wake. The chaos spread quickly as the ogres relentlessly smashed everything in their path, turning the once-peaceful area into a scene of terror and devastation.

"We should probably go help," Kedron said.

Men armed with assault rifles emerged from several side streets, unleashing a barrage of bullets at the ogres. Enraged, the monsters turned their fury toward the attackers, charging them with terrifying speed. The ogres smashed through the front lines, mercilessly slaughtering the men in their path. One of the ogres eventually fell after being repeatedly shot in the face, but the others continued their rampage.

Suddenly, a figure appeared on a nearby building top dressed in a black trench coat, wielding a katana, and wearing a red and white kabuki mask. He paused, walking to the edge of the building, looked down at the chaos below, and leaped off, performing a flip in midair. He slashed out with his sword as he descended, decapitating the nearest ogre in one clean stroke. The creature's head rolled to the ground as its body collapsed lifelessly.

"Now that guy is a badass," James muttered in awe.

The masked man swiftly engaged the second ogre, dodging a swing from its club and slicing deep into its leg. The creature howled in pain, collapsing to one knee as its leg went limp. With agility and precision, the man jumped onto the ogre's back and threw a shuriken at the third ogre, striking it in the face. Enraged and clutching its face with one hand, the ogre blindly lashed out with its club, but the man nimbly hopped off the back of the ogre just in time, causing the club to smash into the spine where he had been moments before. A sickening crack accompanied the impact, and the creature fell to the ground, paralyzed.

Rolling out of the way of another attack, the kabuki-masked warrior hurled a grenade at the attacking ogre's head. The explosion obliterated most of the creature's face, leaving it writhing in agony as it dropped its club to clutch at its ruined features, losing its footing and falling to its knees. Seizing the opportunity, the man darted in and slashed the ogre's throat, unleashing a fountain of bluish blood. Moments later, the monster collapsed, dead.

With only one ogre remaining, the mystery man circled behind it while the remaining guards unloaded their weapons. The man sliced through the creature's Achilles tendons, bringing it crashing to the ground, then moved to its front and slashed at both wrists, leaving the ogre helpless and face-down in the dirt, writhing in pain.

Calmly, the man approached the fallen beast, now unable to lift itself. With a swift, final strike, he raised his sword and drove the blade into the ogre's eye, ending its suffering.

"Holy shit, that was amazing. That guy just killed those creatures almost single-handedly," Jay said.

"Looks like this town has a few more secrets than we realized," Derek said.

Chapter 35

Mysterious Man

Everyone stood in stunned silence, trying to process what they had just witnessed. The mysterious man had single-handedly taken down three ogres. Before anyone could react, he sprinted down a side street and disappeared from view.

"We have to meet that guy!" James said.

"How do you propose we do that? We don't even know what he looks like," Derek said.

"I don't know, but think about what he could do to help with the quest?" James said.

"He would definitely help in fights with monsters," Kedron said.

"But then we would leave this town without him," DeeDee said.

"This town needs to wake up and realize what's happening anyway," James said. "This guy could really help us set things right for the world."

"He's not gonna undo the apocalypse," Bobby said.

"That's not what I mean by setting the world right. I mean, help stop whatever is messing with the vending machines," James said.

"He would be an asset for sure," Tom said. "We can ask around if anyone knows him and go from there."

"Fine, Tom, myself, and James will look around and see if we can track this guy down," Derek said.

"Oh, no way, I'm going too," Kiera said.

"Okay, Kiera too. The rest of you stay here and rest and watch the room. We will return after doing some inquiring to see if we can find out who he is," Derek said.

Everyone agreed with the plan and went to their rooms to rest for a while. Tom, Derek, James, and Kiera headed out with Squirrel to see if they could find the identity of the man in the kabuki mask. Jerky appeared on Kiera's shoulder as they were leaving the room, and she gave him a piece of meat to eat, scratching his head.

Walking downstairs, the first stop was the front desk to talk with Clarice.

"Hello, Clarice," James said in a creepy voice. "I really like saying that."

"Well, hello. Is the room to your liking?" Clarice asked.

"It's wonderful. We really appreciate you setting us up with it," Tom said. "We have a question for you, though."

"Certainly, I'll be happy to do anything I can to help you… What is that?" Clarice asked in a startled voice, pointing at Jerky.

"Oh, that's Jerky. He's my Familiar," Tom replied. Jerky moved to sit on his shoulder and nuzzled his face to show he was friendly.

"Oh… okay, then," Clarice said, clearly uncomfortable with the creature.

"As for what you can help us with, what can you tell us about the masked man who fights off the monsters?" Tom asked.

Clarice's face tightened slightly at the question, but being a good front desk guest relations person, she did not stop smiling.

"Oh, not a lot, I guess. He's a mysterious person who started helping slay monsters in the town when they started appearing. The townspeople call him the masked avenger. I haven't done much digging into his identity since he went to such trouble to hide it," Clarice said. "Plus, when someone starts running around taking care of problems like that, most people just let him do it."

"So, you have no idea who he is?" Tom asked.

"Not a clue," Clarice replied.

"Okay. Can you think of anyone who might know more?" Derek asked.

"Maybe the head of the guard? He is the one responsible for a lot of the security in the town and might have a better idea," Clarice offered.

"Cool. Thank you for the help!" Tom said.

With that, the group left the hotel. Unbeknownst to them, Clarice picked up the phone when the door to the hotel closed.

"Mr. Mayor. Yes, it's Clarice. I'm wonderful, thank you for asking. Listen, those new visitors. Yes, the group in the penthouse. We might have a little problem."

Outside the hotel, Tom, Derek, James, and Kiera stood on the sidewalk with Squirrel next to Kiera.

"Any thoughts where the head of security might be? Should we ask Clarice?" Kiera asked.

"The courthouse. That's where the mayor is, so he's likely there as well. It seems to be the center of official business, so even if we can't find him there, someone will know, and we can talk with the mayor again," Derek said.

"I thought the same," Tom agreed, nodding.

Walking over to the courthouse, the group was greeted by multiple people going about their business with a simple wave. Everyone seemed friendly, which was odd given their recent experiences.

Arriving at the courthouse, the team stepped through the front door. The interior was reminiscent of a police station straight out of an eighties cop show, with desks spread out in the middle of the room and offices lining three of the walls. Ceiling fans hung motionless above, now useless with the lack of electricity, doing nothing to abate the Texas heat. However, the room was still well-lit, thanks to the large windows along the back wall, which allowed natural light to filter in.

Sitting in an office with an open door at the far end of the room was the mayor. He noticed their entrance and exited the office to greet them.

"Hello again, travelers. How might I be of service to you on this fine day?" Jeffery greeted them.

"We were wondering about the masked avenger. He seems like an incredible person. He might be able to help with our quest," Tom said.

"He really is incredible, isn't he? It's too bad we don't know who he is. We would very much like to show him our gratitude for everything he has done for us," Jeffery said.

"You really have no idea who he might be? I would've thought as mayor that you would know your citizens?" Derek said.

"Alas, I do not. There is the distinct possibility that he came here as a visitor and has taken up residence somewhere. I mean, I can't blame him; this is a pretty wonderful town," Jeffery said, gesturing with his hands and smiling broadly at his words.

"I guess that's true. Have you done any investigation to try to find who he is?" Tom asked.

"I certainly have. We wanted to have a party to celebrate his accomplishments. But every avenue I have gone down has left me with exactly zero answers as to the identity of that mysterious man. He just seems to vanish after he fights off the monsters, and no one is too keen on asking him for any answers while he's fighting. That would mean putting ourselves in a lot of danger and possibly interfering with his work," Jeffery answered.

"Alright. Well, we appreciate your help. Can you direct us to the head of security for the town? We noticed you have a well-maintained border, and we're interested in picking his brain about the ideas he has implemented to keep up such lovely appearances and order," Derek asked.

"Why, that is a wonderful idea! We would love to help our sister city of Dallas with some of the ideas we have implemented here. He should be on the second floor of this building. He has an office there," Jeffery said.

"Thank you, Mr. Mayor," Derek said.

"Oh, never you mind the fancy titles. Just call me Jeffery," Jeffery said. "Now, if you'll excuse me, I have some very important business to attend to."

With that, he turned back to his office and closed the door. Moments later, a woman cracked open a door on the same wall, cautiously peeking out to ensure the coast was clear. Seeing no one around, she gestured for the four of them to come closer. Once they reached her, she quickly opened the door fully and ushered them inside.

"You all are looking into the masked avenger?" she asked.

"We are, but who are you exactly?" Tom asked.

"I'm Patty, the mayor's assistant," the woman said.

"Nice to meet you, Patty, I'm…" Tom began, but Patty cut him off.

"It doesn't matter right now—we only have a minute before you need to be heading upstairs," Patty said. "I happen to know who the masked avenger is."

"You do? That's great!" James said.

"SHHHHHH! Not so loud!" Patty hushed him. "The masked avenger is actually the mayor's son. But nobody wants to talk about it."

"Seriously?" Derek asked.

"Seriously! I haven't been here too long. Only got into town a month or so ago. The old mayor of the town was killed on the first day of the strange events that have been happening. Jeffery came along and helped organize everything, and the people here made him the mayor," Patty said.

"We figured something was off," Tom said.

"You're damn right something is wrong. Everyone here is now pretending like nothing ever happened, and the mayor's son has been cleaning up all the messes," Patty said.

"But why wouldn't the mayor want to take credit for that?" Derek asked.

"Because then he'd have to admit something was happening. He wants everyone here to just pretend the world is going on like it was," Patty said.

"Do you know where we can find the mayor's son? We'd really like to talk to him," Tom said.

"He has a place just outside of town in an abandoned church. He stays there to stay out of sight," Patty said.

"Thank you, Patty, you have been very helpful," James said.

"Don't you go blabbing to nobody that I told ya! I'll deny it!" Patty said.

"Mum's the word, we promise," Kiera assured her.

"Now get upstairs. I'm sure the mayor called Edward to tell him you were coming," Patty said. "It'll be suspicious if you don't get there soon."

Leaving the office as quietly as possible, the team made sure the mayor wasn't watching them before heading up the stairs to the second floor. The layout was similar to the first floor, but instead of taking one of the offices, the head of security had set up a desk in the middle of the room.

"Ah! You must be the new visitors. My name is Edward. I'm the head of security for Decatur," Edward said, standing and smiling at them.

Edward was a man of average build wearing a pin-striped suit. His hair was slicked over to the right side of his head, he wore a heavy amount of gel, and he had a very large, curled mustache that almost covered his mouth.

"Yes, we want to ask you about some of the procedures you put in place to keep this town so lovely so that we might consider using some of them in Dallas," Derek said.

"Well, I am happy to help a fellow Texas city. What kind of things do you want to know about in particular?" Edward asked.

"What did you do to keep the city going and working with such efficiency, and how do you keep it safe are our biggest questions," Derek said.

"Well, that's quite simple. Everyone here has a task that they are to perform. Some will help with cleaning up the garbage whenever they see it, others are set to work on removing any bodies so the streets can stay clear. Others will move vehicles, and still others are working on the power situation. Many, many jobs are needed to keep a city in order," Edward began.

"And the security at the borders?" Derek asked.

"That is something we decided we needed when we heard about what was happening in Rhome. We didn't want anyone coming to town who might try to harm the people here," Edward said.

"What if they just lied and said they were good to get in?" James asked.

"We have security wandering the city as well. If anyone is acting out, they will be dealt with swiftly and put in the city jail," Edward said.

"And I'm assuming you have people whose job it is to work at the jail?" Tom asked.

"Why, yes, we do. They are there to keep the inmates in line and comfortable. We aren't animals, after all," Edward said.

"How long will those people be in jail for?" Tom asked.

"That depends on the nature of their crime. But once they have repaid their debt to society, we will release them and send them out of the town," Edward said.

"And then the guards just keep them from coming back?" Derek asked.

"You are a bright one, I can tell," Edward said, putting one finger to his nose and pointing at Derek.

"Well, I am the head of security for our group in Dallas for a reason," Derek said, smiling, but Tom could see the smile didn't quite reach his eyes.

"Ah! A fellow law officer! It is good to meet you. I'm assuming this is not quite as feasible with a town the size of Dallas, though," Edward said.

"It's true, but we are considering zoning off part of the city to implement some of these ideas in a more localized area," Derek replied.

"That definitely could work. Use the buildings as barriers of sorts to keep out the ruffians," Edward said musingly.

"Exactly. I think I need to see a bit more of the town, though, to see the full infrastructure you have put in place. I appreciate you taking the time to speak with us, but we will let you get back to your business and do a little sightseeing," Derek said.

"Very good. If you have any more questions, feel free to find me again, and we can talk more business," Edward said, sitting back down.

Tom, Derek, James, and Kiera walked back down the stairs and left the courthouse.

"So, they're just faking it," James said.

"Definitely. This form of security is sloppy at best," Derek said. "But I didn't want to tell him what we were really after."

"We should walk around and pretend to see some things, but I think it's time to pay a visit to the mayor's son," Tom said.

Chapter 36

Seth

Making their way through parts of the town, they walked along the sidewalks and asked people questions about how safe they felt and the security protocols to keep up appearances. Squirrel got many strange looks, but most people treated him like the group's dog as they walked. Some even asked if they could pet him.

When they reached the edge of the city, they came to another security post where two guards were stationed. Both were wearing tactical gear and carrying assault rifles.

"Afternoon, gentlemen," Tom said.

The men nodded at the group.

"We just recently met with Edward. My name is Derek, and this is Tom, James, and Kiera. Oh, and Squirrel," Derek said to the guards. "We're investigating some of the security methods used here in Decatur so we can make Dallas a safer place for its residents. Do you mind if I ask you a few questions?"

The men brightened at this and relaxed visibly.

"Not at all! I'm Tim, this is Jack," The man on the left said.

"It's nice to meet you both. I noticed that you all are using the barrier arms; how do you make sure people don't come in at other points in the city?" Derek began.

Derek asked questions while Tim and Jack answered them, none the wiser to their true intentions. They talked for about twenty minutes before Derek acted as if all his questions had been answered.

"This has been very enlightening. I truly appreciate all of your help. Your information will be instrumental in us keeping people safer," Derek said.

"It's been our pleasure! We really do enjoy helping people," Tim said.

"Do you all mind if we exit the town for a bit? We figure if we leave and walk around the outside area, we can get a better feel for the size of the secure area and see the city from a different vantage point," Derek asked.

"Not at all! Feel free to come back through this entry point; we'll ensure you're let back in with no issues," Jack said.

"You all are so great. I can't thank you enough," Derek replied.

Both men smiled as they opened the gate, allowing the group to pass through. They walked about a mile until they reached an old, abandoned church. The building had white paneling on the exterior, though the paint was peeling from age. Stained glass windows lined the walls, and a tall steeple rose above with a cross at the top. Out front, a sign read "First Baptist Church of Decatur," with the scripture reference Revelation 6:8 on it. However, the words beneath seemed to have been placed by someone else and read "Do you know what hell is? Come hear our preacher."

"How'd you know this was here?" Kiera asked.

"I saw it from the highway. Seemed to be the only church in the area from what I could tell," Derek said.

"What about those churches that meet in unassuming places they rent out?" James asked.

"Patty said it was an old church. So, this seemed like the most logical one," Derek said.

"You're really good at this," James said.

"At what? Paying attention?" Derek asked.

"Shut up," James said.

"At not talking just to hear the sound of his own voice?" Kiera asked.

"Hey!" James said.

"At making sure they listen to gather information and be helpful to the team?" Tom asked.

"What is this, gang up on James time?" James asked.

"At not mutilating people's genitalia for fun?" Kiera said.

"Now that was a low blow," James said.

"You're one to talk about low blows," Kiera replied.

"…That's fair," James said.

"So, what's the play here?" Tom asked.

"I assumed we'd just see if we can talk to the guy. Knowing nothing about him, we have to feel it out. Hopefully, he's willing to help us," Derek said.

Reaching up and knocking on the front door, the team waited outside for an answer. No one came to the door. Derek knocked again.

"What do you want?" came a voice from behind them.

"GAH!" James yelled as they all turned around in surprise. "How did you do that?"

"Why are you here?" the man asked.

"We wanted to meet you," Derek said.

"Why me? I'm just some guy living in a church," the man said.

"I'm Derek, this is Tom, the scaredy cat is James, and this is Kiera," Derek said.

Squirrel growled.

"Oh, and that's Squirrel," Derek added. "And I think you know that if we're here, we know you aren't just some guy living in a church."

"You here to try to kill me?" the man said.

"What? No! Do people do that?" Derek asked.

"Tried," he said. "No one has succeeded yet."

"Obviously, since you're here talking to us," James said.

"Look, I don't really want to talk to people. Can you just leave now?" the man asked.

APOCALYPSE

"We really need to try to speak with you. We are on our way to try to complete the world quest and could really use your help in completing it," Derek said.

"I'm pretty busy. If you haven't noticed, monsters appear here a lot," the man said.

"Can we at least get your name?" Derek asked.

"It's Seth," Seth said.

"Seth, this issue with the vending machines is making it so anyone left on Earth can't get the items they will really need to survive in this new reality. We need to see if we can help," Derek said.

"I also need to be here to help the people of Decatur," Seth said.

"So, the needs of the few outweigh the needs of the many?" Derek said.

"No, my ability to help the people here is something I can measure. And you don't know that others aren't going to complete the quest," Seth argued.

"And you don't know that everyone else in the world is staying home to do just what you're doing," Derek said.

Seth paused. He stared at Derek for a long moment, his face tightening in his attempt to rationalize the argument.

"What happens when I leave here?" Seth asked.

"I think these people finally have to stand on their own and learn to survive instead of just relying on you all the time," Derek answered. "Maybe these people aren't accepting the fact that something happened because you keep protecting them from it. Your dad is acting like he can just ignore everything and it'll just not exist."

"You don't know anything about my dad," Seth said.

"I know he's a little delusional. He won't even admit that you're his son. He just tells people that he has no idea what's going on and then protects the town by taking anyone who is a criminal and setting them on the outside of the town, and then hopes they don't go on a murderous revenge rampage by sneaking back into the town," Derek said. "He's actually putting people in more danger by ignoring the problem rather than trying to find a solution for it that will actually keep people safe."

"And what exactly do you expect me to do? Run off with you and fight off this threat and let the people here suffer?" Seth asked.

"I would hope, first, you'd confront your father so he could put procedures in place to protect the people here, then go with us, and you can come back as soon as that is done so that hopefully the people here can arm themselves and learn to fight off the dangers as well. If they don't, they'll die eventually when you find a monster you can't beat and it kills you then finishes off the town," Derek said.

Struggling with an internal battle of what to do, Seth silently stood there for a long time. With one hand on the door, he hung his head.

"He won't understand. He has this idealistic view of what the world should be and he'll ignore anything to ensure that happens. It's why I have to fight to keep the people safe. He won't listen to me," Seth said.

"People like that have to experience the consequences of their actions," Derek said.

"At the cost of so many other people's lives?!" Seth said.

"A mayor is an elected position. If he wants to keep up with this farce, then the people can play him at his own game, and if they aren't willing to listen as well and want to continue to ignore the world and its problems, then they are just as guilty of it as he is," Derek said. "They put him in charge and just went along with it because it was easy. That means they're doing the exact same thing."

"They just want things to go back to normal," Seth said.

"We all do, but that isn't going to happen by ignoring the very serious crisis we're in now. The only way that can happen is if they make a new normal for themselves and work together to make it happen," Derek said. "Fighting is now part of life. I get it, most people never had to fight for their lives. They just relied on people like me in the military to do it for them. But the enemy isn't in Afghanistan, Iraq, Russia, or China. It's right outside their fucking front doors."

"Seth, our plan helps people more in the long run. Your fighting is barely a band-aid for the problem. And a band-aid can't heal the kind of giant open wound the world is experiencing now," Tom said.

"Why can't I just trust you all to go handle the issue?" Seth asked.

"You can. But the world-saving business is a team effort, and we aren't nearly as talented as you are. So, we might get the job done, but that isn't a guarantee," Derek said. "We're strong because we're working together. We're just trying to be as ready as we can for the fight we know is coming."

"You're asking me to just let them die until I can come back," Seth said.

"What we're asking you to do is to go into town, tell them the truth, then let them experience it and make a decision on what they'll do. They can fend off monsters together if they fight. But they'll die if they ignore it. Maybe not today, maybe not tomorrow, but if there's something out there strong enough for the System to ask everyone in the world to go handle it, then something will eventually come along you can't beat. And when you die, they all die too— guaranteed," Derek said. "But if you had people fighting *with* you, then you'd be able to weather more storms to come."

"And you're going to be those people fighting with me?" Seth asked. "Fighting in this town?"

"We'll be those people fighting with you at the Grand Canyon. But no, not here. We have our own people to protect. But unlike here, *we* set up teams that fight to protect people who can't. They're back in Dallas right now keeping them safe because they chose to accept this reality and defend people together, not just let Tom or me or Kiera do all the work for them," Derek replied.

"Hey, or James." James added.

"Oh please, you need us more than the people in the Guild building," Kiera said.

"You left the people you're protecting?" Seth asked.

"We did. And we can confidently believe they'll still be fine while we're gone because they're training and learning this Grand System and working to fight for safety," Derek said. "Our jobs are easier, and our survival chances greater, because we're fighting together."

"So, if I do go along with this, how do we tell them?" Seth asked.

"I have an idea for that. Does the courthouse have a bell system?" Derek asked.

Chapter 37

Monstrous Realization

Walking back into town with Seth, the team returned to the courthouse. Seth made sure to wear his trench coat and kabuki mask so that everyone would know who he was. People stopped and stared as he walked through, and the guards were more than happy to let the town's savior through the security checkpoint.

When they reached the courthouse, they went inside and walked over to a box hanging on the wall. Pressing a button inside, the bells sounded from the courthouse so the entire town could hear over a PA system. The mayor ran out at hearing the bells and went white when he saw Seth standing with the travelers.

"What is the meaning of this? Why have you sounded the alarm?" Jeffery asked.

"I sounded it for everyone's good," was all Derek said in reply.

Heading back outside, the party stood in front of the courthouse entrance as people from all over town came to see what was happening.

"Is there a fire?"

"Are there more monsters?"

"We haven't seen anything."

"Is that the masked avenger?"

"We'll be alright as long as he's here."

Cries came from the people as they gathered to understand what was happening. The bells died down a few moments later, and the group addressed the people.

"Listen, we're here to tell you that you cannot continue like you have been. There's a very real danger now that threatens each of your lives. You need to stop pretending that everything is normal and begin working together to fight off the monsters that are appearing," Derek said.

"But we have the masked avenger! We don't need anyone else!" someone from the crowd yelled.

"Yes, why would they need anyone else when the masked avenger could save them? They can go about their daily lives as they always have, safe in the knowledge that they will be fine so long as he is here to save us," Jeffery said, exiting the building behind them.

Removing his mask, Seth showed everyone his face so they would know who the masked avenger was.

"Seth?!"

"What the hell?"

APOCALYPSE

Cries rang out as many of them recognized who it was that had been saving them and now stood before them.

"Yes! I've been the one fighting to save each of you. But I can't do it forever, nor can I do it alone," Seth said to the crowd.

Silence reigned as he paused.

"You all are more capable than you realize. And there's a bigger threat than the monsters appearing here that needs to be dealt with," Seth continued. "Monsters are going to continue to appear and in greater strength, no matter how many times I fight them. Eventually, I will not be able to save you. But that can change! You can get stronger and fight as well!"

"But we aren't fighters! We're just regular people!" a cry came from the crowd.

"So are soldiers! But they go to other countries to put their lives on the line to keep you safe from danger!" Derek called back. "All you need is training and preparation. That's all the military has. You can learn to defend yourself as well."

"And you'll have to. Because I'm going to the Grand Canyon to help deal with the threat that's targeting the entire planet. Many more lives are at stake than just those here," Seth said.

"You really are just going to abandon these poor, innocent people to traipse off to a big hole in the ground because you think you can help more people? What happens if you die there? Then you didn't help anyone, and you doomed this town, too," Jeffery said, walking up next to his son.

"I have to try. And by leaving, it'll force you and everyone else in this town to learn more than just to depend on me all the time," Seth said, looking angrily at his father.

"I forbid it! You cannot just leave and hope everything is fine here! We have worked hard to have some semblance of normalcy in our daily lives, and I will not allow you to undo all that I have done to attain that!" Jeffery yelled.

"You don't get to make that call, Dad. I'm not some child you can just order around anymore," Seth retorted.

"*You!*" Jeffery growled, turning on the party. "This is all your fault! You came here to take away the only chance our poor, defenseless town has of defending itself! You are to blame for the deaths that will come!"

"We didn't even know Seth was here. We really were just passing through. But the people of this town are blindly walking into a situation that'll end up killing not only your son but each one of them as well," Derek replied. "It's *you* who is keeping the blindfold on not only yourself but the people you claim to lead."

Gasps rang out through the crowd.

"You selfish bastard. You hide behind this mask of pretentiousness and pretend to care about these people. If you really cared about them, then you'd be helping to prepare them to defend themselves, not coddling them into a false sense of security about what'll happen!" Derek continued. "If you have even a single shred of care for these people, then you would be putting yourself on the frontline as an example to the others to learn to be better and work together, not throw your son at monsters that'll one day end up killing him!"

Everyone was silent at this.

"Seth is strong. He won't be killed," Jeffery said.

"He's one man against an entire world of creatures that are now slowly throwing themselves at mankind. Eventually, there will be something he can't beat, and it'll kill him. Then it'll march on this town, and if it can kill Seth, what chance do you think you or anyone else in this town will stand?"

Jeffery didn't have a reply for that. He looked at Derek with complete and utter rage. "I will not let you destroy everything I have worked so hard to build here. This is my town, and I will have order!" Jeffery said, starting in a low growl and rising until he was yelling.

"You will get everyone here killed, Father," Seth said.

"How can you say that? After all I've done for you!" Jeffery hissed in rage.

"Because it's true. You had good intentions with trying to make people feel safe, but it's the wrong method. They can't just *feel* safe. They need to *be* safe and know that they are because they're strong. They need to get stronger and work together. It's the only way they stand a chance of survival," Seth said.

"Are you people really going to let this bunch of vagabonds come in here and take the life we have worked for?" Jeffery yelled at the crowd as they looked at each other in confusion.

"If you want peace," Derek said ominously, "prepare for war."

As if his words were prophetic, a terrible shrieking came from the town's west side. A man in tactical gear came running around the corner of a street, eyes wide in terror.

"A MONSTER! IT'S COMING! HELP ME!" the man screamed as he stumbled over his feet and fell.

A massive, six-legged creature emerged from behind him, its body resembling that of a beetle but with the grotesque head of an anglerfish. A long protrusion extended from its forehead, rising straight up before curving back down in front of its mouth as if designed to lure prey into its waiting jaws.

"What the fuck is that?" yelled James.

Tom used Inspect on the creature.

Dangler (Regional Boss)	
The Dangler is a stealthy ambush predator that dwells at the bottom of large lakes, where it patiently lies in wait for unsuspecting prey. When food becomes scarce in its underwater domain, this creature ventures onto land, using its long, powerful legs to pursue terrestrial prey with surprising agility. The Dangler's most lethal feature is the elongated, bioluminescent lure protruding from its head, which it uses to attract prey. This lure can also fire a precise laser shot, making the Dangler a formidable threat both in water and on land.	
HP:	4,026/4,280
MP:	1,000/1,000

APOCALYPSE

SP:	5,540/5,680
Level:	39
Attack:	Bite, Laser Shot

"Holy shit," was all Tom could manage to say.

"They *do* exist," James whispered, awed.

"What the hell are you talking about?" Kiera scowled.

"A Dallas Dangler in the wild," James muttered. "I thought they were only legends."

"Oh, you have *got* to be—" Kiera's next words were suddenly cut off.

"Get these people out of here!" Derek cried as he took his shield and mace out of his Inventory.

Seth equipped his katana while James drew his guns and Kiera readied her rifle. Tom retrieved his greatsword, though he wasn't sure how much use it would be against the massive Dangler. The creature loomed before them, towering at about four stories tall, making it one of the largest creatures they had seen so far.

"Let's go! We have to hold it off!" Derek yelled.

Everyone jumped into action as the sound of automatic gunfire sounded in the distance. Crying out in rage at being attacked, the monster turned a little too quickly and smashed its beetle-like shell into the corner of a building, demolishing it as it turned.

"Kiera, get to a place where you can get shots off and fire at its face. James, you do the same with those peashooters. Tom, you, Seth, and I will go after it directly," Derek ordered.

"How do we kill something that big?!" Tom asked, beginning to get frantic.

"Use your fucking spells, Tom!" Derek yelled.

"Oh, right," Tom said sheepishly.

Darting off to intercept the monster, the team circled around to approach it from behind while Kiera found a vantage point and began firing. Shots from James' guns bounced off the Dangler's tough chitin without effect, but when Kiera fired, her bullet punched a hole in its hard shell, causing purple blood to seep from the wound.

The creature howled in pain, roaring in fury as it turned to face whatever had dared to hurt it. Spotting the team running toward it, the Dangler charged to meet them head-on. Tom attempted to cast his *Fear* spell on the beast, but it seemed unfazed as it continued its advance.

"*Fear* isn't working!" Tom yelled.

"Then fireball it or something! Don't just stop!" Derek yelled back as they moved to flank the monster to attract its attention.

Tom cast *Eldritch Blast*, and the green fire struck the Dangler square in the face. The monster recoiled slightly from the impact, pausing for a brief moment. As it opened its eyes again, a shot rang out, and its left eye snapped shut as Kiera's bullet hit home. The creature roared in agony as a greenish fluid began to leak from the damaged eye, seeping from between its eyelids.

"What exactly are you going to do with just that mace?" James called to Derek.

Ignoring him, Derek ran up to the creature and shouted, *"Divine Strike!"* as his mace glowed with white light. Swinging it with all his might, the blow crushed the hard shell of the creature's leg and sent it flying back into the next leg behind it. Wobbling from the loss of two legs on that side, the Dangler began to fall to the side.

"Oh… *that's* what you're gonna do," James said.

Seth had run to the top of a building and jumped out with his katana in hand. As he fell, he swung down and severed one of the creature's legs, causing ichor to flow freely from the wound into a purple puddle on the ground. He ran around to the front of the beast to try to attack again but found himself staring at the glowing lure as it fired off a laser.

The beam struck him and sent him flying into the building the creature had just smashed part of.

"SETH!" Derek cried out in panic, running to the building to see if he was still alive.

The creature struggled to stand, using two legs on its right side to lift its massive body. Tom, however, was ready. He activated his greatsword's *Cleave* skill, swinging it in a wide horizontal arc. The blade sliced through the lower portion of one of the creature's legs, causing it to wobble precariously. Despite the damage, the Dangler managed to press down with the severed leg, trying to limp forward.

Clearly in pain from the effort, the creature's rage intensified as it whirled on Tom. He rolled out of the way just in time to avoid the sharp end of another leg, dodging repeatedly to avoid being crushed. Suddenly, two of the legs on the beast's left side were severed at the same point where Tom had struck, this time by a powerful greataxe. The Dangler toppled over, crashing heavily onto its right side.

"Come on, you motherfucker! Face me instead! Your sister was a cunt, and your father sucked the biggest cocks he could find!" a yell came from the other side of the creature that Tom immediately knew was Kevin.

The cavalry had arrived. Jay suddenly appeared on top of the creature, though how he managed to get up there was a mystery to Tom. He watched as Jay sprinted along the Dangler's back toward its head. Meanwhile, vines erupted from the ground, wrapping around the beast's body in an attempt to hold it down, but the creature's immense strength caused the vines to begin snapping.

Sliding down its face, Jay let out a yell as he swung his ninjato, severing the lure just above its base. The creature howled in rage and pain as its lure dropped to the ground, the light inside flickering out.

"No more lasers for you, fugly!" Jay shouted, driving his ninjato into the beast's head and dragging it slowly along its face, carving open its skin.

APOCALYPSE

As more people climbed up its side, Tom saw Bobby, Graham, Austin, and Kedron all attacking the Dangler's face, hacking away in a desperate attempt to cause as much damage as possible.

The creature thrashed violently, trying to dislodge its attackers, and managed to throw off Graham and Bobby, who had lost their grip. Austin and Kedron, with their swords embedded in its face, barely managed to hold on until the shaking stopped.

The Dangler scrabbled at the ground, trying to stand again, snapping the vines that had been holding it down. As it thrashed back and forth, the remaining attackers were thrown to the ground, rolling away to avoid being crushed.

Seeing his chance, Tom charged at the creature and leaped onto its face just as it weakly tried to rise. With a battle cry, he thrust his greatsword into its remaining eye, driving the blade deep, popping the eyeball, and burying his arm up to his elbow. The eyelids clamped shut so quickly that Tom couldn't pull out in time, and he found himself trapped as the creature thrashed.

The Dangler slammed its face into the ground, its jaws clamping shut mid-scream. The pressure on Tom's arms eased just enough for him to wrench his sword free, nearly losing his balance as he did so. Steadying himself, he moved to the center of its head between the eyes, raised his greatsword high, and activated his *Cleave* skill again, bringing the blade down where he guessed its brain would be.

The sword sliced through the skin and bone with a sickening crunch. Spasming one last time in its final death throes, the Dangler finally fell still.

Chapter 38

A Change of Pace

Without pausing to rest, Tom, James, and Kiera rushed over to the rubble of the collapsed building. The others, who hadn't been present earlier, stared in confusion, except for Briana. As soon as they reached the pile of debris, they joined Derek in frantically removing the fallen pieces.

After a few tense moments, they managed to uncover enough of the rubble to reveal Seth, who groaned as he sat up, his clothes slightly singed and his hair coated in ash and dust from the debris. He coughed, trying to clear the dust from his lungs, and looked around at the concerned faces gathered in front of him.

"What the hell?" Seth groaned. "That fucking sucked."

"How the hell are you still alive?" Derek exclaimed.

"I have no idea, but I'm still here," Seth replied.

"Shield spell," Briana said, walking up from behind them. "It's really handy."

"Briana with the save again," Kedron said, smiling at her.

"I'd been watching from the window. Fortunately, glass doesn't appear to stop my spells," Briana said.

"She was the one who told us where to go for the monster, and we hurried over as soon as we could," Bobby said. "You guys probably could have handled it, but we figured it was better safe than sorry."

"Not sure we could have. Thanks for the assist," Tom said.

"So, who's this?" Kedron asked.

"This is Seth. He's the masked avenger," Derek said, sitting on the ground in relief.

"You mean that guy that killed the ogres?" Kedron asked.

"Ogre Slayer's my band name. Anyone able to play bass? Drums and guitar, too, for that matter," Seth said, sitting up. "It's nice to meet you. OW!"

Seth grabbed at his side as he sat up, wincing in pain.

"Yeah, I figured something hurt you in that blast. It's amazing you're alive. I would've been in complete disbelief if you'd been totally unharmed. Hold still a moment," Derek said, white light enveloping his hands.

Seth's look of pain softened as the healing took effect.

"Thanks. That feels a lot better," Seth said. "I'm guessing since you're all here that we won?"

"Actually, we're all dead and this is heaven," James said. "Really not everything the televangelists made it up to be. But they have margarita machines in every bedroom."

Seth laughed at the joke. "Those guys were dicks anyway."

"I also think this makes a pretty great point to take back to the townspeople, Seth," Derek said, looking pointedly at him. "If we hadn't been here, you would've been dead, and this town would've been flattened."

"You're right. They can't continue on this way. I'll definitely talk to them again," Seth said.

Standing up, Derek extended a hand to help Seth off the ground. After a brief search to locate Seth's katana, the entire team made their way back to the courthouse and rang the bells once more. This time, when the crowd gathered, the atmosphere was completely different. People were cheering for the heroes who had saved the town, celebrating their bravery and praising their impressive fighting skills.

"Listen! This isn't something to celebrate! I nearly died in that fight, and if it hadn't been for these people here, I would've been killed, and this town would've been destroyed by that creature," Seth said, raising his voice to be heard over the crowd. "You all cannot continue to ignore the world around you and must learn to cope with the changes that've taken place. You'll have to fight, or you all will die."

"NO!" screamed Jeffery from behind them, walking out of the courthouse again. "I won't allow it! You *have* to keep fighting for us so we can continue to live in peace!"

"Shut the fuck up!" Seth screamed at him.

Jeffery recoiled at the vehemence in Seth's voice. He had never been spoken to this way by his son before and didn't seem sure of how to react.

"You just... you don't get it, do you?" Seth said, shaking his head. "You keep acting like you know what's best for everyone, but all you're doing is lining them up to be slaughtered."

He sighed, voice heavy with frustration. "You've been so stuck on your way of doing things that you can't even see what's really happening around you."

Seth's tone softened further, more tired than furious. "Honestly, it's hard to believe anyone's followed you this long. And I'm just as guilty—I've been going along with it out of fear."

His gaze hardened slightly, but it was weighted with resolve, not rage. "But I'm done."

"Seth, I don't know where you got this new rebellious spirit from, but you will stop it at once and act like a proper gentleman," Jeffery said.

"No, Dad, I won't. You'll stop trying to put blinders on these people and wake up to the fact that this world isn't safe anymore, and sitting around here cleaning up the town and going about our normal business won't keep us safe either. They need to be trained to fight," Seth replied.

Jeffery's face turned red as he stared at his son in disbelief. He began to sputter, glancing from face to face in the crowd, only to see their resolve hardening against him as well.

"This is all your fault!" Jeffery said, pointing at the members of Tom's teams. "You came here and poisoned his mind. You are taking my son away from me."

"No, sir. You're doing that all on your own. All we did was take off the chains of childhood and show him that he's able to make his own decisions," Tom said.

"So, you admit that you turned him against me?" Jeffery asked.

"We couldn't possibly have changed his mind if he'd truly been loyal to only you. If there hadn't been a seed of doubt already growing in his mind that this wasn't the right way," Derek said. "You've been slowly setting yourself up for this moment all along. The only difference is that he's leaving with us instead of being the next victim of your poor leadership. All we did was give him a little nudge and help him find the light at the end of the tunnel you kept him trapped in."

"Seth, you will go back to your home and await the next monsters. This is unacceptable behavior," Jeffery tried again.

Nearly everyone in the crowd began shouting at him at this.

"You leave him alone!"

"He's right! We can't keep relying on him for this!"

"He almost died, you son of a bitch!"

"What kind of father sends his son to the slaughter like that?"

Continuing on, the team began to worry that the crowd was beginning to transform into a mob.

"People! You can't let your emotions get the better of you either! You have to be rational," Derek yelled over the calls of the crowd. "You must not react hastily. Let's give him an option. Either change the way you lead to a mindset of preparation for the future, or leave."

"Yeah!"

"Hear, hear!"

"Make your choice!"

Calls came from the crowd in agreement with Derek.

"You all put me in charge because I was doing what was best for all of you," Jeffry tried to plead with the crowd. "I have done nothing but look out for your well-being."

"Liar!"

"Get out of town!"

"We don't want you in charge anymore!" came the crowd's jeers.

"The people have spoken!" Derek yelled again.

Quieting down, the crowd stopped to listen to what he had to say.

"You will leave the town and let someone more competent run things instead," Derek said.

"I will never give up! I am the mayor of this town, and I will decide what is best for these people!" Jeffery said.

"I'm sorry, Mr. Mayor," Edward said, also coming out from the courthouse. "But I can't allow that. The people have chosen, and we can't just ignore what they want. We were chosen to represent them, and we have to abide by their wishes. If you would come with me, sir."

"Even you, Edward? Why would you betray me?" Jeffery asked, pulling away as Edward tried to take him by the arm.

"Because I promised to protect the people, not heed your whims, Jeffery," Edward said. "I know we've been friends for a long time, but you're making a huge mistake, and I can't justify standing with you any longer."

A look of complete betrayal came over Jeffery's face.

"I gave you this job because you were supposed to back me, Edward!" Jeffery yelled at him.

"And I did, but that was at the behest of the people. We now see the truth of what we were doing. And it's wrong. We can't just sit idly by and wait to be killed," Edward replied.

"You'll regret this. Mark my words, you will all regret this!" Jeffery said as Edward grabbed him by the arm and led him off to the cheers of the crowd.

Some of the crowd broke off to follow them and ensure that Jeffery was taken to jail, while most of the others stayed to cheer for the heroes.

"So, what do we do now?" someone in the crowd asked.

"Now, you find someone that can represent you properly, and we'll help teach them as much as we can while we're here. Then you'll have to learn to work and fight for yourselves and not let someone else tell you how you should live," Tom said. "That way, you can grow strong and fend off the monsters."

With the main source of their outrage removed, the people began to talk among themselves, milling about in the street as they tried to figure out what would happen next. Seth walked over to join the team.

"Thank you for what you did," he said.

"No thanks are needed. We did it because it was the right thing to do. We're just glad you could see what was happening. Is there anyone you know that would be good for the position now?" Tom asked.

"I do. I'll approach them and see what can be done. Then we can work with them before leaving," Seth said.

"Good. Because as much as I hate to say it, we have to leave in the morning. I know that's not a lot of time, but we can't delay too long on this quest," Derek said.

"Okay. Let's see what we can do while we still have time," Seth said.

Heading out into the crowd, Seth approached a man surrounded by a group and spoke to him. He then walked back to the party and introduced them to the man.

"This is John Walters. He was the leader of one of the large companies here in town and knows how to manage people. He'll be the best bet for leading this town in the interim. They can decide later if they need someone else," Seth said.

"Alright, John. Let's get you up to speed on everything we know about this new System and how you can make the most of it," Tom said.

The team worked together for the next eight hours to establish some basic infrastructure for the town. Edward eagerly took charge of training people in basic combat and weapon handling. The town's vending machines were used to equip residents with weapons and armor, using the Monster Cores the security team had gathered from the various encounters they had faced while assisting Seth.

People were instructed on choosing Classes and what each Class entailed, helping them make the most of their skills. They also learned how to form parties and set up a Guild, enabling them to utilize the bonuses that would help the town grow stronger.

By the end of the day, the team was exhausted and collapsed into their beds at the hotel where they were staying.

"That was a lot more work than I'd anticipated doing when we stopped here," Tom said.

"But we did a good thing. And Seth is going to come with us," Derek said.

"I guess we'll just have to see what tomorrow holds. We have to get on the road again and make it to the Grand Canyon. You know the roads aren't going to be easy to get through, so it's a long trip," Tom said.

"I know. But I feel good now that we didn't just leave these people to their fate," Derek replied.

Tom noticed a new prompt blinking in his vision. Opening the notification, he was rewarded with some good news.

Level Up:
You have earned enough XP to advance to the next level. You are now level 23! Continue to work hard and push yourself to gain more XP to continue to level up. You receive 10 Attribute Points to distribute as you see fit.

Looking over his character sheet once more, he decided to place five points into Charisma, two into Intelligence, and three into Endurance.

Tom Harris	
Race: Human	**Class:** Warlock
Level: 23	**Total XP:** 531,600
XP To Next Level: 98,400	**HP:** 300/300
MP: 470/470	**SP:** 280/280
Attributes:	**Unused Attributes Points:** 0
Strength: 35	**Constitution:** 30

APOCALYPSE

Dexterity: 30	**Endurance:** 28
Intelligence: 47	**Wisdom:** 40
Charisma: 70	**Luck:** 20
Non-Combat Skills:	
Inspect	**Level:** 6 **Rank:** Beginner
Combat Skills:	
Vehicular Homicide	**Level:** 12 **Rank:** Novice
Swords	**Level:** 10 **Rank:** Novice
Summon Demonic Creature	**Level:** 9 **Rank:** Beginner
Fear	**Level:** 5 **Rank:** Beginner
Corruption	**Level:** 5 **Rank:** Beginner
Spells:	
Eldritch Blast	**Level:** 6 **Rank:** Beginner
Dark Ball	**Level:** 3 **Rank:** Beginner
Dark Healing	**Level:** 5 **Rank:** Beginner
Lightning Strike	**Level:** 5 **Rank:** Beginner
Doppelganger	**Level:** 2 **Rank:** Beginner
Dark Flame Weapon	**Level:** 3 **Rank:** Beginner
Tattoos:	Tattoo of Brute Strength
Tattoo of Life Absorption	

With that, Derek and Tom rolled over and fell asleep.

Chapter 39

Onward

Waking early the next morning, the team gathered their things in their Inventories and made their way to the lobby.

"How was your stay?" Clarice greeted them at the front desk.

"It was wonderful, Clarice. We truly appreciate everything you did for us. The meal was wonderful last night," Tom said.

"I'm so glad you liked it. The town wanted to do something to repay you for your help, so they thought a nice meal would be a good start," Clarice said. "Now, if you would all head outside, they'd like to express their gratitude one more time."

Confused, the teams went to the front door and began to exit. Outside was a sight none of them expected to see. A procession of men standing at attention lined the walkway out of the building. As they began to walk toward the courthouse, each man, one by one, drew swords and held them aloft, forming an arch of steel over their heads as they passed beneath.

"What's this for?" Tom asked as they continued to walk under the swords.

They got their answer when they reached the end, where John awaited them.

"We didn't know how to adequately thank you for what you did for us here, so we thought a form of honor would be the greatest tribute we could offer. We also have a supply of food to send with you," John said. "We owe you so much, especially you, Seth. You put yourself in harm's way time and time again for us, and we are eternally grateful."

John bowed low at the waist to show his respect for Seth and the others. Tables had been laid out next to both of their vehicles, and they had been loaded with food for them to take on their journey.

"This is too much. We can't take all of this from you. We were just doing what we thought was right to help everyone," Tom said.

"And that's exactly why you deserve it. You could've just left this town the way it was and never looked back. We aren't your responsibility, and you were already on your way to solving a global problem. But you still stopped and did what you thought was right," John said. "And for that, we thank you."

Cheers erupted from the crowd that had gathered outside the hotel.

"We won't forget you. And Seth can come back as soon as we're finished. We won't keep him from you," Tom said.

APOCALYPSE

"Seth is free to make his own decisions. If he wants to come back, we'll welcome him with open arms. But if he chooses another path, we'll be okay now," John said, winking at Seth.

Gathering all the food that had been provided, the team stored it in their Inventories and then loaded up into the vehicles, with Seth joining Kedron and his team in the H2. As they set out, they rolled down the windows and waved to the gathered townspeople, who watched as they drove back onto the highway to continue their journey.

Heading north on 287, the team encountered numerous vehicles blocking the road, forcing them to clear a path. While the stretches between towns were relatively free of obstacles, the outskirts of smaller towns and larger urban areas required more frequent stops to remove the vehicles.

Several times, they encountered goblins who had set up ambushes along the road. It appeared that others had already fallen victim to these traps, as evidenced by the tire marks and abandoned vehicles with dried blood splatters on the doors and ground. Rather than stopping, the teams accelerated. The goblins jeered and brandished their crude weapons in a futile attempt to intimidate the travelers. By the time the goblins realized the vehicles weren't stopping, it was too late—the teams plowed through, turning the goblins into a gory mess on the roadway, while their makeshift barricades splintered under the weight of the SUVs.

The next major town they encountered was Wichita Falls. From the highway, it was clear that a battle was raging in the town—not between humans and monsters, but between two groups of people. The teams stopped to assess the situation and saw a chaotic firefight below, with both bullets and spells flying in a deadly exchange. Fireballs and lightning bolts illuminated the scene as they struck buildings and combatants alike, creating a dangerous and mesmerizing light show.

"I don't think this is one of the places we should stop," Derek said.

"What if someone needs our help?" Tom said.

"There probably *are* a lot of people who need our help," Derek said. "But if we go in now, we will absolutely get dragged into a war that we can't afford to be a part of. We don't have the time, credibility, or manpower to discover or dictate who's right or wrong in whatever conflict that's all about."

Tom slumped his shoulders as he knew Derek was right.

"I've been in this situation before when I was overseas. You'll see this kind of thing among tribes out there, and when we did get involved, it would take days or weeks just to figure out which side to help. Everyone has a sob story for why they're in the right, and the other is in the wrong. The short of it is that when the dust clears, there are no real winners, and both sides are usually partially in the wrong," Derek said.

"I just feel bad, though. We could possibly help people get past the arguing," Tom said.

"Look, there was one time my forces entered a small town, and two factions were fighting over a well. They each said they had rights to it based on some documents they had from a long time ago. One of the groups came to us with the body of a young boy that had been shot and killed. They said the other side was taking to killing their children over the feud. We decided to take action against those killing the children and brought them to submission with lethal force. It wasn't until the smoke had cleared and bodies were lying everywhere that one of the women, who was apparently the mother of the boy who'd been killed, came to us and told us that the child they claimed to have been killed by the other side had been shot by the leader of the faction that the child was a part of. People will lie through their teeth to get what they want. We can't afford to be in the middle of a dispute like that," Derek said.

"What the actual fuck?" Kiera asked.

"War is a terrible thing," was all Derek said in response.

"That's horrible! But I see your point, and it makes sense. Alright, everyone, load up! We aren't stopping here," Tom called.

Everyone agreed without hesitation, and the teams took off again. With little in the way to slow their progress through this part of the journey, the team made better time than they had in the metropolitan areas. They still had to remove vehicles and kill off some goblins, but they made it to the outskirts of Amarillo without too much issue. Here, the city seemed to be more established than most of the others they had come across.

"Can we stop for the seventy-two-ounce steak?" James asked. "I've always wanted to try it out."

"That can't still be open, you know," Kiera said. "Not with everything that's been going on."

"You don't know that! Texans are really protective of their meats," James said.

"He does have a point there," Derek said. "How about this? We can drive by and see what it looks like. But if it's closed, we head out of town to camp for the night."

"Deal!" James agreed.

As they drove through the town, it felt similar to how Dallas had once appeared. Though traces of the recent chaos were still evident, the town seemed to be managing the aftermath in a healthier way than Decatur had. When the team arrived at the Big Texan Steak Ranch, they were surprised to see people still dining inside the restaurant.

"Well, I'll be damned. It's open still," Kiera said.

"YES! STEAK ME, BITCHES!" James called. "I wonder if I can kill my own cow?"

The team hopped out of the car and walked up to the entrance. Opening the doors, they were greeted by lanterns lit around the building, and people were sitting and eating their meals in various types of armor.

"Welcome to the Big Texan Steak Ranch! My name is Jennifer, and I'll be your host tonight," a young woman said with a strong Southern accent, standing at the hostess' desk. "How many in your party?"

Her appearance was not what anyone had been used to in their previous life. Where before, they would likely have been wearing some kind of uniform or apron, this young lady was wearing leather armor and carrying a crossbow across her back.

"Umm… thirteen, I suppose," Tom said.

"The only place we have big enough for that many people is out on the patio. Is that gonna be okay?" Jennifer asked.

"Sure," Tom said, still feeling awkward about this encounter and unsure what to say. "Before we go out there, I have to ask. Are you all still actually taking money?"

"Oh no, hon, we're a Monster-Core-only establishment. You'll have to pay with those. Do you not have any?" Jennifer asked.

"Oh, no, we do. We just didn't have money," Tom said, feeling relieved.

"Well, then, that shouldn't be a problem. Now, if y'all would just follow me, I'll show you outside," Jennifer said as she turned to take them out to the patio.

As they walked through the restaurant, the diners barely glanced up from their meals, unfazed by the sight of people clad in armor. To them, it was just another group stopping by for dinner. When they reached their table, they found it arranged as a long dining area with enough space to seat twenty. Taking their seats, Jennifer handed out menus to each of them.

"Now, obviously, we recommend the steak, as it's our specialty, but we have other options such as chicken, hamburgers and Dire Boar. We even have some salads for the weaker folks," Jennifer said. "And if anyone wants to try the seventy-two-ounce challenge, just let your waitress know!"

"Wait," Tom raised a hand. "What was that third thing?"

"Hamburgers?" Jennifer asked.

"After that one," Tom clarified.

"Oh, the Dire Boar." Jennifer nodded. "Well, Texas has been practically overrun with boars for ages now. They've been considered nuisance animals and there were practically no rules governing hunting them." Jennifer frowned. "After this whole System thing came around, the problem took on an even greater level of concern. The pigs are stronger and bigger." She leaned forward, surreptitiously looking to the left and right. "Tastier, too. And we get cores and experience from killing 'em now."

"Wow," Tom tilted his head to one side. "Not bad. Thanks for the explanation, Jennifer."

"No problem, hon. Enjoy your meal!"

She turned away without another word and walked back to her station. A few moments later, another young woman wearing armor came to the table, but she was wearing a sword on her hip instead.

"Welcome to the Big Texan Steak Ranch! My name is Julie, and I'll be taking care of you today. Is this anyone's first time here?" Julie asked, also in a strong Southern accent.

Everyone raised their hands.

"Awesome! I'm so happy y'all came to see us," Julie said. "Can I start you all out with something to drink? Unfortunately, we're out of sodas at the moment, but we have water, sweet tea, and lemonade if anyone wants that."

Everyone ordered their drinks, and Julie left to grab them. Sitting and staring at the menu, most of the team felt uncomfortable with the situation but were still enjoying the normalcy of eating at a restaurant again.

"This is weird, right?" Jay asked.

"Definitely, but good on the owner for adapting the capitalist lifestyle to this new environment. It's genius, really. Thinking ahead to take Monster Cores means people will go out to kill monsters, which makes the city safer while giving them something they'll obviously want, like the normalcy of a restaurant. He makes a profit that lets him pay his people and get what he needs. Wish we'd thought of that," Derek said.

"Capitalism just never seems to die, does it?" Kiera asked sarcastically.

"It's pretty ingrained in our society here. I'm not too surprised to see it continue like this," Austin said. "These prices are a little steep, though, considering what you can get for common Monster Cores."

Julie brought out all the drinks, sat them down, and went to take their orders.

"Now, what'll we be eating this—" Julie began when she was interrupted by a small battle cry that came from the parking lot.

The entire team pulled weapons out of their storage and began to get up.

"Ugh… not again. No, no, y'all just sit and relax; we got this," Julie said as she turned and pulled her sword from its scabbard.

Leaping over the banister that lined the outdoor patio area, she was quickly joined by several other men and women, all armed with various weapons, as they charged into the parking lot.

The team exchanged wide-eyed looks of confusion, unsure of what was happening. From behind the parked cars, the sounds of battle filled the air—clashing steel, cries of pain, and shouted curses—suggesting a fierce struggle was happening just out of sight.

A few minutes later, silence fell over the scene. The waiters and waitresses who had charged into the fray began reappearing, their armor and faces splattered with blood. Julie walked back to the table and exhaled deeply before resuming her duties as if nothing unusual had happened.

"Now, where were we?" she asked, a blood droplet on the tip of her nose falling onto the paper order pad she was holding in her hand.

Everyone just stared at her.

"This happens… often?" Kiera asked.

"More often than we'd like. Those little green bastards are drawn here by the smell of the food. But it's nothing we can't handle. We just want you to have the best experience possible," Julie said, smiling at them, another drop of blood running down the side of her face.

"Hmmm. Decisions, decisions…" James had continued poring over the menu with a critical eye. He hadn't looked up a single time during the absence of their waitress, nor at the battle that had happened mere feet from their tables.

APOCALYPSE

"Fuck it. I'm doing it." He closed the menu with a decisive snap. "I'm gonna do the seventy-two-ounce steak challenge!"

Julie reached into her Inventory and pulled out a cowbell. She held it over her head and rang it.

"WOOOOO! We got us a seventy-two-ounce steak challenger right over here!"

Chapter 40

Steak and Shake

Julie left the table after taking all of their orders. The prices felt slightly unreasonable, but it was hard to tell what the dollar-to-Monster-Core conversion rates were supposed to be. In any case, the team was happy to have a nice meal they didn't have to prepare themselves.

The restaurant even had ice. When they asked Julie how that was possible without electricity, she explained that they had someone who was a wizard in the town and took a spell for ice magic. They used that to create large blocks of ice they chopped up into the drinks. A nice cool beverage hit just the right spot for the party, who had been drinking nothing but water from containers they kept in their Inventory for a long while. Sitting and talking, the team got a better chance to get to know each other.

Briana had been a belly dancer in a previous life, and she even gave them a little taste of what she used to do. Bobby and Kedron had actually both been in the armed forces at one point, and Kedron had been in training to become a chaplain before the world went to shit, which explained his choice of Paladin for a Class. Austin had been between jobs, but was hoping to find another job as a chaplain at a hospital and was even on his way to a morning interview when the obelisks had appeared in the cities.

Clay was an interesting person. At least, that was the way people in Texas would politely describe someone who was quite possibly—completely crazy.

He seemed to be working on a ranch with his family when what everyone was now calling the apocalypse happened. He lived in a backwoods area of Texas but happened to be in Irving visiting his sister, who had moved away from the farm to live in the city. He prattled on about how the government was out to take away everyone's rights and that he thought this might be the way of the universe telling people that there was too much control of everyday life.

DeeDee had been a scrum master at a tech company in Dallas while supporting Graham's career as a medieval fighter. They had been able to travel all over the U.S. for his tournaments because the company DeeDee worked for was a remote-only company, so she was able to work on the road.

A huge fanfare with multiple waitresses came through as they brought out the food and set the giant seventy-two-ounce steak in front of James. They even had a timer for him to eat the food.

Julie smiled brightly. "Okay. Time for the rules!" she projected her voice to the entire restaurant. "Rule number one: The entire meal—which includes the seventy-two ounce Big Texan Steak, loaded mashed potato, chef salad, shrimp cocktail, and bread roll must be completed in one hour. If any of the meal is not consumed, which means *swallowed*... YOU LOSE!" she continued. "Go ahead and cut into your steak, take one bite and make sure it's to your liking, hon."

James cut into his steak, tried a bite, and nodded up at the waitress, his face hard, as though he were preparing to go into battle.

"Great!" Julie chirped. "Since the steak tastes good and is cooked to your satisfaction, we will start the time on your acceptable approval. The time will not stop, and the contest will be on, so make *sure* before you say 'yes.'" She held up a hand to forestall his acceptance. "Once you have started, you are not allowed to stand up, leave your table, or have anyone else *touch* the meal. You will be disqualified if anyone assists you in the cutting, preparing or eating of your meal. This is *your* contest." She was looking directly at James, who nodded. "You don't have to eat the fat, but we will judge this." She set a small trash can next to him with a thick trash bag inside. "Should you become ill, the contest is over, and... *you lose!* Please use the container provided as necessary." the waitress continued, clearly having given this same spiel before. "You are required to pay the full amount up front; if you win, we will refund one-hundred percent." She held out her hand, where James deposited ten Monster Cores. Julie nodded in approval, tucking the cores into her apron. "Next, you must sit at a table that we assign."

Two crew members pulled up a small table next to the rest of the group. James rose and moved over to sit down.

"If you do not win the steak challenge, you are welcome to take the leftovers with you, but no consumption or sharing of the leftovers is allowed in the restaurant once the contest is over. And lastly, if you fail to complete the challenge, you will not be reimbursed for the payment of your meal." She turned toward the rest of the room. "Ladies and gentlemen, let's give a round of applause for our contender!"

A raucous applause spread through the room as Julie turned back to their table. "Alright, cowboy." She winked. "Are you ready? I need a verbal agreement."

"Yes." James growled, his fist clenched around his knife and fork as he seemed to be attempting to cook his steak to well-done with his gaze.

Julie slapped the top of the clock with her hand, beginning the timer. "GO!"

James tore furiously into the steak and ate with gusto, tearing through half of the steak in the first fifteen minutes. In between bites, he was stuffing the baked potato and salad into his gullet and washing it down with the shrimp cocktail. When he got to the second half of the steak, he began to slow down.

Eventually, he stopped and laid back in his chair, waving his hand up in defeat.

"Awww, what's the matter? You full already? I thought you were some kind of eating machine?" Kiera teased.

"Shut up, Mrs. salad and chicken," James said.

"I'm just watching my figure. You might want to do the same," Kiera said, poking at James' overfull belly.

"Stop! Don't do that, or I'll be sick," James said.

"Serves you right for making all the rest of us sick all the time," Jay said.

"Oh, you're one to talk," James said.

"Glad you agree. I do feel I should talk," Jay said.

"Maybe if it had been penis, he would have finished it," Graham said.

"Nah, he'd share with Squirrel and be disqualified, or shot it first and asked questions… never," Kiera said. "That would have been a waste."

Continuing to joke back and forth, the teams laughed and enjoyed each other's company while they relaxed. Once they finished their meal, they paid with their Monster Cores and headed back out to the vehicles.

"You know, these Inventories are amazing. I don't have to figure out where I'm gonna put my doggie bag in the car!" James said.

"They really are useful. Something good came of this apocalypse, at least," DeeDee agreed.

"It's really nice for weapon storage. We can keep way more weapons on us than if we were carrying bags, and it's faster to arm them," Jay said, equipping first a dagger, then a sword, then a gun, and then a throwing star.

Hopping back in the vehicles, the teams drove outside the city to find a place to camp for the night. As Tom drove down the highway, James began snoring softly from the back seat, his belly still full from dinner. The others were sitting silently, lost in their own thoughts when Tom had a sudden idea.

Looking at his skills, he noticed something he hadn't considered before. *Dark Weapon Flame* said it would engulf a weapon in flames, which made him consider the possibilities. Pulling up the information on the GS2, he noticed it, too, had the weapon classification, though as a secondary attribute, after vehicle.

"I wonder if…" Tom thought to himself.

Seeing no reason not to try, he held the steering wheel tight in both hands and activated *Dark Weapon Flame*. The entire outside of the vehicle burst to life in blackish-purple flames with a whoosh that caused everyone in the vehicle to jump all at once.

Screaming and yelling came from the back of the vehicle as every person present panicked and scrambled to understand what was happening.

"PLEASE NO! It's exit only, baby! Take the cuffs off, please!" James, who had been the only one asleep, was nearly in tears with fear as he was jostled by the others while trying to make sense of the situation.

Squirrel, who had been lying in the trunk with DeeDee, was now scrabbling through the seats in an attempt to escape from the fire, his animalistic instincts telling him that his den was burning and he needed to be free. He managed to climb over the third row and stepped on James' crotch, causing him to lash out. Squirrel, in turn, bit James in the face in his panic.

Chaos ensued for another minute as Tom swerved while driving, his own fear taking over momentarily. Kedron and his team, who had been driving behind Tom, stared with confusion at the vehicle, not quite sure what to make of the incident.

APOCALYPSE

When Tom finally had the thought to dismiss the flames, they winked out, leaving them all still screaming but even more confused about what was happening. After another ten seconds of panicking, jumbling, and swerving, the team began to calm down. Everyone glared at Tom as he chuckled nervously.

They did eventually find a place off Highway 40 where they could set up the vehicles as a partial barrier and then pitch the tents they brought with them. Most of the team was still upset with the stunt Tom had pulled, but they were happy to be outside and away from the possibly spontaneously combusting vehicle.

Jay grunted as he settled down into a spot near James, handing him one of the rare beers they'd scavenged. Jay cracked his own as they sat in companionable silence for a long moment.

"Wanna talk about it?" Jay was clearly struggling to fight a shit-eating grin.

James sniffed disdainfully. "I have no idea what you're talking about."

"Yeah, Jay. Don't be an ass," Kiera said as she settled down on the other side of the man.

"Thanks, Kiera," James said, clearly relieved.

Kiera nodded in reply. "Hey, Tom," she called out to the Warlock, who turned to look at her. "Next time, make sure that you get off the highway on a proper ramp? Save the cowboy shit for the movies."

A perplexing dance of confusion and indignation played across Tom's face, before settling into an angry frown. "What the fuck are you talking about?"

"You got off on an on-ramp," she said, as though pointing out the obvious.

Tom looked around as if to ask if *he* was the crazy one here. "No. I *did not.*"

"Oh." It was Kiera's turn to look perplexed. "So, you're saying the ramp we took was…" Her confusion dissipated like a fog under a summer sun as she swung her gaze over to a gradually more and more concerned looking James. "*Exit only?*"

A spray of beer exploded into the air as Jay coughed, falling off of the log that he'd settled on. The man crawled over to Kiera. His apoplectic expression didn't match his manic grin and one hand gesturing to his back with a thumb while simultaneously extending a fist toward the woman.

Magnanimously, she bumped his fist *and* pounded him fiercely on the back as he recovered.

James covered his face with both his hands as he groaned.

Tom rolled his eyes, feeling as though they'd get stuck that way any day now. Resolutely, he changed the subject as everyone in the party made the pilgrimage toward a shamed James to pay homage by way of shit-talk.

"Looks like the next major city we hit is Albuquerque. Wonder what we'll find there?" Tom asked after camp had been made and everyone was sitting around the fire.

"Hopefully, something civilized. I think we could have stayed in Amarillo, but after Rhome, I've been hesitant to say we stay in the town," Derek said.

"I can see why, but seeing as the last two cities we've hit have been better, we can likely trust it," Tom said.

"I know someone in Albuquerque," Kedron added. "We could look them up and see if they made it and find out what the situation is there."

"That would be way better than going in blind and hoping for the best," Tom said.

"It's an old Navy buddy of mine named Carl. I bet he made it. He was a tough son of a bitch back in the day," Kedron said.

"Great! So, we look up Carl and see if he can help us with what's going on. Then we can hopefully find a place to stay the night in the city. We can hit up a vending machine while we're there and try to be as ready as we can for the quest. I'm guessing it's going to be a big fight," Tom said.

"Alright, time to set up watch rotations. James and Clay, you are NOT allowed to be on watch together. I believe Kiera offered to babysit you this time, James," Derek said.

"That's right, you're going to make up for last time," Kiera said.

"For saving you from the bad guys?" James asked smugly.

"No, for fucking off and letting us get captured, dipshit!" Kiera said.

"Tomato, potato," James said, laying back on his bed roll.

"What the hell does that even mean?" Kiera asked.

"Don't go there. The mind of James is a dangerous and terrifying place to be. Best to just let it go and make him suffer," Tom said.

"Oh, he'll suffer alright. Won't he, Squirrel?" Kiera said affectionately, stroking the wolf's fur.

Squirrel growled at James as he stared at him and showed his teeth.

"How the hell is everyone better friends with my pet than me?" James asked.

"Alright, people, let's turn in for the night. We've got a big day ahead of us tomorrow. Get as much rest as you can," Derek said.

With that, everyone turned in for the night except James and Kiera, who had first watch.

Much later in the night, Bobby came over and woke up Tom and Derek.

"We got company," Bobby said in a whisper.

"Where?" Derek asked.

"South. Moving pretty fast, but they're trying to be quiet. Probably goblins, but no telling," Bobby said.

"Alright, get the others up and ready," Derek said.

Once everyone else had been woken and were ready to go, Derek formulated a plan.

"Jay, get out there and stealth around and see if you can find out what we're up against. Don't forget *Inspect*. Anything you can get us information-wise will be helpful," Derek said.

Jay nodded once and took off.

"The rest of you form a half ring with the vehicles at our back and the spellcasters in the middle. When they get close, try to control them with spells while we attack. There are quite a few of us now, so we should be able to handle just about anything," Derek said. "But don't get cocky. The first moment you think you have something in the bag is the time you get killed. Always assume they're stronger, and never stop till they're dead."

The whole group nodded and moved into position to wait. Hunkering down to make themselves smaller against the backdrop of the vehicles, they watched for any signs of movement.

Five minutes later, Jay appeared out of the bushes, running as fast as he could toward the group.

"What is it? What did you see?" Derek asked in a hushed tone.

"It's goblins, alright, but these aren't ordinary goblins. They're more organized. Like they were being led by someone. And they've got scouts. One of them saw me, so they knew which way I went. Almost got an arrow in the back for my troubles," Jay said.

"Looks like we need to work a little more on those *Stealth* skills. Still, great job, Jay. Any info is better than going into a fight blind," Derek said, turning toward the rest of the group. "Alright, looks like goblins, but expect them to be organized and ready, so pretend they're people. Assume they're smart and act accordingly."

About ten minutes later, an arrow suddenly shot out from the trees, aimed directly at the team. Graham quickly raised his shield, deflecting the projectile with a loud clang as it bounced off harmlessly. As the group braced themselves, a pack of at least thirty goblins slowly emerged from the cover of the trees. Despite their familiar, ugly appearance, these goblins were notably better equipped than the ones they had faced before.

From the back of the group emerged a goblin that stood out from the rest, towering over them. He was at least a head taller than a regular goblin. Unlike the others, it was clad in nearly full plate armor and wielded a menacing battle axe.

"Hehehe... We kill now. Take stuff and get stronger," the big goblin said.

"Holy shit, it speaks," James said from the back.

"Yes, me speak. Me smart. Better than other goblins. Me use machine, get stuff. Kill other goblins for money," it said to them.

"Shit, they're learning. It never occurred to me that they would use the vending machines to get stuff, too," Derek said.

"You die now," the goblin said and raised a hand, signaling the other goblins to move forward.

With a flash of green light, vines rose from the ground and grabbed at least a half dozen goblins, and the group charged, yelling battle cries. After she had used her vine spell, DeeDee transformed into a bear for the first time in front of the group and charged in as well.

The goblins halted in their tracks when they saw the bear, their eyes widening in fear. Kevin let out a thunderous yell, activating his rage ability as he swung his weapon, sending the first goblin flying with a powerful blow.

From the back line, James took aim with his red dot sights, firing shot after shot and hitting his targets with precision. Kiera pulled out her lute and played a driving rock tune, buffing the party's abilities. Squirrel, ever protective, stood in front of her, growling menacingly at the goblins.

Tom activated his strength tattoo and stepped forward, unleashing his *Cleave* ability as three goblins charged at him. His sword sliced through them in one sweeping horizontal arc, cutting all three in half without the blade even slowing. Black blood sprayed into the air as the goblins screamed, their bodies collapsing into a lifeless heap, organs spilling out onto the ground.

Next, Tom activated his draining tattoo, sapping life from the surrounding goblins. Noticing the attack, several goblins turned on him, but Bobby, Kedron, Graham, and Clay were quick to step in, fending off the attackers. Graham fought with the precision and force of a seasoned warrior, blocking, slicing, bashing, and tearing through the goblins with unmatched skill. Bobby, too, fought with relentless fury, cutting down goblins left and right.

Kedron was locked in combat with one goblin when another charged at him from behind. Before it could reach him, the goblin fell limp to the ground, a bullet lodged in the back of its neck.

"It's no dickshot, but it'll have to do!" James yelled.

Derek was holding his ground well, blocking the relentless goblin attacks with his shield. However, in the midst of the chaos, he became slightly overwhelmed, and a goblin managed to drive a knife into his thigh. Derek hissed in pain but quickly retaliated, bashing the goblin in the side of the head with his mace. As he fought through the pain, a warm, white light enveloped him—Briana's healing spell. The pain in his leg began to ease as the magic took effect, mending the wound.

"Thanks for the assist!" he called out.

They began to push the goblins back, and the bigger goblin flew into a rage.

"Weaklings! Kill them!" it yelled at the smaller goblins.

Seth ran up to it as he called out.

"Hey there, handsome, how about you and I dance," Seth said and slashed down at him.

The goblin raised its axe just in time, blocking Seth's strike. They exchanged a rapid series of blows, both moving with incredible speed and intensity. The clashing of weapons echoed through the battlefield as the two fought relentlessly. Meanwhile, the rest of the party swiftly dispatched most of the other goblins, leaving the fierce duel between Seth and the large goblin as the last remaining battle.

"Do we step in and help?" James asked.

"I think Seth would be mad if we did," Derek said, smiling.

"What? What do you know?" James said.

"Seth is toying with him. Just watch how he moves," Derek said.

Little cuts appeared all over the goblin's body as Seth danced around him.

"ENOUGH!" the goblin said as a force of power erupted around him, sending Seth backward and falling to the ground.

It stepped forward to slash down at Seth when a shot rang out, and it grabbed its crotch.

"*Dick shot,* motherfucker!" James called.

It looked over at him in rage, grabbed a necklace around its neck that had been hidden under its armor, extended a hand out to him, and shot a fireball toward the group.

"HIT THE DECK!" Derek called as people began diving out of the way to avoid the fireball.

"I already hit the dick!" James shouted, pointing at the wounded goblin.

"I said *DECK*, you moron!" Derek said right before the fireball hit.

The projectile exploded as it struck a barrier that had formed just in time in front of his face. The shield absorbed most of the impact, but cracks spread across it before it shattered, sending flames licking over James' body. Although burned, he survived the blast.

Briana rushed over, quickly beginning to heal his wounds.

Meanwhile, Seth had used the distraction to his advantage. Back on his feet and now fully focused, he attacked with precision. Gashes appeared at the seams of the goblin's armor, and suddenly, its arm was severed, followed swiftly by the other arm, and then a leg. The goblin collapsed, screaming, as Seth methodically cut off its remaining leg.

With cold determination, Seth stood over the writhing goblin and drove his katana into its throat, silencing it for good.

Chapter 41

Albuquerque

"What the hell happened to 'always assume they're stronger' and 'never stop till they're dead,' Seth?!" Derek practically yelled.

"I'm sorry. I just knew he wasn't as strong as me. I didn't mean for anything to happen," Seth said, head hung low in guilt.

"Well, because you assumed wrong, James almost got turned into a charcoal briquette!" Derek said, anger filling him as he began to lose control. "You could have ended that fight in the first few attacks, but you toyed with him long enough for him to use some kind of item."

"I know, I know! I'm so sorry. Is James going to be okay?" Seth asked.

"I'm good. Though I was worried I'd be a toasted marshmallow there for a minute," James said.

"Good thing, too. You wouldn't go well with Graham crackers," Kiera said, hooking a thumb over her shoulder to indicate Graham behind her.

"Next time you have an enemy cornered, you go for the kill, am I understood?" Derek said.

"Yes, sir. I promise," Seth said, looking very sincere.

Letting out a long breath, Derek shook his head and closed his eyes.

"Look, you're strong, Seth. We know this. You'll be a great asset to the team, but you have to be willing to make the hard choices and end things before something bad happens. Battles and fights should be as short as possible. There's no room for error. If you slip up once, your enemy will take advantage. They're looking for an opening in a strong opponent to get the upper hand. It's not some kind of sparring match where you're testing your strength. Treat every fight like it's your last. Or eventually it will be," Derek said.

"You also never know who else on the battlefield needs your help. While you're playing with your opponent, your friends could die from their fight. We're strongest together, and the faster you finish your opponent, the faster you can help someone else with theirs," Bobby said.

"Yeah, I see that now. I'm sorry. I won't let it happen again," Seth said.

"Good. Now, can anyone get back to sleep at this point?" Derek asked.

"I might be able to lie down," James said.

"Anyone else?" Derek asked.

Everyone shook their heads. Adrenaline was running too high now.

"Alright then, let's loot these corpses and head on. They look like they have some good stuff here and we can likely make some use of it," Derek said.

APOCALYPSE

Moving over to the bodies of the goblins, the team began to take the armor off.

"Dibs on the plate armor!" Kedron called, jumping over to the corpse of the goblin boss.

"This will go great with my Paladin Class!" he said as he looked at the metal armor.

"Do you think it'll fit?" asked Bobby.

"I'm not sure. Let's get it off and see what happens. Maybe I can use parts of it?" Kedron said.

As they stripped the boss goblin, Kedron set each piece of armor aside, and when he had finished the job, the armor began to shift. When he began putting the pieces on, they felt as if they had changed size to fit him perfectly.

"Neat! Magically fitting armor? Score one for the new System," Kedron said.

"What did you just say?" Derek asked.

"This armor I took off of tall, dark, and ugly over here? It resized to fit me automagically. So, it looks like if we loot armor, it'll still be useful," Kedron replied.

"That's a great piece of news! But automagically?" Derek asked.

"Well, it was automatic and had to be magic." Kedron shrugged.

"Uh huh… well, I'm glad we figured that out," Derek said. "Take all the armor. We just found out it'll change size for the user. We may not need that blacksmith for resizing anymore. Now they can focus on making new things!" Derek called out to everyone.

Once all the items from the fallen goblins had been collected and placed into a pile, Derek and Tom began sorting through them to distribute among the group. Weapons, potions, armor, and a few magical items were handed out to those in need, while the remaining items were organized and placed into storage.

When they loaded up about an hour later, everyone had at least one upgrade and some new weapons.

"Why are we getting so many weapons again?" James asked.

"Because you can equip weapons directly from your Inventory. Since you don't need to carry all your weapons on your person, that means any situation can be accounted for if you have the right weapon. The more weapons you have, the more situations you can handle," Derek said.

"Situations like…?" James asked, pausing to let Derek fill in the answer.

"Like an armored opponent is best dealt with by a mace or club. But opponents with fleshier bits can have them hacked off with a sword. When you are far away, a gun works best, but up close, you might be better suited for a knife in stealthy situations. It gives you options, rather than just relying on one weapon all the time," Derek said.

"Huh… cool! I like it!" James said.

"You're just gonna keep trying to shoot people in the dick, aren't you?" Graham leaned in and asked.

"Pretty much," James replied.

After loading up the vehicles, the team began to travel down Highway 40 again on their way to New Mexico. They traveled most of the day and into the evening, having to stop periodically to move vehicles out of the road so they could pass, and fighting off monsters that appeared in their path. Most of the monsters were goblins that were still trying to take advantage of travelers, but occasionally, other monsters appeared as well.

When they finally reached Albuquerque, the travelers were tired and ready to find a place to crash.

"Carl lives on the east side of town, so we should be able to get to his house and see if he's there before we get too far into the city. Just follow me, and we can see if he's there or not," Kedron said through the window of the H2 as Tom pulled up next to him.

Driving down some of Albuquerque's suburban streets, the teams reached a single-story house where Kedron stopped. Getting out of the car, they went up to the door to see if anyone happened to be home.

"Why would he be here? No one was staying in their homes in Dallas," Derek said.

"Carl is a bit of a homebody. He really doesn't like going out unless he has to," Kedron replied.

Stepping up to the door, Kedron pressed the doorbell button on the front of the house. Tapping him on the shoulder, Tom got Kedron's attention.

"The power is out, remember? That's not going to work," he said.

"Oh, right. Force of habit," Kedron said and knocked loudly on the door instead.

"Get out of here, Jimmy! I told you before I'm not joining your fucking cult, you son of a bitch!" a voice came from the inside.

"Well, now you've gone and hurt my feelings. I figured you were just the man to come join my cult, you crazy old bastard!" Kedron called back into the house.

"Kedron?! Is that you?" came another yell from inside.

"It's stepdad to you!" Kedron yelled back. "Only your mom gets to call me by my government name!" A long silence followed Kedron's words. "I'm saying I fucked your mom, in case that wasn't—"

"Yeah, yeah, ya bastard," the voice yelled back. "I got it the first time. Suits you, I 'spose. Being a motherfucker an' all."

A minute later, the sound of several locks being undone from the inside could be heard, and the door opened to reveal a man about Kedron's age with a scruffy beard and messy hair. He was carrying a shotgun and had a bandolier filled with knives across his chest.

"What the hell are you doing all the way out here, Kedron?" Carl asked.

"We're on our way to the Grand Canyon. There's a quest out there if you haven't noticed."

"Yeah, yeah, I saw it. But in case YOU didn't notice, it's the end of the world right now, too," Carl said.

"It ain't the end of the world, you twat sponge. It's just the change to a new one," Kedron said.

APOCALYPSE

"That's not what Jimmy and his new cult are telling people around here," Carl said. "Been saying they finally were able to bring about the apocalypse and started this whole shit show, so we need to join them and praise their new overlord or some such nonsense."

"Yeah, that's not what happened at all," Kedron said.

"I figured as much. That's why I haven't joined that cockgobbler and his crazy crew. But a lot of others have," Carl said.

"Seriously?" Kedron asked.

"Yeah, he's been sending people out recruiting, and they are getting quite the following. They call themselves the followers of Zalandar. Say he's some ancient God that's come back to claim this world as his own now and is preparing it for his return with the addition of magic and these fucking monsters that keep appearing everywhere," Carl said.

"Well, that sounds fucking stupid," Kedron said.

"Right?" Carl barked out. "Stupid sack of shit is just on some power trip, I'm sure. But he seems to really believe it. It's been like a plague of Jehovah's witnesses out there ever since."

"Do you think he's dangerous?" Derek chimed in.

"Who the fuck is crew-cut, here?" Carl asked.

"Oh, right, these are my apocalypse friends. Tom, James, Kiera, DeeDee, Graham, Jay, Briana, Bobby, Clay, Seth, Kevin, and Austin," Kedron said, introducing everyone. "Crew-cut is Derek."

"Sure are a lot of you fuckers," Carl said.

"Well, a lot has been going on. We're all part of a Guild, and we're trying to fix the vending machine issue so people can get back to trying to survive. Plus, the twenty thousand XP bonus," Kedron said.

"Got room for one more? I'm ready to get the fuck outta here," Carl said. Kedron turned to Tom.

"You got room in the H2?" Tom asked.

"Not really," Kedron said.

"If it's a matter of transportation, I can have my own vehicle ready. No worries about that," Carl said.

"Then it's fine with me," Tom said.

"Excellent. Let me just go get my stuff. I need to pack a few things," Carl said.

Closing the door again, Carl went back into the house to grab what he needed, locking all the locks on his way back in.

"Cult?" James asked.

"That's what he said," Derek replied.

"That doesn't sound like something we should leave just laying around," James said. "I mean, anyone could step on it, right? Cults are basically the metaphysically religious equivalent of legos."

"That's…" Kiera's eyes widened. "Kind of the deepest thing I've ever heard you say."

"I know, right?" Jay said, drawing his knife threateningly. "Tell us how you took James' shape and show us where you hid the body and I'll make this as painless as possible."

Derek stuck with the tactic that worked best in the face of his teammates' constant attempts of derailment: ignoring them completely. "We don't have time to keep solving things like this for people."

"But what happens if it spreads?" Tom asked.

"You too? I thought you were more rational than that?" Derek asked.

"We can't just leave it here. They can't just be allowed to spread fake propaganda and gain a big following like that. People latch onto crazy like this in these times, and who knows how these sort of things would turn out in this new world of ours," Tom said.

"No, absolutely not. We are not going to get involved. We need to get to the Grand Canyon as fast as we can," Derek said.

"Oh, come on, don't be a party pooper. Besides, don't you wanna go break up some crazy guy's plans and be the hero again?" Bobby asked.

"No, I want to go to the Grand Canyon and be the hero," Derek said.

"Sorry, Derek. It looks like you're going to get outvoted," Tom said, everyone staring at him.

"This isn't a democracy. We aren't voting on these issues," Derek said.

"You're right. It *isn't* a democracy," Tom said, his face a stony mask. He thumbed a finger at himself. "It's a totalitarian dictatorship, and as Guild leader, I say we need to end this before it gets too dangerous."

"Fucking hell," Derek growled. "Fine, we can see what we can do. But this better not take too long. We're already behind."

A few minutes later, Carl came back out of the house with several bags.

"Um, Carl. Why don't you just put that stuff in your Inventory?" Kedron asked.

"Well… quite frankly, because I didn't think of that, Kedron. It's all still a little new to me," Carl replied, taking the bags off and putting them in his Inventory.

"Alright, lead us to Jimmy, Carl," Kedron said.

Looking up at Kedron with confusion, realization hit Carl at what he was being asked for.

"Well, shit. Fine, but you guys are not gonna like this," Carl said.

Chapter 42

Under Where?

Carl went back into his house one last time and opened the garage door. He started up a beautiful FLH sparkling blue nineteen seventy-three Harley Davidson motorcycle. Roaring to life, the sound of the engine made some birds in a nearby tree fly off in protest. He pulled up next to the team and motioned for them to follow him.

Loading up in the GS2 and the H2, the teams took off down the street behind the motorcycle. Carl wore a black full-head helmet and a black leather jacket, with a back patch that said "Born to Ride," with his jeans. He appeared exceptionally comfortable riding through the streets and around stalled vehicles.

"We need to form a biker gang! Look how easily he avoids the cars!" James said.

"Yeah, but he can't plow down goblins on that little bike," Tom said.

"But we don't look nearly that badass either," James countered.

"If you want a motorcycle, I'm sure we can find one. But I'm not giving up the Goblin Slayer," Tom said. "It's too useful, and I can upgrade it."

"I wonder what kind of upgrades a Harley gets?" James asked, beginning to get excited.

"Maybe some phallic grips and some sack-shaped footrests?" Graham interjected.

"Yeah, something like… hey wait…" James said.

Continuing to wind through the streets of Albuquerque, the teams eventually stopped in the middle of the street in the heart of the city. Carl stopped his motorcycle and took his helmet off. He looked back at the groups and then down at a manhole cover on the ground.

"Wait, he wants us to go where?" Jay asked.

"Looks like it's into the sewers, folks" Derek said, looking pointedly at Tom.

"If it has to be done, it has to be done," Tom said, opening the vehicle door after pulling off to the side of the road.

"We're gonna have to ride with the windows down for the rest of the trip," Kiera said, putting her face in her hand. "And Squirrel is gonna smell the worst."

Squirrel looked over at her and whined.

"Yeah, I'm talking about you. It's not your fault. It's our fearless leader's idea," Kiera said.

"Hey, you all agreed with me, except Derek," Tom said.

"And let the record show I still think it's a bad idea," Derek said.

"Duly noted," Tom said.

Walking over to the manhole where Carl was standing, the teams gathered around.

"Is everyone ready for this? It's not going to be fun, but their hideout is underground. Jimmy left me a map because he's been pressuring me to join for days," Carl said.

"No," James said.

"Not really," Kiera said.

"This sucks," Austin added.

"Oh, come on, guys. It's not any different than mucking out a barn," Clay said.

"That's the spirit, Clay," Tom said. "Let's get to it."

Carl produced a manhole cover lift out of his Inventory and pried the metal disc out of the hole. He pulled it back and set it down with a clang, depositing the lift back into his Inventory.

"So, who's first?" Carl asked.

"Shouldn't you lead since you know the way?" Tom asked.

"I will, but I ain't goin' in first. No idea what's down there these days," Carl said. "So, hop to it."

"Yeah, hop to it, oh, fearless totalitarian dictator who makes the calls," Derek said sarcastically.

"Fine, let's go," Tom sighed, and he began to climb down into the hole.

Rotting fish and excrement were the smells that hit Tom's nostrils first. He almost gagged as he climbed down the metal rungs of the ladder set in the wall of the sewer. The squeaking of rodents could be heard as he put his feet down on the pavement below, reaching the bottom of the climb down.

"See anything?" Derek called down.

"Define 'anything,'" Tom called back up.

"Something that hasn't come out of the backside of a mammal," Derek retorted.

Tom looked around once more. "Nothing!"

Still, no one came down. "You're saying there's no shit down there?"

"Oh, no," Tom called back. "There's plenty of that, just not much else."

He heard the man curse above him.

Derek began climbing down after him, never one to leave his friends behind. Once everyone was in the sewer, Carl removed the keys from his Harley and joined them. The sewer was a main line with two ledges running along either side of the central spillway. The tunnel was much larger than Tom had anticipated, as he had initially thought he would need to duck to walk through it based on what he knew of sewers.

"Is this normal? Should the tunnels be this big?" Tom asked, looking up at the nearly ten-foot-high top of the pipe.

"No," Derek said, equally confused. "These pipes normally aren't this large. Must have been something with the magical changes of the world that altered them."

APOCALYPSE

"Shouldn't look a gift horse in the mouth," Carl said, interrupting their thoughts. "We could be walking hunched over through the sewage in the bottom."

"Shouldn't look this gift horse in the other end, either," Jay coughed, holding a sleeve up to his nose.

"So, which way first?" Tom asked.

"That way, then we take the first left," Carl said, pointing further down the tunnel.

"Couldn't we have gotten in down there?" James asked.

"The turn is before the next manhole. I did the best I could to keep us near the places we needed to go. I don't want to be down here any more than you do," Carl replied.

"Alright, let's do this, then. Like you said, we don't want to be down here any more than we have to," Tom said, and took off walking down the tunnel.

"Also, a word of advice, try not to fire off any guns in here. Ricochet and all that," Carl said.

"What if I'm really close to the bad guy?" James asked.

"It might come out the back of him and ricochet. I'd rather not get hit by a stray bullet just because you got trigger-happy," Carl said.

"Ugh… fine," James acquiesced.

Walking for about a block and a half, the team came up to the left turn and had to jump across the drain in the middle to get to the other side of the sewer. They continued following the directions Carl gave them as they made a right, then a left, then a right, then two more lefts over the period of about two miles.

Coming to a wall in the tunnel, they were forced to stop.

"Well, this is a dead end," Jay said. "Did we get lost?"

"No, it's just got a secret door. Here, let me find it," Carl said.

"Actually, I have a skill for finding hidden objects. I can help," Jay said, and they set about looking at the wall together.

Investigating the wall, Jay and Carl felt around for some kind of switch or ledge that would open the door to the other side. After about fifteen minutes of searching, Jay hopped over to the other side and found the switch hidden in a broken brick high up on the wall.

"Well, that's why it was so hard to find," Jay said, and he pulled on the switch.

The door popped open on the side everyone else was standing on, and Carl pulled it open.

"For fuck's sake. We'd have never found it without you," Carl said.

"I honestly don't even know why I went to search over there," Jay said. "Just felt something pull me in that direction. Must be the skill."

"Whatever it was, it worked. Now we can keep going," Tom said, stepping through the door.

As Tom entered the room, he was suddenly tackled from the side and slammed to the ground. Someone leaped on top of him, raining punches down on his head. Tom yelled out to his friends between blows, trying to shield his face with his arms.

Derek burst into the room, grabbing the assailant and yanking him off of Tom, only to be attacked from behind by another person. Chaos erupted as more of the team rushed into the room, joining the fray, while more mysterious attackers emerged to confront them.

Jay, quick to react, pulled knives from his Inventory, and the rest of the team followed suit, drawing weapons to fend off the attackers. The tables turned as the instigators, now outmatched, fled the room, leaving three of their men dead on the floor. Tom, Derek, and Bobby were also down, bleeding from wounds sustained in the fight. Tom quickly healed himself while Briana tended to Derek and Bobby. Soon, they were back on their feet, surveying the aftermath.

"What the hell was that?" Tom asked, still holding his head a bit from the blows.

"Part of the cult. People waiting to see who would come here, I would suspect. This was why I wanted nothing to do with them. They're thugs, trying to bully people who they can't bring in with scare tactics or by giving them some kind of weak hope," Carl said.

"Well, we need to be on our guard. We didn't think they were this dangerous. I mean, we knew what they were trying was dangerous, but not that they were out here ready to attack people," Tom said.

"Yeah, and now I'm pissed. They're using cheap blows to get the drop on people. Time for some payback," Derek said.

"Well, they ran off that way," Kedron said. "Go get them."

"With pleasure," Derek said, walking off in the direction that Kedron had indicated.

"Dude, I didn't think he would do it. I thought he was playing tough," James said as the others started following after him.

"Derek doesn't like getting jumped," Tom said. "I once saw him send a guy to a hospital in a bar fight when he jumped on his back to try to help his friend. The first guy was harassing a waitress, and Derek stepped in to stop him. The fight broke out, and his buddy thought he could help him win by sneaking up on Derek. That was a mistake on his part."

"Damn straight," Derek snorted.

"Sneak tactics are effective. He should use them more," Jay said.

"It's not that. In the civilized world, he wanted a fair fight. It's just who he is," Tom said.

"Cops get involved?" Kedron asked.

"Yeah, it was a whole mess. But the waitress explained what happened, and he was let off with a warning. The obnoxious idiots threatened to sue, but nothing came of it once the police report was written," Tom replied. "Guessing no one would take the case."

"Good on him for helping that waitress," Briana said. "I wish more people were willing to step in like that."

"People get sue-happy, so it's hard to step in. But Derek has always been that way," Tom said, smiling at the thought of his friend.

After passing through the wall, the sewage pipe transitioned into a brick-lined tunnel that seemed to stretch on endlessly. The group walked for nearly half an hour before reaching a right turn that led into a large, open room. Derek, with a determined look on his face, entered first. As he stepped into the room, a thug suddenly lunged at him from around a corner.

Derek swiftly dodged back, caught the thug's arm, and hurled him to the side. As he moved to the right, another assailant who had been lurking on the opposite side of the doorway took a swing at him. Derek dodged the strike, pulled out his mace, and delivered a solid blow to the man's shoulder. The man cried out in pain as Derek then swept his legs out from under him, sending him crashing to the ground.

Hearing the commotion, the rest of the team rushed into the room, this time with their weapons drawn and ready. More people dressed in black emerged from the shadows, attempting to ambush the party. However, the battle quickly turned one-sided as the group, now fully prepared, fought back using tactics and coordination rather than being caught off-guard.

"ENOUGH!" a man yelled from the far side of the room.

All fighting stopped as Carl looked up to the far end of the room at who had called out. A snarl came to his face.

"Jimmy," Carl said through the snarl.

Chapter 43

Cult Play

"Carl? Is that you?"

"Yeah, it's me, Jimmy. Come on out here," Carl said.

A man wearing red robes walked forward into the dim light given off by glowing moss growing on the walls.

"What the hell are you doing down here? I thought you didn't want to join us?" Jimmy said.

"I don't. I was just joining up with these guys and they aren't fond of what you're doing here. Figured I'd tag along to watch the fun," Carl said.

"Fun? You mean where they try to beat the crap out of my congregation?" Jimmy said.

"Congregation, fanatical followers—whatever terms you want to use, I suppose," Carl said.

"We are *not* fanatical! We are devoted to Zalandar, who was called out of his thousand-year slumber to bring about the apocalypse!" Jimmy yelled, getting angrier as he spoke.

"Then why has no one ever heard of Zalandar, eh Jimmy? They had records a thousand years ago, and nothing ever talked about Zalandar or any other all-powerful being that needed to be worshipped," Carl said.

"Jesus Christ has joined the chat," James muttered.

Kiera elbowed him in the ribs.

"Just because you and so many others are ignorant of the master's glory doesn't make him any less real, Carl!" Jimmy continued. "He is the all-powerful being who has returned to give us the powers that we now control. And you are naive in your scorn of his blessed gifts!"

"No, Jimmy, the Grand System gives the gifts. It was right there in the tutorial, you complete and utter fuckstain," Carl said.

"And where did the System come from, huh? That's right, it is the great Zalandar's vessel of power!" Jimmy said.

"Wrong again, Jimmy. There are Administrators who run the System. Just because you don't understand something doesn't mean your 'god' created it," Carl said, making air quotes around the word "god."

"Surely, his greater followers will eventually rise to the level of Administrator, and I will rise to the top by praising him and bringing him more followers!" Jimmy went on.

APOCALYPSE

"There's no talking to you, Jimmy. So, we should just get down to the fighting now, I guess. I'm gonna enjoy making you shut up," Carl said.

"Oh, nay, nay. It is *you* who will be doing the shutting up, Carl. For Zalandar has given me an additional gift. And that gift is the control of one of his ancient beasts. COME FORTH MIGHTY TYRANTUS!" Jimmy screamed at the end of his rant.

The ground trembled as something heavy stepped down.

"Jesus has left the chat," Jay whispered, his eyes wide.

"Nooo," James moaned. "Jeebus, save me!" His voice was tinged with unease as he peered down at a small puddle that rippled with each quake.

Again, the ground shook, each tremor growing stronger as whatever approached drew closer. The vibrations became a steady rhythm, a harbinger of the beast that soon emerged from the far end of the room. With a mighty roar, it opened its jaws wide, the sound echoing off the walls as it defiantly challenged all who dared to face it.

"IS THAT A FUCKING T-REX?" James screamed.

"Well… shit," Carl said.

The men in the black robes around them backed away, almost giggling.

"Behold the beast of Zalandar, Tyrantus! He will crush you and devour all those who do not believe!" Jimmy said.

"It's a fucking T-rex. How the fuck did he get a T-rex?" James asked, almost frantic now.

"Shut up, James. It's not any bigger than the last monster we took down. We can handle this," Tom said, only half believing the words he was saying.

Tyrantus
Tyrantus is a fire-breathing T-rex gifted to the fanatic cult that worships the great being Zalandar. This monstrous beast stands as a symbol of Zalandar's fiery wrath and unstoppable power. Covered in scales as black as the void, Tyrantus' eyes glow with an infernal light, and the heat emanating from its body is enough to scorch the ground it walks on. The cult of Zalandar uses Tyrantus as a living weapon, unleashing it upon their enemies to bring fiery destruction and chaos. Created through ancient and forbidden rituals, Tyrantus was once a mighty T-rex until the followers of Zalandar captured it and transformed it into a living embodiment of their God's fiery fury. This beast is more than just a creature of destruction; it is a testament to the cult's willingness to harness the most dangerous forces in the universe. When Tyrantus is unleashed, it leaves nothing but ashes in its wake, spreading the cult's terror far and wide.

HP:	3570/3570
MP	500/500
SP:	2960/2960

Attacks:	Bite, Inferno Breath, Molten Stomp, Roar of Zalandar

Just as Tom finished using Inspect on the creature, the beast put one foot forward—the brick turning red hot beneath its step—opened its mouth at the party, and breathed a stream of fire at them.

"IT BREATHES FUCKING FIRE TOO?" James screamed as he threw his hands over his face to fend off the attack, however futilely.

Briana was ready with a shield that stopped the fire and caused it to spread to either side of the party.

"Well, that complicates things," Derek said.

"FUCK THIS!" Tom yelled as he stepped forward. He used his skill *Corruption*, then used *Fear* right after it on the beast.

The T-rex first stopped, then took a step back from the party, its gaze uneasy as it stared at Tom.

"SIT!" Tom yelled at the beast, and to the shock of everyone present, it did.

"How are you doing that, Tom?" Derek said out of the side of his mouth to Tom.

"HOW ARE YOU DOING THAT?" Jimmy yelled.

"I figured if you were controlling it, it's some kind of summon. And who is better at summoning than a Warlock?" Tom called over.

"What!? It's not a summon! It's a beast of Zalandar! Only his chosen should be able to..." Jimmy began and then paused. "Wait, do you worship Zalandar?"

"No, of course not," Tom said.

"Then you shouldn't be able to summon..." Jimmy stopped and put his hands over his mouth.

"AHA!" Tom yelled. "I knew it!"

"Well, no matter. The cat's out of the bag. But if you can control it, that means your Charisma is stupid high," Jimmy said.

"It's my highest stat currently," Tom said. "What I don't understand is why your creature is so big when mine aren't."

"What do you mean yours aren't?" Jimmy asked.

Casting his summon spell, Tom called forth one of his creatures. This time, as opposed to an Abyssal Chicken or a Dretch, a creature that appeared to be half man, half elephant with long tusks protruding from its elephant-shaped head, appeared on the ground next to him.

"What the fuck?" Tom asked, surprised at the new summon.

"Seriously? *Those* are your creatures?" Jimmy asked.

"Well, this isn't what normally happens, but I still wish it was something that big," Tom said, pointing over at the now cowering T-rex.

<table>
<tr><td colspan="2" align="center">Demonic Mastadonian</td></tr>
<tr><td colspan="2">Mastadonians are formidable creatures, half man and half elephant, hailing from a distant plane where strength of arms is revered above all else. Towering at nearly eight feet tall, their powerful frames are covered in thick, leathery skin, with the head and tusks of a mighty elephant. Their eyes gleam with an intense focus, driven by an unquenchable thirst for battle and the desire to prove their strength in combat. Mastadonians live by a strict code of honor, valuing fair fights, loyalty, and the prowess displayed on the battlefield. The Mastadonians come from a war-torn plane where constant battle is a way of life. From a young age, they are trained in the art of war, their society revolving around martial prowess and the pursuit of glory on the battlefield. Despite their fearsome appearance, Mastadonians adhere to a strict code of honor, refusing to strike down an unarmed opponent and always seeking to test their strength against the strongest foes.</td></tr>
<tr><td align="center">HP:</td><td align="center">1025/1025</td></tr>
<tr><td align="center">MP:</td><td align="center">750/750</td></tr>
<tr><td align="center">SP:</td><td align="center">840/840</td></tr>
<tr><td align="center">Attacks:</td><td align="center">Can wield weapons, Trunk Slam, Battle Roar, Tusks of Vengeance, Honor's Shield</td></tr>
</table>

"This really isn't fair, you know," Jimmy said.

"Fuck fair. I play to win," Tom said, motioning for the Mastadonian to attack Jimmy.

Launching itself across the room, it jumped on Jimmy, who went down in a flailing ball of screaming man and elephant. Punching and kicking at him, the Mastadonian beat the absolute shit out of Jimmy until he finally used a spell to throw the creature off him.

"I WILL NOT BE BEATEN BY THIS… THING!" Jimmy screamed.

"What about that one?" Tom asked.

Jimmy turned to his right, where Tom pointed, to see a Dretch standing beside him, and let out a girlish scream. The Dretch smiled at him as it let out one of its toxic farts.

"OH MY GOD IT SMELLS SO BAD!" Jimmy said, trying to cover his mouth and nose with his robes.

"Well, I've had just about enough of this," Carl said as he ran over to Jimmy and hit him in the head with a baseball bat.

Jimmy fell to the floor unconscious. The T-rex vanished as soon as he did. Everyone stood there for a moment, no one speaking.

"Soooo… Profit?" James finally said, unable to bear the awkward silence.

"You have beaten the beast of Zalandar," one of the people dressed in black said from the side of the room.

"Sure, why not," Tom said.

"You must be truly powerful indeed. What God do you hail from?" another asked.

"We don't hail from a God. And neither did that turdburger," Tom said.

"So... Zalandar isn't real?" the cultist asked.

"Well... I didn't say *that,*" Tom hedged.

"..."

"Even the System mentioned the guy by name, so he has to be real. But it's obvious, if you think about it." Tom huffed. "Zalandar was this guy's fucking Patron. Sure, Patrons might be powerful *somewhere* else, but here? Their actions are severely curbed and are reliant on their vassals. Zalandar person—real." Tom locked eyes with the cultists in turn. "Zalandar-God? Fake."

"Then... what do we do now?" another asked.

"You go back to your homes and try to get on with your life. You can't really be so gullible that you need to follow this queef cloud around, are you?" Kiera asked.

"But... the apocalypse. We don't know what to do now that it's happened," said a man who stepped in front of the others.

"You do what we did. You form a Guild, and you bring people together to get stronger. You don't worship some made-up being in hopes that they will rain favor down on you or shoot rainbows and sunshine up your ass or whatever," Tom said. "You try to work together to make this place better for everyone. And Jimmy was not doing that."

Looking at each other, the thugs all shrugged slightly and then looked at Tom.

"Do you have a Guild?" the one in the front asked.

"We do. But it's in Dallas," Tom said.

"We could go to Dallas," the man said, looking at the others who nodded at him.

"Well... You really want to go that far?" Tom asked.

"We don't know how to run anything like this. We are better suited to following. Could we join your Guild? You seem strong," the man asked.

"I mean... I guess? You'll have to be vetted by Brian, our Guild Admin. But if he thinks you're good enough, I don't see why not," Tom said.

"Is this Brian your boss?" the man asked.

"What? No. He's the Guild Admin. Kind of like an HR person," Tom said.

That seemed to make sense to the meatheads.

"So, what do we do with Jimmy over there?" Derek asked.

A shot rang out from where Jimmy had fallen.

"Got it!" James said, giving the room a thumbs up.

Everyone stared at him in disbelief.

"What the hell, James?" Tom yelled at him.

"Oh." He looked sheepish. "You wanted to do it?"

APOCALYPSE

"NO! I meant, why the hell did you just shoot the guy like that?" Tom asked.

"Oh." James blinked. "That's easy. We couldn't do anything else with him. Jail isn't really a thing. I figured better to end it now than have him pop up on us later," James said, putting his gun away. "I always hated those characters the good guys let go and they kept coming back later in the story with a new plan to kill them."

The party all looked at each other, each expecting the other to have some kind of argument against it.

"I mean… we can't just go shooting people like that, can we?" Tom asked.

"After everyone I've shot and killed so far, *this* is where you draw the line?" James asked. "What a load of shit."

"I mean… I guess?" Tom said.

"Come on, let's see if he has anything and then get back to the vehicles. We have places to be, people!" James called.

The black-robed thugs moved over and searched Jimmy's body for the team, seeming to see Tom and his people as their de facto leaders now. They brought over what they found, and Tom took it from them. Still a bit confused as to what was happening.

When they had finished gathering everything up, one of the thugs approached Tom.

"What do we do with the treasury?" he asked.

"Treasury?" James asked, his ears perking up.

"What treasury?" Tom asked.

Motioning for them to follow, the thug led them to the back of the large room and opened a hidden door. Inside were weapons, armor, gold, Monster Cores, and jewels stacked almost to the ceiling.

"Jackpot!" James said, moving into the room.

"Holy shit. Where did all this come from?" Derek asked.

"We had been gathering it. Jimmy said we needed all this stuff for Zalandar's return, and we should have it ready for him," the thug said.

"Well, we should take it with us, I guess?" Tom asked, looking at Derek.

"We can't leave it here. Well, the gold is probably not worth much now, but maybe someone back at the Guild can find something to do with it," Derek replied.

After gathering up the items and adding them to their Inventories, the team, along with the followers of Zalandar, made their way back through the tunnels to the manhole they had entered earlier. One by one, they climbed up, emerging into the open air. As they stood there, they exchanged glances, each person reflecting on the journey they had just undertaken.

"If you're serious about joining, then head to Dallas. The Trammel Crow Center is the Guild building we have. Tell them that Tom sent you and they'll help find a place for you. Otherwise, you can form a Guild here and try to help people," Tom said to the man who had shown them the treasury. "I never got your name, by the way."

"It's Jack," the man said. "We'll go to Dallas. You seem like someone who knows what they're doing."

"BUUURRR!" James made an incorrect buzzer sound. "We're all flying by the seat of our pants—full dicks out for Harambe kind of situation."

Tom placed his entire hand over James' face. The man's shoulders slumped.

"Not necessarily," Tom replied. "I just try to do right by people. The rest is all from people working with me to help make things better."

"Well, however you do it, we can help," Jack said, extending his hand.

Tom took the hand and shook it.

"Alright, everyone, time to load up. Next stop, the Grand Canyon... hopefully," Tom said.

Chapter 44

Red Flagstaff

Jack managed to secure several fifteen-passenger vans to transport everyone back to Dallas. The new recruits expressed deep regret for their previous actions, explaining that they had just been looking for someone to lead them through the chaos of the apocalypse. Tom understood, to some extent. Jimmy had all of the trappings of power: perceived competence, strength, and most importantly—easy answers. He felt confident they were genuinely eager to learn and was happy to have them join the group.

Before they left town, Carl suggested a place where they could spend the night and start fresh in the morning. After dealing with the cult, everyone was exhausted, so the idea of resting was appealing. Near the edge of the city was an old hotel that had been repurposed to provide shelter for travelers.

The crew hopped into their vehicles and followed Carl, who led the way on his Harley. After a short drive, they arrived at the hotel, which appeared to be housing a small group of people. Carl led them inside to speak with the receptionist.

"Welcome to the Albuquerque Holiday Inn. How can I help you, Carl?" the lady at the desk said.

"Hey, Rose, good to see you're still here. Think you have some rooms for me and my friends here?" Carl asked.

"Sure thing. If you wanna head upstairs, I can give you these keys. Each one has double beds. Should be enough for all of you," Rose replied.

"Thanks, love. We'll be out in the morning, headed on our way," Carl said as he turned to head upstairs.

Everyone split up the keys and went to rest for the night, knowing they had a long day ahead of them and were tired from the day's events.

Early the next morning, the teams met in the parking lot to get ready to head out.

"Provided we make similar time to what we've been doing, and there are no more delays…" Derek paused to look at Tom.

"I'm not sorry for the stops we've made," Tom said.

"Even so, we should make good time to Flagstaff, Arizona, like we did from Amarillo to Albuquerque. We can stop there, and it should only be a short trip up to the Grand Canyon. I want us to be at least as rested as we can be when we arrive, so we will stop there to rest," Derek explained.

"That sounds good. I know some places in Flagstaff that might still be a good place to stop. Might be some monsters around, since Flagstaff isn't as big of a city as Albuquerque; but shouldn't be anything you lot can't handle," Carl said.

"Cool. Because I could use a little more practice," Austin said. "That last fight where they got the drop on us kind of messed with my head."

"It's not your fault that happened," Bobby said. "It happens to everyone. You get surprised and you lose a fight. Don't let it get you down."

"Thanks, man. I appreciate that," Austin said. "Especially since you got your ass handed to you too."

"Oh, really? I wouldn't have gotten jumped if I wasn't in there trying to pull your ass out of the fire," Bobby said.

"Well, that's funny because I was only in there when Derek was getting the shit kicked out of him," Austin said.

"And I was only in there because Tom got jumped," Derek said.

"I never said I was a fighter. I was just trying to be a good leader and take the initiative," Tom said.

"True. We can't fault you for that. No one else wanted to go first. And you can heal yourself. So, better you than someone else," Derek said.

"Heavy is the head that wears the crown," James said.

"I am NOT wearing a crown. This is just me trying to be willing to take on responsibilities," Tom said.

"That's respectable," Carl said. "I'm glad to hear that our leader is willing to put in the work for the Guild."

"Well, I think we've wasted enough time. Shall we away?" Derek asked.

"Agreed. Let's go," Tom said.

The team jumped into their vehicles and hit the road again, headed for their next destination. Carl took the lead, as he knew the route to Flagstaff better than anyone else.

As before, they had to clear vehicles blocking the way, and Carl was content to let the others take the lead in dealing with any goblin-made roadblocks. Carl would hold a hand in the air when he saw the blockades, pull off to the side, and the SUVs would surge ahead, destroying their would-be robbers.

As they traveled through the desert, they began to spot larger monsters roaming the sands—creatures so massive they looked like small mountains, yet still distant on the horizon.

Relieved to avoid those beasts, the team pressed on toward Flagstaff. When they finally reached the road signs marking the city limits, everyone was eager to rest after a long day of travel and hard work.

As they pulled into the city, it looked like a ghost town. Not a soul was in sight. They stopped at what seemed to be an abandoned hotel and cautiously began searching for any signs of life.

"What's with this place seeming so desolate?" Kedron asked.

"No idea. It's normally not like this. Though the population is lower than other towns, it's not *this* quiet," Carl said.

"Over there, I saw someone moving in that window," Bobby said.

"Are you sure?" James asked.

"Yeah, I'm sure. They definitely were watching us, then ducked down out of sight," Bobby said.

"HEY OVER THERE! WE AREN'T HERE TO HURT YOU WE JUST WANT TO REST FOR THE NIGHT!" James yelled at the place Bobby had indicated.

"Smooth, James," Derek said. "I would definitely want to come talk to someone yelling at me."

The door to the house cracked open slightly, and a woman poked her head out.

"You were saying?" James asked.

"Keep your voices down," the woman hushed them. "They'll hear you."

"Who will hear us? This place looks abandoned," Tom asked.

"The raiders," she said in a harsh whisper, becoming agitated.

"Raiders? There shouldn't be any raiders yet. The apocalypse just happened like two weeks ago. Who the hell got their shit together that fast to do raids?" Derek asked.

Rolling her eyes, the woman waved them over to the building she was in.

"Get in here and be quiet. We don't need them coming in early because you jackasses won't shut the hell up," she said.

"Wow, language…" James said.

"Oh, you're one to talk, Mr. I can't go one sentence without swearing," Derek said.

"Fuck you," James said.

Derek held his hands out as if to an imaginary jury. "I rest my case, Your Honor."

Moving to the building, the teams entered, and the woman hurriedly shut the door behind them. Tom clicked the button on the remote to lock the GS2 out of habit, and the horn honked.

The woman gave him a withering gaze.

"Sorry, force of habit," he said, holding his hands up placatingly.

"Look, the raiders come through here almost daily looking for things to steal. They harass people and kill anyone that gets in their way," the woman said.

"But where did they come from? Like I said, it's too early in the apocalypse for anyone to have found the time to coordinate raid groups and vehicles to attack people like this," Derek said.

"They're a nomadic people that live out in the desert. They broke away from society about ten years ago to live in a lawless state together where there are no rules, and they reject any government interference," the woman said. "The local police had many run-ins with them as they tend to be drug addicts or sovereign citizens that believe they've found some loopholes in the constitution that means they don't have to follow the rules like everyone else."

"Oh. So, crazy people," James interjected.

"Essentially. They had been gathering supplies and building up stockpiles in the desert for years, and now they see this as their opportunity to take whatever they want from people," the woman continued. "They come and raid the city, trying to take anything they can to keep up their supplies. They were ready for something like this to happen and are just taking advantage of the rest of us."

"We're so sorry to hear you've been dealing with that," Tom said. "This apocalypse is hard enough without having to worry about crazed lunatics coming in and trying to steal everything not nailed down. My name is Tom, this is my team, and we're on our way to the Grand Canyon to try to help with the worldwide quest so we can set things back to normal."

"Don't you say it, Tom," Derek said.

"But maybe we can help here as well," Tom said.

Derek facepalmed.

"I'm Sarah. I'm not sure what you could do here, though. If you're passing through, I'd suggest getting going now. Those vehicles are something the raiders will be looking to take with them," Sarah said.

"Why haven't you left yet?" Kiera asked.

"And go where? It's an apocalypse. I don't know where to go. No one does. With communication shut down, we can't just call our family and plan a road trip. We need to know where to go," Sarah said.

"Well, we can't just let our vehicles get stolen. Guess we'll have to do something about it," Tom said.

"If by 'do something,' you mean keep driving, then that's a great plan," Sarah said.

"See, she has sense. Listen to the sense," Derek said.

"We should probably try to defend them," Tom said.

"That's a bad plan. There are a lot of raiders. Hundreds of them," Sarah said. "And there's what? A dozen of you?"

"I think we're up to fourteen now," Tom said.

"Oh, that should make the difference," Sarah said, sarcasm dripping from her voice.

"Touchy much?" James asked.

"You try living in constant fear of being attacked daily for two weeks, and then come tell me how you feel about it," Sarah quipped.

"Fair point," James said.

"Look, we've been on the road for a long time and need to rest. We should be stopping here. These people can't just go out and do whatever they want like this," Tom said.

"And if we fight them off, we haven't rested at all," Derek said.

"Maybe not, but we made a difference in people's lives," Tom said.

"Or we send the raiders off with their tails between their legs, only to come back with even more forces, and they will completely burn the town to the ground out of revenge," Derek countered.

"You all seriously think you can fight off the raiders?" Sarah said.

"We've fought a lot recently," Tom said. "It's kind of our thing."

"Much to our detriment," Derek said.

"We've done nothing but get stronger and improve our teamwork through the fights," Tom countered. "It prepares us for this bigger fight coming up."

"It *delays* the bigger fight coming up and puts us in danger," Derek said.

APOCALYPSE

"We're always in danger, Derek. It's a fucking apocalypse," Tom said.

Derek was quiet for a moment. Tom had a point. He just hated that they were still sticking their necks out for people.

"I get you hate that we keep doing this, but if not us, then who? You said it yourself to Seth," Tom said.

"I said that to get him to join us," Derek said.

"Hey!" Seth said.

"Oh, you needed to hear it too. You were being Tom just for that one town," Derek said.

"Look, I appreciate you looking out for us. You are our constant voice of reason and one of my best friends. But we need to do this. I can't leave people to suffer like this," Tom said.

Letting out a big sigh, Derek nodded.

"I know. I'm just trying to be sure we don't do something stupid. Which I will say this is," Derek said. "So, what's the plan?"

"We need to set up some traps for them. Jay, you think you can help with that?" Tom asked.

"Why? Because I'm the Rogue?" Jay asked.

"Umm, yes?" Tom said.

"…Fair. I can, actually, but I don't like being stereotyped," Jay said.

"Duly noted. Probably going to happen again," Tom said, looking at the others. "We're going to give them a surprise they won't forget."

Chapter 45

Raiders

A few hours later, the teams met back up after carrying out their individual tasks. Jay had taken a team to begin setting up traps for the raiders after getting some more information from Sarah about how they attacked.

"Each day, they drive into town mostly in trucks because they can carry people and items in the beds. They drive through the town, firing their weapons and yelling to let people know they are coming. Then they raid buildings seemingly at random to try to find any supplies they can," Sarah said. "People try to live in the buildings they've already hit, but they seem to have picked up on that and go back to some of the previously hit buildings to take what they can. As long as we just give them our stuff, they leave us be. But if anyone fights back, they're dragged out and killed where people can see."

"Derek, can you take point on setting up the plans?" Tom asked, looking directly at his general.

"Sounds like traps are definitely our biggest advantage. Jay, we need as many as you can rig up. Everyone else needs to get their weapons ready so we can pick some of them off before things get hairy. DeeDee, you should also be able to help with those vines," Derek said.

"I can do that. I can also make the vines grow thorns to try to take out tires," DeeDee added.

"That's an excellent idea!" Derek said. "Do that to stop as many vehicles as you can. We need them out on foot. Kiera, you'll need to be in a high-up position and pick off as many as you can with your rifle. You'll be a key player in the on-foot stage. Do you have enough ammo?"

"I stocked up really well. I'm good for a long time," Kiera replied.

"Excellent. Briana, you'll make some barriers to stop vehicles that get through or funnel them to this one area in the middle of town," Derek said, looking at a map of the city that Sarah had drawn on a piece of paper for them.

"Seth, I need you to take out any troublemakers. Don't get bogged down in any one fight, and move in and out as fast as you can," Derek said.

"You got it. No playing with them this time," Seth replied.

"The rest of you, we'll be going in and taking out groups one at a time, so be ready to run from place to place and watch each other's backs," Derek said.

Traps were set and everyone was in position, ready to go. All they had to do now was wait for the raiders to arrive. As the sun began to set, the sound of approaching vehicles and a rising cloud of desert dust appeared on the horizon. Gunfire echoed in the distance, growing louder as the raiders drew near. The crew could hear the whoops and hollers of the men in the backs of the trucks, whipping themselves into a frenzy.

"We're as ready as we can be. Everyone stick together and follow the plan. But remember that no plan survives contact with the enemy, so we'll adapt as best we can," Derek said.

Nodding in agreement, everyone took up their positions. From what Tom could see, there were about twenty trucks, which meant over a hundred raiders were heading into town, judging by the number of people packed into the truck beds. The convoy split into two groups, each taking a different route through the city.

On the right side, the first set of trucks rolled over a hidden trap. Two stones, tied to a chain, were triggered, shooting up into the air and catching the raiders standing in the truck beds. The taut chains slammed into their chests and necks, yanking them out of the vehicles.

Hearing the cries of pain behind them, the drivers glanced back and slammed on their brakes. As the trucks came to a halt, Kiera took her shot, picking off the drivers one by one. Some trucks lurched forward as the dead drivers' feet slipped off the brakes, only to roll over thick vines strewn across the road, each vine bristling with huge thorns that shredded the tires, leaving the trucks immobilized.

Across town, DeeDee was busy deploying vines across the roads, creating the same clothesline effect to catch other raiders as they drove through. Graham and a few others jumped out, using guerrilla tactics to eliminate any raiders who fell, then quickly retreating into side streets or buildings with secondary exits.

James moved swiftly from building to building, targeting drivers, and if any trucks started moving, they would run over a bed of screws the team had found in a hardware store and scattered across the roads. The raiders lacked any coordinated tactics or a clear leader, leading to mass panic within their ranks. The plan was going smoothly. The raiders were completely disorganized, and the teams picked them off one by one.

Then the second wave arrived.

Alerted by the sounds of gunfire, the second wave of trucks barreled into town after the first had triggered most of the remaining traps. The first few trucks sped past their halted comrades, trying to reach their friends who were being slaughtered on the ground, ducking under the now-visible clotheslines. Most of the trucks, however, stopped behind the first wave, and the raiders jumped out, guns ready to shoot anyone unfamiliar. The spikes or screws still caught those who drove in, but most were cautious enough to avoid the traps.

For the raiders, the real problem was their overwhelming numbers and the few members of Tom's team darting in and out of cover. They couldn't fire at them without risking hitting their own. Swearing and screaming filled the air as fights broke out among the raiders when they accidentally shot each other.

As chaos consumed them, Tom's team found themselves doing less and less work as the infighting claimed almost as many raiders as their own attacks.

Unleashing an *Eldritch Blast*, Tom ignited a trail of lighter fluid that encircled the back of the town, trapping the raiders in a ring of fire with no escape. As the teams continued their hit-and-run tactics from the alleys and backstreets, the raiders—now firing wildly with automatic rifles—only ended up killing more of their own as their panic escalated to outright terror.

Seth was a blur of activity, effortlessly weaving in and out of buildings, cutting down the largest raiders with his katana. Kevin, doing what he did best, charged out from a building at a smaller group of raiders who had been cut off, bellowing his war cry. In a matter of seconds, he slaughtered six of them with his greataxe before disappearing into another building, gunfire narrowly missing him and striking the walls instead.

The raiders, increasingly terrified by the relentless hit-and-run tactics, began to group together, backs to each other, trying to watch all sides. Kiera, lying prone on a tall building's roof, started picking off those who seemed to be giving orders.

James found a broken window and engaged in a gunfight with a group of raiders, like an old western shootout, popping up to fire and ducking back down between shots.

Even Jerky joined the fray, appearing on the shoulders of raiders to bite at their necks, then turning invisible before anyone could retaliate. Squirrel darted in and out of hiding, tearing at the groins of unsuspecting victims, executing his own hit-and-run tactics without engaging in direct combat.

With their numbers rapidly dwindling and unable to find clear targets, the raiders finally broke. Fear filled their eyes as they scrambled to jump into any still-drivable vehicles. When those filled up, they turned tail and ran.

Jay and Kedron appeared in the GS2 and H2, blocking the road out of town and cutting off their retreat. Jay ran over one unfortunate raider, bashing the poor bandit with the bumper spikes and cattle guard as he tried to flee ahead of the group. The retreating raiders were funneled into a single street leading south, only to be cut off by attacks from behind and Briana's barriers. Desperation drove them to trample over each other, using anything or anyone as a shield.

The battle turned into a slaughter as the teams charged in, outnumbered three to one but empowered by the raiders' panic. Still firing wildly, the raiders ended up killing more of their own, sealing their defeat in a chaotic frenzy.

As the battle neared its end, the remaining raiders—about a dozen—threw down their weapons and raised their hands, begging for mercy. However, one raider remained defiant, spraying bullets wildly at one of Briana's shields while screaming at the people on the other side.

He backed away from the advancing team, his desperation palpable, but his escape was cut short when he stumbled into Seth. Without hesitation, Seth drove his katana through the raider's back, the blade erupting from his chest in a gruesome spray of blood. He gurgled as the katana punctured a lung, blood spilling from his mouth as his assault rifle slipped from his now limp hands. He collapsed forward as Seth ripped the blade out.

With the immediate threat neutralized, Tom pulled out handcuffs from his Inventory, and the team set to work restraining the remaining raiders, seating them on the ground.

"So, that went well," Tom said.

"We got lucky. If they had another wave coming, we would not have done so well," Derek said.

"Don't be such a sour puss. Take the win," James said.

"I'm just trying to be realistic about… James, you were shot!" Derek exclaimed.

"What?" James asked, looking himself over and noticing he'd been hit in the arm. "Well, I'll be damned."

"Hold still, I'll heal you," Derek said, moving quickly to his side.

"I sure do get hurt a lot with this stupid apocalypse," James commented. "I guess the adrenaline is still…"

James began to wobble on his feet before losing the battle to remain upright. Derek caught him and laid him carefully on the ground before going to work healing him. A white light began to glow over his arm, and the bleeding stopped before the bullet was pushed out of his skin, tinkling lightly on the ground. The wound closed, and his eyes fluttered open as the light dissipated.

"Soo… dark…" James whispered weakly. "Kiera? Is that you?"

"I'm here," Kiera said, her voice filled with concern.

"Kiera, I was… hoping for one last thing before I… go on into the light," James' voice was clearly losing its strength. "Kiss me."

"I… Okay, James. Just this once."

Smiling, James puckered his lips as a shadow fell across his face.

A long, wet tongue licked its way from James' chin to his hairline as the smell of ten-thousand asses suddenly blasted into his puckered face.

"Ugh, *gross,* Squirrel," James shouted, suddenly sitting up and pushing the wolf away from him. "Did you lick every dead raider's asshole?" He grunted, pushing at the dog and wiping his face clean. "Get *off* me."

Kiera was grinning from ear to ear.

"Yeah, alright," James admitted. "Good one." He looked toward Derek. "Thanks, man."

"Don't mention it. Just try to be more careful," Derek replied, helping him back to his feet.

"So, what do we do with them now?" Kedron asked.

"We need to ask a few questions," Tom said.

Moving over to the group of raiders, Tom put his hands on his hips and looked down at them.

"How many more of you are there?" he asked the raiders.

Many of them wore armor that looked cobbled together from scraps, as if they'd scavenged it from the trash. Others sported makeshift protection like football pads or hockey gear, looking like they had stepped out of an old apocalypse movie. The silence was thick, and no one dared speak, many still looking up at them defiantly. Rolling his eyes, James fired a shot into the air, causing all the raiders to jump.

"There were about six hundred of us out in the camp," one of the raiders said, fear in his eyes that were beginning to fill with tears.

"And how many of you came here?" Tom asked him.

The man looked up at Tom, the tears now beginning to fall down his dirt-stained face.

"About two hundred and fifty," he said. "Look, man, I don't wanna die. I just joined these guys because they kept raiding the town, and I needed food."

"So, you thought it was okay to come in here and just take whatever?" Tom asked.

"I just wanted to survive. I saw them kill some of my friends, and I couldn't go out like that," he said through sobs.

"And what if you killed someone here?" Derek asked in a harsh tone.

"I didn't kill nobody! I just stood in the back and helped them load things into the trucks," the man continued. "Promise! Please don't hurt me. I don't wanna die!"

Derek sighed as he looked over to Tom.

"This was another thing I worried about. Some of these people are just doing what they think they have to in order to survive. We can't just kill them. But we can't let them go back either. They'll tell the others and bring them all at once," Derek said.

"We could raid the raider's camp," James offered.

"There will be women and children there. You want to kill all of them too? We likely killed husbands and fathers here already," Derek asked.

"No," James replied, looking down and feeling a little ashamed.

"We did what we had to do," Tom said.

"I know that. But the next step is slippery. More will come. We can fight them off, but we'll eventually run into a point where we're dooming the others left because we're cutting off their suppliers," Derek said.

"They'll have to figure that out themselves. They started this, and they can figure out how to survive without raiding other innocent people," Tom said. "We need to get Sarah to gather the rest of the people still here so we can show them that they can defend themselves now."

Sarah managed to gather most of the townspeople into one place. The sun had set, leaving the area normally lit by street lamps shrouded in darkness, but the team had lit fires in old barrels to illuminate the space. The townspeople surveyed the devastation around them with a mix of disgust and horror. A few couldn't hold back and vomited at the sight of the raiders' bodies piled together. Yet, despite the gruesome scene, no one said anything to the team. Instead, they were silently grateful for the help.

"People of Flagstaff. We have solved the first half of the raider problem for you," Tom said to the gathered people, which numbered about three hundred. "Now, you have to work to defend yourself from whatever comes next. The number of their fighters should be low, but others will likely come. We'll be staying here tonight should another strike come, but we cannot stay forever. You'll need to work to defend yourselves as well. Life as you knew it is over. This is the way of the world now, and you're going to have to get stronger."

"You must be willing to protect what's left of yours. You can do this. The weapons of the raiders, we leave to you to use in your defense. But you must make the choice to defend or leave," Derek said.

Turning to Sarah, she smiled at them sadly.

"Thank you for what you did. But most of us aren't fighters. We'll likely be leaving to find another place to stay," she said.

"That's understandable. But eventually, many will have to become fighters. This world is not a safe place anymore, and you can't pretend it is," Derek said.

"I know. And I appreciate you looking out for us. We'll do our best and go where we can. Where are you all from?" Sarah asked.

"We're from Dallas. It's quite a journey, but we welcome anyone that wants to make the trip," Tom said.

"Dallas, that *is* far. But if you made it this far, I'm sure some will want to join you," Sarah said. "For now, I'll show you where you can stay, and if we need you before the morning, we'll let you know."

Chapter 46

Canyon Bound

Sarah led the team to a hotel that was mostly intact. There were plenty of rooms, and although the bedding was disheveled, it was still usable. As they collapsed onto the beds, the team let out collective sighs of relief. The world had already gone to complete chaos, but they were grateful for a place to rest after all the travel and fighting. They made the most of the minor comforts they could find.

After a good night's sleep, the team woke up and prepared to hit the road again. As they gathered at their vehicles, the townspeople came out once more to see them off.

"What's all this for?" Tom asked.

"The people wanted to thank you. We don't have anything to offer you, but we came to say goodbye," Sarah said.

"We don't need anything. But we appreciate the offer," Tom replied.

"The people felt they should do something, so they came. Some of them will actually be leaving for Dallas because of you," Sarah said.

"I hope they know it's a long and dangerous journey. But we have cleared a path of cars on one side of the highway. If they follow that, they should be able to get there reasonably fast," Derek said.

"That's even better. Thank you for everything you've done," Sarah said.

Shaking hands with people and graciously accepting their thanks, the team met with those gathered before loading up into their vehicles, and with the sound of the motorcycle ignition drowning out most other sounds, the team headed off from Flagstaff for the Grand Canyon.

Following 40 west, they eventually came to 64 going north and turned off to continue along this highway, which would take them directly into Grand Canyon National Park. The drive was mostly smooth, as there had not been much traffic on the road when the world events happened.

Finally reaching the entrance to the national park, they encountered a herd of elk blocking their path. The animals quickly scattered at the sound of the approaching motorcycle, clearing the way to their initial destination. Kiera rolled down the rear window to shoot at one of the elk.

It fell to the ground, dead from a perfect shot to the heart. Smiling at the memories that flooded her of the time she spent with her grandfather, she motioned for Tom to stop. Exiting the vehicle, she moved to the creature and cut it into small enough pieces to fit into her Inventory.

APOCALYPSE

"This will be good for us to have for some extra food. Shouldn't waste the opportunity when it's literally crossing the road in front of us," Kiera said when Derek came to offer to help.

Upon arriving at the gate, it was clear the park had been abandoned, as no one was there to manage the entrance. The arms of the gates were down, blocking their path, so the team had to get out to lift them to let the vehicles pass.

"This truly is a beautiful place," DeeDee said. "The air is so clean and fresh with all the pine trees."

"I came here as a teenager with my family once, on a road trip, and it still seems mostly the same," Tom said. "We ate at that Pizza Hut there while we were here."

Tom indicated a restaurant attached to a theater near the entrance.

"It really is beautiful. I wish Texas was more like this," Kiera said, taking in the picturesque scenery around them.

Driving into the park, the team found a place to park near the canyon's edge.

"So, where is this vending machine we're supposed to be looking for?" James asked.

"I'd imagine it's near there, where all those people are gathered," Derek said, pointing to the bottom of the canyon.

A group of about a hundred people could be seen camping near the canyon's basin, on a ledge that jutted out of a cave. Tents were set up with a fire in the middle of the camp, showing they were working together in some fashion, but the tents were separated into what appeared to be groups of people within the group below.

"Guess we should go down and say hello," Tom said.

Everyone got out of the vehicles and went to the edge of the canyon.

"Sure is a long way down," Graham said.

"How the hell do we get there?" Kedron asked.

"There will be a trail here somewhere. They offered guided tours on donkeys to the bottom. We just have to find it," Tom said.

"Over there," Derek said, pointing further along the edge. "We can follow that path down to the bottom."

Moving to the trail Derek had pointed out, the team stared down at the narrow path beaten into the side of the cliff.

"Well, that doesn't look safe at all," James said.

"If donkeys can make it, why can't we?" Tom asked.

"I can think of some very load-bearing and four-legged reasons why," James replied.

"Don't be a princess. Get your ass moving," Jay said.

"After you, old man," James said, making room for Jay to go.

"Fine. I'll show you how it's done," Jay said, moving forward.

"You realize you just let the guy with likely the highest dexterity go first, and he'll make you look bad, right?" Derek said to James.

"Hopefully he'll find the hazards as a Rogue, too," James said, smiling at Derek.

"Was… was that an actual strategy you just used?" Derek asked, completely surprised.

"I may not have many ideas, but when I do, they tend to be doozies," James replied.

"I don't think we're thinking of the same kind of doozies you are," Jay said as he continued to stare into the canyon.

Walking down the semi-treacherous trail, the teams watched every step they took as small stones fell over the sides of the trail and bounced down to the bottom of the canyon. Tom stared down the side at the rocks as they fell and the speed they picked up, and his head began to spin.

"Don't look down. It makes it worse," Bobby said as he followed his gaze.

Tom turned back to face the canyon wall and closed his eyes for a moment.

"Not a fan of heights, I take it," Bobby said, not really asking a question.

"Not afraid of heights—that's stupid. I'm afraid of the sudden stop at the bottom of the fall," Tom said.

Laughing, Bobby put a hand on his shoulder. "I know that feeling. When we were parachuting into a warzone, I was completely terrified. The commanding officer had to literally toss me out of the plane. You can do this. You don't just get over it, but it gets easier as you go down." He picked up a stick and made a small circle around himself. "Just keep your focus inside your three-foot world."

The team continued zig-zagging down the trail as it wound back and forth along the cliff face until they finally reached the bottom. Several members let out sighs of relief upon arrival. From this lower vantage point, it was much harder to spot where the group of people was gathered, but Derek remembered the location and led the way toward the camp.

Even at the bottom of the canyon, the river running through it made the journey challenging, and they had to be careful not to fall in at certain points where the water was deep and the rapids were strong. The camp was set up about two miles from where they descended into the ravine. With no choice but to press on, the team continued forward.

"Are we almost there?" James complained.

"We'll get there soon. Let this be a lesson about how out of shape you are," Derek said.

"Look, I shoot guns at things. I don't need to be in shape," James said.

"Wrong, you need to be ready for something to come charging at you and work on yourself. This isn't the same sit-on-your-ass-and-eat-donuts-at-work kind of world. You have to be ready to fight," Derek countered.

"But I like donuts," James whined.

"We all do, but Krispy Kreme likely didn't survive, so you're just gonna have to do without," Tom said.

"It's really depressing thinking about all the places that didn't survive. I could really go for some Taco Bell right now," Bobby said.

"And get diarrhea on this lovely walk? No, thank you," Austin said.

"We never ate at them fancy restaurants. We always had to eat what we grew on the farm," Clay said.

"That sounds horrible," James said. "And you think Taco Bell is fancy?"

"Why? Beef is awesome!" Clay said. "We could have steak anytime we wanted because we had our own herd of cattle."

"Okay, maybe horrible was too strong of a word," James said, thinking about the steak he had eaten in Amarillo.

"It's hard work. Especially when the government kept invading my cousin Tripp's field to mess with his Mary Jane plants," Clay said.

Everyone stopped and stared at Clay in confusion for a moment.

"You all grew weed on your farm?"

"Hemp is a great plant for all kinds of uses. It can be made into rope, clothes, flour, milk, lip balm, soaps, and so many other things. Of course, those damn cops came and burned it without thinking and got all the animals on the farm so high that they started eating their pens because they got the munchies," Clay said.

"That's some funny shit," James said.

"We didn't think so at the time. That got most of them out of their areas and into the fields, where they started eating the crops. But looking back at it, yeah, that is pretty fucking hilarious," Clay said.

As they walked, they continued to talk about their lives and the things they missed most from before the System integration.

"It's hard to believe everything happened only about two weeks ago," Tom said.

"Life is so different now. If you had asked me if I would be walking through the bottom of the Grand Canyon two weeks ago, I'd have said you were completely nuts," Kiera said.

"So many people died," DeeDee said, unable to stop the sadness she felt. "I don't even know how my family is doing."

Silence fell over the team for a moment as they thought about all the death they had seen in the recent weeks.

"I think we've all felt the loss in some way or another. It's hard to believe we're only finding like ten percent of people still alive when we get to places," Tom said. "It doesn't bode well for most cities."

"Well, we can't think about that now. We're almost there," Derek said, trying to redirect the topic.

The team looked up and saw the ridge of the precipice hanging over the canyon ahead. A narrow path on the far side led up to the flat top. As they approached the path, they were greeted by the sounds of people talking and noticed a man standing guard at the entrance.

"State your business here," the man said.

"We're here to see if we could help with the quest to restore the vending machines," Tom said.

"We probably got enough people. But you're welcome to come and see. You'll want to speak with Jake. He's the guy taking control of the whole area because he and his team got here first," the man said and moved to let them pass.

The group entered the camp together, and as they did, most of the people around stopped what they were doing to stare at them. It was a bit unnerving, as the expressions on many faces made it clear they weren't there to make friends.

One man broke away from the others and walked over to introduce himself.

"Hey, I'm Zach. Nice to meet you. You all here for the quest as well?" Zach asked, extending a hand to shake.

Tom took the hand. "We are. I'm Tom, and we thought we could help by coming here. Though it looks like most of these people aren't too keen on getting much help."

"You got that right. Everyone is here mostly for the XP. Fucking selfish bastards. Sorry, I don't mean to sound too harsh, but I know their plan isn't going to work," Zach said.

"And what plan is that"" Derek asked.

"Throw parties at it until they win. We've already had about eight parties that never came back," Zach said.

"Eight?!" Tom asked incredulously.

"Yeah, they go in, but they don't come out. Not sure why, though," Zach said. "But come this way. I'll introduce you to Jake. Then you can get a better idea of what is going on."

Chapter 47

Jake and Bob

Walking over to a large tent set in the center of the camp, the team was instructed to wait outside while Zach went inside to speak with Jake. This tent was markedly different from the others, which looked like they had been hastily stolen from a sporting goods store. The central tent was an imposing structure made from heavy-duty, dark green PVC, like most temporary pavilions, and was clearly designed to withstand harsh conditions. It was rectangular in shape, with tall, reinforced poles anchoring the corners, giving it a solid and almost military appearance.

The entrance was covered by a canopy that extended outward, providing extra shelter and adding to the tent's sense of importance. The flaps at the entrance were hanging loosely, blocking the view of the interior, and the entire setup suggested that this was a command tent or a central meeting place, built for more than just casual camping.

There was some talking inside the tent, and Zach reemerged with a tall man in tow. They walked over to the party, and Zach made introductions.

"Tom, this is Jake, the leader of the Panthers. Jake, this is Tom. He and his group just found us and are looking to help," Zach said.

"We don't need help. We'll finish this shortly," Jake said, looking down with almost a sneer on his face.

"That's great. We aren't here to steal anyone's thunder. We just want the vending machines to go back to normal so we can equip ourselves properly," Tom said.

"Then I expect you won't have to wait long. My team is up next, and we'll kill the monster," Jake said.

"Up next?" Derek asked.

"We drew lots for which teams would take on the beast in the Dungeon first, then formed trial orders. My team is next. We're stronger than any other team here and will put a stop to this. So, your help won't be needed," Jake said.

"I hope that's true. It would mean less danger for us, and we've seen enough of that already in this world," Tom said.

Jake simply nodded once and turned back to his tent. Before he went inside, though, he stopped and spoke over his shoulder.

"Feel free to find a place to set up camp. You can watch us win from out here," he said and then disappeared behind the flap of his tent.

"I bet he's such a tender lover," James said softly.

"He's not that bad. He's just trying to look out for his team," Tom said.

"Well, he should absolutely look at a course on sharing. I can recommend a good kindergarten teacher to help him figure that out," James said.

"If we don't have to get in harm's way, I see that as an absolute win for us," Tom said.

"But… loot," James said.

"That would be nice, but what can we do? And I'd rather not start anything with this many people around," Tom said.

"We get all the way here and *now* you listen to my advice?" Derek asked.

"The other times, we didn't have the same options. This time, there's a chance we don't have to get involved," Tom replied.

"We always had options," Derek said.

"True, but the options were usually do nothing and let people die," Tom said. "There weren't other teams of adventurers lining up to deal with the other problems."

"With so many teams not coming back, technically doing nothing might be letting people die," Derek countered.

"But they aren't helpless people. They are people who can fight. It's apples and oranges," Tom said, trying to dismiss the topic.

"Look, I'm not trying to step on your toes here. I'm just checking your logic and resolve. I'm happy you want to help people, but we always need to be sure the juice is worth the squeeze," Derek said.

"The what?" James asked.

"The juice is worth the squeeze. It means that the risk is worth the payout," Derek said.

"I know. But I also have to listen to my conscience and heart. I don't know that I could live with myself if I just let people die when I knew I could do something to help," Tom said.

"Well, it would have sucked if *we* had died trying to save those people only for them to die right after we did. But I see your point and why you felt that way," Jay said.

Moving to the edge of the camp, the team began to set up tents and make camp for themselves. Once they had finished settling and discussed their plan, night had begun to fall. They moved over to the fire to find out more about what was going on.

The camp was a rough, makeshift settlement, with tents scattered haphazardly in groups that had traveled there together around a central fire pit. The ground was uneven, littered with rocks and debris, giving the area a disorganized feel. In the middle of the camp, a large fire crackled, casting flickering light and long shadows across the faces of those gathered around it. The fire was built from scavenged wood and scraps, its warmth drawing people close in the cooling night air.

As they gathered around the fire, they spoke with several of the camp's inhabitants. Some were completely drunk, slurring their words as they recounted their tales. Despite their varying states of inebriation, they all gave the same grim response: no one could defeat the monster. It was simply too strong.

"People go in there and are just torn to shreds. We've been trying to level up out here, but nothing we do seems to help in beating it," one man said.

"It doesn't seem like there's going to be an end to this. It just seems like it's unbeatable," another group said.

"Hey, you're a woman. You're pretty. Do you think a centaur has a human stomach, or a horse stomach? And where is it located?" one of the drunk men asked Kiera.

Deciding to take a different approach, they began asking about the people around the camp, focusing specifically on Jake. The responses they received were widely varied, which only added to the man's air of mystery.

"Jake's a good guy. He's a hardass, but he is fair. He's taken to organizing people around here to make sure everyone gets their shot at the monster," some said.

"He's a real dick. Just came in and started ordering people around like he could just run the whole show and was better than anyone else," others said.

"Wasn't he here first?" Tom asked.

"….Shut up," the man replied after not being able to come up with a good response.

"Hey, if horses wore pants, would they be able to sit down?" the drunk man slurred as he spoke again to Kiera.

"How do you keep finding me?" Kiera asked, exasperated at his persistence.

However, they gained the best insight into what was really going on when they found one of Jake's team members. The man's name was Tim, and he was the team's Rogue.

"Jake is definitely a good guy. He comes off harsh, but he has a heart of gold. He cares about his people but definitely wants to make sure that they're strong enough to survive in this world, so he pushes us to be our best," Tim said.

"So, he's just trying to make sure everyone is safe?" Tom asked.

"He wants people to be okay, but he's still focused on being strong. He has a moral code he follows, so he isn't just in this for the desire to make sure everyone gets along. He wants that XP and any rewards that come from the fight. But his honor won't let him cheat or do something wrong to get there first," Tim said.

"He sure comes off kinda rough, though," Tom said.

"That's just because we've been here for a while now, and he's had to deal with so many different assholes only here for the XP and not to get the job done. He knows what needs to be done and stepped up to be sure it's done fairly," Tim said.

"That makes sense. Do you think you all have a chance in there?" Tom asked.

"I don't really know. We're likely the best team here, so we stand the best shot. But I've seen teams go in and come out beaten to hell, and I've seen teams go in and never come back," Tim said.

"So, this is a Dungeon?" Derek asked.

"Yes. The System seems to have formed a Dungeon around this to make it orderly. It may not have been before, but it is now. It appears to be different, though, because unlike other Dungeons we've been in before, it acts like more than one team can go in. Most people here don't want to work together, so only once did two teams go in together, and they didn't come back out. But they were some of the weaker teams," Tim said.

"So, it could be like a raid Dungeon?" Derek asked.

"Maybe. But you'd likely have better luck getting peace in the Middle East than getting teams to work together out here," Tim said.

"Do you know anything about the creature? Anything we can learn about?" Tom asked.

"It's some kind of shadow creature. So, it's hard to pin down. Not a lot more than that has been able to be shared. You might have some better luck talking to Bob, though. He claims to be an expert here," Tim said.

"Bob?" Tom asked.

"Yeah, you can't miss him. He's wearing a jumpsuit with his name on it," Tim said.

"If he claims to be an expert, why aren't more people listening to him?" Tom asked.

"Because he's a little loose in the head. You'll see when you talk to him. Most people don't believe him," Tim said.

"Do you believe him?" Derek asked.

"I didn't. But the more time goes on, the more I feel like maybe he has a point," Tim said.

"Thanks for talking to us, Tim. We appreciate the info. We're still trying to understand what's going on around here," Tom said.

"Don't mention it. Glad more people are coming still. We're likely to need the help," Tim said.

Walking around for a while longer and talking with people as they became available, Tom finally spotted Bob off by himself, sitting and eating a meal from a camping plate. He, Derek, and James approached the man while others were busy talking with some of the other teams in the area.

"Hi, Bob. My name's Tom. I was wondering if we could ask you a few questions?" Tom asked.

With his mouth full, Bob motioned with his hand that was holding a fork at the log near him, which was being used as a makeshift seat around the fire. Taking a seat and waiting while the man ate, they looked at him expectantly. When it finally appeared as though he wouldn't say anything, Tom spoke instead.

"What is it you actually do here? Why have you come to the Grand Canyon? It doesn't appear that you're part of any of the teams that came," Tom asked.

"I'm a vending machine repairman," Bob said through the mouthful of food.

Looking expectantly at him, the three waited while he continued eating.

"Like… from before the apocalypse?" James asked.

"Sure. But also, now, too," Bob said after swallowing his food.

"Oh… wait, what? Really?" James asked.

"Yup. I fix the machines when they stop working. Came here to try to fix this one. Can't get near it, though," Bob said as if it was the most casual thing in the world.

"I thought the System kept the machines up?" Derek questioned.

"They do, from a software standpoint. But when they break, they need someone to fix 'em," Bob said. "That's where I come in."

"I don't understand. How do you fix the machines?" Tom asked.

"With tools, usually," Bob said.

"No shit, genius," James said.

"I guess what we mean is—how do you know *how* to fix the machines?" Tom asked.

"Well, I was fixing a vending machine when the big screens in the sky broadcast that message. There was a shock that went through the machine while I had it open, and it seemed to try to meld me with the machine. When the System realized I couldn't be joined with the vending machine, I was given a new Class. Vending Machine Repairman," Bob said. "That meant I got the information for fixing them downloaded into my brain, and now I know everything about them."

"And nobody believes you?" Derek asked.

"Well, it sounds a little crazy. Plus, I have no way of proving it right now. The others seem to be mostly concerned about the fighting, anyway," Bob said.

"Well, there was no Class called Vending Machine Repairman in the tutorial, so it does sound a little off," Derek said.

"That's true," Bob said. "But it's not something you can choose. I'm guessing I'm the only one in the world now. If not, I'm one of only a very few."

"And it's not a Profession?" Derek asked.

"Nope," Bob replied.

"I don't really see why anyone wouldn't want you to be there. They just don't like you?" Tom asked.

"Beats me. Oh, and if we can't get this fixed soon, the whole world is going to end because the IFP doesn't want these machines falling into the wrong hands," Bob said.

"Now, that does sound made up. We haven't heard anything about that," Derek said.

"And you won't. They'll just do it all of a sudden. The mana core they put in the planet is also a bomb. They can trigger it at any time," Bob said, taking another bite of food as if nothing was wrong.

Stunned to silence, the three men sat there staring with wide eyes at Bob. No one could believe what Bob was saying. It was all just too much to take in.

"That must be why they don't believe him," James said.

"Maybe. I have no idea. But whether you believe me or not is of no real consequence," Bob said through a cheek full of food. "You don't have to believe me. But I would suggest these people hurry up and figure out how to get rid of that monster."

"Probably don't like him telling them to hurry up either," Derek said.

"Can you tell us anything else about the vending machines?" Tom said.

"I can tell you tons of things. You don't have enough time for me to tell you everything I know about them," Bob said. "We'd be here for weeks."

"Do you have a place to call home, Bob?" Tom asked.

"Not really. Been traveling ever since the System was implemented," Bob said.

"How'd you like to join us at Vanguard?"

Chapter 48

Vending Machines

"No, thanks," Bob said.

"What? Why not?" James asked.

"I feel like I can do better," Bob said.

"So far, it seems like you aren't doing anything at all. You can't exactly be picky. Not a lot of offers flying around out here," James said.

"Look, I know nothing about you. You showed up today and haven't made any impression and haven't done jack shit," Bob said. "Show me you're worth joining, and I might change my mind."

As they were saying this, the sound of stone grinding on stone sounded out near the cave entrance.

"It looks like it's opening again. I wonder what we'll see come out this time?" Bob said, turning to look at the entrance with everyone else.

A door further back in the cave was lowering into the ground from the ceiling, which had been blocking further access. It continued slowly until it melded into the floor of the cave seamlessly. Everyone waited anxiously to see what would happen.

After about five minutes of waiting and nothing happening, Bob turned back around to the fire.

"Shame," Bob said.

"What does that mean?" Tom asked.

"If no one came out by now, no one's going to," Bob said.

"What?!" Tom said. "They just died?"

"No, I'm guessing they were killed. It's not the first time," Bob said, bringing another bite to his mouth.

Through the quiet of the stunned camp, the sounds of boots stomping and metal armor rustling could be heard as Jake and his team moved forward with stoic faces. Turning to watch them move, the entire camp held a collective breath as they headed toward the cave entrance. Pausing at the mouth of the cave, Jake turned back to the camp over his shoulder and smiled a grim smile.

"Time to clean up this mess," he said as he turned back and walked inside.

"He's really going in there with only five other guys?" Tom asked.

"He is. And nothing anyone can say will deter him or change his mind. He's sure he can handle all of it and that his team is better than everyone else here. Damned fool," Bob said.

"So, you don't think he can win?" James asked.

"No one else has; why would he?" Bob asked in return.

"What if he's stronger?" James asked.

"Everyone who came out said they barely scratched the creature inside. He won't fare much better," Bob replied, taking another bite of his dinner.

The stone-on-stone grinding echoed through the camp again as the door closed behind Jake and his team. Once the door was fully shut, the collective breath that many had been holding was released in unison. Conversations quickly broke out among the camp members, with some speculating that the fight was already over, while others voiced their readiness for their own turn against the monster.

"Since we have some time, what's the deal with these vending machines, Bob?" James asked.

"A rather vague question. Got anything more specific?" Bob asked in return.

"How do they work? And why put the Source Machine here?" Tom asked.

"Well, all the vending machines in the world are hooked up to a singular mana network. It's powered by the mana core that was placed in the Earth's core to give the people here access to magic. Items are created here in the Grand Canyon at the Source Machine for anything they need in the Item Bank. That's then sent via the network to any machine for whatever the Class is that the user has," Bob explained. "As for why it's here, that seems to be because it's a big hole in the ground to hide it in, but one where a repairman could get to if need be. I don't know the full reason, as they didn't see fit to tell me. The creature in that Dungeon has accessed the mana core via the Source Machine, which is what has given it the power it has."

"So, it has an infinite amount of power now?" Tom asked, suddenly very concerned.

"No, that's ridiculous. The body of any living creature can only contain so much power. It does feed it constantly, so it was able to grow faster, but even Dungeon creatures can only contain so much power based on a number of factors," Bob said.

"And how do you know this? I thought you were just a vending machine specialist," James asked.

"When I got the download, I learned much more about this System than just the vending machine specs. I have to know a lot as someone who has far more access than others," Bob replied.

"Just how much access do you have?" Tom asked.

"Not as much as an Administrator, but definitely more than all of you," Bob answered.

"Okay, so that means you can just take things from the machines?" James asked.

"I could, yes, but that wouldn't serve me any purpose," Bob said.

"You could be rolling in Monster Cores. You'd be rich," James said.

"And what exactly would I do with them? The only thing on Earth that takes Monster Cores are the machines. And if I can take what I want, I don't need to buy them," Bob said.

"You could trade them to people," James tried.

"For what? I can get anything from the machines. And the machines can make anything," Bob said.

"Well… you could…" James began but was cut off by Bob.

"Look, boy. There's no point. I could have all the stuff I wanted, but then I'd just have stuff. Nothing to do with it, nothing to gain from it, and it would be stupid and pointless. You're not really thinking this through. You're just thinking like someone from capitalist America with a dream of owning a yacht and four hundred cars because they saw people on TV doing it. It's completely fucking worthless now," Bob scolded James. "It's why most people will never be given that kind of power. They're selfish and irrational."

"Bob, you said the machines can make anything, but we've only seen adventuring gear. So, it can make, say, toilet paper if someone needs it?" Tom asked.

"Sure can. Anything Earth has to offer, it can sell you. Just have to go into the right menu on the screen," Bob said.

"The screen you have to have your hand on to access it?" Tom asked.

"The screen you simply have to touch once so it can read your Class. You can take your hand off the screen to see the menus after. Are you telling me you've had your hand on the screen the whole time?" Bob asked.

Tom, Derek, and James looked at him sheepishly.

"It just says put your hand on the screen to change options. We didn't realize it only needed it for a moment," Tom admitted.

"Well, I can see why you'd think that. You didn't try to attack the machines or anything, did you?" Bob asked.

"No, there was a warning about that when we were first talking about the machines. We don't know exactly what happens, but we weren't willing to risk it," Tom said.

"Good. It'll summon a shit ton of monsters to your location to kill you if you do. You won't survive. The System will make sure of that," Bob said.

The trio blanched at that.

"Really glad we left that alone now," Derek said, looking at James.

"What the hell? I wasn't going to do it… Once I found that out, anyway," James said defensively.

"Why isn't the System sending down hell on this monster, then? Isn't it messing with the vending machines?" Tom asked.

"Technically, I don't think it is. It seems to just be feeding on it. At least, as far as I can tell. Can't say for sure without getting in and having a look at it," Bob replied.

"What about moving a vending machine? If a building didn't have one and they wanted to put one in their Guild building, for example, could they do that?" Tom asked.

"No, it would stop working once you removed it from the power source. If it goes offline, that could be seen as an attack, and monsters might start spawning," Bob said.

"Note to self: leave machines alone," James said.

"Since you left your hand on the machine, I suppose that also means you aren't looking at the upgraded items for your Class as well?" Bob asked.

"What? No, we just assumed it was showing us the best items at the time," Derek said.

"Yeah, it does do that, but it's not based on your level. It shows you the lowest-grade items first. Stuff just about anyone would be able to use. As you level up, you can change it to better items through the menu and purchase those. Of course, they're more expensive, but they're better items. You just have to search for them based on rarity," Bob explained.

"I'm definitely glad we found you. Do you have any advice on the Dungeon situation?" Tom asked.

"I'm guessing it's a raid boss. You'll need multiple parties to beat it. It's just too tough for a single party," Bob said.

"I thought so. Why has no one else tried that?" Derek asked.

"Greed, probably," Bob said as though he didn't care at all. "People are fickle. You can't get people to do anything they don't want to."

"If we do fight this thing off, do you need to be in the party that goes in to fix it?" Tom asked.

"No, I'm not a fighter. But I can go in once the Dungeon opens again to get the access I need," Bob said.

"Is there something you could do to get the monster away from the Source Machine to possibly make defeating it easier? If we gave it a distraction?" Derek asked.

Bob paused mid-chewing and thought about it for a moment.

"Actually, that's not a half-bad idea. But I would be in danger without protection… Yes, I believe there *is* something I could do about that," Bob said, looking at Derek in a different light. "That's not a half-bad idea at all, boy."

"I bet we can get a few people to join up with us to form a raid party. We have enough people with us for almost two full teams. How many teams are allowed in a raid party?" Derek asked.

"Five, normally," Bob said. "All depends on the boss, but this isn't a world boss, so I'd guess it's the standard number."

"World boss?" Derek asked.

"Yeah. Big fuckers. But that's not important now. What is important is that you get other teams to help, or you're doomed from the start. If you can convince them to help, I'll help you all as well," Bob said.

"Fair enough. Thank you, Bob. We'll see what we can do to get some other teams involved," Tom said.

Getting up from the log, the trio wished him well and moved off to talk to some other teams. Zach was their first stop, as he seemed to be the friendliest of the people they had talked to so far.

"Zach!" Tom called when he saw him across the fire.

Turning to see who called his name, Zach smiled when he saw Tom and acknowledged him with a head bob, excusing himself from the conversation he was having.

"Hey, Tom. How's it going?" Zach asked, walking over to where they were.

"We talked with Bob and think we have a plan to end this whole situation. But we need three more teams to join us for the plan to work. Would you be willing to join us, and is there anyone else that might join up?" Tom asked.

"I'd be more than happy to help put an end to this. But I'm not sure that any others would be willing to join up with us. This is a tough group of fuckers," Zach said.

"Can you point us to which people we might talk to?" Tom asked.

"Sure, I can take you. But what is it you have planned?" Zach asked.

Tom explained the plan of taking Bob into the Dungeon to get the monster off the Source Machine, and using the teams to protect him and fight off the monster. As he explained, Zach thought hard about the plan, and by the end, he was smiling.

"That sounds like it just might work. Let's go talk with Jeff. He has a team that would be good for defense. He can help with protection, and we can look for others that would be willing to join. Come on, I'll show you where he's at," Zach said.

As Tom, James, and Derek moved to follow him, the sudden sound of stone grinding against stone echoed behind them as the Dungeon began to open. They quickly turned to see what was happening, but nothing could have prepared them for the sight that awaited them.

Chapter 49

The Massacre

Tim, Jake's Rogue, crawled out of the Dungeon's entrance, dragging his shattered legs behind him. Blood oozed from a dozen different wounds, staining the ground as he moved. His legs were twisted unnaturally, clearly broken, and his body was battered and bruised, with deep gashes across his arms and torso. His face was a mask of pain and terror, eyes wide with horror as he clawed his way forward, using only his hands to pull himself along the rough stone ground. Each movement was slow and agonizing, his fingers digging into the dirt as he desperately tried to escape the Dungeon's grasp.

Seeing him, others in the camp rushed over, and a few Clerics quickly began casting healing spells, their hands glowing with soft light as they tried to mend his grievous wounds.

"It's not working!" one of the Clerics yelled.

"I'm dark aligned, you fuckwit," Tim groaned out.

"What does that mean? I've always been able to heal people before," the Cleric said.

"There are a few types of Classes that your magic can't heal because it comes from light-aligned sources. You need dark healing to help," Tim said through gritted teeth.

"Move! I can heal him!" Tom called.

Pushing through the throng of people gathered around Tim, Tom made his way to the center of the crowd. Once he reached Tim's side, he knelt down and began to cast Dark Healing. As the spell took effect, Tim visibly relaxed, some of the pain easing from his strained expression.

"Thanks, man. That really sucked there for a bit," Tim said.

"I can't heal all of your injuries right now. My healing isn't very high, but that should at least keep you alive," Tom said. "Bone mending is a tricky healing that I can't fully do. This is meant more for HP regeneration than repair work. Works wonders on flesh, not so good for bone."

"Hey, I'll take it…" Tim began to laugh but broke out into a coughing fit as he winced in pain again.

"Don't move too much. I have no idea how much internal damage was done. Your legs will likely have to be set before they heal, too," Tom said.

"I'll just take not-dying for now. That was absolutely stupid of us. We never stood a chance," Tim said, a sadness overtaking him.

"And everyone else is…" Tom started but trailed off.

"Dead," Tim said.

Gasps and shocked murmurs ran through the gathered crowd. Some people had thought Jake's team had the best chance of winning, while others acted as if they knew they couldn't do it. A couple of teams even walked away to prepare to go next.

"Bob was right. You need to do this together!" Tim said.

A few people moved to pick Tim up as gently as they could, and he was moved over to his tent to rest. Tom followed him to see if he could find out more.

"What exactly happened, Tim?" Tom asked.

"We found the main machine. It was huge. The creature is some kind of shadow that attaches itself to the machine and seems to feed off of it. Even when we dealt it damage, it just seemed to heal itself and gain its power back," Tim began. "It launched attack after attack at us, never letting up. Even our strongest powers couldn't kill it."

"What else?" Tom pressed him, speaking in a low tone.

"Monsters. It could summon other smaller versions of itself to harry us at the same time," Tim said. "Don't do it. Don't go in. We can live with the machines the way they are!"

"Bob says we can't. They're going to blow up the planet if we can't get it fixed," Tom said, his heart sinking as he made the declaration, unable to look Tim in the eyes.

"Then… we are well and truly fucked," Tim said, his head falling back onto the ground in defeat.

"It's not over yet. We have a plan," Tom said, determined not to wallow in the pity of the moment.

Getting up and moving over to Zach, Tom leaned in to speak with him quietly.

"We need to figure out if we can get enough people on our raid party idea ASAP," Tom said.

"I've got some feelers out, but I think that this new development will help turn people to trying with us. They're likely going to warm up to the idea of trying a group effort now that Jake is dead," Zach said. "Still can't believe he was so cocksure about going in alone. That bastard."

"Go talk to the teams again. Be sure you can get the ones you want before anyone else goes in. We can't just keep having teams throw themselves at a pointless fight. And if they're worried about the XP share, when we completed a Dungeon before, we all got the XP," Tom said.

"Are you sure everyone gets the XP for this dungeon? It seems different," Zach asked.

"Well, no, but it might motivate people to join if they know we have some experience with Dungeons and that we might all get our own XP," Tom replied.

Nodding, Zach walked off to speak with some of the other teams. Everyone waited around, reluctant to enter the Dungeon after witnessing the massacre of Jake's team. The next team scheduled to go in actually decided against it. They packed up their gear and quietly left the encampment, choosing to return home instead.

A while later, another team, confident they were tougher than Jake's, decided to enter the Dungeon. Despite warnings and attempts to reason with them, they wouldn't listen. As they disappeared into the Dungeon, the camp grew eerily quiet, the once lively atmosphere now replaced with a somber mood. People milled about, unable to shake the growing sense of dread. It was becoming painfully clear how dangerous this Dungeon was, especially now that someone they admired hadn't returned.

After about an hour, with two more teams having entered the Dungeon and none returning, Zach reappeared, this time accompanied by a man in armor.

"Tom! This is Isaac. He's the leader of another team here and has agreed to join our attempt at the raid," Zach said.

A tall black man in full plate armor extended his hand to Tom. The armor, polished to a shine, reflected the light and emphasized his commanding presence. His eyes showed an intelligence that belied his tough exterior. His grip was firm as they shook hands in greeting, a mutual respect passing between them as they acknowledged each other.

"We have a mostly defense-based team with a lot of our group focused on being able to take hits and get back up. Figured in this world, being tougher to kill meant living longer," Isaac said in a deep voice.

"That's exactly what we're looking for in the raid. We just need one more party to make it work," Tom said.

"So, what's the plan when we do get in? There hasn't been much luck with the assaults so far, and from what Tim says, there isn't much hope right now," Isaac said.

"Bob thinks he can take the beast off the machine if we can get him in. So, he will be in one of our teams. When it's off, that should cut its power source, which will weaken it and make it so it can't heal itself. We need your team to keep Bob protected. Take the hits and defend him while he works. Meanwhile, the other teams will keep the creature distracted until it's detached, and then we will hit it with everything we have," Tom said.

"And the minions?" Isaac asked.

"Same as the big guy. We murder them with impunity. DPS builds should be able to help keep them in check," Tom said.

"Sounds good to me. We're in. Time to pay that monster back for all the death it's caused," Isaac said.

"Plus, the whole stopping the planet from exploding bit," Tom said off-handedly.

"What the fuck did you just say?" Isaac asked, Zach looking equally confused.

"Bob didn't tell you? The IFP is planning to blow up the mana core if we can't 'fix the glitch,'" Tom said, making quotations around the movie quote.

"Holy shit. No, we didn't know about that. This makes things much more urgent. I need to go talk to some people. I think you'll have more volunteers shortly," Isaac said, quickly moving off to find someone else.

"Are they really going to blow up the whole fucking planet?" Zach asked.

"Not really sure. But I'm not going to sit around with my thumb up my ass having a tea party while we wait to see what happens. So, we need to do this soon," Tom replied.

"That sounds right to me. I'll go get my team ready. If we move quickly, we can likely move up in the order," Zach said and walked away to meet with his team.

Moving back to where his teams had set up camp, Tom spoke with them to prepare them for what was to come.

"Looks like we may get our chance to go sooner than we had hoped," Tom said.

"You think we stand a chance?" Kedron asked.

"As long as we stick to the plan and nothing goes horribly wrong like it always does," Tom said.

"Fucking hell. You just had to jinx it, didn't you?" Kiera said.

"Yup. Might as well get it out of the way before James does," Tom replied.

"That's fair," Graham said.

"What the hell? Seriously, I'm not that bad," James said.

"You're right. You're worse," Kiera said.

"Now, listen here, lady…" James started when Squirrel started growling at him.

"Et tu, you hairy fucker?" James asked in mock offense.

"Who's a good boy? Yes, you're a good boy!" Kiera said, scratching the wolf's head and back while Squirrel closed his eyes in pleasure at the praise.

"Jerky? Where are you?" Tom called out.

Jerky appeared on his shoulder a moment later.

"I want you with Bob. We need to go introduce you so you don't surprise him, but Bob must stay safe at all costs, do you understand?" Tom asked.

"Jerky understand. Jerky protect old guy," Jerky replied.

"Good. We all have to work together on this. It's not going to be easy, and we need to pull out all the stops," Tom said.

The team nodded solemnly, everyone taking this utterly seriously.

"Now, get yourselves ready. We're moving in soon, hopefully," Tom said.

"Tom," Zach called from off to the side.

Moving over to where Zach was standing, he met another man standing with him.

"Tom, meet Chris. Chris has a pretty good team made up of defense and magic users, so he should be able to help with the fighting team alongside yours and mine," Zach said.

"Great to meet you, Chris. This isn't going to be easy, so we need all the help we can get," Tom said, extending a hand to shake with Chris.

"Zach and Isaac told me what's at stake now, and I'm absolutely on board to help however I can. Some of us have families back home, and we'll do whatever we need to keep them safe," Chris said.

"We're so glad to hear that, Chris," Tom said.

"Because a lot of us may die," James said.

"Not helping!" Kiera scolded him as she pulled him away from the talk by his ear.

"Ow, ow, ow, fucking OW!" James screamed as he was drug away.

"Sorry, ignore the idiot," Tom said.

"It's fine. I've got one too," Chris said, chuckling. "Now, can we go over the plan one more time?"

"Zach, can we have Isaac join us? I'd rather finalize everything with all of us here," Tom asked.

"Sure thing. I'll go get him," Zach replied.

Zach jogged off to find Isaac, and Tom turned to his team.

"Kedron, come over here," Tom called, and Kedron came to join the others.

A few minutes later, Zach came back with Isaac, and they all gathered around to discuss strategy.

"Alright, so here's the plan…"

Chapter 50

Entering the Dungeon

After going over the plan in detail three separate times, the teams felt like they were ready to begin as soon as the Dungeon doors opened.

"I'll go talk to as many of the other teams as we can to see if anyone minds if we go next into the Dungeon. The last two teams that went in didn't come back, and I don't like the chances of the one that's in there now. I doubt we'll have much trouble with a request to go next," Zach said and walked away to talk to people in the camp.

"We'll get our teams ready, too," Isaac said, looking at Chris, who nodded back to him.

"I don't exactly know what chances we have, but I like these odds way better than just running in there with only my team like the others have been doing," Chris said.

With that, Chris and Isaac moved off to be with their teams as well.

"You all ready?" Tom asked.

"Of course. We aren't afraid to die here. If we do nothing, we die anyway, so this is just us giving it one last try at surviving. We see it as if we are going to die either way; we might as well die trying to stop it from happening," Kedron said.

"Thanks for being with us," Tom said.

"You're welcome. We're happy we can stand with friends in the end," Kedron said.

"Fuck, man, don't call it the end. That's dismal as shit," Tom said.

"I was trying to sound fucking heroic, you douche canoe. Give me this fucking moment," Kedron said.

"You just were bringing down the whole mood, you cockholster. We don't need to talk like that. We can win this," Tom said.

"Right. Like all those other teams did. Seriously, man, lighten up and take this moment to sound like a hero," Kedron said.

"You played way too many video games, didn't you?"

"Oh, you're one to talk, Mr. I worked for a big video game developer."

"If there was a fan here blowing your hair back in the wind, it couldn't be more perfect for the hero pose you were going for. Come on, puff out your chest and do the Captain Morgan pose for me," Tom said.

"Fuck you. At least I wasn't some emo whiner about the situation," Kedron said.

Both men paused, then erupted into laughter.

"Fucking gallows humor. I'm so glad you were the one to find us and not some other asshat who takes things too seriously," Kedron said.

"Yeah, me too. People suck sometimes," Tom said.

Kedron slapped Tom on the back, and together, they walked back over to the group.

"You two are in a great mood. I'm guessing you were just talking about how we are likely to die horribly as well?" James asked.

"Yup. We specifically mentioned how your ass was likely to go down first when we scatter and leave you to fight the creature by yourself. It's gonna be fucking hilarious," Tom said.

"Wait, for real? You guys are joking, right? I'm squishy," James said, a small hint of panic in his voice.

"Relax, dick boy. We got your back," Graham called over.

"Phew. Thanks, meathead. I need your fat frame in front of me to take all the hits," James said.

"Anytime, shithead," Graham replied. "We can't all be good at something."

"I'll have you know I've become a pretty good shot," James said.

"Yeah, but if this creature doesn't have a dick, you're fucked," Kiera said.

"Besides, I doubt your little bullets are going to be that effective," Bobby said.

"And I'll have you know I got a skill for a powered shot that uses my mana to deal extra elemental damage," James said.

"Great, because we are gonna have to unleash everything we have. Don't use that until Bob gets the creature off the machine, though. It can heal itself until then. Once it's off, though, we give it fucking hell with everything we have," Tom said.

Zach came back over to the group as they were bantering back and forth, working on lifting their spirits.

"Everyone's willing to let us go next. Isaac and Chris said they would meet us by the entrance. Whenever you're ready, just join us there. I'm going to get my team ready now, too. Bob should already be there. He seems eager to go inside," Zach said.

"Understood. We'll see you all there shortly," Tom said.

Zach left them again, and Tom turned to the team.

"Well, you heard the man. Pack your shit up, and let's get going," Tom said.

The teams quickly packed up what little they had left, storing everything in their Inventories. They then retrieved their weapons, readying themselves in advance, and moved together toward the Dungeon entrance.

As promised, Zach, Chris, Isaac, and their respective teams were already there, waiting. Each team had a full squad, except for Kedron's, as Bob had joined Tom's team as their eighth member. As they stood ready, another man approached from the camp behind them.

"Anthony? What are you doing here?" Zach asked.

"I noticed you're one man short. I figured I would offer my services," the man, apparently Anthony, said.

"You're willing to help us?" Zach asked, clearly confused by the man's request.

"Wait, what's wrong with him joining us?" Tom asked. "Seems like we could use all the help we can get."

"Anthony has been one of the ones who was really ready to jump in. He seemed reluctant to let us go first until I told him about the whole planet exploding thing," Zach said.

"I'm sorry for that. I thought you were just trying to get ahead of your turn unfairly. I've been waiting for days to go with my team. They were starting to get restless. I didn't mean to sound like I was against your idea," Anthony said. "I just want to help put an end to this shit. We want to make sure the world doesn't end just like everyone else."

Anthony stood over six feet tall, a towering figure clad in full plate armor. His broad shoulders and heavily muscled build were evident even beneath the thick metal, giving him an imposing presence. The armor, meticulously crafted with intricate engravings, spoke of both strength and attention to detail. He carried a large shield strapped to one arm and gripped a formidable sword in the other, both showing signs of use. His stern expression and the confident way he moved suggested he'd been in his share of fights, fully prepared for whatever lay ahead.

"I'm happy to have another beefcake to stand in front of me," James interjected.

"Anyone willing to fight with us is welcome. So long as Zach doesn't object," Tom said, turning to look at Zach.

"I agree. I was just worried he was coming to try to stop us. If he wants to help, then I say welcome aboard, mate," Zach said.

Kedron sent Anthony a party invite, and Anthony took his place with the others.

"Alright, Bob. Do we just walk to the entrance, and it will let us all in?" Tom asked.

"No, you haven't formed the raid party yet. It's in the party menu," Bob said.

Tom pulled up the menu, and sure enough, there it was.

"It wasn't there before. What the hell?" Tom asked.

"It only appears at Dungeon entrances. I'm guessing you never looked at the party menu while there? Now that you're here, it becomes available to use. Go on, set it up, boy," Bob replied.

Tom selected the "Raid Party" option, extending the offer to join to all the party leaders. One by one, each leader accepted, and Tom's display shifted. The interface now showed the names of all the party leaders, each accompanied by a row of tiny red bars representing the health of every one of the forty party members.

At first, the sudden influx of information was overwhelming. The screen was crowded with red bars and names, making it difficult to focus. Tom took a moment to adjust, moving the health bars to the edges of his vision. This subtle change helped clear the clutter, allowing him to concentrate on the center of his display while still keeping track of his team's status.

As the interface settled into this new arrangement, the task of monitoring everyone became more manageable. The health bars, now neatly aligned along the periphery, provided a constant reminder of the entire group's overall status.

"Alright, now all we have to do is wait for..." Tom began but was interrupted by the sound of stone grinding on stone behind him.

The entire raid party turned to watch as the Dungeon door slowly began to open. As the massive stone barrier descended, darkness greeted them, spilling out from the stone corridor beyond. The shadows seemed to stretch endlessly, giving the impression of a vast and foreboding space within.

Tom stared up at the door as it continued to lower, finally grasping the true scale of the Dungeon. The entrance was enormous—twenty feet high and nearly as wide—its sheer size making the party members seem small in comparison. The stone appeared ancient, worn smooth in some places, yet it still exuded a sense of strength.

As the door settled into place, the team waited in tense silence, eyes fixed on the gaping maw of the Dungeon. They watched for any movement, any sign of life from within. But the darkness remained undisturbed. No one came out.

"Damn. Another team killed," Zach said.

"Unfortunately, we don't have time to mourn them. Jerky, get over to Bob. Keep him safe," Tom said.

Jerky appeared on his shoulder, causing some of the people on the other teams to jump at the sight of him—one man even pointed his sword at Jerky.

"Jerky keep old man safe," Jerky said.

"I'm not that old! I'm fifty-one!" Bob protested.

Jerky jumped from Tom's shoulder and bounded over to Bob, where he climbed up onto the man's shoulder.

"And just what exactly is this... thing supposed to do for me?" Bob asked.

"He's a lot more useful than you think. Plus, he'll keep an eye on your back while you work," Tom said. "Can't have you getting shot or stabbed or blown up or cut to ribbons while you do what you need to do."

"That instills me with such confidence, thanks," Bob said sarcastically.

"Time to get in there, mates. We can sit here and shoot the shit till the world ends... literally. But let's get going and see what we're facing," Zach said.

"Right. Time to go in." Tom said.

As Tom turned back to the groups, he noticed that the entire camp had gathered behind them. The men and women stood in silent solidarity, their weapons raised in the air as a gesture of support and a wish for good luck. The sight of the entire camp united in this way was striking, a powerful reminder of the stakes they all faced.

As the teams took in the sight of the assembled crowd, a voice rang out from the back, cutting through the tension.

APOCALYPSE

"GIVE 'EM HELL!" they shouted, and the rest of the gathered people let out battle cries.

The teams stood there, unsure what to do in the awkward moment. James seemed to have a response.

"Oh, yeah! We got this, don't you guys worry! We're gonna kick that thing's ass and be back for tea time!" he said.

The teams facepalmed, then turned to enter the Dungeon. Darkness began to swallow them when Tom received a prompt.

Dungeon of the Devourer

The Dungeon of the Devourer is a nightmarish realm ruled by a malevolent entity known only as the Devourer. This Dungeon is infamous for its shifting shadows, relentless traps, and creatures that feed on fear and despair. It is designed to test the limits of any adventurer's resolve, with dangers lurking around every corner. Only the most prepared and coordinated parties should dare to enter.

Raid Mode Available:

- This Dungeon can be entered with a standard party or as a raid, allowing for multiple parties to work together. Raid entry is required for parties larger than the standard limit.

Warning:

- **High Risk, High Reward:** Only experienced and well-prepared adventurers should attempt this Dungeon. Failure to adequately plan and execute strategy could result in significant losses.

Dungeon Difficulty: Rare

Recommended Level: 15+

Objective: Defeat the Devourer

Current parties in the Dungeon: 0

Current completions of the Dungeon: 0

Recommended Party Composition: Due to the extreme difficulty, a well-coordinated raid party is recommended, with a balance of Tanks, DPS, Healers, and Support roles to handle the Dungeon's varied challenges.

Enter?

Yes	*No*

The message pulsed softly, its letters shimmering with an ominous red hue that matched the gravity of the decision. The words "Dungeon of the Devourer" seemed to almost pulsate, as if alive, adding a sense of foreboding to the prompt. The question hung in the air, waiting for Tom's command.

Tom selected "Yes," and the prompt disappeared.

"Devourer, eh?" Tom said.

"What are you, Canadian, now?" Jay asked.

"Just surprised at the creature's name. Apt," Tom said.

Continuing in silence, the team moved deeper into the corridor. As they advanced, the heavy Dungeon door began to close behind them. The familiar sound of stone grinding against stone echoed through the passage, signaling the door's slow ascent back into place. The final thud as the door sealed shut left them in momentary darkness.

Suddenly, torches along the walls flared to life, their flames flickering to cast a dim, wavering light on the rough stone walls. The warm glow illuminated the way forward, guiding the adventuring team deeper into the Dungeon's depths.

As the parties progressed, distant, indistinct noises broke the silence. The faint sounds seemed to echo from deep within the Dungeon, creating uneasy tension. Up ahead, the path bent sharply to the left, leading to a set of stairs descending into the darkness.

As they began to descend the stairs, more torches along the walls lit up, seeming to await their movement to activate.

Reaching the bottom of the stairs, they noticed something unsettling. The shadows on the walls began to twist and crawl, moving as if alive. Yet, despite the eerie motion, the corridor remained empty—the adventurers were alone, or so it seemed.

"I don't like the look of this," Tom said. "Anyone have some light magic?"

"Why light magic? The torches seem fine," James asked.

"Not for *seeing* with. Because the monsters might be fucking shadows, you twat waffle," Derek said.

"Aww, Derek, you do care," James said.

As James and Derek were talking, a shadow detached itself from the wall, lunging at them with sudden, predatory speed. The creature moved silently, seizing the opportunity to strike.

Just as it was about to reach them, a brilliant flash of light burst from behind, streaking through the air and slamming into the shadowy figure. The creature let out a piercing scream as the ball of light collided with it, its form disintegrating on impact.

In an instant, the shadow exploded into a cloud of black, ash-like substance, which quickly dispersed into the air, leaving nothing behind.

James and Derek had both jumped back and put their hands up defensively in response.

"What the fuck was that?" James asked in a panic.

"A shadow creature, you nitwit!" Derek answered. "Thank you to whoever used the light magic."

"No problem," a man from Zach's group said as he gave a small wave. "And I'm Steve, by the way."

"Steve. Thanks again. Glad you were ready," Derek said.

"Yeah, no worries," Steve said with a smile.

"Everyone, have your weapons and spells ready. We need to be prepared for anything ready to jump out at us," Tom said. "Don't let your guard down and we'll get through this. We have to."

The parties raised their weapons into a ready position as they continued deeper into the Dungeon.

Chapter 51

The Dungeon of the Devourer

Staying ready this time, the forty members of the raid party remained vigilant as they descended deeper into the Dungeon's depths. Every footstep echoed in the narrow corridors, heightening their awareness.

Eventually, the team reached their first room at the end of a long passage. The chamber was dome-shaped, with walls that appeared perfectly smooth, curving upward to meet at a rounded apex above them. The room had an unnatural precision, its design almost too flawless, which only added to the unsettling atmosphere. At the far end of the room, two doors stood closed, their dark wood contrasting sharply with the stone walls.

As the last member of the team stepped inside, a door suddenly shot up behind them, sealing them in much faster than the entrance door had moved. The sound of the door slamming shut reverberated through the chamber, leaving the team momentarily stunned.

Torches hanging on the walls flickered, casting an ominous orange light that filled the room. The shifting flames caused the shadows to dance along the smooth stone surfaces, creating eerie shapes that seemed to move of their own accord.

As the team watched in tense silence, the shadows began to morph, taking on the forms of various creatures. Some stood on two legs, others on four or more, their dark outlines stalking the outer edges of the room. The creatures' shapes were indistinct but menacing, as if they were waiting for the perfect moment to strike.

"Form up! Defensive people along the outside! Shields up and be ready for an attack!" Tom called out.

Immediately moving into action, the teams formed a defensive circle, with fighters positioned on the outside and spellcasters protected in the middle. The coordination was sloppier than Tom would have liked, but they obeyed without question, which was all he could ask for at this moment. As they turned to face outward, the shadows along the walls shifted, their dark forms facing the team before beginning to slither up the walls toward the ceiling.

"They're going to dive into the middle! Light casters, prepare spells!" Derek called out, his voice steady despite the tension.

Four team members began casting, their eyes following the sinister movements of the shadowy beasts. As the creatures reached the top of the dome, they started to peel themselves from the stone, transforming into three-dimensional monsters. Some took on the shapes of wolves, their forms twisted and malevolent. Others morphed into hideous, warped figures resembling humans, while still more grew additional legs, becoming grotesque insects, spiders, and other nightmarish creatures.

One creature, resembling a monstrous wolf, released its hold on the dome and plummeted toward the party. Another spider-like being descended slowly, hanging from a thread of pure darkness. As the creatures started their descent, they opened their gaping mouths, revealing rows of sharp, shadowy teeth and fangs.

As they neared the group, three balls of light shot out from the spellcasters, striking the descending creatures. Each impact caused the monsters to explode into the familiar puff of shadow ash, just as the team had seen before. The fourth spellcaster took longer to cast but successfully erected a shining barrier of light over the center of the group, providing a crucial defense.

The shadow creatures hissed and screamed, shielding their faces as they continued to fall or descend, but the light barrier repelled them with brutal efficiency. Those that collided with the barrier burst apart, the cavern echoing with repeated firecracker-like sounds as the creatures disintegrated.

However, some of the creatures were clever, releasing their grip on the ceiling farther from the center to avoid the barrier. These monsters fell upon the fighters, who dodged and fought back as best they could. Some were tackled to the ground by the creatures, struggling beneath their weight. Chaos erupted as weapons flashed out, stabbing, chopping, smashing, and cutting at anything that resembled a shadow.

Cries and screams filled the chamber, a mix of shadow creatures' shrieks and human shouts. Spells flew through the air, striking the creatures from the sides, backs, and heads as the team fought desperately to hold their ground. Though the barrier held strong, the shadow creatures were adapting, beginning to rain down on the team from positions further out, evading the light and pushing the battle to the edges of the formation.

Eventually, the onslaught began to slow as the creature limit seemed to have been reached. The relentless rain of shadowy beasts ceased, and no more fell on the raid party.

Despite this, the battle was far from over. The fighting continued with furious intensity as the team struggled to maintain their formation, fending off the remaining monsters with everything they had. The air was thick with the sounds of clashing weapons and the cries of both warriors and creatures, each side determined to overpower the other.

"Tom! The tattoo! Use the tattoo!" Derek called.

Tom activated his Tattoo of Life Absorption, feeling a surge of power as life force drained from countless enemies at once. The energy flowed into him, invigorating his body and mind. Some of the shadow creatures began to shrink, their forms weakening as their life was siphoned away. Sensing the source of their depletion, many of the shadows turned toward him, their malevolent eyes focused on nothing else as they clawed and crawled, desperate to stop the drain.

Others, however, were intercepted by the relentless wall of fighters who stood between Tom and the advancing shadows. Swords, axes, and spears hacked and slashed at the creatures, cutting them down before they could reach their target. Tom continued to battle the monsters around him, swinging his greatsword in wide, sweeping arcs that cleaved through the bodies of the shadow creatures with brutal efficiency. The Tattoo of Life Absorption replenished his SP, HP, and MP with every strike, allowing him to swing faster and harder, channeling the influx of energy into increasingly powerful attacks as he also activated his Tattoo of Strength for an added boost.

When team members were injured too severely to continue fighting, they were quickly pulled back into the center of the formation, where Healers worked tirelessly to mend their wounds. The air was filled with the sounds of chanting, the glow of healing magic, and the clash of steel against shadow.

Isaac fought like a man possessed, his full plate armor not losing its gleam even in this darkness, as he cut down monster after monster. His roars of anger echoed through the chamber as he struck with unrelenting fury, each blow delivered with precision and force.

Meanwhile, Kevin had found a kindred spirit in Kirsten, a fellow Barbarian clad in an Amazonian outfit that barely covered her. The two fought side by side, their greataxes whirling in rage-fueled fury. They carved through the shadow beasts in a synchronized dance of destruction, their powerful swings felling enemies before they could even get close.

As the number of beasts dwindled, the raid party began to converge on the remaining creatures, ganging up on any that were left in the room. The air was thick with the sound of slashing and hacking as they relentlessly pursued their foes. Finally, the last shadow creature was struck down, its body disintegrating into a cloud of dark ash.

When the dust settled, and the shadows had dissipated, the room was left in grim silence. Blood stained the stone floor, a stark reminder of the battle's cost. Three of the team members lay incapacitated, while two others had fallen, their lives claimed by the relentless assault.

"Dammit! No wonder no one was coming back. This would have been nearly impossible for a party of eight," Kedron said, breathing heavily as he rested his hands on his knees, trying to get his breath back.

"The Dungeon does change slightly based on the size of the party," Bob interjected. "I'd imagine there weren't nearly this many monsters for that small of a party."

"Still, I was expecting to just find the boss and kick his ass," James added.

"That's a bit unreasonable for a Dungeon," Bob said. "There are always other challenges first."

"It doesn't matter. We need to take a moment to rest after that. Can we heal anyone still alive?" Tom asked.

"Yes, but it'll take some time," Derek said. "Resting is a good option."

"We can't rest too long, or the Dungeon will reset," Bob said.

"We won't be here that long—just enough to heal and regain stamina," Tom said.

"And what do we do with the dead?" Zach asked.

"Take their gear, and we'll have to come back for the bodies. We can't drag them with us. It'll slow us down and make us vulnerable," Isaac said. "I know that sounds harsh, but we can't afford to take the risk."

Most of the team members sat down to rest while they had the chance, their bodies and minds weary from the intense battle. A few quietly began to strip the gear from the fallen, gathering what could still be used. Meanwhile, the Healers continued their tireless work, tending to the injured and doing their best to stabilize those who had been gravely wounded.

"I ain't never seen shadows move like that before. Damn CIA tactics sons of bitches!" Clay said.

"At least the majority of us made it through okay," Seth said, sitting next to him.

"True. Gonna take more than the dark to kill me off," Clay replied.

"Anyone else notice that the doors didn't open?" Isaac called out.

Sure enough, none of the doors, even the one leading them into the room, were open. Several people moved to the doors leading further into the Dungeon and tried to open them, but they didn't budge.

"So, it's likely some kind of puzzle to get out of here?" Tom asked.

"Likely," Bob said. "Just have to figure out what kind and solve it."

"But there's nothing in here. Even the walls are nearly smooth," Chris said.

"There are always clues," Bob said. "Just have to find them."

"Alright, we need to fan out and see if we can find anything at all. Anyone with the Rogue Class, start using any abilities you have to find if there's something hidden we've missed," Tom called out.

Everyone spread out across the room, searching for a switch, lever, or any clue that might reveal how to open the doors. Some team members felt along the walls, their hands tracing the smooth stone surfaces, while others scoured the floor for hidden mechanisms. A few even looked up at the ceiling, hoping to spot something that might have been overlooked.

After about thirty minutes of searching, someone called out from near one of the two doors. There, they had found a section of the wall that appeared slightly different from the rest. Jay quickly moved over to investigate. Using one of his skills, he was able to detect something behind the unusual wall section. Without hesitation, he smashed through the smooth outer layer, revealing a small hidden door.

Inside the compartment was a narrow space, and at the very back, a button was visible. Jay reached his arm in, almost up to his shoulder, and pressed the button.

Immediately, two massive doors on either side of the presumed exit began to slide apart, the movement cracking and breaking the plaster on the surrounding walls. As the doors fully opened, two enormous statues emerged on tracks. The statues depicted a grotesque beast, shaped like a sphere with a wide, gaping mouth that stretched across its entire middle, lined with sharp teeth. The statues moved forward until they positioned themselves at the entrance of the now open doors, standing as silent sentinels.

Suddenly, a trapdoor in the floor between the still-closed exit doors creaked open, and a pedestal rose from the opening. Atop the pedestal was a stone tablet, its surface engraved with words. Derek stepped forward to read the inscription, the room falling silent as everyone waited to hear what the tablet would reveal.

"Beware the Devourer who feeds on all. Destroyer of worlds, it answers the call. To these great Gods, must you leave a sacrifice. Only that which is given freely will completely suffice. The life of your own, must you freely give. In hopes it won't find you and that you may live," Derek read.

"Is it saying we have to sacrifice someone to it?" James asked.

"No, that doesn't sound right," Austin said. "It says you must freely give. So, something related to life that someone would freely give might be blood."

As Austin said this, two bowls moved forward from within the mouth of the beasts. They came to rest at the edge of its jaws near its teeth.

"Uh huh… so we need to bleed someone to get out. Nice," James said sarcastically.

"If it's the only way, I'll do it," Tom said.

"I will as well," Zach said. "Just have the Healers on standby for us."

Zach and Tom approached the bowls, each prepared for what came next. Zach called out for someone from his team to join him, and a woman named Jane stepped forward, ready to assist. Tom, aligned with dark magic, didn't call for anyone. He knew he would need to rely on his own abilities to heal himself.

"So, blood brother style?" Tom asked, pulling out a knife and looking over at Zach.

"What? No, don't be daft. Jane here has some medical supplies. She has an IV drip we can insert into our arms to drain the blood easily. Were you really going to cut yourself? That would be terrible," Zach said.

"Well, I was. Until you made it sound like a stupid idea," Tom said.

"That's because it is a stupid fucking idea, shit for brains. It would be super painful," Zach said.

"How was I supposed to know you had medical equipment for bloodletting?" Tom asked.

"You could have asked someone if they had any ideas besides splitting yourself open and hoping for the best," Zach said.

"…Touché, salesman," Tom said. "Alright, let's do this, then."

Jane first assisted Zach, setting up a blood drain that began to drip steadily into the first bowl. Once it was in place, she moved to help Tom do the same. Blood flowed into the bowls, the crimson liquid gradually filling them until they reached about the halfway mark.

At that point, the platform they were standing on tilted forward slightly. With a sharp click, a hidden mechanism was triggered, and both of the exit doors began to slowly open.

Jane quickly moved to help both men stop the bleeding. Tom, relying on his dark magic, healed himself, but he still felt a wave of dizziness wash over him as the effects of the blood loss set in. He sat down, trying to steady himself as his body began to recover.

After they had regained themselves from the healing, the parties looked at the two doorways.

"Now, what?" James asked.

"Send men down both tunnels. We need to see what's ahead of us. Jay, you take the left. Send another scout down the right," Derek said.

Nodding, Jay headed off down the left tunnel while another man named Mike went down the right.

Chapter 52

The Devourer

A short while later, Mike came back from the right path, his face pale with dread. "It's a dead end," he muttered.

Tom's heart skipped a beat at the unsettling news. Jay should've been back by now. Something wasn't right.

"Where's Jay?" Tom asked, voice low and tight with anxiety.

"I don't know," Derek responded, his brow furrowed. "The other path was blocked, but we were planning to go through this door, anyway. Mike's report says there's nothing on the other side."

Tom nodded grimly. He was hoping Jay would've made it back by now. "Alright, let's head down the other way and see what's going on. Hopefully, he's okay."

Tom turned and approached the group, briefing Zach, Isaac, Kedron, and Chris. It took mere minutes for them to agree, but the air was thick with an uneasy tension. They could only hope Jay was safe—or at least alive.

The corridor they entered next was far narrower, forcing the group to move in single file. Each footstep seemed to echo, amplifying the silence as they walked. The walls felt close, almost oppressive. Tom's pulse quickened with every passing second. The deeper they went, the more isolated they felt from the rest of the world.

As they reached the end, they emerged into a gargantuan chamber. The sight of it stole their breath. The room stretched upward, at least six stories high. The size was disorienting, a cavernous abyss of stone, dust, and a faint, otherworldly glow. At the far end, stood the Source Vending Machine, a behemoth of metallic, dark beauty.

It loomed over them, a thousand feet wide, with an endless number of rows packed with every product imaginable. Each item was perfectly packaged, gleaming beneath the strange internal lights that flickered eerily. The sight of it was almost too overwhelming to comprehend.

"I've never seen anything like it," Bob breathed, his voice quivering with awe as his gaze drank in the enormous machine.

For a split second, the entire group was spellbound, drawn into the machine's unnatural radiance. It was magnificent, otherworldly, like something birthed from the deepest pits of legend and fantasy.

APOCALYPSE

But the serenity didn't last. The lights above them flickered, the air growing inexplicably colder. A low hum filled the cavern. That's when they noticed it. From the shadows, at the edge of the machine, something was stirring.

A great, bloated shadow slowly oozed out from the crevices of the vending machine like thick black smoke, swirling and twisting, condensing into a mass of dark, malevolent energy. The swirling mass began to solidify, shaping itself into something grotesque and unnatural.

The Devourer.

Tom felt his breath catch in his throat. A monstrous figure stood before them now, its presence overwhelming. It was a towering, horrific apparition—its body bloated, its form shifting in unnatural ways, as if the shadows themselves had given birth to a beast from some forgotten nightmare.

"GWAAAAAHHHHHH!" the creature screamed, a sound that shook the very ground beneath them. It was an agonizing, deep roar that vibrated in their bones, reverberating through their skulls.

"You dare disturb me in my sanctuary?" the beast growled, its voice a low, grinding noise like the sound of centuries-old stone being dragged across iron.

The creature stepped forward, each movement a tremor in the air. And then Tom's blood ran cold. He saw Jay—unmoving, hanging limp in a corner of the room, suspended in some twisted energy, his body unresponsive and far out of reach.

"JAY!" Tom shouted, panic gripping him like a vice. "Jay, are you okay?"

Jay's voice, faint but defiant, barely reached them. "Just peachy… But if someone could get this fucking shitburger to let go of me, that'd be great!"

A shot rang out from behind them, the sound of a gunshot splitting the air. The bullet struck the Devourer's hand, causing it to recoil in pain. For a split second, the beast's grip on the spell faltered, and Jay fell to the ground with a heavy thud, the impact forcing a sharp grunt of pain from him. He quickly scrambled to his feet, his movements unsteady but urgent.

"And if you pick him back up, the next one goes right in your fucking eye, you giant cock sucker!" Kiera shouted from the back of the group, her voice seething with rage.

Jay pushed past the front lines, adrenaline driving him forward, and joined the others with a grimace of pain. "I'm fine, I'm fine," he said, though his voice was strained. "Let's just kill this thing."

The Devourer was slow to react, but when it did, it was with explosive fury.

"You will pay for this insult!" it snarled, the words dripping with malice. "You disgusting, pathetic excuses for life!"

It raised both hands high, and the shadows on the ground began to writhe and coil, snapping upward like dark tendrils, taking shape. From these tendrils emerged smaller shadow creatures—vicious, malevolent beasts that lunged toward the group. They were everywhere now, multiplying like a plague.

"Execute the plan!" Tom yelled over the noise, his voice a sharp command. "Defensive team, keep Bob safe! Everyone else—distraction tactics! Draw the creature's attention!"

The battle exploded around them. Spells, arrows, and bullets flew through the air, whizzing past the melee fighters and impacting against the Devourer's hulking form. The beast hissed, but the barrage didn't seem to faze it. Meanwhile, Isaac's team quickly made their move, moving toward the vending machine with Bob at the helm.

"Hold back on major spells until it's clear of the machine!" Tom barked. "We need it free—Bob, keep moving!"

The melee fighters clashed with the swarm of shadow creatures, steel against shadow. Every blow felt like it could be their last. The line of defense pushed forward, gritting their teeth, determined to keep the smaller monsters at bay long enough for Bob to reach the machine.

Bob finally reached the vending machine, but the defensive team was under intense pressure. They formed a semi-circle around him, fighting desperately to keep the shadows at bay. Jerky perched on Bob's shoulder, eyes darting around, alert for any threat.

"Bob, hurry!" Isaac shouted, his shield raised as he took the brunt of a vicious strike from one of the shadow creatures.

Bob yanked open the side panel of the vending machine, revealing a complex tangle of circuits. His hands trembled, but he forced himself to focus. This was the only shot they had.

Jerky screeched, "LEFT!" warning Bob just in time as a bolt of dark energy shot toward him. Bob leaned, narrowly avoiding the strike, but the sheer weight of the situation was beginning to wear on him.

"RIGHT!" Jerky screamed again, his little body shaking with urgency. Bob moved with lightning speed, twisting his body just enough to avoid the bolt.

Each warning from Jerky was another close call. Bob could feel the sweat pouring down his face, the urgency of the task threatening to overwhelm him. But he pressed on. Every second counted. As he worked to rewire the machine, Jerky kept a lookout, his frantic calls echoing in the chaos.

On the front lines, the melee team had nearly dealt with all the additional shadow creatures. They managed to fend off the attacks with skill and resilience, keeping the pressure off the ranged fighters and sustaining minimal damage themselves. Their coordinated efforts were beginning to turn the tide of the battle, clearing the way for the final phase of their plan.

"Is that the best you got?" James yelled at the boss creature as he continued to fire rounds at it.

"You really have to antagonize it?" Derek yelled back to him.

"Hey, are we the distraction team or the cheerleading squad?" James asked.

Looking at James, the giant shadow creature quirked what could only be described as an eyebrow, and then turned to look directly at where Bob and the defensive team were.

Suddenly, the Devourer let out a roar of fury. Tom saw it happen in slow motion—the creature was charging, its enormous hand reaching out toward Bob, intent on crushing him.

APOCALYPSE

"SHIT!" Tom yelled and fired an *Eldritch Blast* at it.

Flinching slightly as the green fire hit it, the creature moved toward where Bob was sitting.

"If you're going to do something, now is the time, Bob!" Isaac called over his shoulder to him.

"Almost done, just need a moment longer," Bob said, his hands moving furiously.

"GWAAAAAAAHHHH!" the creature screamed again as it reached out, headed for the defensive team.

"Got it!" Bob yelled suddenly, plugging something into the board he was working on.

Lights flickered throughout the machine as a shock of electricity flowed across the front window of the machine and connected with the creature as it moved toward them.

Screaming in pain as the electricity flowed through its body, it disconnected itself from the machine and fell onto the floor, shaking the entire cavern.

Barely keeping their feet, Tom looked over at the monster, now fully exposed as it lay on the ground.

"UNLEASH HELL!" Tom yelled as he activated his strength tattoo and charged the creature.

Members of the raid party began to glow in shades of blue, red, green, and yellow as they activated their abilities and charged at the creature. A barrage of fireballs, lightning bolts, and colorful orbs of various sizes shot from the magic users, streaking through the air before crashing into the beast where it lay. The creature let out a deafening cry, feeling pain that wasn't instantly healed for the first time. Large chunks of its shadowy body exploded into ashy fragments, scattering across the ground.

Writhing on the floor, the creature struggled until it managed to regain its feet, thrashing violently. It swung its massive arms, swiping at the melee fighters and tossing them aside like ragdolls. Squirrel, quick and nimble, had leapt onto its back and was furiously tearing at the creature's neck. The beast roared in pain, then swatted Squirrel off with a flick of its massive hand, sending him crashing into the cavern wall. Squirrel hit the ground and lay still, unmoving.

In a desperate attempt to recover, the beast began re-forming its shadowy body, shrinking noticeably as it tried to regenerate. Now nearly half its original size, it continued its assault, swiping at the melee fighters with brutal force, sending more of them flying. Tom dove to the side, narrowly avoiding a blow, and sprang back to his feet. With all the strength granted by his abilities, he activated *Cleave* and swung his greatsword in a powerful arc, cutting through the side of the beast and opening a deep, gaping wound.

The creature roared in agony, its eyes filled with fury as it lashed out wildly, swiping repeatedly. Fighters with shields did their best to defend against the relentless shadow claws, but the sheer force of the attacks pushed many back. Fixing its gaze on Tom, the beast formed a massive fist and swung down, intending to crush him. Tom barely had time to react—he raised his sword to block, but a shimmering blue barrier formed over him just as the fist was about to make contact.

The shield held, but just barely, as the beast poured its weight into crushing it. Tom glanced over and saw Briana standing with her staff held out in front of her, both hands trembling as she channeled her shield spell. Blood trickled from her nose as she strained to maintain the barrier, forcing more mana into the spell with every ounce of strength she had. The beast reared back and brought both fists down in a crushing blow.

Tom dove to the side just as the beast's fists came down. The shield shattered with a resounding crack, and Briana cried out, collapsing to the ground, unconscious from the feedback of the spell. Tom gritted his teeth and slashed at the creature again, drawing another furious roar. In retaliation, the beast turned its attention to the spellcasters, swinging its massive claws. A third of the casters were thrown aside or killed instantly, their bodies scattered like broken dolls. The remaining casters continued their assault, quickly drinking mana potions to replenish their energy as they launched spells in rapid succession.

A shot rang out, piercing the air and striking the beast directly in the eye. The creature recoiled, a shriek of agony tearing from its throat as it clutched its face. It spotted Kiera, who had taken the shot, positioned with her rifle. With a roar of pure rage, the beast rushed toward her, its clawed hand outstretched, ready to rip her apart. Kiera's eyes widened in horror as she realized the beast was coming for her, its intent clear and deadly.

"KIERA!" Tom yelled out.

Just as the creature's claws were about to reach Kiera, Seth leaped in front of her, his katana flashing as he intercepted the attack. He swung his blade with precision, slicing into the creature's hand and forcing it back momentarily. Snarling in frustration, the beast lashed out repeatedly, its swipes coming faster and harder. Seth stood his ground, deflecting each strike with his katana in a desperate struggle to hold the line.

The creature, growing more furious with every blocked attack, changed its approach. With a powerful swipe, it aimed directly at Seth's weapon, knocking his katana aside and leaving him vulnerable. In the split second that followed, the beast brought its other claw forward in a brutal strike.

Seth was tossed aside like a mere toy, the claws tearing gashes across his face and body. When he hit the ground, he rolled to a stop and tried to rise. He only made it to his hands and knees before the Devourer picked him up in one hand and brought him toward its face.

"NOOOOOOOOOOOOO!" Kiera screamed as she aimed up at its face and let round after round loose into its head.

"YOU FUCKING CUNT!" Kiera continued to scream as tears came to her eyes. "DIE AND BURN IN HELL! CRIES OF REMORSE, FEED ME STRENGTH! YOUR TIME HAS COME, AND YOU WILL PAY FOR YOUR SINS!" Kiera screamed, shooting another spell at the monster.

When this spell hit, it latched onto the creature and shone brighter and brighter as she fed mana into it.

"What the hell is that?" Tom asked.

"I have no idea, but it's coming from Kiera," Derek said in awe of the power she was using.

When the light finally winked out, Kiera fell to the floor unconscious.

"FINISH IT!" Zach called as they renewed their attack on the creature.

"No, no, no, NO!" the creature yelled as the barrage began anew. "This cannot be! I will not be defeated!"

The creature raised both hands into the air, and a powerful wave of energy exploded outward, knocking everyone off their feet and sending them sprawling onto their backs. As the dust settled, the creature's form shrank again, now only about the size of the troll Vanguard had fought. Without hesitation, it turned and rushed toward the massive vending machine it had been feeding on, Seth still grasped in one hand, blood running down his face.

"Don't let it get back to the machine! It'll heal itself!" Bob shouted urgently.

Isaac charged in from the side, his shield raised. With a powerful shield bash, he slammed into the creature, knocking it off course and sending it sprawling to the ground. Tom quickly got to his feet, casting his *Doppelganger* spell. An image of himself split off, mirroring his movements.

The beast regained its footing. "ENOUGH!" it roared its defiance as it threw out both hands and sent a shower of shadows out to cover everyone present.

Everyone save Tom, who was still behind the creature. Instead, Tom's doppelganger was dogpiled in swarming shadows, seemingly unconcerned that the person they were attacking was insubstantial.

Seth, bloodied but still held in the creature's grasp, looked Tom in the eye. "Go to the machine, Tom," he said, his voice hoarse but urgent. "Get what you need to stop this thing!"

The plea hit Tom like a fist to the gut.

The Devourer stood defiantly in its victory. Looking out, it surveyed the party of adventurers all bound to the floor by shadows.

"Please," Seth almost whispered as the creature began to squeeze.

Tom's heart hammered in his chest, a war raging within him. His mind screamed at him to move, to act, but every part of him wanted to run to Seth—to throw himself at the Devourer, to save the man who had fought beside him. Seth's pain-filled eyes were etched into his memory, his plea for Tom to leave him behind echoing in Tom's mind like a broken record. But there was more at stake now. More than just Seth's life.

The monster's roar still echoed in his ears, and he could feel the weight of the situation pressing down on him, suffocating him. If he didn't get to the machine, they all would die. Kiera, Isaac, Zach, James, Derek, and the rest—they wouldn't survive unless he made it to the Source Machine. But Seth... Seth was right there, so close.

Tom clenched his jaw, torn between two impossible choices. *Save Seth*, the words screamed through his veins, but at what cost? Everything he had fought for, everything he had sacrificed to protect them, would be lost. He would lose them all.

His gaze flickered back to Seth, and for a moment, the world seemed to pause. He could feel the weight of their shared short history, the bond they'd forged in battle. Seth had been there for him. But if he didn't act, everything would be in vain.

The sound of the Devourer's footsteps drew closer. Time was running out. He knew what he had to do, even if it meant tearing his own heart out.

"Foolish mortals," the Devourer snarled, black spittle spraying from its wounded maw. "You believe that you are heroes? Powerful? Capable? No." Its voice was laced with venom, but somehow soft—not quite comforting, but final. "I am the final black. The embracing darkness behind the lidded eyes of countless corpses. I am the Avatar of the Destroyer. The weapon that was crafted to slip between the ribs of the 'Grand System' itself." Its use of the System's title was dripping with scorn and sarcasm.

"You? Who squabble in the streets for scraps?" It hissed. "Who raise the petty sums of Monster Cores with trembling hands toward the altar of packaged goods and paltry rewards?" It's laugh was a hideous, twisted thing that dug into the mind and took root. "Why do you fight back against that which *will*, which *must,* come to be? Why raise your weapons in futile effort when you can bend the knee in subservient supplication?

"Tell me, mortals." It squeezed Seth, bloodied nails digging into the man's ribs as he shook him at the fellow raiders in demonstration. "You. Each of you are gripped by the fist of Fate. Your destiny was writ among the Cosmos before the foundations of your very being, and yet you rebel in hopeless defiance against the one who would free you from the chains you so willingly bear?"

With a final, tortured glance at Seth, Tom turned. His legs moved before his mind could catch up, his body already sprinting toward the vending machine. The decision had been made. Everyone else—they were counting on him.

Tom's heart pounded as he reached the vending machine. He placed his hand on the screen, his eyes scanning the shelves frantically, searching for any item that might give him a chance.

Before he could make his purchase, a powerful blow smashed him to the ground, ripping him away from the machine. His body fetched up against the wall a few meters distant.

The creature was no longer charging, but instead stood tall, its eyes filled with cruel amusement. It stared at Tom with cold, derisive contempt, a wicked sneer twisting its grotesque features.

"Do not hate the cleansing fire that sweeps away the gnarled and rotted deadwood, for it lays the foundation for a new and majestic world." The creature's words were hypnotic—compelling in their fervent belief. "For those courageous few—boldly embrace the gentle night."

APOCALYPSE

The Devourer's glowing eyes blazed as its voice rose in crescendo. "And for those of you for whom fear and doubt have turned your wallowing will into water?" A demonic grin split the fiend's face. "Allow *me!*"

With a tortured, deliberate motion, the Devourer raised its hand and crushed Seth in its grasp. A sickening crunch echoed through the cavern as Seth's body twisted in the creature's hold, his mouth open in a silent scream. The beast's eyes never left Tom's as it squeezed the life out of Seth, an evil sneer curling on its lips. It was taunting him.

Tom's stomach churned. His throat tightened, bile rising. Anger surged through him, boiling and furious. His hands, once trembling, were now steady with rage, every fiber of his being consumed by the need for vengeance.

"NO!" he roared, a guttural scream of pure fury. His mind exploded with rage as the sight of Seth's broken body filled him with a burning hatred.

Suddenly, Tom remembered Bob's words from earlier that day as though he were standing next to him and speaking them once more. 'You can take your hand off the screen to see the menus after.'

Tom looked down at the hand he'd used to touch the Source Machine, his eyes wide. Quickly, he shut them, mentally accessing his System screens and… *there!*

Appearing in front of him was the selection screen for the Source Machine. It was still on the same page he had been on when he'd been struck by the Devourer, and right there at the top, he saw what he needed.

He wasted no time making his purchase

The monster was still standing, waiting. And Tom could feel the weight of the moment pressing in. This was it. It had to end here.

"And *you,*" the Devourer locked eyes with Bob, who was still elbow deep in the guts of the Source Machine. "It is time to end your pathetic struggles." He reached out to wrap his blackened claws around the repairman, who had his tongue sticking out as he turned his head to the side to reach further inside the machine.

As the creature's claws drew nearer, Bob almost casually reached out with a sparking wire of copper that had been stripped clean of its protective shielding. The copper inside was thicker than Tom's wrist. As it touched the Devourer, the creature froze, electricity arcing through its frozen body as it gyrated in time with the electrical current flowing through it.

With a furious snarl, Tom sprinted at a diagonal angle to the Devourer. As he drew closer, he passed by the Source Machine. Practically without pausing, he ripped the can that he knew would be there, resting at the bottom of the machine, from its compartment and tore the thing open.

As quickly as the item appeared in his hand, he hurled the flash grenade at the Devourer, the light bursting outward in a blinding explosion. Caught between the consuming light and the ravening power of the Source Machine's electricity, the shadows recoiled, screeching as the explosion of the grenade filled the cavern with an earth-shattering crack.

For the first time, Tom saw the creature stagger, its form flickering as the light burned away its darkness.

The distraction was brief—but it was enough.

"NOW!" Isaac screamed as the shadows of their bonds shattered and the blinding light tore through the air. Tom took a deep breath, his hands still shaking but steadying. He equipped his sword and charged, his rage fueling his every step as he prepared to finish this once and for all.

Tom didn't hesitate. With a battle cry that echoed through the cavern, he charged toward the Devourer. His greatsword, crackling with the energy of the flames that engulfed it from a spell he fired off without thought, was raised high. The beast was still disoriented, its form staggering from the Flash Grenade's blinding burst.

"Tom, get him!" Isaac shouted again, his voice a desperate plea.

Tom's feet pounded the stone floor as he leapt into the air, the weight of the sword a reassuring presence in his hands. The ground beneath him shuddered from the force of the Devourer's movements, but Tom was faster. He swung his greatsword with all the force he could muster, the edge of the blade slicing through the air, aimed directly at the Devourer's neck.

The creature roared, but it was too late. The sword cleaved through its shadowy form, leaving a jagged gash in its massive neck. Black mist poured from the wound, like smoke escaping from an old, cracked furnace. The beast's screech reverberated through the cavern walls, a sound filled with agony and pure rage. It staggered back, its body writhing as if trying to fight the very essence of its being.

The ground shook beneath Tom's feet as the Devourer reeled, its massive hands swiping in all directions, each strike sending shockwaves through the cavern. But Tom wasn't backing down. His eyes burned with determination as he shifted his stance, preparing for the next strike. He could see the monster struggling to regenerate, its form flickering and shrinking as it tried to reform its shadowy body.

The Devourer staggered back, its shadowy form flickering, weakened by the slash that had torn through its neck. But it wasn't defeated yet. The beast hissed in fury, and Tom could see the black mist pooling around its wound, desperately trying to stitch itself back together.

Tom's breath was ragged, his muscles burning with exhaustion, but his resolve was unshakable. He could feel the flames of fury still raging within him, the need to end this fight once and for all. The beast was regenerating, but it was slowing. This was his chance.

The ground shook as the Devourer's massive claws swung again, but Tom was ready. He dodged to the side, his body moving with the precision of a practiced warrior. The creature's claws slammed into the stone floor with a deafening crack, sending debris flying in all directions.

Tom didn't waste a second. He surged forward, his greatsword raised high, the flames around it dancing wildly. He could feel the weight of every strike, the intensity of the magic flowing through him. This would be it.

"Die!" he shouted, his voice thick with rage. The sword came down in a powerful arc, cleaving through the Devourer's arm as it swung to strike him. The creature howled in pain, but Tom was already moving, his blade flashing in the dim light.

He didn't stop. With each swing, he delivered blow after blow, each strike cutting deeper into the creature's dark, shifting body. The Devourer swiped at him, but Tom was faster. He ducked under one strike, pivoted, and drove the sword into the creature's chest. The blade sank in with a sickening, wet sound, the flames roaring as they burned through the darkness.

The Devourer screamed in agony, but Tom wasn't finished. He pulled the sword free with a savage jerk and swung it again, aiming for the creature's other arm. It didn't have time to react before the blade slammed into it, severing the limb with a burst of black mist. The beast howled once more, staggering backward, its form flickering violently as the shadows tried to pull themselves together.

But it was too late.

Tom saw the opening. With a final, furious scream, he leaped forward, using every ounce of his remaining strength. He thrust his sword forward with a final, vicious blow, driving it deep into the Devourer's heart. The creature let out a shriek of pure, unrelenting rage, but as Tom's blade pierced its core, the shadows began to unravel.

The Devourer's body shook violently, as if it were fighting against its very existence. Black mist poured from the wound in torrents, and the cavern filled with a deafening roar. But in the end, it wasn't enough.

With one last, guttural scream, the Devourer exploded into a cloud of shadowy ash, the remnants of its monstrous form scattering across the floor. Silence descended over the cavern.

Tom stood there, panting heavily, his greatsword still crackling with the residual energy of the flames. His body ached, every muscle screaming in protest from the battle, but he had done it. The creature was gone. And with it, the threat to his friends.

The cavern was still, save for the faint echo of the Devourer's final death throes. Tom let out a shaky breath, lowering his sword. He looked around, his eyes scanning the damage—the fallen comrades, the destruction, the shattered remnants of the battle.

But they had won.

Tom's legs finally gave out beneath him, and he dropped to his knees, his breath ragged and heavy in the stillness of the cavern. He had done it. They had done it. The monster was gone, and he had kept his promise to fight until the very end.

Chapter 53

Losses

"SETH! Where is Seth!" Tom cried out after making sure the beast was finished.

"He's over here!" called Jay.

Tom ran toward the Healers, urgently pushing his way through the crowd that had gathered. Men and women were laid out on the ground in a long row, some groaning in pain while others lay eerily still. Healers moved frantically from person to person, doing what they could to save those who were still clinging to life.

At the far end of the row, Tom spotted Jay kneeling beside Seth's body. Unlike the others, no Healers hovered nearby to help. Tom's heart sank as he rushed over.

"Seth! Seth! Speak to me!" Tom called out, his voice tinged with desperation as he reached the end of the row.

Jay looked up, tears streaming down his face, and met Tom's eyes. He shook his head slowly, his gaze returning to Seth's lifeless form. Seth's body bore four massive wounds in his abdomen, each one a gaping hole that had nearly cut him in half. His chest remained still, no breath filling his lungs, and his skin had turned a deathly pale. Blood soaked his clothes and armor, the deep red stains stark against his lifeless body.

Tom knelt beside them, feeling the weight of the loss settle heavily on his shoulders. Seth was gone.

"No, no, no, no, no! This is all my fault! We led him here, and he trusted us!" Tom cried as tears began to fall from his own eyes.

"It wasn't your fault. He chose to come with us. We all knew the risks when we joined," Derek said, putting a hand on his shoulder.

"But it should have been me! We convinced him to come, and now he's gone!" Tom continued.

"We can't think like that. We all did what we had to do. Because of him, Kiera is still alive. If he hadn't come, she wouldn't be here," Derek said. "He died bravely, saving someone in return. He would be happy with his lot."

Tom wept over Seth's body, his shoulders shaking with grief. Others joined in mourning the loss of their comrades. Nearly a third of their number now lay dead, with many more injured, as the Healers moved tirelessly among them, doing their best to mend wounds and save those they could.

APOCALYPSE

The mood was heavy and somber as the Healers worked, the quiet murmurs of the living mixing with the pained groans of the injured. Those who could be healed were tended to, while the fallen were left to rest in silence. The surviving members of each team gathered the belongings of their fallen comrades, dividing the gear among themselves as a practical necessity and a final tribute.

Tom's team, however, set Seth's gear beside him, untouched. They stood together in a moment of silent reverence, unwilling to take what had belonged to their friend, honoring his memory in their own quiet way.

"We'll have to take their bodies out of the Dungeon. Once we exit, we can bury them," Derek told the teams.

"Where's Bob?" Tom asked.

"I'm over here, Tom," Bob said.

"Were you able to fix the machine?" Tom asked, still finding it hard to speak.

"I was. I figured out what happened and fixed the issue. Everything should go back to normal now."

<table>
<tr><td align="center">Quest Complete: Destroy the Corruption</td></tr>
<tr><td>Congratulations! You have successfully defeated the Devourer and completed the quest.

Rewards:

    •   20,000 XP per party member
    •   Rare Monster Core (x1) per party member

The Devourer has been vanquished, and the corruption has been purged. Your bravery and skill have earned you these rewards. Continue to grow stronger, adventurers!</td></tr>
</table>

"A hollow prize for the sacrifice we've made," Tom said.

"It will help so many others, though. Now, we can be sure that the rest will get the items they need," Derek said. "Come on, Tom, we need to get ready to leave the Dungeon to let the others know."

They waited silently as the Healers finished their work, preparing the bodies to be taken out of the Dungeon. When everything was ready, the parties marched back the way they had come, the heavy weight of loss hanging over them. No one spoke as they moved, their footsteps echoing through the narrow corridors. Along the way, they paused to gather the last of the bodies they had left behind, determined to bring everyone home.

The mood remained heavy as they continued through the Dungeon, the sorrow palpable in the air. Each step felt like a reminder of those they had lost, and the burden of grief pressed down on every heart. Yet, the knowledge that they had made a difference kept them moving forward—a flicker of resolve amid the darkness. Tom carried Seth's body himself, while Jay followed close behind, cradling Seth's gear. Tears streamed down Tom's face, carving clean streaks through the grime and blood smeared on his cheeks.

As they approached the Dungeon entrance, the door began to slide open, the familiar grinding of stone on stone echoing through the space. When the door had fully lowered, the raid party was met by the entire camp waiting just outside the cave entrance. A cheer erupted from the crowd as they saw the adventurers alive and returning. But the celebration was short-lived; the cheers quickly faded as the camp saw the expressions on the faces of the returning parties and the bodies they carried.

The crowd parted to allow the group to pass, their heads bowing in respect as they mirrored the somber mood of the raid party. Though there was much to be thankful for, the sting of loss was still fresh, a shared sorrow that transcended any victory.

Gently, the party laid the bodies down in a row outside the cave. The entire camp sprang into action, gathering around to show their respect for those who had fallen. Someone suggested funeral pyres instead of burial, so that the families would have something to take home, and the teams agreed this was the better solution.

While materials were gathered, a few members of the camp constructed a pile of stones, placing a single tablet at its front. They carefully engraved the names of all those who had fallen, including Jake and his team, creating a lasting memorial to honor their sacrifice.

In honor of those who gave their lives so that so many could live.
"Greater love has no one than this: to lay down one's life for one's friends."

Frank Marshall
Jennifer Hall
Alex Stevens
Laura Chambers
Victor Morales
Grace Thompson
Gene Sullivan
Sophia Collins
Phillip Paulson
John Erics
Emil Folks
Andrew Cordon
Jack Silvers
Emily Hanson
Joshua Thorn
Wesley Starr
Jake Weathers

APOCALYPSE

Steve Miller
Harold Hanover
Edward Burgess
Forrest Tripp
Seth Stone

May their bravery be remembered, their sacrifices honored, and their spirits forever guide us.

After the pyres were prepared, everyone gathered as those who had died were laid upon the prepared wood. One of the mages cast an ember spell and held the flame in their hand.

"Today, we gather to honor the brave souls who gave everything in the battle against the shadows. We stand here not just as comrades, but as family, bound by the sacrifices we've made and the courage we've shared. Each of the names we remember today belongs to someone who stood shoulder to shoulder with us, who faced the same fears, and who fought with unwavering resolve to protect what we hold dear.

"These are not just visages amongst the faceless crowd. They are our friends, our mentors, our brothers, and sisters. They are the heroes who answered the call when it mattered most.

"Their valor was not in the absence of fear, but in their willingness to push forward despite it. They stood firm when the odds were against us. They faced the unknown with strength, and in their final moments, they gave us a chance to continue, to fight another day. It is because of them that we are here, and it is because of them that the path ahead is clearer.

"Though we mourn their loss deeply, let us also celebrate their lives, the joy they brought, the strength they shared, and the legacies they leave behind. Each flame that rises tonight carries the spirit of a warrior who fought with all they had. As we light these pyres, let us commit to carrying their memories with us, honoring their sacrifices by continuing the fight they believed in.

"May the flames guide their spirits to peace, and may their courage continue to inspire us. They will not be forgotten. Their legacy will live on in every victory we achieve, in every life we protect, and in every battle we fight.

"Let us stand together, united in their memory, and let these fires be a beacon of the strength they showed and the hope they gave us. Farewell, dear friends. Your fight is over, but your courage endures. Rest in peace, knowing that your sacrifice was not in vain. We will honor you by living up to the standard you set and by continuing the battle you so bravely fought," the mage said.

With those words, he knelt and lit the fire, watching as the flames spread across the carefully prepared wood. The fire grew quickly into a roaring bonfire, its light flickering and casting long shadows as it consumed all that it touched. The crowd stood in silent reverence, many shedding tears as they remembered their fallen friends. Drinks were passed around, and the shared solemnity of the moment united everyone in their grief and gratitude.

As the flames continued to burn, new logs were added to the fire, and food was brought out from every party that had gathered. Everyone shared what they had in honor of those who had given their lives, a tribute to their bravery and sacrifice. Everyone ate, drank, and raised their glasses in toasts to those who had made the ultimate sacrifice. Some sang songs of warriors from ages past, their voices lifting into the night, while others danced around the fire, celebrating the lives and the courage of their fallen comrades.

The night became a mix of mourning and celebration, a poignant reminder of the bond they all shared and the courage that had brought them together. Though loss weighed heavy on their hearts, they honored their friends with every laugh, every song, and every shared memory around the fire.

At one point Kiera got up, pulled out her lute, and sang a song by Manowar called "Army of the Dead," and by the end, there wasn't a dry eye in the camp.

The celebration continued late into the night as everyone ate and drank their fill. Laughter and songs echoed through the camp, blending with the crackling of the fire and the occasional clink of glasses raised in tribute. As the hours passed, the funeral pyres gradually burned down, their flames reduced to glowing embers, and the campfire dwindled to a soft, warm glow.

One by one, people retired to their tents, setting up their sleeping arrangements and eventually drifting off to sleep. The camp grew quiet, the night settling in with a peaceful hush.

Tom remained by the fire, staring into the dying embers, lost in thought. Sleep eluded him, his mind still processing the day's events and the weight of the losses they had endured. Before long, Derek, James, Kiera, and Jay joined him, silently taking seats around the fire. They sat together in the quiet, finding comfort in each other's presence as they shared the quiet moments of reflection, bound by the experiences of the day.

"You guys should just get some sleep. We have to travel in the morning," Tom said.

"Nah, we'd rather stay here," Jay said.

"Yeah, you're not getting rid of us that easy," Kiera said before taking a swig from a bottle of wine.

They sat there in silence for a moment while they drank their booze.

"I remember when we first met Seth," Derek began. "He was truly amazing. He had such talent for someone so young."

"He was such a sweet soul," Kiera said. "I still can't forgive myself for what happened."

"You didn't do it. You were fighting the same monster he was," Tom said.

"But he died saving me," Kiera said.

"He stepped in to make sure you were okay. He's a hero for that," Derek said. "Don't tarnish his sacrifice by saying things like that. You have to grieve, but you also have to remember how brave he was."

"He truly was brave. That little shitbag was always protecting those people in Decatur," James said.

"He was so much more. He was the best of us," Tom said, holding his bottle of whiskey in the air.

"The best of us," the rest said, joining Tom in raising bottles of drinks.

"Remember when I got burnt to a crisp because that fucker was playing with the goblin?" James said, laughing.

"You sure got the bad end of that stick. You looked like Anakin Skywalker before Briana healed you," Kiera said.

"More like someone roasted a nutsack instead of a marshmallow over a fire for too long," Jay said.

"Oh, you're one to talk—you look like a nutsack right now," James said.

"Weak comeback," Jay said.

"Look, I'm a little drunk. I'm trying here," James said.

"I'm sure you've said that to a lover before," Derek said.

Laughing and joking, the team stayed up together until the first light of dawn crept over the horizon. Exhausted but unwilling to break the moment, they finally shuffled off to their tents as the rest of the camp began to stir. They collapsed into their beds, still buzzed from the drinks, and quickly fell into a deep sleep, their minds eager to escape the weight of the previous day's events.

When they awoke later, the smell of freshly prepared food greeted them, and they gathered to eat, trying to shake off their hangovers. As they ate, the reality of their losses returned; the ashes of their fallen comrades had been carefully collected and placed into containers for each team to take back with them. These were handed out solemnly to the team leaders, who accepted them with quiet reverence.

Tom received Seth's ashes, gently placing them in his Inventory. He turned to his team and promised, "We'll stop in Decatur on our way home. We'll speak with his friends there and let them honor him, too."

With the ashes distributed, the teams packed up their tents and gear, preparing to leave the Grand Canyon. Before they departed, the other members of the teams they had fought alongside gathered to see them off. Handshakes, hugs, and words of gratitude were exchanged, a shared understanding of the battles they had faced and the bonds they had forged.

"Before you go, we wanted to say thank you," Zach said.

"We all experienced loss, but we know that we did the right thing and wanted to thank you for getting us all together to stop that monster," Isaac said.

"We'd still be up there fighting for the next turn if it wasn't for that," Chris said.

"We just did what we thought was right," Tom said.

"We know, but we wanted to thank you. We appreciate what you did," Zach said. "You also put up a hell of a fight. You guys are pretty amazing."

"You all weren't so bad yourselves," Derek said. "We make a hell of a team. If you're ever in Dallas, look us up."

"Dallas, eh? We'll definitely look you up at some point," Zach said.

"Thanks, friends. We're so happy to have met you all as well. We have to get back to the Guild, but we hope to see you again one day," Tom said, each of them shaking hands in turn.

Chapter 54

Final Notice

Crackling, whirring, and popping could be heard from somewhere in the camp behind where the teams were saying goodbye.

"Come in, I repeat, we have completed the quest to set the machines right. We are now safe from the danger it posed," Mike said through a portable HF radio he had brought with him.

There was a long pause on the radio before a response finally came through.

"Copy that. This is Joe of the Guild Vanguard in Dallas, Texas. I read you loud and clear," Joe's voice came through on the radio.

"Wait, Vanguard? Where have I heard that name before?" Mike said.

"By any chance, did any of our team members make it to your location for the fight? They left a while ago, and we haven't had any contact with them," Joe said.

"Who did you send? There are a pretty good number of people here," Mike replied.

"There were eight of them in total. They were led by a man named Tom," Joe replied.

"Tom? Oh, yeah! He was here. He helped lead the raid party that finally took that son of a bitch down," Mike said.

"That sounds like our Tom," Joe said. "Is he still there with you, by chance?"

"He was just about to leave. Let me see if they're still nearby. Hold, please," Mike said and moved away from the radio.

Tom had just finished shaking hands with the other team leaders when Mike came running over to them.

"Mike? What's up, man? Came to say goodbye?" Tom asked.

"No, no, no. Well, I would like to say goodbye, but there is someone on the radio who claims to be with your Guild. Says his name is Joe," Mike said.

"Really? That crazy old bastard got a radio working?" Tom asked.

"Well, he was a prepper. It would make sense that he had one in his supplies," Derek said.

"He wants to talk with you if you can be available," Mike said.

"Sure, we don't have to leave right this instant. Lead the way," Tom replied.

Leading the way back to his tent where the radio had been set up, Mike walked over and picked up the mic.

"Hey, Joe, you still with me?" Mike asked.

"Sure am. Did Tom already leave?" Joe asked.

"Yup, that's Joe, alright. I would know that voice anywhere," Tom said.

"He's right here, Joe. I'll pass the mic over to him," Mike said, reaching out to hand Tom the mic.

"Hey, Joe, how ya doing, you old coot?" Tom said, depressing the button and talking into the mic.

"Tom? Oh, thank God it's you. Are you all alright?" Joe asked.

"Yeah, we're alright. So, you had a radio in your supplies, I would guess?" Tom asked.

"Boy, them's fightin' words. Doubting a man's HAM radio capabilities is like doubting his ability to satisfy his old lady," Joe replied irritably. "I won't have it, ya hear?"

"Roger that," Tom chuckled. "Well, it's still good to hear from you. How's everyone else doing there?"

"Oh, they are doing as well as they can be. Of course, we're still fighting off monsters, but I'm sure there's no one in the world who isn't. Brian has been doing an amazing job of getting people integrated into the Guild. Some people have shown up saying they met you and wanted to join," Joe said.

"That's great! Did they say where they were from?" Tom asked.

"The first group was from Irving," Joe began.

"Awesome! Kedron will be super happy to hear that," Tom interrupted.

"Another group came from Decatur. Then, a few people from Albuquerque just showed up, telling some wild stories of what you did there. A brutish bunch was leading them, but they listened to everything TJ said. He had to beat the shit out of one of them, but the others were ready to listen," Joe continued.

"That's our TJ. Glad everything is going smoothly," Tom said.

"Oh, and Harold got the power back on for the building. It went a lot faster than he first thought when everyone else began pitching in with what they knew," Joe said.

"So, he figured out the machine he was working on?" Tom asked.

"I don't really know how it all works. He tried to explain it to me. Something about having some kind of mana collectors on top of the building that feed into like a battery or something in the basement. Then it goes through some kind of magical converter that changes the mana into electricity to power the generators that were already a part of the building. But apparently, we have to be careful with how much magic is used in the area. Normal use seems fine. But if a bunch of people start casting spells, it could deplete the ambient mana enough to stop the whole damn thing from working," Joe said.

"What does that mean for our fighters protecting the building?" Tom asked.

"Harold and some of the others have a theory that the mana collector thingies on top of the building will be pulling enough mana from the air to stop the monster spawns. It seems that they were appearing so often because of that mana. With less in the area, it should drastically decrease the number of monsters that appear," Joe said.

"That sounds like good news to me," Tom said. "What about the rest of the Guild? Everyone else doing okay?"

"Well, some people have gotten hurt, but Rebecca and a team of Clerics have been working in the area set up as the hospital ward and have been able to heal everyone so far. We also found some people who were interested in farming, and they were able to get Professions in it, so they have been working on growing food. They actually have some magic that makes the plants grow faster. A new project to expand into a plot behind the building is already underway."

"That sounds amazing! How much faster are they growing?" Tom asked.

"Seems to be that they can grow a crop in about a week if they use their spells daily. There is some worry about taking the mana from the collectors as the operation grows, but Harold is already working on a solution to increase the mana that can be pulled. A new person from Decatur joined. He's a contractor, and he's working with Paul, the architect, to build the protections for the expansion of the plots behind the building," Joe replied.

"Wow! A crop a week! That's unheard of. Magic is truly something else. That means our food problem is solved?" Tom asked.

"Not quite. Protein is still a big lacking factor. We have hunters going out for now to bring back game. But we'll have to find a way to get livestock eventually," Joe said. "But for now, we are sustaining ourselves fine. And the farming team is making plans for livestock. It'll happen at some point."

"So, it sounds like everything is going smoothly. The rest of the team will be so relieved. We were worried that something might go sideways while we were gone. I'm glad that isn't the case," Tom said. "Oh, and get this! We found a vending machine repairman while we were out here. Hoping he wants to come back with us as well."

"A vending machine repairman? How would that help? All the vending machines changed," Joe said.

"No, he's a repairman for the current vending machines. His knowledge is invaluable to us in this world," Tom said.

"That's definitely good to hear. We still have so many questions that need answers," Joe said. "But I didn't reach out because everything is all sunshine and rainbows, Tom."

"What do you mean, Joe? It sounds like everything is going great," Tom said.

"You remember Shandra? From that other Guild in Dallas?" Joe asked.

"Yeah? Though I thought she was coming out here. Come to think of it, I haven't seen her here," Tom said.

"Yeah, apparently, she decided against it. She came back and has been holed up in her tower. She hasn't just been idle, though. She's been taking her people out to fight monsters as well. We just thought that she was working on building up her forces to keep her people safe," Joe said.

APOCALYPSE

"What aren't you telling me, Joe?" Tom asked.

"Well, until recently, she had been cordial and was just working on her team. But she started approaching some of the members of our advance teams to join her. She was not happy when they continually turned her down," Joe said.

"I imagine not. So, she's trying to poach our people?" Tom asked.

"It gets worse. She got pissed when some of the newer people came and started joining our team. You need to get back here fast, Tom. Shandra has declared a feud between our Guilds, and it looks like it may break out into a war before we can do anything about it," Joe said.

Tom froze. Unable to say anything else, he spoke the only words he could feel at that moment.

"Shit."

End of Book 1

Special Thanks:

To my incredible wife—thank you for your unwavering support, your patience through the long hours, and your constant belief that I could bring this story to life. Your encouragement meant more than I can put into words, especially on the days when doubt crept in. This book exists because you stood beside me every step of the way.

To Jay Beraz and Geneva Agnos—thank you for being constant sources of inspiration, both in character and in spirit. Your emotional support kept me writing even when I felt stuck, and your wonderfully weird selves reminded me that I'm not alone in my strange little corner of the world. You made this journey a lot more fun—and a lot less lonely.

To TJ Lombardi—thank you for being someone I could relate to, someone who truly got it. Your uplifting words and quiet encouragement carried more weight than you probably realize. Having you in my corner made this process feel a little less daunting, and a lot more possible.

To Jez, Chrissy, and Geneva at Legion Publishing—thank you for believing in me and giving this story a real home. Without your support and faith, this work might still be buried on Royal Road instead of reaching the audience I always dreamed it could. You made something feel possible that once felt distant, and I'm beyond grateful for the chance you gave me.

To everyone who has read this story—thank you. Whether you left a critique, dropped a comment, or simply kept turning the pages, your feedback and encouragement helped shape this book. Your support kept me going more times than I can count, and I'm endlessly grateful for every one of you.

To Nick a.k.a "Bosloe"—thank you for your unwavering support and for walking this path alongside me. We went through this journey of publishing together, shoulder to shoulder, and carried many of the same burdens. Without you, I would've surely wavered, maybe even given up. Our talks and your steady encouragement were like a rock I could cling to in the midst of the storm we weathered. I'm proud we made it through together..

 War

Book 2

Grand System Vending

By

Ryan Maxwell

The good news: The vending machines aren't trying to kill them anymore.

The bad news: Pretty much everything else is.

After debugging the apocalypse and stopping the corruption infecting Earth's last supply chain, Tom thought survival might finally get easier. He was wrong.

With civilization hanging by a thread, the real threat isn't just monsters—it's people. Between power-hungry guilds, a self-proclaimed ruler who collects slaves like trading cards, and the ever-mysterious System pulling the strings, the only certainty in conflict.

Now, Tom and his friends have a new mission: get back to Dallas before the world burns down around them. But when the city is already a battlefield, the difference between a hero and a warlord is just a matter of perspective.

Peace was never an option.

Pre Order Now!

<u>Welcome to the Dark ages</u>

Morgan and Merlins excellent Adventures

Book One

By

Malory

When Merlin needs a hero to save the world, he gets... well, me.

Fan-bloody-tastic.

I was supposed to be dead. Instead, I wake up face-down in Dark Age mud, possessing some poor bastard's body, while the ghost of history's most famous wizard rambles on about being murdered, cosmic energy and the end of all reality.

Just one tiny problem: I know about as much about cultivation as a pig knows about particle physics.

Now I'm fumbling with mystical energy that feels like juggling nitroglycerin, trying not to get shanked by everyone and their grandmother, and dealing with Merlin's constant "helpful" commentary.

Something dark is rising in Arthurian Britain.

Something that made even Merlin scared. They say fate has a sense of humour. Turns out it's the kind that laughs while setting your hair on fire.

Welcome to the Dark Ages, where cultivation meets chaos, and the only thing sharper than a sword is my questionable wit.

<u>Read Now!</u>

<u>Theft of Decks</u>

By Lars Machmüller

When the deck is stacked against you? Change the game!

In the frontier town of Isarn, Chase will never be more than the lowly Darkborn thief he is. Banned from training, banned from acquiring better cards, if the Lightborn had their way, he'd be banned from life itself.

He's not alone though, and the one thing he and his friends have is determination. Losing a hand to a brutal punishment only fueled his obsession to get access to his own amazing, reality-bending cards.

That is the path to power and a future for them all. Nobody cares where you came from when you're rich enough. For now, though, they're facing both established powers, churches and age-old prejudices. It's time to get to work, and if the Lightborn won't share and play nice?

Sometimes the only way to get dealt a better hand is to steal the whole damn deck!

<u>Buy on Amazon</u>

Quest Academy

By Brian J. Nordon

A world infested by demons.
An Academy designed to train Heroes to save humanity from annihilation.
A new student's power could make all the difference.

Humans have been pushed to the brink of extinction by an ever-evolving demonic threat. Portals are opening faster than ever, Towers bursting into the skies and Dungeons being mined below the last safe havens of society. The demons are winning.

Quest Academy stands defiantly against them, as a place to train the next generation of Heroes. The Guild Association is holding the line, but are in dire need of new blood and the powerful abilities they could bring to the battlefront. To be the saviors that humanity needs, they need to surpass the limits of those that came before them.

In a war with everything on the line, every power matters. With an adaptive enemy, comes the need for a constant shift in tactics. A new age of strategy is emerging, with even the unlikeliest of Heroes making an impact.

Salvatore Argento has never seen a demon.
He has never aspired to become a Hero.
Yet his power might be the one to tip the odds in humanity's favor.

Buy on Amazon

<u>Wandering Warrior</u>

By Michael Head

A divine quest to deliver justice.
One year to accomplish his mission.
After nineteen planets, there's something different about this one.

James Holden has reached the maximum level there is for a human. That's perfect, since he's the only one of his kind. A wandering warrior, without control of his destination, tossed between universes by gods who've failed to tell him why. James is the lone Judge on a new world in need of someone to balance the scales. He isn't afraid to do so with extreme prejudice. As the Chief Justice, he has to right the wrongs the innocent can't fix themselves.

As James quickly discovers, the roots of corruption run deep. Guilds choose to protect themselves rather than the people. Monsters roam the wilderness unchecked. Judgment is usually a decision between right and wrong, but nothing is ever that simple. This time, being the strongest human won't be enough to punish the guilty. James might have to recruit some new blood, even if he prefers to work alone.

On his twentieth world, he is going to win, no matter the cost. James will have to find a way to break past the limits of the system if he's going to have a chance at making a difference.

<u>Buy on Amazon</u>

Knights of Eternity

By Rachel Ní Chuirc

When Zara awoke in chains she thought she'd gone mad.

She was Zara the Fury - mistress of flame and fear. Her name was whispered across the land, from ramshackle taverns to the royal court. Even the heroic Gilded Knights thought twice before crossing her path.

She was feared—*respected.*

Now she was curled up on a dirt floor on her fiancé's orders. Valerius, leader of the Gilded, mocks her cries for help. And the kingdom is on the brink of war over the missing Lady Eternity…

But that wasn't why Zara thought she had gone mad.

The reason why is that the last thing she remembered was blood, an arcade screen, and the gun that changed everything.

**But no chains can hold the Fury, and when she gets out?
The world is going to *burn.***

Buy on Amazon

<u>Scarlet Citadel</u>

By Jack Fields

Gormon Hughes is 19, thin as a broom, and has—not for the first time in his life—been swept into the path of trouble. Poor, recently heartbroken, and indebted to the sort of people who file their teeth into needle points and devour wriggling bloated spiders for fun, Hughes sets his sights on salvation.

That salvation is the Scarlet Citadel, a wealthy organization of pageant fighters, monster hunters, and secret keepers. With the aid of strange oracles, rare good fortune, and a unique power that bubbles like champagne in the core of Hughes' being, he must join the Citadel and advance himself.

But the ladder of progression is harsh and dark. The rungs are slippery.

And falling means disaster…

<u>**Buy on Amazon**</u>

<u>LITRPG!</u>

To learn more about LitRPG, talk to other authors including myself, and to just have an awesome time, please join the LitRPG Group

<u>www.facebook.com/groups/LitRPGGroup</u>

Facebook

There's also a few really active Facebook groups I'd recommend you join, as you'll get to hear about great new books, new releases and interact with all your (new) favorite authors! (I may also be there, skulking at the back and enjoying the memes…)

https://www.facebook.com/groups/LitRPGlegion/

https://www.facebook.com/groups/GamelitSociety

https://www.facebook.com/groups/LitRPG.books

https://www.facebook.com/groups/LitRPGforum/

RYAN MAXWELL
RHINO WRITING

www.ingramcontent.com/pod-product-compliance
Lightning Source LLC
Chambersburg PA
CBHW070737190726

48292CB00002B/307